THE
HONEYS

Ryan La Sala

PUSH

Copyright © 2022 by Ryan La Sala

This book was originally published in hardcover by Scholastic Press in 2022.

ISBN 978-1-338-74533-7

10 9 8 7 6 5 4 3 2 1   23 24 25 26 27

Printed in the U.S.A. 40

This edition first printing 2023

Book design by Maeve Norton

TO THE GIRLS WHO TOOK ME IN
WHEN THE BOYS KICKED ME OUT

We came as one and left as many.
We came with nothing and left with everything.

—ANONYMOUS CAMPER,
ASPEN SUMMER ACADEMY, 1923

I

CHAPTER 1

My sister wakes me with a whisper.

"I love you, Mars." Her voice crumbles in her throat. In the moonlight from my window I can see the gleam of tears streaked over her jaw. She hovers so close I can smell her. Not her usual shampoo, but an unright odor. The rich sweetness of decay, like molding flowers.

"Caroline? You're back?" I'm confused. The summer night swells with cricket song and the curtains billow against her hunched form, like the outside is trying to take her back. I used to leave that window open all the time when we still snuck out onto the balcony connecting our bedrooms. On nights like tonight, I used to wait for Caroline to *tap tap tap* on the glass, a book and a flashlight ready. But Caroline and I haven't met on our balcony in a long, long time.

It's her, though. Only Caroline would know I still keep the window unlocked, just in case.

"Caroline?" I ask the shadow. The overripe stink.

No answer.

"Why are you home?" I'm too sleepy to hide the hope in my voice. Despite everything from this past year, I'm happy to see my sister. I've waited so long for her to come back for me.

She lifts something above her head. I recognize the shape, the catch of soft moonlight on rough metal. It's my iron sundial. She must have grabbed it from my bookcase. I use it as a bookend because it's so heavy.

She stifles a sob, heaving the sundial high. I reach for my phone on the nightstand.

"Caroline, what's going on—"

"Forgive me," she sobs.

Caroline brings the sundial down on my hand, crushing nail and bone into metal and glass. I'm about to scream when she lifts it again, and this time she brings it down on my head.

———————

Pink lights.

Pink walls.

The blood in my eye turns the clean brightness of the upstairs hallway into a rosy nightmare as I run from my room. From crashing and chaos.

I am slow and I am stumbling. I cradle one hand with the other, feeling familiar skin bent into unfamiliar carnage. The knuckles of my hands don't match anymore, their twin-hood out of alignment. Like Caroline and me.

She storms behind me. She's so close her stink overwhelms me. All I can hear is her screaming.

Mars. Mars. Don't go. Don't go.

It's not her voice. It's not my sister. It's something wearing her skin, filling her flailing body like a pressurized water hose. She overtakes me before I've made it to the stairs, and the pink world whirls as we hit the floor. Upside down, I see the door to our parents' room open, see Mom in her nightshirt halt. Gasp. Scream. Dad calls up from downstairs.

I barely dodge the next hit, the iron sundial smashing into the floorboards beside my head. I blindly drive a hand upward into a slippery jaw and the sundial tumbles away, down the stairs with gunshot thuds. My vision is fucked up, but in the brightness of the hallway I can see Caroline now. She is filthy, her brown hair clumped with dust and debris. Her clothes cling to her, black with mud, but the plastic Academy logo still shines on her uniform's sleeve. She pulls something from her waistband and holds it over us.

A knife. My sister has brought home a knife.

But what scares me more are her eyes. Later, I will try to convince myself that there was no sign of my sister in that wild stare. But my dreams will replay this moment with cruel clarity; trap me within it like a bug preserved in amber. I will want to believe I am being killed by a monster, but in the stare of my attacker I don't see monstrosity. I see my Caroline. Lucid. Herself. So recognizable that my agony—even my shock—dissolves into relief. This is the first time since this awful year began that I've looked into her eyes and seen her—seen *her*—looking back.

Caroline cringes, and it's all the warning I have before she plunges the knife toward my face. I twist but a seam of fire rips open in my ear. Now I scream, but I can't hear it, can't hear anything through the white-hot pain. I feel the house tremble under my back as Dad hits the top of the stairs. I feel Caroline get dragged away. I roll to my side and use my good hand to heave myself onto the banister. I stare into the chandelier that hangs into the great drop of our entryway. The lights are still pink, the world still blurry. The whole house spins beneath me like I'm the center of an unbalanced carousel.

I am powerless as I watch Caroline kick and bite at our dad. Not Caroline. Not our dad. Strangers. Actors. Unreal characters that have broken into my life for this improvised horror. Mom stands in her doorway, another imposter. She claps both hands over her mouth, frozen. I want to scream at her. Want her to help. To fix this.

Caroline sinks teeth into the meat of Dad's hand. He's a big man; he flings her off with violent disgust, driving her into the mirror at the top of the stairs. The glass shatters over her, but she never stops moving. Not for a second. She plunges toward me, the carpet twisting beneath her shoes as she tries to get her footing. But she's too close, too out of control. I know what will happen before it happens.

Caroline trips. She falls into me, arms hugged tight around my shoulders. The banister snaps and we hurtle backward. Then down. The ceiling fills my view. We fall through the chandelier; then the chandelier is falling with us. Like dancers, we spin in the brief infinity of the drop, a storm of light and crystal and blood.

When we hit the floor, Caroline hits first.

She breaks beneath my body. I'm close enough to hear her snap, to feel her stiffen, and to know she's gone too still. I am wrapped in her arms, her hair, in the sweet stink she brought home. The silence and the stillness scare me more than anything else.

I struggle free, broken crystal biting flesh from my naked thighs, my knees. In the wreckage, I stand.

I look at my sister.

She's covered in my blood. Her body curls into itself. Her face is the last thing to stop twitching. One eye half-lidded, the other flung wide open like a doll.

Caroline is looking at me when she dies. And she is smiling.

CHAPTER 2

When we were five years old, Caroline gave me a little pink calculator.

It was shaped like a cat and had candy-bright buttons. She liked it, but I loved it, and she loved me, so it became mine. Growing up, she was always like that. Generous and maybe a little too insightful about what people wanted. I played with that calculator endlessly, and when I lost it, she surprised me with a new one. It was our dad's accounting calculator, stolen from his desk, and because she was Caroline, she'd drenched the buttons in sticky pink nail polish. Just for me.

Caroline got in trouble, and I got a hobby. She gave me lots of strange devices after that, and I bought her every color of nail polish I could find. It was our joke. One year it was an old-school abacus in exchange for neons. Then the sundial for thermosensitive metallics. And finally, my favorite: a 1987 Mayfair Sound Products calculator, made in Japan. A blocky device bigger than my hand. Pleasantly heavy, with noisy buttons. And all I gave her was royal blue. Painfully inadequate, but she wore that color all the time, even after we stopped talking.

In the aftermath of Caroline's attack, I find the Mayfair at the very bottom of my room's wreckage. It is utterly smashed. Ruined. But what gets me—what finally shocks me out of my stupor—is a perfect, bloody fingerprint on the device's one unscathed corner. She must have picked it up, considered it, and put it back before reaching for the sundial to wake me.

I don't understand why. I don't need to understand why. I sob as I sift through the mess and, searching for each piece, I learn something.

Death isn't the end of a life, but the division of it. When someone dies, their soul scatters into all the things they've ever given away. Love. Bruises.

Gifts. You struggle to piece together what's left—even the things that hurt—just to feel haunted.

It takes me until sunrise to find every broken bit of the Mayfair calculator. The house is quiet by then, Mom and Dad with the body at the hospital. I face the pieces alone, laid out on my desk in the weak morning light. There's the brushed metal frame, the popped-out buttons, the emerald guts of circuitry veined in copper. Cleaning the grime off was the easy part. Now I'm trying to figure out how this goes back together. If it goes back together at all.

I don't know how anything in so many pieces could go back together.

Caroline is dead.

My sister is dead.

There are no pieces, no parts, that can be assembled to make sense of the absence my sister has become. There is just a sudden, shocking emptiness where her life used to be.

I try to count the voids. To trace their shapes. When a person dies, you do this. You try to account for what's gone. Some of what's missing will be clear right away. The missing sound of their voice, or the to-do lists they'll never complete, or the new blankness that sits in their chair at breakfast. Those I'm ready for.

But so much worse are the small, infuriatingly small gaps—really just pinprick holes—that Caroline leaves everywhere else. Emptiness, fired through my memories like buckshot, so scattered that I can't quantify what's gone. I can't count it. I can't measure it.

My sister becomes a constellation of voids.

And, like the broken calculator, I'm incapable of adding it all up, of making any kind of sense out of it. So I sit at my desk, for days and days. And I stare at the pieces floating in the muted light of each sunrise. Bent metal, plastic buttons, emerald guts, copper veins. Pieces, parts of a former whole.

But now all I see is the new emptiness that separates them.

When I fear something, I study it. Caroline would dance about it or probably write a poem. Something dreamy and creative. But I'm our logical half. A killjoy, but smart. Our necessary evil—we used to joke growing up—as our joint fears pushed Caroline toward art, and me toward research. Toward data and science. Maybe even an anecdotal account from a primary source, if I got desperate.

No one will talk with me about what happened. I become desperate.

So I research death.

I learn about sky burials and water burials. I watch videos of dances and parades, and even ashes being turned into fistfuls of beautiful blue-green beads. I learn about the Jewish custom of covering mirrors so that a mourner's contemplations reach inward, not outward.

I cover my mirrors, too, but it's because every time I see myself, I see her. I glimpse her final, twitching grin, like a translucent film laid over my own face. Our face. We're twins. Not identical, but close enough.

We are twins.

We *were* twins, I guess.

That happens, too, according to my research. When someone dies, suddenly you've made an enemy of the past tense, but the past tense is all you've got now and it feels like it knows it.

Well. Fuck the past tense, I guess.

Oh, and also: Fuck the upstairs banister. After that night, I avoided even looking at the splintered breach where Caroline and I fell. Then one morning I woke up to men in boots bounding up and down the stairs, and suddenly it was fixed. That was somehow worse. An ugly feeling burned in me when I put my hands over the new wood, something like betrayal. I didn't get why, but it's that same ugly feeling that I feel now, a week later, only eight days after Caroline fell to her death in our home, as I watch a truck pull up our driveway to deliver a brand-new chandelier.

I watch the men hoist the crystal sculpture into place. And as I watch it rise, I think, *As far as death rituals go, Caroline would've loved this. The drama alone.*

Not the chandelier, but the fact that our parents couldn't go two weeks without replacing it despite the death of their daughter. Same with the banister. I should commend them for even going a day, but then I look up chandeliers online. This one is custom, the kind of shit you have to pull a string to get in less than six weeks. As the installation team turns it on, I force myself to look directly into its cold, bright guts.

When our parents ordered their new chandelier, was their daughter even officially dead?

My mind answers in Caroline's airy voice.

Probably not, Mars, she laughs.

We hold the funeral in our home a day after the new chandelier goes up.

Like all things with my family, the funeral is a careful performance of obfuscation. It's the Matthias family way. Mom's a New York senator, after all, so it's all of our jobs to keep up appearances. Our lives are beholden to the public eye, and I guess that means our deaths are, too.

As family and friends enter, there will be no sign of what happened here. The crystal has been swept up, the debris vacuumed away, the blood scrubbed from the grout. I secretly think Mom and Dad planned the funeral around the chandelier's delivery, and not the other way around. It radiates a joyful warmth, boasting that there's nothing to hide and, even if there was, there's nowhere to hide it. The light fills every corner of our spacious colonial mansion, which has been bedecked with calla lilies; poster-huge photographs of Caroline, fresh from Staples; and a sweet perfume from the beeswax candles Caroline loved to burn.

What attempted murder? What accidental suicide? Not in this *Lovely American Home. Here, enjoy a canapé, why don't you?*

"Mars, sweetie?" Mom calls from inside the house, and it barely reaches me outside on my balcony. The same one Caroline crawled over to get into my window. I'm hiding out here, fiddling with the still-busted Mayfair calculator. "Mars? Are you up?"

I climb inside. I'm supposed to help direct the catering staff during setup, and later I'm on welcoming duty at the front door. *Welcome! Come on in. Drinks are that way; the body of my sister is over there. The reenactment starts at four o'clock, don't be late!*

Officially, Caroline did not die in our house. She died two days later, in the hospital, when it became clear she wouldn't wake up. When the doctors scanned her, they found a milky mass in her brain, and we all learned a new word: *glioblastoma.* The tumor accounted for her "uncharacteristic behavior," said the doctors. Her death was inevitable, coming for her no matter what, once that thing took root. In a way, the swiftness of her death could be seen as a mercy.

They said that. But they didn't know about the attack. No one does, and no one will unless I tell them. Dad took me to a twenty-four-hour urgent care center somewhere outside Westchester County while Mom rode in the ambulance with Caroline. Dad answered questions for me while they checked out my hand and swabbed blood from my hair.

Officially, I was crushed by my bookcase. Dad was ready with the lie when the physician's assistant asked. When they asked me again in private, just me and the PA, I said, "I know I look bad, but you should see the bookcase."

Like I said: a performance of obfuscation. And without Caroline here, I'm now unquestionably the lead. I hate it. Our duet has become my solo. For all my sardonic theatricality, I never wanted this stage to myself. It'll be like this for the rest of my life. I wonder if it will ever not feel like its own form of death.

It certainly feels like death today.

A million times during setup I stop to look for her among the staff filling our house with chairs and tables; filling the tables with pastries and cut fruit. A million times I don't find her, and I shiver when I remember that she's in the one room I refuse to enter: the parlor, transformed with drawn shades and dimmed lighting, an entire wall crowded with tribute bouquets from everywhere—from school, from the hospital, even from Aspen. And at the center of the arrangement, a casket of polished cherrywood.

"She would have loved this," Mom actually said as the coffin was being dragged in through the solarium. The same thing I thought when I watched the chandelier rise like a cold sun. I was being sarcastic, the language Caroline and I shared behind our parents' backs. Mom is being sincere.

She would have loved this.

As if Caroline spent countless hours vision-boarding her big day. Her "Celebration of Life," which is printed on the programs in big, loopy letters.

Caroline would've hated all this—the performance, the programs—but especially the term *Celebration of Life*. Caroline was a highly accomplished seventeen-year-old, but she was seventeen years old. There is very little life to celebrate, certainly not enough to go around. In my mind, I joke to her that there's nothing more gothic than a celebration that hinges on the guest of honor being dead, and she says, *Mars, please, don't make me laugh.*

And I remember the way she laughed.

I stop talking to her after that.

CHAPTER 3

After setup and before guests arrive, I'm sent upstairs to get ready. Mom, or more likely one of her aides, has laid out a garment bag on my bed, and inside it I find a simple black suit. I lie beside it in a damp towel, looking at the ceiling, holding Caroline's knife to my chest. If we'd called the police it would have been confiscated as evidence, but instead I just picked it up from the mess and cleaned it myself. I discovered that it's not a knife. It's just knife-like. It's a flat blade of metal, one end square and sharp, the other hooked. It's a beekeeper's tool, meant for prying open the wax of a hive. I press it against my body until the cold metal is as warm as my skin. I stay like that until I'm dry.

For once Mom told me I could wear makeup. Usually she pleads with me to "tone it down" when I'm in public, but not today. It's not because she's warming to my fluidity. It's because all the other signs of what happened—the banister, the chandelier—have been swept up, patched, and hidden away. I'm the evidence that remains. Laced in my mother's permission is the demand that I do my duty as a Matthias and hide myself, too.

I sit at my vanity and stare into my face. Our face. Our wide jaw and high cheeks, our sharp Cupid's-bow lips and downturned nose. Our hair is brown. Caroline kept her hair long and in her face. I keep mine long and pulled back, usually, but I let it fall forward now. It hides more when it's down.

I'm great at makeup but let me tell you, not even a drag-queen-level contour can hide that I've clearly been through some shit. Diligently, I blot away my bruises and pin my hair to cover my bandaged ear. I flip my septum piercing up into my nose. I can't do anything about the plastic splint holding my hand together, except maybe bedazzle it, but even that's a bit much for the eccentric Matthias twin.

My splinted hand catches on my sleeve as I pull on my jacket, and I hiss in pain. Even small movements hurt, sparks of fire lighting up in my nail beds where the sundial smashed. There's nothing I can do but wait for my knuckles to heal and my broken nails to grow.

And who knows if I'll ever hear right again? I still wake up each morning with an earful of blood. Even now, as I apply a fresh bandage, I feel a wet tickle as it begins to soak the gauze.

When I'm ready, I take up my post in the foyer, where I politely welcome guests dressed in dark suits and dark dresses.

I'm so sorry for your loss.

My heart goes out to your family.

You're in our prayers.

I accept the sad words. I shake one hundred hands, thankful Caroline crushed my left hand and not my right. More than once I catch myself tucking away certain observations so that I can trade with her later, like we always do at the end of Mom's fundraisers. I shiver, sad all over again, and I'm about to excuse myself when a trio of girls march up to me and one says: "Mars, right? Fuck, you look just like her."

The girl who speaks doesn't shake my hand. She pulls me into a hug and I am struck by the overwhelming familiarity of this perfect stranger.

"You probably don't remember us. We're Caroline's friends from camp. I'm Bria."

"I'm Sierra."

"Mimi."

They each hug me. They are the prettiest girls I have ever seen. Mimi is small, round, and pale in a peplum-waisted dress. Sierra is tall, tan, and sleek in a black jumpsuit. And Bria wears a crimson sweaterdress despite the heat, though her brown, marble-smooth skin doesn't appear to even have pores. They're completely different, but together emanate a harmonizing beauty. Their loveliness puts me on high alert, as does the fact that they're from camp. They mean Aspen. As in the Summer Academy at the Aspen Conservancy, where Caroline was when the tumor began to dissolve her sanity.

Allegedly.

If they are who they say they are, what ended in this foyer—right where we're standing—began with them at Aspen.

"This is . . ." Bria looks around the grand entryway, at the guests and their expensive mourning splendor, at the lilies and the glossy photos, and finally at the new chandelier. ". . . so strange. Like, too much, you know? She'd be so mad. Oh, Mars, it must be terrible to have to deal with this without her."

"I . . ."

A sob cracks in my throat, surprising me. It's the first emotion I've shown all day. Bria takes my hand and holds it; squeezes it, willing strength into me. I regain myself.

"Listen, Mars," she says. "I know it can't mean much, but we're so, so sorry for your loss. Everyone at Aspen loved Caroline. We were worried when she left so suddenly. And then we heard the news and . . ." Bria holds my hand even tighter, like it's the only reason they drove (or more likely were driven by one of the many chauffeurs smoking in our driveway, holding the news vans at bay) two hours from the Catskills.

I pull away. Their hypnotic beauty fades. Finally, I feel what I'm supposed to feel. Anger. The snarling grudge I've been tending to summer after summer, as Caroline fled to Aspen without me. *With* them. She chose them—these rich, glossy dolls—over me, over *us*, and I've hated them from afar for years. But now that they're here, my resentment withers in their warmth. They feel like she felt. I want to hug them like I didn't get to hug her.

My breath shakes up through me. I have so many questions for them.

"Caroline loved Aspen," I say. "She said it was her favorite place in the world."

Sierra and Mimi exchange a look behind Bria, whose expression stays plain and considerate. I go on. I'm suddenly desperate to know what they know.

"She may not have been acting normal in her last couple weeks. They say the tumor was putting a lot of pressure on her brain. She might have been pretty confused?"

I make it a question, but Bria just nods sympathetically. It's Mimi who gives me what I want.

"That explains it. She was *so* different. Like, *so* paranoid. Even toward us? Usually she tells us everything—well, at least *me* everything—but then in her last week she—"

"We're sorry," Bria cuts in. "Mars, you probably don't want to hear this. Not today."

I tuck this moment away for inspection later. Caroline used to be the most easygoing person, always up for anything. She looked forward to Aspen every year, except this past year something changed. She became anxious, and it only got worse as summer closed in on her. Caroline felt something bad coming with the season. She saw signs none of us could see. Maybe she felt that thing growing in her head.

"You used to attend Aspen with her, right?" Bria asks.

I stiffen. How much do they know about my disastrous departure from Aspen? I only answer with: "Yeah, forever ago."

"Why'd you stop?"

It's a good question. It's uncommon to stop attending Aspen once you get in, assuming your family doesn't blink at the five-figure, eight-week tuition (plus mandatory fees for private tutors, excursions, and transportation). But the way she asks it tells me she knows the truth. Maybe not all of it, but enough to know my falling-out wasn't a matter of money.

"Just didn't feel like the right place for me anymore," I say, gesturing at my body. Dressed in this suit my parents picked out, I look mostly boy, but if Caroline told them anything about me, they'll know what I mean.

They nod in unison.

"Yeah, people can be assholes," Sierra says, speaking for the first time.

"It's not so bad now that we're older," Mimi says. "They renamed Battle of the Sexes to the Village Victory Cup. It's, like, all the same gender warfare stuff? But still."

"You should come visit," Sierra offers. "Like, a redo. And you can bring home the rest of her stuff."

Mimi shoots Sierra a wide-eyed look. Bria, quick and smooth, asks, "Do you ever think about coming back?"

I do, all the time. And I could go back, if I wanted to. But not attending Aspen has turned into a protest that I refuse to end. Still, I miss it every year when Caroline leaves in June, and I resent her every year when she returns in August, kissed brown by the sun and overflowing with private memories baked golden by the hot summer air.

They are waiting for my answer. When they blink, it's a cascade from left to right, like they're one large spider.

"Not really," I say, unsure of what I just saw.

"Fair," Bria says. "We brought you something. Sierra?"

Sierra opens her bag and pulls out a heavy cylinder wrapped in paper. I know what it is right away. A candle, like the ones we have lit all over the house. I can smell its waxy sweetness on the paper.

"We found it in her bunk with your name on it."

I stare at Caroline's handwriting. *For Mars.* I bite into my cheek to force the tears back. The girls hug me one at a time before slipping into the crowd, and the next grieving party takes their spot before me.

It's only during a break an hour later that I unwrap the candle, careful not to rip the paper where Caroline wrote my name. The wax is a rich yellow, molded with a honeycomb pattern. Caroline used a metal lettering tool to impress my name into the wax, too. The letters are messily spaced. It's cute. It's terrible.

I turn it over carefully, knowing there will be a wax bee melted into the side.

I gasp, nearly dropping the candle.

There is a bee all right, but its body has been crisscrossed with gashes, as though carved by a red-hot knife.

CHAPTER 4

They open Caroline's casket for the ceremony—the *Celebration*—so that people can line up and pay their respects to the departed and the departed's family. I can't look at her, afraid she'll still be trapped in that half-lidded stare, that smile. I can't stop thinking about the candle she left for me. She wasn't even at camp for a week, so she must have just made it. What was she thinking? Who was she by then, as the tumor grew?

The ceremony ends. Then, like a winding millipede, the guests merge into a procession with a thousand hands, each one reaching to touch me as people whisper more blessings and prayers and condolences. As a politician's child, I have a lifetime of training in polite deflection, and I use all of it until finally—finally—the hands run out. The staff puts out coffee and a lunch buffet in the dining room. The parlor empties.

In the kitchen, my mother waves me down. She sits at the granite island with my aunts.

"Oh, Marshall, sweetie, I'm so sorry," Aunt Michelle coos, pulling me into a hug. Then she catches herself. "Oh, I mean *Mars*. You're going by Mars now, right? Sorry, dear, old habits die hard."

I don't remind Aunt Michelle that the family has always called me Mars, even in baby videos, because Grandma said it was the only way she could tell between me and her wrinkly little husband, Grandpa. Marshall Matthias the Second. I'm the third attempt, evidently.

I've only ever been Mars. Aunt Michelle's just being an idiot.

"Either is fine," I say, and she relaxes like I've just spared her life. I suppress an eye roll. I'm gender fluid, not a grenade.

"Mars, sweetie. Listen," Mom says, rubbing my arms. "You don't need to be down here if you don't want to be. I know you didn't want to have the ceremony in the house but . . ."

"Tradition. I know."

"Yes. But traditions are for all the old people. And the important part is over now. Why don't you make an ice run or something?"

I shrug. "But Dad."

Mom shrugs. "I'll handle Dad."

"But you."

Mom's eyes are rimmed red, her skin paper-thin like the grief is dissolving her from within. But at my concern, she only smiles. She hugs me, rubbing my back through my starched white shirt. I'm conscious of the eyes watching the senator hug her child. Her only child now. I watch the crowd back, my eyes landing on Bria, Sierra, and Mimi.

Caroline called them "the Honeys."

I pull out of the hug.

"I'm staying," I say. I search my mom's face for signs of relief, but I don't find them. I put together too late that she was hoping I'd go. Vanish, like I usually do.

"If that's what you want," she says, and her performance is perfect. Caroline would tell me I'm being too hard on her, and maybe I am. I can't help it. My mind has become a storm of doubts and cynicism these past days. My defenses against my natural paranoia are at their weakest right now.

Maybe I should vanish, after all.

I excuse myself from the kitchen. There are people everywhere, except the parlor. I duck in there, cross to the wide French doors without looking at the casket, and slip out into the solarium. It was my job to attend to the plants while Caroline was away this summer, and until she died I wasn't too serious about it. Now I'm obsessed. I take my time checking

20

soil moisture, watering, and snipping away dead growth. The bok choy keeps trying to flower, but I pinch off stalks like Caroline told me to. I collect the crushed bulbs and clippings in a battered bucket already half full of all the things I've picked away. It calms me down, and I'm about to reenter the parlor when I freeze.

Through the warped glass of the French doors, I see people bending over the open casket. It's Bria, Sierra, and Mimi. The Honeys. Something about their posture makes me nervous. I think it's the way they're leaning in, like people inspecting a buffet, figuring out which morsel they'll take for themselves.

Sierra and Mimi turn away, shielding Bria as she digs her hands into her black curls and removes her earrings. Then she leans into the casket and fastens the earrings to Caroline, tilting Caroline's frozen jaw with sure hands, like she's practiced this many times. The movement is so quick—so strange and invasive in the soft quiet atmosphere of the parlor—I almost doubt I saw it right at all.

The girls leave, pinkies hooked and swinging between them. My calm has evaporated into the hot air of the solarium. Sweat dots my upper lip. I slip back into the parlor and approach the casket. Whereas before I looked only at the mosh of flowers all around it, my eyes now finally fix on the pale thing within. Caroline. She is cocooned in pink and white. Everything about her looks wrong—her jaw is clenched and her skin is too rosy and her lips are slightly puckered. My mind flashes between this ugly, pretty thing embedded in softness, and the eerie smile she gave me among the crunching crystal and swinging light.

I lean in. For a moment I smell that horrible, sweet decay. The scent from that night, permanently woven into my sheets. I hold my breath and get even closer. I am inches from Caroline's frozen face. Her makeup is fuzzy, like pollen. I can make out Bria's fingerprints where she adjusted Caroline's jaw. I reach into the casket and brush away Caroline's hair, wincing when my knuckle grazes the cool, dead flesh of her cheek.

A small earring glints among her mouse-brown curls, pushed through the lobe of Caroline's ear. It's a golden bee, so finely detailed I expect it to move. Was it there before, or did Bria place it there? I know I need to stop, but I run a finger over the gold. It's still warm. The warmth from someone else's body.

And then something crawls from Caroline's ear.

I snatch my hand away, jostling Caroline's head, and out from the casket buzz a trio of black dots. They weave toward me. I bat them away, frantic, then lose them in the busy backdrop of flowers. I can hear them circling me. Then I feel something tiny and fast crawl along the ridge of *my* ear, like it's trying to burrow beneath my bandage.

I cry out, clasping my hands against my ears, trying to crush it. Pain blossoms behind my eyes and I know I've reopened my wound. Arms catch me—people waiting. I flail until the buzzing goes away. I see the dark shape of the bees cut through the dim light above the casket, landing on Caroline's throat, her lips, her eyelid.

And, though people are pulling me away, I am close enough to see the insects dart down the curve of her cheekbone and wiggle their way back inside her head.

CHAPTER 5

The Honeys.

That's what everyone at Aspen calls the girls in Cabin H. It's been that way for decades, Caroline said. Caroline resented the term—she insisted it was dehumanizing—but she also resented the girls themselves for adopting it so enthusiastically. She mocked their odd, exaggerated girlishness. Said it was nauseating, the way they held pinkies. Yet when Caroline was placed in that illustrious cabin, she accepted it without protest.

Because everyone knows it's an honor to be invited to Cabin H.

There's history to all the cabins at Aspen, as there is with all the playgrounds of the rich. Historically Cabin H was considered a charity. It was all the way out near the wetlands, where Aspen keeps an apiary of beehives, and the girls on scholarship were forced to live there and walk into camp for their meals and activities.

They were called the Honeys, as in worker bees, as in working class. It was meant as an insult. Then those girls grew up, and they used their connections to one another to grow rich. Their children attended Aspen in their place. Then their children's children attended. Coated in the golden glow of nostalgia, and no longer stinking of charity, Cabin H became a symbol of industriousness and rustic glamour. Each new generation of girls built on the elitism of the last, cultivating a coy power as thick and ample as the honey they were named for. And all the while, year after year, they took care of those bees, planting flowers they knew the bees favored and harvesting the sticky rewards.

With power comes exclusion. Rituals. Initiations and tests of loyalty, or so people said. It's all supposed to be a secret, but the sort of secret everyone's meant to whisper about. The girls, meanwhile, feign oblivious-ness, hiding in their outward prettiness. The pet names and the chained pinkies—it's an act. Specifically, the act of a predator. Like a stinging insect cloaked in the satin bell of a flower.

No one ever questions them. Not that I ever saw, at least. And it makes perfect sense not to. Those who find the act charming see no reason to look through it. Those who find it problematic dismiss the girls with righteous quickness. And the adults of Aspen idolize them. The Honeys embody the very merits of beautified resilience that the camp sells to wealthy parents looking to toughen their pampered children while ensur-ing their exposure to the *right* people. The Honeys are the *right* people.

Caroline hated the Honeys until she became one. And for a while, I hated Caroline because she had what I wanted most, and she didn't even care.

She dismissed those girls so easily. That was her way, though. Caroline wore detachment fashionably, like the slick skin of a seal, the grip of real-ity sliding off so that she always appeared cool and unbothered in the hot, frantic world. I'm not like her—I catch on everything. Every small want grows out of me like thorns, making me impossible to embrace. I look tough but I moonlight as pathetic. But not Caroline. She was invin-cible in her isolation, needing nothing, needing no one.

Needing things, she once told me, *means you can be controlled. And I never want that. To be controlled. To need things. To need anyone other than myself.*

That was her way. She was strong alone yet never alone. I resented her for it.

I wanted—I have always wanted—what the Honeys had. It was an instant, unconscious wish anytime I saw beautiful girls. I coveted not just their beauty, but their freedom to embody beauty. Their sororal close-ness, too, and the power it gave them. I wanted in on the act, and I'm not sure that Caroline ever understood why. Whenever I tried to talk about this incoherent need, or the frantic, harsh static that writhed under my skin—when I saw girls, saw myself, saw the difference—she would shrug unhelpfully. Like this yearning was only mine. Odd. Alien. And I began to feel like an alien.

I think this is where our divergence began. Our bodies were changing, mine lumbering in a direction that set me further and further apart from my sister, from girls like the Honeys. Eventually, the binary of the cabins at Aspen felt insufferable. A constant question I couldn't answer.

Who am I?

What am I?

And then . . . well. And then I had to leave Aspen. For everyone's safety, they said.

And Caroline stayed.

No, it was worse than that. She *begged* to stay. And our parents, who were skeptical about Aspen from the start, let her. That's when I lost her, I think. When I left her alone at Aspen and she came home months later, a newly minted Honey.

My body betrayed me. Then it was my sister's turn, I guess.

Meanwhile, I tried out summer at home, pining and furious, pretending I'd never cared. Trying to adopt Caroline's iconic dismissiveness. I swore off the great outdoors and turned toward the inner workings of computers. Logic. Math. I mocked Caroline's little camp projects—the friendship bracelets, the dipped candles—like it wasn't exactly what I wanted. Caroline let me. She played along with my whole *Aspen is a sexist, capitalist cult* protest, but I could tell she loved those girls more than anything. At dinner her phone buzzed—literally buzzed—with texts from their group chat. They talked incessantly at night. And in the winter months they would send one another these insidiously cute "Aspen Prep" care packages.

Trust me when I tell you there is nothing more alarming than seeing the one you love slowly become enamored with cutesy scrapbooking tutorials and hand-painted picture frames.

I wanted Caroline to hate what was happening to her, but there was no room for hate among those girls. Just a sisterhood I resented, envied, adored, and despised all at once.

But something went wrong. In the woods. In the cabin. I know something went horribly wrong.

Caroline came home last August, and something had changed. Her easy joy jumped and skittered, like a warped record. She didn't want to talk about camp with me, and I got the sense she didn't want to return. That was confirmed as the months passed and any mention of the Aspen Conservancy caused Caroline to fumble her words. Something repelled her from camp, or maybe it was the girls themselves. I found her Aspen Prep packages unopened by her desk; she stopped with the scrapbooking, the group chats, the late-night calls. She never said why or why not.

And it will haunt me until the day I die that I never asked her *what* was wrong.

Whatever it was, Caroline was scared. So scared that her fear occupied her fully by the spring. It walked around in her skin, a doom clothed as my sister. Some seed of dread planted long ago was now blooming in her body.

Then it was June, and Caroline left for Aspen.

And days later Caroline returned, breaking into my bedroom.

And then Caroline died.

And then the Honeys arrived at my house.

And then . . .

I still don't know what I saw the day of the funeral. I'm afraid to even think about it. Each time I try, the memory grows blurry under my inspection. It's clearest if I don't think too hard about it and let it guide me from the periphery of my mind, like an instinct.

And my instinct is what causes me to pack my duffel bag two days after the funeral and announce over Saturday brunch:

"I'm going back to Aspen."

Mom puts down her phone next to her plate. Dad looks up from his laptop.

"What? Why?" Dad asks.

I take a deep breath. I need to keep it cool for Phase One of my plan.

"The girls from Caroline's cabin offered to let me visit. And it was Caroline's favorite place. I want to go, and see it all again, and . . ."

My voice cracks. I thought I was lying, but I realize I'm not. Yes, I have my suspicions and of course I have a level of paranoia that only I, Mars Matthias, could summon, but . . .

But it's true. I really do want to explore Caroline's last days in the place where she was happiest, and see if I can piece her back together from *that* instead of our horrible final moments. If I'm going to survive her death, I need a final version of her I can live with.

Dad sighs, putting a hand over mine. Mom's expression is unreadable, which I know means she's trying to think of a way to out-argue me on this.

"I think a drive through the camp might be nice," Mom says eventually. "We can go together."

"I want to stay, though. By myself."

"For how long?"

For as long as it takes me to figure out what those girls did, I think. Instead I say, "You already paid Caroline's tuition and housing for the whole summer, so the camp will be inclined to let me stay if they can keep the money."

My parents are studying me like I'm speaking pure nonsense. Their hesitance stings. They never attended Aspen, but they grew up going to camps like it every summer. They've always had an easier time understanding Caroline's adoration over my protests. Even after what happened to me, they urged me to go back. Show some resilience like the Matthias that I am. But the time for resilience has ended, I guess. That it took Caroline's death for my family to finally doubt Aspen . . . it burns new brightness into my resolve.

"And they owe me," I say finally. "Remember how they begged?"

I know my parents don't want to get into who is owed what, which is why I bring it up. Bringing it up will force them to progress past the *how* of my attendance to the *why*.

Mom offers a reconciliatory smile. "Mars, what's this really about?"

I glance at the parlor. It's been reset, but each time I go near it my ear feels the phantom tingle of that bee crawling on my skin.

"I can't be here," I finish. "I can't spend summer in this house."

Mom sighs. We are, all of us, remembering the scene I made at the Celebration of Life. I'm using that now, as a threat. If there's one thing Mom will do anything to avoid, it's a scene.

"Heather," Dad cuts in, giving her a long look. They're communicating in their unspoken parent language. Mom's face smooths, unreadable. In unison they turn toward me.

"We'll talk about it."

Wonderful. Phase One complete. In fencing, this is a feint. A move meant to draw the opponent into an attack, which I will be ready for. I hide upstairs for the rest of the day, reading about Aspen, readying my counterattack. In fencing it would be known as a riposte, but this isn't fencing. This is a family weakened by grief, hyper-considerate of optics. This is why Phase Two involves me standing in front of my bathroom mirror, sawing through my hair with the kitchen scissors.

"Mars? Can we talk to you?"

Both parents arrive at my door. I drink in their shock as they look at what I've done to my hair. Mom gasps. Dad looks like he's going to curse, but he just steps out into the hall.

Sitting on my bed, my mom holds my hand and stares.

"Why, sweetie?"

"Aspen has a grooming policy," I say, keeping my voice flat. Emotionless. "They'll put me in the boys' cabins. Boys have to have short hair."

In the silence, I can hear the wet swallow in my mom's throat as she tries to find the right words to tell me I'm not going, but she can't. I've stunned her. My riposte is working.

"Did you talk to Aspen?" I ask.

"We did, yes." She recovers a bit, like she's reciting a dream she's just remembered. "They were excited about you visiting."

"Visiting or attending?"

"We didn't specify," she says slowly. "Mars, listen, sweetie. You're right. The camp policy only allows for them to put you in a bunk with other . . ."

With other boys, is what she doesn't say. If she did, it wouldn't hurt me. My cropped hair is supposed to prove that—that I am as much boy as I am girl, that I morph as I see fit, that hair has nothing to do with it. My mom's hesitance just goes to show that she still hasn't put her mastermind toward understanding that my fluidity is an advantage, not a hindrance.

"That's fine," I assure her. "That's what I figured. I literally don't care. I'll even wear the boys' uniform."

Mom's eyebrows go up. "Even the cargo shorts?"

"Nothing below the knee, but yeah, even the cargo shorts."

This wins me a sad smile. She says, "Mars, sweetie, Aspen is two hours away, and you'll be alone there. And after what happened the last time . . ."

"That won't happen again," I say.

She doubts this. I doubt this, too. I add, "It would be a PR nightmare if Aspen let anything happen to me again, *especially* now. I'll be safe. I promise."

Dad has taken up sentinel at the door. He clenches and unclenches his jaw, watching us. He and Mom exchange another long, silent conversation with just their eyes.

I move past their hesitance for them.

"When do we go?"

Mom sighs again. I wish it was love that earned her resignation, but it's not. It's optics.

"Tomorrow," Mom says. Dad huffs. Mom stands, my hand sliding from hers, and she's gone. Dad looks at me for a few seconds too long, like I'm a strange vase in a museum.

"She's worried about you, Mars."

"I know."

"Is this really what you think your sister would have wanted?"

Caroline would want to be alive. The retort smolders in my throat, but I swallow it down. I just say, "*I* want this."

My father finally enters my room and passes a large hand over my butchered hair. He looks around, his eyes landing on my bookshelf, then the sundial, placed high up and out of reach.

"Can't say I blame you. But can we get this haircut cleaned up in the morning? Even in the woods, you're still a Matthias."

I smile. I nod. Dad leaves my room.

I breathe in, breathe out, and let my heart level. I slide down into my sheets, then reach under my pillow. I pull out the candle, inspecting the carvings in the wax. I press it to my nose, and I'm sure beneath the sweetness I detect a hint of rot. Something unright.

Officially, Caroline died from a tumor. Unofficially, she died in an act of violence brought on by that tumor. An accident. The grisly marriage of madness and gravity, and me, the heavy thing that crushed her.

But I know my sister.

She wasn't crazy, but she *was* scared. She was scared for the entire year leading up to Summer Academy, yet she went anyway. And in that

30

moment in the hall, when she had me pinned, she was lucid.

The chaos from that night hums in my mind. I hear her screams as I stumble down the hall. I see again the shocking brightness of our home, dyed pink by the blood coating my eyes. We fall. She breaks.

Mars. Mars. Don't go. Don't go.

It was a command. A threat. Or so I thought. Now I think it was more. A warning, so important it drove Caroline all the way to the edge of her sanity, then right off into whatever waits beyond.

Don't go. Don't go.

"I'm sorry, Caroline," I whisper to my empty room. "But I have to go back."

CHAPTER 6

The barbershop opens early at Dad's request and they negotiate my hack job into a boyish fade. They're extra careful around my ear. While the clippers sing against my skull, I watch hair fall into my lap and try to convince myself none of this matters. I'm still me.

Well, a kind of beaten-up version of me. I avoid looking at myself at the end but Dad's lilting smile of encouragement tells me exactly how pathetic the final result is. Mom sighs. There's a lot more sighing as we pack the car and head out toward the Catskills.

Both parents join for the ride, which is rare, but I sense that they're eager to visit Aspen, too. Maybe they have questions they want to answer in person, just like me. Mom takes conference calls while Dad drives and I lie on the back seat, texting a few friends about what's up with me. I fire off a few updates to social media, too, letting everyone know I'll be offline for a while. Quickly I'm bombarded by hearts and messages saying *Take all the time you need*. I turn my phone facedown on my chest and let the thrum of the highway lull me to sleep.

Miles later I sit up, stiff necked, a glare slanting through the sunroof. The dream I was having dissolves in the tinted light, my spine popping as I stretch. My phone is an endless barrage of sympathy, and I swipe it all away without reading.

We're slowing. That's what woke me up. Now we've parked in a shimmering plaza of baking cars.

"What do you think? Will this do, Mars?"

I think Dad is expecting me to have some sort of reaction to where we've pulled over for lunch. It's an Applebee's. I cannot imagine having an opinion on Applebee's.

"This is fine."

My hand goes to pull at my hair, but of course it's gone. I marvel at the prickling fuzz of my scalp. As we walk inside, I watch my reflection leap and pinch across the chrome of the parked cars. Then my reflection is on the dark glass of the front doors, watching me like a detached shadow. Then it's bound in a bathroom mirror, and I'm trapped looking at myself for the first time in a long time.

The gash on my forehead shines. The bandage on my ear is visible from every angle now. I dance my fingertips along the surgical tape, feeling for even the smallest opening. Anything an insect could crawl into. I check my hand next. I must have done something in my sleep, though, because a clot of crimson has gathered beneath one of my nails. I dab it with a wet paper towel, wincing when I shift one of the nail fragments. My eyes water. Someone tries to open the door.

"One minute!" I shout.

In the mirror I am a mess. A spiky-scalped, monstrous thing hunched in the yellow light. I'm marbled with old bruises and misty eyed and, oh wonderful, now I'm bleeding into the porcelain sink. I know people think being queer is, like, very fabulous and full of witty repartee and all that, but sometimes it's also crying in the bathroom of an Applebee's somewhere near Margaretville, New York, while Rihanna's "S&M" plays on the speakers for the early-bird crowd.

A mess, basically. And not even a hot one. Just a mess.

Which is unlike me. I've never ever in my whole life been able to pull off messiness. If I'm out of my own control, I'm within someone else's—that's what Mom used to tell us. She meant that the moment we lose our grip on a situation, it becomes an opportunity for someone else to take advantage of us. I heard it another way. I heard: It is up to you to demand people see you as *you*, or they will almost always decide you are someone else. Maybe someone weak, or vulnerable, or dismissible.

I can't afford to be those things. I don't do mess, not when my first stint at Aspen showed me exactly how bad things can get when my story is controlled by others.

And yet here I am, a mess. A justifiable mess, sure, but a mess I can't afford to be. And even worse, I'm *scared*.

Aspen is only a few miles away. Minutes. Moments, after years of distant wondering. I can't even imagine being hungry right now. No 2-for-$20 combo for Mars Matthias.

I splash the blood down the drain and give myself a stern glare. I glare until the mess is smothered out, and only Mars is looking back.

Back in the car, I reread the last couple of texts between Caroline and me. Our chat is buried beneath a mountain of mourning from family and classmates, mostly unread, all un-responded to. Caroline's text is a photo of our parents posing with the Aspen sign that I only sort of remember.

Take care of these two for me! See you on the other side!

We're close now. They'll take my phone when I arrive. I memorize the text and the photo, then stare out into the vanishing suburbs and widening fields.

We pass farm stands advertising corn and firewood. Huge trucks sit inert upon overgrown lawns. Houses retreat into the land, sometimes accompanied by big, burly-looking barns. We go faster, and suddenly the neat fields dissolve into waves of wildflowers, then thickening bramble, then the forest rises like a tsunami. I watch the sky wink through the closing treetops, and it's like the farther we drive, the farther into the earth we sink. The forest is thick now, a verdant chaos pressing against our car as we swing up the snaking turns of a mountain. Sometimes, right as the turns break, the tree line whips back to reveal a green abyss, and it makes me reconsider Caroline's text.

See you on the other side.

I know it's not what Caroline meant, but as we career through the forest, I feel as though the other side is rushing to meet me. The jaws of the forest close over the narrowing road.

Mom loses her signal and her call drops. Dad pops on the radio and it's just fuzz. We turn off the paved roads and onto dirt ones, finally crunching past an elegantly painted sign that reads:

Welcome to

ASPEN CONSERVANCY SUMMER ACADEMY

est. 1923

Oh, shit, I nearly think out loud. Mom sighs.

I thought I was ready for the violent familiarity of that sign, but I am not. Brutally nostalgic is how it feels. And the same uncanniness emanates from everything after. The trio of boulders at the turn, then the wooden posts regaling visitors with Aspen's values:

TRADITION

CHARACTER

SPIRIT

Each new sight is the scalpel digging open waxy scars. The cracks in me widen, and I fully feel the deluge of anticipation—dread, excitement, hope, and fear—I've been stifling all day. I take such a big breath, Mom gives me a cool glance in the driver's mirror. She's looking for—has been looking for—any excuse to turn this car around and go home.

I give her a smile and a *big* thumbs-up. *So* excited! I earn another sigh.

I look back out the window.

With all the strange familiarity, I sense an unexpected nearness to Caroline. For a moment, she feels so close that I expect to see her through the trees, glowing in a pool of neon-green ferns. Watching me as I enter the world she ran away from days ago.

I wonder: How *did* Caroline escape? How did she get all the way home? Did she take a bus? Or hitchhike? We don't know. My parents don't want to know, but I need an answer to this, and to all the unknowns I've inherited. It feels almost like an obligation, to bear witness to what happened to her. A last, desperate attempt to be with my sister at her end.

We begin the hairpin turns cutting down into the valley, teasing glances of the aspen groves for which the Conservancy is named. The lake, flat and lustrous, winks like a promise in the distance. Then come the gates, flung open, and after that the Welcome Center. Like many of the camp's buildings, it's a rustic cottage that appears to grow up from the pine needles. It's shabby and lovely, but expertly so, and too huge to qualify as quaint. This goes for most of Aspen, which is designed with the same derelict, woodsy illusion in mind.

Wendy, one of Aspen's co-directors, surprises us in the entryway. I nearly shout when I see her, almost invisible in the dim interior. She's standing so still, like she hasn't moved an inch since the last time I saw her, right in this exact spot, when she waved me goodbye. The symmetry of the two moments—my departure, my return—converges when she clasps my hand and says, "Told you we'd see each other again, Mars."

She gives a chummy wink and a little shrug, like, *Isn't life so strange?*

Wendy feels much, much older. The taut authority that's always crackled just beneath her cheer is more obvious now. I check, and yes, she still has a small mole embedded in the thin hair of her temple. Caroline used to tell me it moved.

Wendy small-talks with my parents about the drive up as she leads us through a den, past a kitchen of milky tile, and into a sitting room that spills through a wall of lacy French doors, out onto a patio dusted in pollen. There is not a single light on in the house, but the bright sun pushes into every corner like a presumptuous guest. It's the smell that is most familiar to me, though: a woody mustiness baked by the heat, spritzed in citronella and dotted with sunscreen. Something sweet sneaks in, beneath it all. Something overripe and pungent.

It's burned away by the smell of coffee as Wendy pours three mugs. The steam lingers in the light too long, like the air is slow. It occurs to me that things are different here out in the woods. Even physics.

The adults vanish into an office. I'm sure there's been tons of communication between Aspen and my parents since Caroline's death, but this is Wendy's time to really express remorse in person. I don't want to see more of that.

I take the chance to explore the room. Lace doilies creep over the ancient wooden furniture like sugary fungus. A vase of leaning lilies (real) sits on a credenza that boasts framed photos of past campers, past directors. I find myself studying each scene, seeing Caroline in all the sunburnt smiles, even in the ancient sepia photos taken, according to the placard, nearly a hundred years ago. Then I stare up into a framed painting that spans an entire wall. It's a hand-illustrated map of Aspen.

The Welcome Center is a blank square in the lower left edge. The road winds on, connecting with a network of paths and buildings that make up the central campus around Big Lodge, where the original owners used to stay. That's where all the main buildings are, too, like the dining pavilion and the rec center. Up the hill are the fields, the pool, and the tennis courts. Down the hill, rolled up against the lake's edge, are the boathouse, the docks, and the waterfront.

If you go left at Big Lodge, through the woods is Hunter Village, where the older boys stay. It's a minified version of Aspen swept up into the hills, a lodge and two burly cabins—Bear Hut and Eagle House, notorious and whispered about endlessly among the younger campers. The cabins squat atop tree-thick stilts that make a flat, sturdy sense of the land's incline. I left before I could be dragged there, but it's where I'll be staying for . . . I'm not sure. However long I last, I guess.

My eyes find their way back through the woods, past Big Lodge, and to the other side of camp. Near the boathouse I find Amazon Village, where the older girls stay, a lowland reflection built to mimic what the boys have always had.

Aspen keeps a strict binary to the two villages of Hunter and Amazon. That's just for the oldest kids, though. The younger campers are kept in adjoining clearings close to Big Lodge, in newer, friendlier cabins built about thirty years ago. Cabins with just letters for names and no mythic titles. The youngest campers are called Bandits. The next age group up is called Scouts. Bandits and Scouts get to do stuff together. They only divide for swimming and sleeping. But then, after the age of fourteen, the space between the gendered communities rips open. Boys become Hunters, girls become Amazons. And those in between?

In between, on the map, are miles of eerie, unnavigable woods.

"How fitting," I mutter.

I stand back from the map, observing it all at once. I've been reading all about Aspen since I decided to come back here. Like the other Great Camps, Aspen was built and run by a single family with legions of staff. The grounds were self-sustaining, and for every room you'd find in a house, they built an entire building. A rec hall for play, cabins to sleep, and an entire pavilion to dine. Even more woodsy amenities were erected as it became its own private village. There's a mill for the baker, and a shed for the groundskeeper. A leatherworking cabin. A pottery barn (literally a converted barn for pottery), a stable of horses and their riding ring, and a smith shop beside it. This last one isn't on the map, but I know it's there. If I scraped the painted trees away, I'd find it hidden below. And if I picked off the roof, I'd find Mars, aged eleven, hiding. Caroline and I used to meet there when she was avoiding mucking out the horse stalls and I was avoiding boys, or counselors, or swimming lessons, or literally any one of Aspen's many tortures.

My eyes drift to the other side of the lake, which is curiously bereft of details. But that's where Cabin H is. Across the lake and up a sunlit slope of wildflowers. I used to stand on the docks and watch that meadow, pretending I could see the air clouded with honeybees, pretending I could see a bronzed leg kick out over the back porch. Sometimes I really did hear them. It was when they laughed. For some reason, that sound always carried to me across the lily-choked waters.

The map paints the impression of a flowering field, but the cabin itself has been omitted. What happens there, unobserved? What do the girls of Cabin H laugh so loudly about?

Above everything, painted upon a curling scroll, is Aspen's slogan. I read it aloud.

"We came as one and left as many. We came with nothing and left with everything."

The quote is unattributed. It feels like it's the voice of the camp itself, of all the campers, past and present, rising in unison. One, as many.

Something bangs in the house.

I lose my balance—I didn't realize I was on my toes looking into the map—and I fall into the photos, downing them like dominoes. Heavy, entitled footsteps launch a boy my age into the living room.

"Mars! Buddy! You made it!"

First I register teeth—perfect and white and too many—and then there's a boy smiling down at me. Dark green shirt, a lanyard jingling with keys. A counselor. He introduces himself with a seismic handshake. "Wyatt. It's good to meet you, man. Me and the other guys are really looking forward to having you in Bear Hut. Did you just get here?"

Man. Other guys.

It begins.

The office door opens and out come Wendy and my parents. Wyatt stands at attention—clearly he knows who I am, which means he knows

39

who Mom is. His teeth flash as he introduces himself, making expert small talk with the adults as we walk from the Welcome Center to the car. Then Wendy pulls him away, giving my family room to say our goodbyes.

We hug. Mom sniffles just a little when I let her go, and the sound clatters around in me, finding all the old dents of guilt. I do, for just a moment, doubt everything about what I'm doing.

Mom rubs my arm. "If you want to come home, just let Wendy know. No explanation needed. We'll come right away."

"Okay."

She swallows back tears. Her composure re-forms around her, a coolness that presses back against the muggy air.

Dad clamps a hand on my shoulder. "Have fun. Make friends. And—"

"*We before me*," I finish. A Matthias mantra. Basically, *your actions reflect on all of us.* I give a consenting nod. "Of course."

"Very good." Dad does that thing where he claps his hands together, the way dads ceremonially announce it's time to move on. "Well. That's it, then?"

That's it. Wyatt and Wendy appear on a golf cart, and Wyatt heaves my bags up beside Wendy. My parents ease into their car, the engine dampening the buzz of insects that have gathered in the awkwardness of our goodbye, and they're gone.

Wyatt and Wendy are looking at me, maybe expecting a tear or two, but I smile to show I'm fine. They don't look convinced. I'm not either.

"I'll drop these at the cabin," Wendy says. "You boys okay to walk into camp?"

We nod. Wendy rumbles off and we follow after, stepping into the golden cloud of dust, pollen, and light. Aspen's light, thick and reaching, like a demanding embrace.

II

CHAPTER 7

We walk slow, but not slow enough.

Aspen stalks us from behind the dense forest. Coy. Carnivorous. Through the trees I glimpse neon fields, stone walls laced with ivy, and red-stained buildings aflame with afternoon sun. The invisible bugs envelop us in their chanting. This is how Aspen has felt to me all these years away; like the specter of summer itself, a warmth that could be recalled but never felt.

Now it reaches for me. I'm not ready, but it doesn't matter. The forest slides away and all the winking details—the glimpsed buildings and the walls and the fields—crash together, forcing apart the brambles so that the sky rushes in, so big and blue you could choke on it.

I clench my jaw as the camp locks into place around us. The heat of the forest was smothering, but this heat under the open sun is invasive. I feel the last particles of cool air—from the car, from the restaurant—burn from my lungs as summer swallows me from the inside out. I am claimed. The uncanny familiarity is within me now; there's no going back.

Wyatt talks—has been talking—this whole time. He's a year older than me, and a Leader-in-Training. An *LIT*, hence the dark-green shirt. He remembers me from when we were both Bandits. He'll be my guide and I'll stick with him while we sort out my daily itinerary. If anyone gives me any shit, he's got my back. He totally gets what I'm going through. He's . . .

"You're Wendy's nephew," I remember suddenly.

In the glare of present day, Wyatt is on the cusp of being unrecognizable from the cheery, round-faced boy I remember. But the eyes give him away. One brown, one brownish blue. I squint at him as the present eclipses the past.

Wyatt's easy smile turns self-conscious. I'm totally right.

"So you do remember me. That's great! Didn't think you would. You look super different, too. Have you been working out? I see those guns."

His grating eagerness returns. I clock the phoniness. I'm mad it took me this long to realize I've been saddled with Aspen's best salesperson. A windup camper, drilled on Aspen codes and credos from birth. I'll have to be careful about what I reveal to Wyatt.

"They just packed up the farmer's market before you got here. It'll be back next Sunday. And . . . you probably remember a lot of this, so stop me if I'm boring you," Wyatt is saying as we reach Big Lodge. The building is an overgrown confusion of mossy logs and squinting, milky windows, all belted by low, shadowy porches. It's monstrous. It thrusts right up through the treetops, yet still feels curled into itself, like it may wake at any moment and trudge back into the lake. Around it are smaller, similar buildings, like a scattered litter. They reach out to one another with covered paths. Wyatt points out the recreation hall, the dining pavilion, the culinary center, and the Eco-Lab.

"Basically I live there when I'm not at Bear Hut. The Eco-Lab actually used to be a library, but we converted it to an ecology studies center with a grant from SUNY."

I stare at Big Lodge. The stillness of the building against the ever-waving trees is unnerving. The shade, too. I forgot shade could look like that. Here, under the open sky, the shade is bright black. Impenetrable. Clean prisms of darkness wedged beneath the eaves, the porticos, the low porch ceilings.

I want to throw myself into the shade. The air has no business being this *hot*. But the shade wouldn't be safe. I gaze into the cool prisms, looking for them. I catch two faces in an open window, and then the shine of an oiled leg kicking out from a railing. I hear the squeal of a swinging chair. Someone invisible calls to Wyatt and he waves.

Then I do see them. The other campers in their white uniforms, gathered in the shade like drifts of unmelting snow. Their faces are grinning blurs. They watch us walk by and I'm swamped in self-awareness, feeling every blot of sweat seeping through my black tank top, feeling their eyes on my shoulders, my jaw, my hands, my height. Trying, at a distance, to pry my secrets right off my body.

I know what I look like. I know how people see me. I used to play sports to offset my femininity, but the result is a muscular frame that makes my swish that much stranger. And now with the shaved head I'm sure people are even more confused.

Or not? Bria said Aspen had gotten better. Maybe it's my own demons that are filling in all the blank stares.

Then we walk by a group of little kids sprawled over a large banner they're painting. I recognize the curiosity that silences them as they wait for me to pass so that they can huddle together and giggle at the mystery of me. A few steps after we go by, they laugh.

I'm sweating everywhere now. I want to dive into the shade and hide.

Wyatt must notice. He talks louder, walks faster.

"Wendy will make sure your bunk is all set up, so we've got some time to kill. Want to see what the other Hunters are up to? Ready to make some friends for life?"

I almost say *No, thanks*. But that's the messiness I saw before. The fear. That Mars won't last here. He'll break. I know from experience. So I say, "Sure."

We leave Big Lodge and detour through the woods. Wyatt reminds me that majors are in the morning—those are a camper's individual programs—but the afternoons consist of group activities. Wilderness Workshops. Village Challenges in everything from dodgeball to watercraft

45

construction. Hut Hikes. Village Cleanup. And, if there's nothing planned, free swim before dinner.

"Hope you brought your floaties," Wyatt jokes, looking at my arms.

"Actually, I'm allergic to water."

"You are?"

"Yeah, you didn't know? Queer people dissolve in water. That's how all those divers make such small splashes at the Olympics."

"I—oh, you're making a joke." Wyatt says this like he's telling a toddler *Good work on this ugly-ass drawing of a dog.*

I resolve to make no further jokes.

Blessedly, the hike into the hills inspires breathy silence, and I give up on ever not being a sweaty mess for the next five-ish weeks. The uphill tapers, and suddenly we're in a maze of pale stalks—trees, thin and shivering. They have bone-white bark swirled with black, half-lidded eyes.

"Mars, meet the aspen," Wyatt says with a grand sweep at the trees. "The world's oldest organism."

"Really?"

"Yeah, aspen colonies are estimated to live thousands and thousands of years."

I look at the trees. The way they seem to look back unnerves me. I keep waiting for one to blink.

"Which is the oldest?" I ask.

Wyatt grins. "None of them."

I cross my arms. Wyatt clearly wants to deploy some fresh, hot nature facts.

"I said aspen, right? Not *aspens.*" His grin broadens. "It's 'cause all these are clones. Just one huge organism connected at the roots. Pretty cool, right?"

I have to admit, he's not wrong. I'm still not sure about the eyes, though. We resume walking through the grove and after a minute Wyatt says, "Don't repeat that."

46

"Already lying to impress me?"

"No. I mean that's really how the aspen works, but we can't officially say this clone is the oldest organism on earth. It's highly contested."

"By *who*? The Old-Ass Tree Society?"

"Ha, close. Other conservancies. Ecologists. People like that. It's possibly true, but it's technically a guess 'cause the clones don't live that long. But the root system does, so we don't *know* know."

"Right," I say. "And it would be impolite to ask Ms. Aspen her birthday."

Wyatt chuckles, this time catching the joke.

"Your secret"—I wink—"is safe with me."

We enter a denser region of the woods, the afternoon's brightness reduced to just gold-white shafts against the dim heights. The temperature drops. Finally, we arrive upon a group scattered on rocks and fallen trees, wearing helmets and harnesses, necks craning as they watch a boy teeter on a wobbling bridge fifty feet in the air. His brown arms wheel as the group lazily encourages him to *do it, do it, you got this, Mitch.*

"Hunters, attention! This is Mars Matthias. Mars, I present the men of Bear Hut. And that's Brayden managing the ropes. He's our cabin's Leader."

A handsome college-aged guy with a patchy mustache shoots me a nod, only glancing away from Mitch for a second. A soft hail of greetings are thrown my way before the guy in the sky makes a wrong step and everyone's attention snaps back to him.

"You brought sneakers, right?" Wyatt asks me. "The sandals are cool but you can't climb without sneakers. If you want, I can radio Wendy to grab them from your bag."

"No!" I nearly shout. Wendy can't go in that bag. "It's fine. I'll just watch."

"Wait, I have an idea."

Wyatt immediately unlaces his own sneakers but I stop him.

"It's cool," I insist, holding up my splinted hand. "Besides, I can't."

"Oh." Wyatt stands. His phony eagerness has given way to an outright naked need for approval. Is he nervous? It makes me nervous that I make him nervous. That usually doesn't go my way, with boys.

"Sorry, forgot," he says. "But when you're healed, we'll get you on the ropes, okay? Unless of course you're allergic to those, too."

I smile. I say, "Nope, got my shots," and it makes Wyatt smile, too. Settled, he turns to Mitch in the sky, rousing a cheer from the boys with powerful claps of his big hands. I sit and watch, but I keep replaying Wyatt rushing to give me his shoes. I don't know why this should fill me with a tickling heat, but it does. When Wyatt takes a turn on the ropes, he flashes me an eager smile, and I look away.

The sounds out here are old and new, so different from home. The chant of bugs is incessant, a lush and frenzied bass underpinning the treble of birdsong and wind. Atop it all is the tremulous echo of shouts, screams, and laughter carrying over the lake. I stand and stretch, then wander a bit into the woods. No one notices. I move, following the distant shouts toward where I think the lake will be. We're high up; I should be able to see across it. I can hear something else, too. A dull, aching grumble, like the sky is hungry. Thunder, I think.

It gets louder as I pick through the forest. I forget about the heat and the sweat, focusing only on that rumbling. I picture it, like massive static in the distance, gray-blue clouds twisting into themselves as they spread over the horizon.

No, not static. A hum? A hum. It oozes from the air. Low, pulsing, lush.

EARTH

I wave a bug away from my ear.

I am at the top of the hill now, looking down at Aspen from a great height. There are no clouds; this is not thunder. Thunder boils, but this

48

hum simmers. I turn and turn, trying to find a source. I close my eyes so I can listen, but in the dark of my mind I see myself, alone and spinning in the woods. Like I'm peering through the unblinking eyes whirled into the white stalks of the aspen trees.

I watch myself stumble, catch myself, charge up a great hill. Watch myself burst onto a bald rockface that juts into an open drop, watch myself reaching toward the lake in the distance, reaching after the hum that vibrates off its knife-bright surface.

"Hello?" I call back.

MARSEARTHTO

There are words in the air, and a warning within those words, but the hum drowns it all out. Within the hum I hear what I've been searching for, finally. Laughter. I can hear them laughing. They're—

MARSEARTHTOMARS

I realize the words are different from the hum. Competing. A separate, deadening tone that cuts into my hypnosis and pulls my eyes downward. I stare at my feet, standing at the edge of a cliff. I stare down through a gap in the treetops below, just wide enough for a body to fall through.

And that's when I see her, sprawled on the forest floor, almost invisible if it weren't for the soft glint of the chandelier crystals frosted around her. They wink like starlight. It's Caroline, her ruined body, her eyes two black holes pulling me close, so close that I'm right there, right before her, when she screams:

EARTH TO MARS!

I jolt awake just as I fall forward. The sky swallows me and my feet punch through air. Then a hand thrusts into the blue oblivion and pulls me backward, onto scraping stone. Safe, at the edge of the cliff.

"Whoa, close call there!" A red face fills my vision. Wyatt! His hand squeezes my forearm. He lets go right away, like I'm white-hot.

"Did you say that?" I ask.

"Say what?"

I don't know. I don't know what I'm asking. My name, someone shouted my name. I was walking, I was listening, I was about to fall, and someone shouted my name. I squeeze my eyes shut. The afterimage on my eyelids, printed in a throbbing negative against the sunlight, is a girl.

Caroline. I saw Caroline, her body in the precise pose from her fall, on the forest floor fifty feet below me.

Impossible.

But if I'm so sure it's impossible, why am I afraid to look again?

"Mars?" Wyatt's hand finds my shoulder. I jump. He jumps. I should feel fear, but I feel a rushing emptiness where that hum used to be. And then I feel angry with myself. Hot, furious humiliation. That Caroline was taken was bad enough, but that I should have to relive it in my nightmares? My daydreams, too? If anything feels impossible, it's living the rest of my life like this.

"I'm sorry," I say, realizing I'm about to cry. "I thought I heard someone calling my name."

"Yeah, I've been calling after you for, like, a hundred feet. You're fast, Matthias. Those sandals got turbo boosters?"

My sandals are clotted in muck. My hands are filthy, like I've been crawling. I twist to look back toward the trees, expecting the sturdy woods of the ropes course. Instead, it's just a wall of white, the aspen grove shimmering in the heat. My tears never fall, because that's when the fear finally blooms.

"I'm sorry," I whisper.

"Don't be sorry," Wyatt says, pulling me away from the edge. "Just be safe."

CHAPTER 8

The hike back to the ropes course is baffling, longer than it should be and down a hill crisscrossed with fallen trees that I must have scrambled through. Wyatt and I are silent as we pull ourselves through the jagged spokes of dried branches. I'm thankful. It gives me time to decide what just happened. There are a few explanations for my sudden, nauseating reverie—grief, I have learned, cracks us into pieces that make all sorts of strange, alarming shapes—but I decide upon heatstroke. The sun is inescapable out here. The air thick enough to chew. Probably also Applebee's didn't help.

A part of me wonders, though, just as we leave the white grove, if a splinter of whatever drove Caroline into her frantic delusion has found its way into me. But then we're back in the tall pines, and the shade shields me long enough for rational thought to prevail. Aspen is a place. Just a place, if I don't make it into more than that. I need to get my shit together.

Before we reach the Bear Hut boys, Wyatt goes all stern.

"So look, I'm sorta in charge of making sure you're okay," he admits finally. Guiltily. "I don't want to crowd you or anything. It's mostly for safety, since you missed orientation. I don't know how much you remember, but in the woods we stick to the paths for a reason. Lots of ravines and gullies. And cliffs like that one. It's easy to fall, especially at night. Last week one of the landscapers . . . he . . ."

He doesn't finish. He doesn't need to. I remember the stories about hunters and hikers who underestimated these woods. The cruel topography of Aspen chewed them apart. People go missing in the mountains too often.

"I'll be more careful. Sorry that I scared you."

"You got a watch?" Wyatt asks.

"What? Why?"

Wyatt holds up his wrist, showing me a garishly large watch. It's blocky, full of buttons and wheels.

"Christmas gift last year," Wyatt says. "Fully waterproof. Military standard durability. And it's got a compass. We're in the woods a lot out here and it's easy to get turned around, but I'm never getting lost. Here, want to try it on?"

He undoes it deftly, shoving it at me. I can't help it—I laugh. It seems Wyatt is determined to dress me. He cracks a smile, too. The tension fades between us.

"I'm so sorry, Wyatt, but this I am *definitely* allergic to."

"What? Too straight?"

I pick at it with two fingers. "Is that *camouflage*?"

Wyatt takes it back, feigning offense. "I'm surprised you can even see it. Must be defective."

I laugh again, and Wyatt beams like he's scored the first point of the day.

Back in the group, a hand claps over my shoulder, scaring me. I forgot how much guys love to just touch one another.

"Mars, man, it's great to meet you!"

It's Brayden, the counselor. Or Leader, in Aspen-speak. He shakes my hand with a hot, chalky grip while he snaps off his helmet. "You got up here okay? You been keeping Wyatt busy?"

"Sure have." I smile sweetly.

"Cool, cool. Welcome to Aspen, man. You're part of Bear Hut now, the best cabin ever. You meet the boys? Good. You'll get to know everyone soon enough, my man. Don't you worry. Lots of time for all that. Here, want to walk with me?" Brayden throws some signal to Wyatt before leading us back down the path. He wants me alone. I brace myself.

It begins with small talk. How is it to be back? What activities do I remember? What am I looking forward to? Then it goes quiet, and I think he's about to bring up Caroline, but he doesn't. We just stay in uncomfortable silence until Brayden says, "If you need anything, you let me or Wyatt know, okay? We want your time here to be awesome."

Awesome. I consider feigning an allergy to Awesome.

Brayden guides us all the way to Hunter Village.

"I bet it's weird being back here. Or I guess you never stayed in Hunter Village, did you?"

"I was a Scout when I left," I say. It's the first thing I've said in minutes.

"Nice. Nice. Lots has changed probably. We got a new sports complex and they finally finished the indoor pool. And there's a new theater, too. State of the art." Brayden gestures vaguely in the direction of Big Lodge, invisible from this deep in the forest. Instead, much closer, small huts dot the path. Brayden doesn't point those out, but I know what they are. Cure Cottages, from back when Aspen was a makeshift sanatarium. People came here to escape tuberculosis, thinking there was magic in the mountain air. Now they're staff housing.

"You picked a good day to arrive," Brayden says, perhaps also thinking about the heat. "Weather's been up and down."

I remember how this sort of heat seems to draw all the morning's coolness up into late-afternoon storms that hammer the forest with rain, then cease into a sticky, dripping dusk. I listen for thunder again, but can't hear it. I can't hear anything—no birds or bugs or wind. Life deadens as we walk into Hunter Lodge's shadow. We stomp up the porch, into a dark and cold interior that spreads into a massive meeting room. It smells like cedar and animal musk, probably because all over the walls and the shelves are mounted animals heads. They follow us with glassy black eyes as Brayden rushes through a quick tour.

"We use the lodge for Village meals, and activities when the weather sucks. This is the dining hall, that's the activity center, and upstairs is for Donovan, our Village Leader, and the hunting parties that come through. The rec room is open nightly after dinner, and a lot of the guys hang out here. You play poker?"

"Actually, I play poke-him."

"What?"

"Never mind. Yes, I know how to play poker."

"Cool. Any sports? You look like a wrestler, maybe?"

"Nope, no sports," I lie. The last thing I need is to be dragged into every random micro-masculinity contest. I'll be dead if I win one by accident.

"That's too bad. We've got a competitive bunch this year."

See? My instincts are as sharp as ever.

We head out the front, down a sloping lawn that meets the edge of the lake. Two cabins border the lawn. Brayden brings us to the farther one and announces: "Welcome to Bear Hut!" Next to the screen door is a carved bear standing on two legs. Someone has placed a bucket hat on its head. Brayden gives it a chummy slap on the ass.

"That's Bernard, our mascot. Not much of a talker but he keeps us safe," Brayden recites.

Everything in Bear Hut is made of wood. The floor, the walls, the ceiling, the furniture. All wood. Except for a huge, scorched fireplace rising up the back wall. That's brick, but inside it? Wood. And actually, nothing about Bear Hut could be called a hut. It's a cabin bigger than most people's houses, many of the interior walls knocked out to create a communal area. A circular chandelier of antlers hangs over us. Pendant fans churn the muggy air.

The smell. A close, damp must. The smell of summer, and cedar, and boy sweat, closed into the dark corners of the cabin and baked into a fungal tang by the heat. I clench my jaw against the memories it stirs, phantom bruises waking beneath my skin.

"We call this area the den," Brayden says, referring to the couches and recliners around the fireplace. "Kitchen's over there, but no one uses it. Bathroom and showers are that way. Wyatt and I sleep through there, and you'll be on the second floor with the rest of the . . ."

Brayden's face twists up.

The rest of the boys, he was going to say.

"They said you were cool with the sleeping arrangements." He gives me a worried glance.

"They said that . . ." I draw it out, relishing his spooked look. "Because it's *true*."

Brayden gives a nervous laugh, quickly moving us up the stairs to a massive loft lined in bunk beds, between them bureaus and small couches. All wood. Shoes and clothes clutter the corners, and I can smell mildewed towels. There's also a large plaque over the entrance that says: INVITE THE OUTSIDE . . . IN!

Brayden brings me to the last bed, where my bags are waiting on the plastic mattress. His friendliness is fading.

"So, some quick ground rules. Wake-up is every day at seven, and lights-out is at eleven. Boys from Hunter Village are allowed in the bunks until sundown, but no one else. That means no girls."

Brayden mumbles this last part. I suppress a grin. I think he just got my poke-him joke.

"As you probably know, we're pretty strict about what gets brought into camp. No outside food, no electronics, and we have a zero-tolerance policy for alcohol and drugs. Medications are administered at the infirmary. We do bag checks randomly throughout the summer, too. Aspen is a haven away from the rest of the world, and we really want everyone to feel present. And safe. Now, Mars, answer me honestly: Is there anything in your bag that you think may keep you from being safe, or that might threaten another person's safety?"

"No," I lie.

"May I check?"

"Of course."

Outsmarting the bag checks is an ancient art passed down between campers at Aspen. We'll see if I've still got it mastered.

Brayden unzips my bag, peeling my clothes apart like something among the folds might sting him. He finds a bundle, gives me a nervous glance, and unwraps it. He is left holding a sports bra.

Brayden stuffs it back into my bag and even zips the bag up, unable to look me in the eye.

"You're good," he declares.

My plan worked.

Brayden makes short work of his other official counselor business. He takes my phone and puts it in a bag with my name on it, letting me know I can use it for emergencies only, or in exchange for a made-up currency called Bear Bucks. I get Bear Bucks by doing chores. There is a chore chart. There's a curfew, an *Aspen Manual*, and so on.

Then Brayden opens a dresser drawer with a fresh label sporting my name. My full name. Marshall. And a dumb little smiley face.

"Uniforms are in here. Laundry is picked up every three days. A fresh uniform is mandatory during the day on weekdays, but you can wear your own clothes after dinner so long as they comply with Aspen's dress code." This is said with a pointed glance at my tattered tank top, which is not compliant, which is why I wore it. "So, get changed, and let me know if you need a different size. Linens are in the bottom drawer. Don't worry about making your bed. We'll be back here after Embers, just hanging out."

Embers. Each day at Aspen ends with a reflective, fireside meeting known as Embers. Sometimes it's a camp-wide meeting at the big amphitheater, sometimes it's the cabins meeting separately. I remember a smoke-choked fire, and an acoustic guitar, and enough sing-alongs to unnerve a show choir.

I shiver.

"Any questions?" Brayden asks.

"Nope."

"Cool. Get changed. The boys should be back soon. And welcome to Bear Hut, man."

Before Brayden leaves the loft, he turns, and I see that the fraternal warmth has completely vanished.

"One more thing," he says. "You're a Hunter now, Mars. You're not a kid anymore, and we expect our more mature campers to be just that. Mature, responsible, independent. That goes for policing your own behavior and the behavior of others. I'm not going to monitor your every move. Same with the other boys. We operate on an honor code at Aspen, and we expect campers to resolve their conflicts as best they can before escalating issues to the cabin leadership or the directors."

I grip the post of the nearest bunk bed. I nod. I recall well Aspen's hands-off approach to resolving conflict. Negligence, Aspen would argue, builds the most outstanding character. But why is Brayden making such a point of this?

"Wendy briefed me about your last summer here," Brayden adds. "Your side of it, I mean. I knew those boys. They were good guys. It's a shame things couldn't get resolved before Wendy got involved and people got kicked out."

The muggy odor of the cabin is suddenly suffocating, and I have to fight to keep breathing. Brayden hasn't asked a question but he waits, like he wants an answer. No, I know that look in his eyes. Flat. Expectant. Dangerous. Brayden wants an apology.

I say nothing.

"I don't want to see any of my boys get kicked out this summer," Brayden says finally. He looks me up and down, and I wonder if he includes me among his boys. I'm guessing not, based on what he says next.

"Wendy mentioned that you were . . . that you are . . ."

"Gender fluid."

"That's cool, man." Brayden resumes his fratty, dismissive persona, just like that. Now that I've seen him out of it, it doesn't quite fit. I can see the dark thing squirming beneath. He says, "Don't expect special treatment, though, and no one will give you a hard time. If they do, let me know. But leave Wendy out of it."

I nod.

"And Wyatt. He's her nephew. You know that, right?"

"I know."

"Good. Assume she knows what he knows. Are we clear, then?"

Brayden watches me for the long seconds before I manage to say, "Yes, crystal clear." And then he goes.

I sit on the unmade bed, thinking about the cascade of threats hidden in his little orientation: Don't act up; handle your shit yourself; don't tell Wendy; avoid Wyatt.

I don't want to see any of my boys get kicked out this summer. As if I'm a danger to their little club.

Maybe I am a grenade, after all.

No one is watching me, but I force calmness into my every movement as I peel off my sweaty clothes. I grab a uniform and lay it out before me, considering what I'm about to do. Who I need to become to survive here.

The last time I was at Aspen, I was small and unsure. I floated through the camp's rituals with easy acceptance, a twig swept through a river's currents. Like when Caroline and I got cast in the Bandit musical as Thing One and Thing Two, and they made sure I wore a bow tie, and her a hair bow. Or when I tried to sign up for dance and they laughed at me until I said I was joking. Or the whole Battle of the Sexes meltdown. All those concessions I didn't know any better than to make.

Now I feel heavy with an identity that causes the camp to warp around me. I'm not that twiggy little kid anymore. That's good and bad. I'm stronger now, but that makes me much harder to accept.

I rip open the plastic of the uniform and dress without further hesitation.

I know I will need to change if I want to last here. And if I'm going to uncover whatever lurks beneath the Conservancy's surface, integrating is imperative. I can't debate it every time.

And besides, Caroline would point out, *you change all the time.*

She'd be right. Long ago I had to learn that my body isn't who I am; who I am is how I feel. A pressed polo shirt won't change anything. Still, I hate how I look after I've dressed. What little androgyny I'm able to hold on to fades as the clean white lines of the uniform reveal my square shoulders, my flat chest, my narrow hips. At least I brought extra-short shorts. Still, not even a five-inch inseam is going to help me baffle the binary.

Oh well. I'll think of this as dress-up. Mars Matthias's latest performance of *dude*, a Golden Bear Boy in Brayden's ensemble.

Alone, eyes closed, I raise my arms into a ballerina's pose. I didn't get to dance but Caroline still taught me all her lessons. I probably practiced them more than she did. I skip and twirl in my socks, making sure to point the toe like she'd tell me. Then I flop onto the bunk bed. I consider my shoes—you're required to wear closed-toed shoes outside the cabins. Dad made me pack sneakers and even hiking boots.

But I pull on my gladiator sandals. I kick out my feet, enjoying the black leather straps cutting across the white socks. I won't be able to run, but if I play my cards right, I won't have to.

CHAPTER 9

The boys return from the ropes course, filling the cabin with shouting and shaking as they shower before dinner. The smell of sweat diffuses to steam, then grassy soap and detergent as fresh uniforms are pulled over damp bodies. I busy myself putting away my clothing among the uniforms already in my drawers, hiding Caroline's beekeeping tool between layers of fabric, next to the Mayfair calculator. I don't know why I chose to bring it, other than the solitary fingerprint Caroline left on it before she went for the sundial. That there's meaning to this—that it's all somehow significant—is a hope I can't seem to shake. Just another way I'm chasing her, I guess.

I brought the candle, too, but I don't hide that. I stash it in my cubby, by my pillow, pausing to place my thumb over the bee in the wax, hiding the gash that divides it.

"You can't light that," Wyatt tells me, as if I just struck a match. He lets me keep it, though.

We assemble outside, counting off. I'm told my number is twelve, and as we walk down the path toward Big Lodge, I meet the other eleven. There's Mitch, the boy who was climbing, and Andrea, who is from Italy. Ray is loud and charming. Brian has ice-blue eyes and a soft voice. Trent provides only his name and avoids shaking my hand, and Xavier blinks at my painted nails. I miss three names, and then two different boys introduce themselves as Charlie. The second one is shouted down by the cabin, who declare him *The Chuckster*. He meekly denies this but I sense actual fury around the joke, which I'm guessing has plagued him for a while now.

"Sunday night is cookout night," Wyatt tells me, but I can already smell the sizzle and see the smoke solidifying the dusk light bouncing off the lake. We pass the dining pavilion, finding a paved patio teeming with people. Our cabin gloms into a shapeless line and soon we're facing down a steaming buffet of sweating kitchen staff serving us with bright, tired smiles. I accept a hamburger and corn still wrapped in a scorched husk. The line surges past glass aquariums of lemonade, sliced fruit floating behind frosty glass. Then I'm washed against a table of condiments, a low tide of bottles and bowls advertising their contents with laminated signs. Not just ketchup, but organic ketchup from Heaven's Bounty Farms. The mayonnaise is described as "small batch." I dare not read the entire paragraph describing the relish.

The lawn is covered in colorful picnic blankets that swirl and overlap like a deflated circus tent, and everywhere campers sit cross-legged. I scan, looking for any sign of Bria or the other Honeys. It's known that the Honeys don't always come to Big Lodge for meals, but then I see a group of older girls sprawled near the flagpole. My confidence fades as I step onto their blanket.

"Uh, hi," a girl says with a menacing chew of her hot dog.

All the faces look at me with matching disgust.

"Hi," I say. I don't recognize any of them. I feel the ever-present compulsion to apologize for myself. They seem to want that, too.

"Sorry," I say. "Just looking for a place to sit."

"Keep looking. No boys allowed," one says.

"Okay. Sorry," I say, and I go to leave.

"Wait," one of them says. "You're new, aren't you?"

Some variable slides into place and her eyes widen with realization. Then, like I'm not standing right in front of them, the girl whispers to her friends: "It's *her* brother."

They stop chewing. Their disgust closes into something else. Pity, and curiosity. They don't know what to do, what to say. I spare them the choice and rush off, their whispers joining the din thickening around me. People chewing, staring, laughing. My vision tunnels, now just looking for an escape. Then a waving hand catches me. Wyatt, reeling me over to where the Huntsmen have settled.

I keep my head raised as I walk, but on the inside I'm withering. I wonder: What rumors about Caroline have I made true, arriving all bloody and bruised? Who does she become to these people, now that they can see the marks she left on me?

I feel ashamed, like I'm failing her again.

I reach the boys. My arrival silences whatever they were talking about. Then, as soon as I bite into my hamburger, the questions start. Softball small talk, Dad would say. *Warm-ups*, Mom would add. I tell the boys I'm from Westchester. My full name is Marshall Matthias the Third, but you can call me Mars. I don't play any sports but I used to do tennis, and fencing, and I went through a bouldering phase. I'm looking at colleges in the Northeast but will probably end up at Cornell, like my parents. I want to study mathematics or physics. My dad is a doctor; my mother works in the government.

They are very, very careful to avoid asking anything that might bring Caroline up. It's like they can see the voids in my life, the portions that have been punched out by her death, and they ask around them.

Or maybe I'm being paranoid again. Purposefully vague small talk is an art among the rich, a test of how little you can say about how much you have. The result is a coy, pointless dance like this one, where status is smuggled into conversations through sly intimation.

For instance, Mitch shows off a rope burn on his hand from a riding rein, and then offhandedly mentions that none of *his* horses have so many vices. The Chuckster does an imitation of his aunt who throws cookouts like these, and who is alarmingly rude to the caterers. This reminds Charlie to tell a story about his bar mitzvah's after-party. The point of his story is to complain about a hot waitress who wouldn't give him a hand job, but by the time he gets there we've learned the party was on his family's yacht.

Well-crafted hints and calculated afterthoughts, seeds cast nonchalantly in the hopes they grow into status. All of it pointless. Aspen is one of the nation's oldest and most exclusive camps. The camp itself is considered a National Heritage Site, so valuable to our nation's history that it must be protected by law and managed by a conservancy, whatever that is. And here we are among all this wild majesty, this stately heritage, feigning humility through bites of macaroni salad.

Thank god the bugle sounds, announcing dinner's end. We're ushered down to the waterfront for an evening activity: an ice-cream social among a forest of tiki torches that snap in the gathering wind. Wyatt goes to organize a cornhole tournament, and the second I'm alone, someone calls my name.

It's a group of guys sitting around a firepit on the sandy beach. I recognize some from my cabin, but the guy who called me over, lanky and attractive, is a stranger. He's grinning, but as I approach he smuggles away his laughter to feign polite scholarship. I brace myself.

"Hey, so, me and the guys were wondering," he says. "What's up with you?"

"What's . . . *up* with me?"

"Yeah, like, what's your deal?"

The guys all keep the same stoic mask, but laughter licks at the edges. My fingers itch to play with my hair but it's gone, so I make a fist.

"Are you asking if I'm gay?"

The boy shrugs. "Straight, gay, boy . . . girl."

On *girl* one of the guys spits out a laugh. Another punches his shoulder, but all of them are starting to crack up. I take a deep breath and lift my chin, ignoring them as I lean in toward the leader, playing along with his act of childish curiosity.

"I'm sorry, what's your name?" I ask.

"Uh. Callum?"

"Well, Callum, I appreciate the inquiry but . . ." I drop my voice to its lowest. "I'm not going to have sex with you. You look bad at it."

The table's shaky silence erupts. Everyone laughs except Callum. He's shaking his head, theatrically disgusted, but I've turned it around on him. His boys are laughing at him, not me. By the time he figures this out, I've left them behind.

Not for the first time—in fact probably for the hundredth—I wonder how Caroline stomached this place. These people. I know that our home could be cold, our parents constantly shoving us through the choreography of very visible, highly achieving childhoods. Caroline always talked about escaping it and vanishing somewhere deep in the woods. How could she have meant here? How could this be better than home?

I find a rock jutting from the water's edge, sit on it, and stare across the dark lake. I'm very busy feeling petulant when Wyatt finds me.

"Mars, I want you to meet someone." He steps aside, revealing a boy so fiercely attractive I'm immediately back on high alert.

"Mars, this is Tyler. He's in Eagle House. Tyler's great. You two are totally going to get along *fabulously*."

Tyler and I exchanged a quick handshake. Terse hellos. But invisible to anyone else is the moment we both reach a grim understanding as to why we're being introduced. We're both gay. For most straight people, this is an infallible, determining factor of friendship, as if queer people are magnetized. If Callum and his goons are watching, which I'm sure they are, Wyatt has just given them plenty more to laugh about.

Tyler's eyes dart from my painted nails to my exposed thighs to my sandals, and never return to my face. I'm no better. He's wearing not one but several woven bracelets. And a super-nice watch. Wyatt couldn't know what he's done, but there's a vastness between Tyler and me that's just been pressurized. It's immediately uncomfortable.

"See? I'll leave you to it, then." Wyatt walks away so that we can continue to get along fabulously. Tyler politely introduces me to a few people and makes sure to mention several times that he has a boyfriend and they are going to Syracuse together, someday. We join in on a game of cornhole. Even though Tyler and I win, he proposes we switch up the teams.

I consider throwing myself in the lake but decide to save the histrionics for when a lifeguard is on duty. Tyler asks if I want to check out the dessert bar, and when I say sure, he sighs, clearly wishing I would just get the hint. I end up listening to him complain that nothing here is "keto" while I cover my own gloopy ice cream in sprinkles.

"Ketosis is a metabolic state," Tyler informs me. "It's really hard to achieve."

"Maybe the ketosis was the friends we made along the way," I say.

Tyler isn't listening. He and everyone turn toward a sound barely audible over the din. Laughter, bright and sparkly.

Their laughter.

A ripple of awareness sweeps through the crowd on the beachfront, pulling attention back to the group of girls who have suddenly appeared upon the lawn, playing a dusk-lit game of croquet. They're too far for me to make out faces, but I know it's them. It's the way the rest of Aspen—the people, the stretching shadows, the snapping flames of the tiki torches—is drawn toward them.

No one looks, but everyone watches the Honeys.

"Do you know those girls?" I ask.

"Cabin H," Tyler says with derision. "Yeah. They're total bitches."

"Was my sister?"

Tyler's mouth pops open like he just remembered who I am. He doesn't get to answer, though, because I'm already over him.

"Enjoy ketosis," I say before heading in their direction.

I hover near the girls for a few minutes, and when they abandon the croquet game I follow them to a well-lit picnic area atop the hill, under a towering pergola dripping with wisteria. Most of the older girls hang out here, clumped upon picnic tables and Adirondack chairs, a firepit spitting up embers. The Honeys glom together at the far edge, arranged like a Renaissance painting of exposed legs and messy buns. I intend to walk right up to them, but then I feel it—the reason no one talks to them. A nearly physical pressure that repels the body but pulls the eye.

Just walk up and say hi, Mars. These girls were in your *house* only a few days ago. Bria is right there. Sierra at her right, Mimi at her left. They invited you here, I remind myself.

But now it feels like I made it all up.

I step under the pergola and weave around the firepit. I end up standing before Bria, clutching my bowl of gloop, trying to think of how to say the word *hello*, when abruptly she does it for me.

"Well, hello, dear."

I am so shocked to be spoken to, I don't manage a response. But then I realize they're not talking to me. Bria is looking at a girl who has approached from the other side.

"Hi," she says. She's nervous. She's brought two friends with her and they push her forward.

"I was wondering if . . . well, my cabin was wondering if we could use the dance studio on Mondays?"

Bria still has her croquet mallet. She rolls it on her lap, causing the head to spin. "Why?"

"To practice. We were hoping to perform at the Jubilee."

"But we perform at the Jubilee," Bria says.

"Yes, but . . ." The girl turns to her friends, but they just nod her along encouragingly. "We noticed Cabin H is on the schedule but doesn't show up, so we thought—we *hoped* you maybe wouldn't mind."

Bria looks to Sierra, who looks to the larger group and asks, "What do we think?"

Suddenly they're all talking:

"But where will *we* practice?"

"Lya, you don't need to practice, you're basically a genius."

"At jazz! But we're doing contemporary for the Jubilee."

"I know we already snapped on it but I was thinking we could do some hip-hop."

"Snaps are final."

"But what about the *Mondays*?"

"Maybe every other?"

"I like that. Every other Monday."

"Okay, so, every other?"

There's a bubbling of *okay!* and *fine* and *let's just snap on it already*. Bria raises a hand and snaps her fingers, the rest snapping quickly after. Then they turn expectantly to the trio of girls who have been watching the discussion, waiting.

The trio of girls hesitate, then also snap their fingers in agreement.

"Great!" Bria says. "Snaps are final. Studio is yours tomorrow. And every other Monday."

The trio of younger girls clutch one another as they walk past me, excitedly whispering *I can't believe they let us have a snap* and *That went sooo well.*

"And what do you want?"

It takes me a moment to realize "you" is me. Instantly, I forget all of English, even swears. Bria turns her attention toward me, as though I've been waiting in line. Two girls sitting behind Bria on the table roll a croquet ball back and forth without looking at it. They're staring at me. All the Honeys are staring at me with the same intelligent disinterest, their aura totally chilled compared with how they treated the other girls.

It's happening again. I'm about to apologize for myself but I think: *No, they invited you here. You just have to say hi.*

"Hi."

"Hi," Bria says. Now all the girls under the pergola are paying attention. On reflex I go to touch my hair and then realize it's not there.

"I got a haircut," I blurt.

"Congratulations, I'm still a lesbian," Bria says, turning her back on me.

"No, I mean you probably don't recognize me. It's me—"

Bria shrieks. I jump. Suddenly the Honeys are all smiling.

"Oh my god, Mars? Mars *Matthias*?"

Bria throws back her head and fills the night with laughter. For a second, I think I'm going to evaporate from embarrassment, but then she leaps up and hugs me.

"Oh, you look so different! I thought you were just another one of the Hunter boys. They've been trying to get me to break all session. God, that was rude. I'm so sorry." She turns to the many people watching, and like a dousing spray, the inquisitive stares flicker away.

Bria gives a faultless smile, but behind her I notice the girls of Cabin H exchanging unsure glances. I can see them whispering through their grins.

"Welcome to Aspen," Bria says. "I mean, welcome *back*."

For some reason it feels like many more than a dozen girls watch me from the Cabin H table, like I'm the focal point of hundreds more eyes. I feel nervous and elated, and for once in my life I'm shy.

"But why are you here?" Bria asks.

"I . . ." My mind slows down, just one thought at a time plinking into the long pause that follows Bria's question. "You invited me."

"I did?"

"Sierra did. At the . . . Celebration of Life. For Caroline."

"Oh, right. *Right.*"

Bria throws Sierra what I'm sure is the Honeys' version of a death glare, and Sierra, very subtly, shrugs. I turn to stone. Or I want to. I would like to toss my statued body into the lake and stay down there until everyone watching this interaction has been dead for hundreds of years, and only then will I rise.

The bugle sounds. Bria rushes back to the table as everyone starts to get up. It's time for Embers.

"Welcome back," she says with a pinched smile, and they glide away.

I am absolutely irradiated with humiliation. First Callum, then Tyler, now this. For a second, I even think I'm going to cry, just right there next to the picnic tables as the rest of the camp flows around me. What did I expect? I left Aspen for so many reasons. Why am I surprised they're all still here, waiting for me?

I decide no on the crying and follow the campers to the other side of the waterfront, where a footbridge leads a short way over the lake to an island of noble pines. It's not a big island, and it only contains an amphitheater of wooden benches and a squat stage. The trees have been cleared at the far side of the island, unveiling a perfect view of the lake's liquid blackness beneath the last of the violet sunset.

I sit at the edge of the bench with the rest of Bear Hut and join them in pretending I don't exist.

From my memories of the Embers ritual, I know it'll involve a quick review of the day's activities, announcements, and a prayer. Always a prayer. It's not called that, though. It's called Embers, the last glowing bits of light before the day is extinguished.

The campers quiet down as someone takes the stage. I'm looking through the rows lit by firelight. After a minute of searching, I spot Bria's dark braids, her head tilted down so another girl can whisper in her ear. Cabin H sits together, strangely close, strangely intertwined through held hands and hooked legs. It's hard to see where one girl ends and another begins.

And then Bria looks up. She looks at me. We lock eyes, and a chill caresses my bare skin as she smiles. It's a wild smile, like she's on the verge of screaming with laughter. And then all the Cabin H girls turn, too, in unison, smooth and quick like a cluster of owls. A wave spreads, and within seconds the entire camp is staring at me. They are quiet. Waiting. Smiling. The sounds of the crickets fill the air.

"Mars? Do you mind standing up and saying hello?"

Wendy. Co-director Wendy. She's on the stage. She says my name like she's repeating it, and her hand is outstretched to me. I put together that she must be introducing me, and that's why everyone is looking at me. Nothing strange. But when I glance at the Honeys, there's amusement twisted into their lips.

Total bitches, Tyler said.

I stand. I breathe. I give a wave to the two hundred faces watching me. I try my best to collect my scattered thoughts into something resembling confidence.

"Hi, my name is Mars. My pronouns are he, him, they, them, or she, her. Whatever, really."

I pause, waiting for either a rash of whispers or, worse, an errant *Yas queen!*, but Aspen gives me neither.

"I'm in cabin . . . Bear Hut."

More, I have to say more.

"I'm . . . really happy to be here, and I'm looking forward to meeting everyone."

The camp responds with a garbled *WELCOMEHELLOHIMARS*. I'm about to sit down but Wendy beckons me to join her out in the middle of the amphitheater, among the benches. I set my jaw, resisting the itch to make sure my nose ring is hidden as I float to her, the heat of every human eye in a ten-mile radius pushing into my skin. Then I face the camp, but I don't see faces. Just a sea of golden eyes shining in the dark, the firelight flickering within them.

I jump when Wendy takes my limp hand in hers. "Here at Aspen, we are a family. A loss of one is a loss for everyone. We were devastated by the news of Caroline's passing, and I would like us all to engage in a moment of silence. Please, everyone, will you join me?"

Wendy places one hand on my shoulder now. With her other, she reaches out into the sea of faces. Hands reach back, grasping her. Grasping me. Crawling over my shoulders, layering atop one another, knuckle on palm on wrist, so that I'm knotted into the center of a monstrous, heavy huddle. It happens so quickly I can't even think about running. And then it all goes quiet. All the eyes close. All sound ceases except for the crackling fire and the calls of loons off the lake. I am overcome with the urge to shout into the silence. I don't want more silence surrounding Caroline. I'm going to be crushed by it, by these hands, by their pulsing grip. I want to scream, but the thing about screaming is you have to let yourself breathe first. And I won't. The air will taste like warm skin.

And then it gets worse.

Wendy squeezes my hand. "We have a small surprise for you, Mars." The silence broken, all the hundred hands retract. I'm suddenly light enough that I could float, but Wendy keeps me tethered. She gives a signal and a quartet of campers pops up. They unfurl a wide roll of paper across the back of the stage.

WE LOVE YOU CAROLINE, it says in large, lopsided letters. And it's streaked in handprints. Bloody handprints, as though ghosts push through from the other side. I squeeze my eyes shut, and when I open them, I see that it's just paint. Handprints of cheap craft paint turned to muddy crimson by the firelight. It's the banner I saw the little ones making this afternoon, nothing scary about it. Each handprint is signed, and many include long handwritten notes.

I'm sorry. I'll miss you. You were beautiful. Rest in peace. Goodbye. I'm sorry. Goodbye. I'm sorry.

Now I want the silence back. Anything instead of this. The crinkle of paper bulging toward me in the breeze and the cacophony of dead-quiet, hollow remorse. Loopy letters. Bloody fingerprints. I hate it. I hate them. I want their silence vanquished. I want my sister back. I want to tear her memory away from these bloody, soiled hands.

"Caroline left an impression on so many of us," Wendy says to the camp. "We will remember her always. She lives on, like a handprint on our own lives. And though her loss leaves a hole in the heart of Aspen, we are overjoyed to welcome back her brother, Mars. I truly believe that Caroline would want this. All of us, together, like the family we are."

I am too self-conscious to cry, or even react. By the strained tenderness in Wendy's speech, I know she wants me to match her, to perform my grief for her. It's like I'm outside my body again, watching myself with everyone else's eyes, waiting for me to move or react or even inhale.

I manage a pained smile. "Thank you." It escapes as a whisper, not because my sadness has made me small, but because I'm brimming with fury. These people weren't her family. *I* was her family. They have no right to use her memory to bring themselves closer together. To touch me, as if my grief could be grasped by anyone else.

But maybe I'm not being fair. Maybe, in the end, they knew her just as well as I did. Or maybe none of us knew her, and we're making her up now. A girl in the shape of our guilt.

The banner crinkles as another breeze contracts it. Wendy squeezes my hand, then turns back to the crowd. "This week, I expect each and every one of you to do your part in making sure Mars feels at home here at Aspen, starting with a BIG Aspen welcome. Please, everyone, let us join together in welcoming Mars home."

She raises our held hands, and like a congregation the camp rises to their feet. I force myself not to run, expecting all one hundred of these white-clad children to charge after me, splashing and writhing into the lake like knotted moon-white leeches.

They begin to stomp and clap, a rough rhythm that eases into something like a chant. Wendy holds me in place, fiercely. I'm trapped between the campers and a paper wall of their bloodred remembrance. Then I am awash in the Aspen cheer. Half sung, half shouted, it booms across the lake:

> *We came as one!*
> *We left as many!*
> *We came with nothing!*
> *We left with everything!*
> *Aspen before and evermore!*
> *Aspen before and evermore!*

CHAPTER 10

I wake to a twinkling sound, like crystals pinging off a stone floor. It stops the moment I open my eyes. I'm in a new room now, strange light reaching up into the beams of a strange ceiling. I sit up and stare back at the stormy whorls and knots in the wooden walls, like unblinking eyes watching me sleep. For a moment my dream hangs thickly around me, and the eyes bulge and droop. Then I'm awake.

I expected to wake up disoriented—this unfamiliar ceiling, these new walls—but Aspen feels most familiar in the morning's light. Like a painting of itself. And I feel relieved to wake up in a bed that's not my own at home, which still hides the phantom stink of my own blood.

This is better, I think as I rub the dreaminess from my eyes. *This is new, so this is better.*

The cabin sleeps around me. Quilted sheets over anonymous lumps, tufts of messy hair embedded in sleep-sculpted pillows. They look like soft mountains.

I pick through the shoes, down the stairs, to the kitchen. I pull a ceramic mug from a doorless hutch, rinse out the dust, and then refill it in the deep, milky basin. The water should taste metallic or mineral, like the walls of the well it probably comes from, but it's sweet. Filtered. Like all the forces of nature, this, too, has been refined by Aspen's wealth.

A dizziness hits me as I stand at the faucet. It's not physical. It's the reeling sensation of falling through time, brought on by the water's taste. My body remembers something, a moment anchored in this sweet water. I drink again. To feel more.

The memory is incomplete. I smell dust and leather, and feel heat on my eyelids. I am lying in grass, eyes squeezed shut, laughing toward the sky. If I'm laughing, I must not be alone, and if I'm not alone I must be with Caroline.

That's all I get. That, the warmth on my skin, and the aftertaste of sadness. The new, blue fringe that edges all my memories of Caroline.

I leave the mug in the sink and head to the bathroom to shower. Brushing my teeth, I watch the blur of myself in the steamed mirror as I replay the memories of last night. The chanting, the firelight, the banner, but especially the way Bria and the Honeys turned to me first, finding me in the crowd before Wendy had me stand. It gives me chills, the way those girls looked at me. A single sight separated into many eyes.

I step into the stillness of the cabin, everyone asleep, and I'm wondering just how early it is when the dizziness returns. The trigger this time is the chill of the cabin wrapping around my raw skin. The combination catapults me backward again.

I'm on the hill, in the grass. I'm holding a hand up to catch the sun from going in Caroline's eyes. She's doing the same for me. A game we used to play, a test of loyalty. We're together, and she feels so solid, like I could reach into the memory, wrap my arms around her, and pull her out with me.

Her eyes watch me from the band of shade in the shape of my hand. It's like she's right there.

I bite into my cheek to stave off the sudden sob that builds in my chest, but it doesn't work. I choke on it as I rush down the stairs, out the cabin's back door, to the porch facing the woods. The nausea of being in both the past and present splits me, and out come red-hot tears. Soundless and surging. Ugly. They shake me so hard I think the porch will collapse, so I hold the railing and wait for the wave to crest, break over me, and hiss away.

It does pass, eventually. Just not easily. And when the grief ebbs, I feel parts of me go with it.

I finally see what I've been staring at, out here on the porch. The forest is bone white. All aspen trees. They watch me with the same eyes I awoke to. Sightless black eyes whirled into bark. The sideways light of dawn lids them in shadow, and dew sparkles in their seams. Like tears. Like they're crying with me. I can't say why, but I feel a kindness in their quiet solidarity. Then I feel a little embarrassed. Twice now these trees have watched me vanish into my grief. The first time was when I nearly plunged off a cliff, and now this. I'm still only wearing a towel.

I wipe at my cheeks. I can still taste the over-sweet water. I spit, and spit again, then head inside. I'm halfway across the upper floor when I freeze. Everyone still sleeps around me, but I sense something about my bed looks changed.

I see it.

In the drained pastel of morning, the small flame is garishly vivid.

Someone has lit Caroline's candle. It wavers, like it can feel the chills coursing over my bare skin.

I check again and no one is moving. Nothing else in the cabin is disturbed.

I pinch out the flame just to make sure the fire is real. It is, though the wax is barely melted. It wasn't lit long. And it certainly wasn't lit by me. I slide back under my blankets. Someone must be playing a prank on me, I decide, as I watch the whorls in the wood. They watch me back.

Then one of them blinks.

I sit up.

I don't breathe.

I think I've imagined it, but no, the knot blinks again. This time I can even hear the creak of the wood twisting. I scream, but like my sobs no sound comes out. Just a hissing static from deep within me, and then up from my lungs burst the jovial tones of a trumpet. The morning bugle on the cabin's ancient speakers.

It startles me awake, and I sit up, almost hitting the bunk above me. The boys stir. My mouth tastes sweet and coppery. My brain swims through the fog of a vaporizing dream.

I push my hands into my eye sockets, finding them wet, like I've been crying in my sleep again. Drifts of the dream linger. The memory of Caroline, the eyes, and . . .

When I glance at the candle, I find that the wick is black, the wax still warm when I touch it. I begin to shake. I look at the walls next. The knots look back, but now they're lifeless, betraying none of what they saw from their wooden sentry.

———————

Breakfast is in Hunter Lodge. French toast. The kitchen staff are even wearing striped shirts and black berets. The chef has penciled on a curly mustache. This only adds to the surreality of my morning, though everyone pretends it's normal. And I guess it is. Aspen has a renowned theater program and a vast costume closet. It's not uncommon for the Leaders to dress up as cowboys for a camp-wide gold rush, or to see a younger cabin sweeping about in *Lord of the Rings* cloaks, their Leader dressed like Gandalf. Part of the camp of camp, I guess.

I sit at the far end of one of the long banquet tables. I pick at my food, trying to shake the uneasy sensation of being watched that I woke up with. It doesn't help that the few times I glance up, Callum is glaring at me.

"Mars! Earth to Mars!"

I whip around, knocking into Wyatt. He puts up his hands in mock surrender.

"Did I scare you? Man, you look half-asleep still."

"*Earth to Mars*," I repeat. "My sister says it all the time. She used to, I mean."

I'm making things more awkward. When I finally manage to

78

glance up, Wyatt is looking at me not with pity, but with scrutiny.

"Are you wearing lipstick?"

"Lip gloss," I correct. I'm feeling femme today. "Why?"

He cocks his head.

"Just wondering. Anyway, important question for you. How do you feel about trees?"

"Love trees. Huge fan of their second album."

"Glad to hear it, 'cause you're coming with me to Eco-Lab today. Maybe tomorrow, too. Depends on if you decide you want to pick a major. Anything come to mind?"

There are hundreds, literally hundreds, of things I would rather do than look at trees with Aspen's Best Boy, but I just give a nonchalant shrug and say, "Trees are pretty cool."

"I agree."

Wyatt bounds off, joining Brayden at the head of our table. Hunter Lodge is shushed for morning announcements from Donovan, Wendy's husband and the other co-director. He oversees Hunter Village. Literally, he oversees it. He is humongous, bearded, and barely bound by his XXL green shirt.

"All right, Huntsmen, listen up," Donovan bellows. "Today is the start of a new week, so you'll all need to sign up for new electives if you have an afternoon slot open. Check in with your LITs before you leave for majors so we can submit your top choices to Derrick. We'll let you know at lunch where you're going for your afternoons this week. Also, as you all know, our Hunter Village Challenge continues today—"

The boys erupt in competing cheers. Donovan regains control with a wave, saying, "The winning cabin will get out of dinner duty on our upcoming Outbound, which leads me to my next announcement: Outbound begins this Thursday, and we won't be back on campus until Saturday morning, so make sure to let your clinic instructors know. And please, boys, hand over your laundry. I'm talking *today*. We're heading into the wild, and some of you haven't swapped out your uniforms even once. I can smell Eagle House from the lake."

More hollering.

"Last, but not least," Donovan bellows, "if you haven't already, please take this chance to introduce yourself to the newest Huntsman, Mars. Mars isn't in our chore chart yet, so can I get a fellow Huntsman volunteer to show him the ropes?"

No one moves. When the silence stretches on sufficiently, Donovan asks, "Looks like the new recruit's got the boys shy. Well, then. Mars, any preference for chores?"

I scramble to think of anything I'm remotely interested in doing. The single task that comes to mind is finding that banner from last night and burning it, but I can't reasonably suggest petty arson. And yet . . .

Wyatt puts up a hand.

"Mars is with me. We're heading to Eco-Lab early. We'd love to help with chores but, well, nature calls!"

In the split second of silence, I notice Brayden's expression darken. But Donovan looks relieved, as do the tables of silent boys. I'm hot with discomfort. What did Donovan think was going to happen? A heated debate to recruit me to scrub toilets? What about this lip color indicates I would be any use during chores?

And now I'm stuck with Wyatt again. Special treatment. Brayden's grudge has just grown deeper.

With a powerful clap, Donovan ends breakfast.

"Great. All right, men, let's hop to it, then!"

With nothing to do, I stand back as the boys clear the plates and wipe down the tables. At one point Tyler and I make eye contact, but he looks away quickly. I can't help but watch the way he blends in perfectly with the other guys, and I realize that maybe this is why he doesn't care to be around me. I'm a tough color to blend, and maybe he's worried I'll rub off on him.

I roll my lips together. The gloss felt like such a small thing when I put it on. The sandals, too. Now I'm not so sure.

I head back to Bear Hut. First I check and, thank god, the candle is not magically lit. Then I stand before the mirror in the upstairs bathroom, a wet towel hovering over my pursed lips.

I still feel watched by those eyes in the walls. Some invisible predator is toying with me already, and it hasn't even been twenty-four hours. But I have no right to self-pity, not after I got myself into this.

What is *this*? This is a maze I've failed once before, yet reentered willingly; I'm determined to reach the center of it this time. But what path do I take? Do I integrate, or do I defy?

Whichever path, I can't afford to be intimidated this early on.

I leave the lip gloss on. Bright things in nature are often poisonous. Let that be my defense, then. Let Aspen watch, and predators prowl, and all the waiting jaws yawn wider.

I will be a ruin to consume.

CHAPTER 11

Wyatt tells me all about the trees as we walk down to camp.

"This stuff is like magic," he says, stripping a silvery ribbon of bark off a birch tree. "It burns wet, so if you're trying to start a fire in the rain, use it for kindling."

"Have you ever actually had to do that?"

"Oh, man, all the time. I grew up camping around here." Wyatt hands me the strip of bark, then bounds off again.

"You went camping in the rain?" I'm huffing. Somehow his impromptu tree tour has led us off the path, and I'm struggling to keep up.

"We went camping *outside*, Mars. It rains outside. And snows."

"Wow! And here I thought inclement weather was just a conspiracy to get people to buy milk and bread."

Wyatt glances back at me. "Really?"

"What? No, of course not. I'm not *that* sheltered."

The look Wyatt throws at me, specifically my gladiator sandals, indicates that, yes, I perhaps am the most sheltered thing he's ever seen. I wind the strip of birch bark between my fingers. It's waxy and flexible, the color a shifting silver-brown-silver, like mummy's flesh.

"Do you really go camping in *winter*?"

"Every family holiday."

"Your family is nuts."

Wyatt chuckles. "Oh, no. They're mostly city people. They think *I'm* the crazy one. Sometimes my brothers will come with me but usually they just stay in the cabins here, so it's just me. Wyatt in the wild."

I stop, like I refuse to go one step farther with the self-declared maniac.

Wyatt just grins and then leaps across a pit of mud, the keys on his lanyard jingling. I pick around the edge.

Main Camp is quiet when we arrive, everyone still wrapped up in chores. We head to the Eco-Lab. Wyatt explains that even though he's close to my age, he's basically a full-time employee helping out with the Ecology major. When he uses a fob to unlock the lab, I whistle and say, "The perks of being a wildflower," but I don't think he gets it.

Inside we find a cool room of scuffed tiles and low tables crammed with equipment. The walls are decorated in wildlife posters. Along the back wall is a painting of an eagle with its wings spread, an X taped to the floor indicating where you stand so that you can see how your arms compare.

"So you're basically a counselor?" I ask, eyeing the keys around his neck.

"Leader-in-Training," Wyatt corrects. "LITs still have majors, but we're expected to help out the instructors and be role models. Next year I'll be a full Leader, and after I get my degree, I'll be able to come back as an instructor. My Aspen major is Environmental Science but that's what I want to do for, like, real life when I'm older."

"No offense, but Aspen isn't exactly what I'd call real life."

"Maybe not Summer Academy, but Aspen has programming year-round. This forest is home to thousands of species of flora and fauna, and some really cool ecosystems. If it wasn't for the Conservancy, it'd all be developed by now. No offense, but I prefer this to whatever your *real life* involves."

"Fair," I say.

"What about you? If you stay for the session, what will you major in?"

I don't answer right away. Until a second ago, I felt crowded by Wyatt's unrelenting enthusiasm for all things Aspen, but after seeing him use that fob I think I need to reevaluate. He probably knows things about Aspen that no one else knows. I just need to corrupt him, if such a corruption is even possible.

"Maybe Environmental Science," I say. I feel like a snake lying so easily, but it's kinda the truth. I'd planned on doing whatever got me close to the info I needed.

"Oh, no way!" Wyatt brightens. "We could use the help. Today we're talking samples." Wyatt toe-taps a surge protector, causing a row of old desktop monitors to boot up. Then he starts pulling plastic bins out of a closet. I don't have a job yet, so I inspect the posters on the walls. They're the illustrated sort, showing a hundred varieties of mushrooms, or beetles, or butterflies. On the counters are bell jars with the real things: spiders and bugs and frogs pinned in static yoga.

The bugle sounds, and the campers arrive a short while after. My nerves twist inside me as they slump into the chairs, but none are the girls from last night. Then our instructor arrives—Wyatt introduces her as some sort of scientist from a nearby SUNY school—and soon we're sent back into the woods with a list of samples to collect.

For a while, Wyatt just recites more nature facts, mostly about the plants. Then he stops us so we can look at a spiderweb that, as he describes it, is *super-freaking-perfect*.

"Watch your language, SpongeBob," I scold.

"Look," he says, pointing out the spider at the web's edge. "Orb weaver. You can tell by the web's design. It looks cool, but once she catches her prey, she'll wrap them up and then suck out their insides."

Wyatt makes a grotesque slurping sound, almost scaring me into the web.

"Nature is so evil," I say, waving away phantom threads.

"Nothing evil about eating," Wyatt says. "All anything in nature wants is to survive. Nothing evil about that."

"What are you, her lawyer?" I joke.

While we keep walking, Wyatt starts reciting spider facts. The most poisonous species we need to look out for are the black widow and the brown recluse.

"I heard daddy longlegs are poisonous, too," I say.

"Those aren't even spiders."

"Too kinky?"

Wyatt turns so red that even his shoulders blush. I stroll after him.

"Okay, nature boy. Question. If a spider could wink," I ask, "would it use one of its eight eyes, or four of its eight eyes?"

"Spiders can't wink," Wyatt says tersely. "They don't have eyelids."

"I said *if*."

Wyatt gives a long sigh, but he's smiling. I like that I can clear away his gregarious counselor act and get a real reaction.

"Fine," he says. "Answer: one out of eight."

"Why?"

"Because you wink to, like, let someone know about a secret, and one eye is more discreet than four. Though I guess it depends which eye. Spiders have different-sized eyes typically, so maybe the eye they wink with could indicate the level of secrecy."

"Like the difference between a white lie and a national security secret?" I offer.

"Well, I don't know about that." Wyatt swipes his nose with his thumb, considering this. "I don't think a spider would ever be given clearance for *national* security. They're pretty environment specific."

"Spider-Man has clearance."

"Spider-Man has eyelids."

I laugh. Actually laugh. Wyatt seems as surprised as I do. He looks grateful, too, like he wasn't sure I had the ability until just now. Resuming our walk, he glances up into the treetops and says, "Your turn."

"My turn?"

"Yeah. I've been spitting pure nature facts. Tell me something about whatever you're into."

"What I'm *into*? Spitting? Pure nature *facts*?"

"I'm serious," he says with a grin. "What are you interested in?"

"I don't know. Math, I guess. Physics. Psychology."

Wyatt scrunches up his face like I just confessed cannibalism. So strange is my answer that I'm almost sure I've killed the conversation, and I rush to think of some fascinating fact from my world to share. Something Wyatt will find astonishing.

"Oh!" I clasp my hands together. "Okay. Listen to this. Francis Galton, he's a famous statistician, right?"

"I didn't know statisticians could be famous, but go on."

"Okay, well. In 1800 he was at a county fair. You've been to one of those, I assume."

Wyatt has picked up a stick. He swings it at the air, cutting through a cloud of gnats. "More often than church," he says grimly.

"Great. Okay. So. At the fair, there was a contest to see who could correctly guess the weight of an ox. Galton was there and he analyzed the answers, and he found that while hardly anyone guessed correctly, the average of all the answers was spot-on. Just dead-on accurate."

I wait for a beat. Wyatt lets out a whistle that is half-sincere, half-sarcastic. I ignore the sarcastic half.

"It's just not how we think of crowds, right? Like crowds are, in general, not to be trusted, but in this case the aggregate intelligence of the crowd trumped individual expertise. And a similar phenomenon has been used to predict all sorts of stuff. Like one time a bunch of people found a lost submarine. And sometimes the stock market—"

"Hold up, Mathlete." Wyatt stops me with a raised hand. "They found a submarine? Like, a sunken submarine?"

"Yes. They located it on the floor of the ocean."

"So you're telling me a crowd can just . . . predict things?"

"Certain crowds. Certain things. In the right conditions, humans can behave like supercomputers and predict all sorts of stuff."

"Isn't it the other way around?" Wyatt squints at me. "Humans have been around a lot longer than computers. Who behaves like who?"

"Error," I intone, giving a robot jerk to my limbs. "Error."

For a while we meander, and then Wyatt quits his safari tour when we reach a brook that, according to him, is perfect for sampling. I lean against a tree and watch him kneel over the slick rocks.

"Your family," I say. "They've owned Aspen for a long time, right?"

"Yeah, my great-great-grandfather was the original caretaker, way back when it was built. And then he bought it from the owners for dirt cheap when they lost their fortune. Then my family technically sold the land and the buildings to the Conservancy, but we still run it. I basically grew up here."

"And you said you come here in the winter?"

Wyatt sits back on his heels, holding up a tube of murky water. "For holidays. And to help Wendy run Winter Academy. Here, why don't you take the next sample?"

I crouch next to him and dig a tube into the muck. He watches me like he's expecting me to complain or gag or something. I focus on the water and ask, "There's a Winter Academy?"

"Yeah. Caroline never told you about Winter Academy?"

"She only came here in the summer. In the winter, she went on ski trips to—"

"Windham? Yeah, that's near here. Lots of Aspen kids come back for Winter Academy. It's an unofficial Aspen tradition, just a few long weekends reserved for Aspen families only. You can do ice skating and hikes and stuff, but most of us just go skiing."

The more we talk about it, the more I'm sure he's right. Caroline never asked me to join her ski trips. I figured it was just another way we were growing apart, but I'm not surprised to find Aspen at the start of that split, too. I bet if I scrolled far enough into Bria's or Mimi's social content, I'd find cozy photos of them posed around a brick fireplace like the one in Bear Hut, in matching long johns and hats crowned in puff balls.

"Mars?"

Wyatt hands me another tube. We hike upstream for a little while, and I'm so lost in thought that I slip on a rock and plunge my leg into the muck. The tubes roll into the water, but Wyatt snatches them up.

"You know you shouldn't be wearing those sandals, right? Won't you let me get you sneakers? I bet—"

"It's cool. I'll be careful."

I'm quiet as I think about what it means that Caroline returned to Aspen throughout the year under the charade of ski trips. Were there other excuses, too? I hate that we spoke so little this past year that I hardly noticed the weekends she was around versus the ones she was away.

Wyatt lets me be quiet. No more nature facts or winking-spider scenarios for us. Then his (hideous) watch peeps and we start back toward the group.

"How'd you like Eco-Lab?" he asks.

"Do we always collect samples?"

"No, we do a lot. After we collect samples, we analyze them in the Eco-Lab, record the data, do fieldwork, and so on. All the Aspen majors seek to leverage the ground's many natural resources and man-made enhancements," he recites.

"What about the apiary?"

Wyatt slows. "What about it?"

I sense I should be careful asking about the beehives out by Cabin H.

But without knowing why, it's hard to navigate my line of questioning. Let's try playing dumb, then.

"I was looking at the majors on the Aspen website, but I didn't see Apiculture anywhere. I figured it would be part of Ecology."

Wyatt is suddenly very focused on the expanse of lawn glowing through the forest ahead. He slows even more, like he doesn't want to have this conversation out in the open.

"It's not safe," Wyatt says. "It's not safe to work with the bees unless you have special training."

"Oh, that's so weird. Caroline said she handled them all the time. She made it sound like there was a whole Apiculture major here. Maybe I misunderstood her, though?"

I stop. Wyatt stops, too. He's irritated, but why? I can either keep playing dumb, or just go for full directness. Or there's a third option. I scandalize my tone, like it's all a joke to me.

"Is it like a secret or something? Be honest, would a spider wink about this? If so, with which eye?"

"No, no, nothing like that," Wyatt scoffs. He doesn't laugh at my joke. Farther up the path some other campers are walking toward us. Wyatt watches them. "Apiculture isn't on the website because it's always full. Every year. The hives are right next to Cabin H and the girls always make a big fuss if Wendy tries to add anyone into their cabin, or the major. It's a whole thing. Why do you care anyway? Suddenly you're interested in bees?"

I shrug, a little crestfallen. "The Honeys were Caroline's friends."

"*The Honeys?*" Wyatt shakes his head. "If that's why you're here, let me stop you right now. They're not worth your time, Mars."

I step back a bit, because for the first time since I met him, Wyatt is exhibiting actual anger.

"What'd they do to you?" I ask.

"Nothing. They ignore me, like they do all the guys," Wyatt says. He kicks at the ground, like a kid. "Actually, I don't even think they realize they're part of Summer Academy. I mean, this place is all about making friends and encountering nature and trying new things, but those girls just treat it like a summer vacation."

I realize I'll get more if I just let Wyatt talk, so I find a banal way to agree with him.

"Yeah, they were . . . super standoffish at the social last night, even though they told me I should come back."

"Right, see? They toy with people." Wyatt adjusts the bin of test tubes as we resume walking. "They don't even care about the bees. Leena just does all the work and the girls lie around, but then the second Wendy asks them to come into camp for activities and stuff they're all like, 'But the bees!' and Wendy gives in. And then they act like being all the way out in H is such a struggle, but they literally all request it every year. And if we try to split them up, the parents get involved. It drives Wendy *nuts*."

Wyatt is really heated about this. I tentatively throw down some bait.

"They remind me of, like, a secret club or something."

Wyatt gives a dark chuckle. "They would love that. But the truth is, they're just a clique of bored, pretty girls. And I know your sister was in that cabin, but trust me, Mars, she was nothing like them. I never got why she hung out with them. She actually had a brain."

At the mention of Caroline and her brain, I take a quick breath. Wyatt must know why because his voice softens. We stop before entering the Eco-Lab.

"Sorry. I guess I'm just trying to say that Summer Academy has so much more to offer you than a wannabe sorority."

"Like tubes of sludge?"

"Like actual friends," Wyatt counters. "Look, Mars. Wendy has her doubts, but I think being here could be really good for you. We've got a great cabin this year. I bet you'll really like them if you just give them a chance. Maybe focus on that?"

I think of Callum's smoldering glare after I humiliated him. And the lit candle, and the way no one wanted my help with chores, and how Tyler brushed me off last night.

"Yeah," I say. "Sure."

Wyatt heads inside, leaving me to think about what he's said. I watch a black-winged shadow swoop between the beams above the awning.

"Do you have an opinion for me, too?" I ask the bird.

It considers me, then wiggles into a hidden nest. Safe, in a home woven from scraps.

———

Lunch is in the main dining hall, next to Big Lodge, and it's pure chaos. Or really it's picturesque chaos. The hall's windows are pushed open, showing a panoramic view of the lake. Clouds of sun-kissed campers tumble inside, surging through the oak banquet tables. They yell to one another over the flurry of hands passing platters of mac 'n' cheese, barbecue, and spring mix salad. A younger cabin of boys starts a water-chugging contest, the chants blurring into the ruckus of another table seized in debate, I don't know what about.

After lunch, Wyatt and I head to his elective this week, which is sailing. I'm not allowed on the boats because I'm not CPR certified. Wyatt offers to stay on the docks with me, but I refuse, thinking of Brayden's warnings about special treatment. When he's safely on the water, I meander to the boathouse deck to get a better view of the other side of the lake.

"Hey," a girl says from the dark blue of the shed where they keep the kayaks. She's got a clipboard. I think she's the Leader who signs out equipment.

"Hey?"

"Mars, right?"

"Right."

"I'm Sylv."

Sylv pauses, maybe wondering how to give me that Big Aspen Hello that Wendy encouraged from everyone last night. I brace myself, but she just says, "We're out of kayaks."

"It's okay. I'm just here for the view."

Sylv looks out over the lake. It must look dull to her, from her post, though I wonder if I imagine the hunger in her eyes when her gaze passes over the distant meadow.

I watch the other side of the lake for a few more minutes before hiking back to Big Lodge, our meeting spot. I find room after room of heavy, upholstered furniture itchy with heat. Dust chokes the meager light squeezing through the thick curtains of the study, which is where I spend the most time exploring.

I find books so old their skin is cloth soft, and the titles are just a shatter of foil on the spines. I'm looking for clues. Notes tucked away. Circled words that make up suspicious sentences. I end up in the common room leafing through a stack of melting *National Geographic*s, avoiding the gaze of a taxidermy elk. Finally the bugle sounds, and a few minutes later the Bear Hut boys barge onto the porch. It's time for the Hunter Village Challenge, whatever that is.

We're led out past the athletic fields, up to the old stable. It hasn't homed horses in forever, I gather, because the walls are sticky with rock-climbing holds, and a gymnastics floor has been put down. A raised runway cuts through the center, and we circle up beside it.

"Boys! Listen up!" Brayden and the Eagle Leader, Quinn, get us to quiet down. "Today is the ultimate Village Challenge. A tournament to find the most valiant Huntsman among you. A *fencing* tournament."

I guess several boys were expecting this because they let out self-satisfied cheers. Some, like me, glance nervously at the exit.

The counselors introduce a short, slender man who is Aspen's designated fencing instructor. His name is Rudi. He runs through the rules and safety procedures of a fencing bout while Brayden dons the full-coverage protective gear, exemplifying each item. It's a suit of stiff white fabric, and a full-head helmet with a face of black metal mesh. It reminds me of a beekeeper's suit, but it's tighter. Brayden looks goofy in it, but you can tell he feels awesome. Then they actually do a demo, which Rudi ends in seconds. Just a flashing swish of Rudi's sword and a buzzer sounds above us.

"All right," Brayden says, pulling off his helmet. "We're doing this sudden death style. You're in until you're defeated, and the last man standing wins it for his cabin. Who wants to go first?"

Hands shoot up. Not mine. From experience, those fencing jackets are hot, and this gym isn't air-conditioned. If they actually do make it through all the matches, which they won't, I can just use my hand as an excuse. I slip away unnoticed, getting as far as the barn doors before I stop. I can see the dance studios at the bottom of the hill. Some girls are down there warming up, or maybe already rehearsing. They snapped on it, and snaps are final.

I sway in the wide doorframe. Dandelion spores pirouette on a sweet breeze like a prophecy, or a temptation. Wyatt said I should give the boys a shot, to at least pretend I'm not just here to study the Honeys. Maybe he's right.

I decide to stay.

Two boys have suited up. The rest of us cheer them from the edge of the raised strip. Wyatt of course is the loudest. I realize I'm watching him—watching his hands again—and I stop. I focus on the swishing blades, the shuffling of feet, and the cry of the buzzer.

I'm glad I stayed. The bouts tell me a lot about the boys. It's unlike the fencing tournaments I used to participate in. It's not dignified or beautiful. I'm captivated by the careless nature of it all. The rushing. The bravado. From beneath the black mesh, their laughter contorts to sneering so quickly, like sportsmanship and bloodlust share a subtle seam. The boys fling themselves at one another, crash, and break apart as though they can't be hurt, and I wonder what it must be like to walk through life with the assumption that you are indestructible.

The tournament progresses quickly. At first Bears lead, then Eagles throw down their final, secret weapon: Callum, who clearly knows what he's doing. Callum brings it down to a tie, and the playful cheers crinkle, growing sharp. The boys, I note, are no longer having fun. It's all urgent now. Important and bitter in a way that scares me. Then Callum bests our last viable player, The Chuckster, and the Eagles roar out a mocking victory cry. Someone—I don't hear who—shuts it down by pointing out that, actually, it's not over until Mars loses, too.

Oh, wonderful.

The guys stop their shit-talking and glance at me with less-than-amused incredulity. When I hold up my splinted fingers, they roll their eyes, like, *Of course.*

"Actually," I hear myself say. "I'll do it. I'm a righty."

"You're wearing sandals," an Eagle boy says.

"*Gladiator* sandals," I say, which gets a chuckle from the Bears.

A dark joy sparks to life in me. Spite. That's what drives me to get up and don the heavy fabric armor. I pull on the jacket, the metallic vest. It's humid with the sweat of the other boys. The glove's grip is sticky. The mask's mesh is warm with breath. It's gross but I don't care.

Show them, I whisper to myself.

Callum is grinning back at his cabin-mates. He's going to hate me even more for this, but oh well. In an ecosystem of boyish egos, there's always got to be a sacrifice, someone shoved to the bottom. All the boys here underestimate me, but it's Callum's poor fortune to be the one to suffer for it. If Wyatt wants me to participate in the games boys play, so be it.

Callum pulls on his helmet and mirrors me on the strip.

"I'm not going easy on you," he says, just for me to hear.

"Funny," I say with mock intrigue, "your dad liked it rough, too."

Rudi begins the bout.

"Allez!"

Callum lunges; I parry. He tries again; I parry again. Rudi laughs, but I don't take my eyes off Callum. He's mad and getting madder. Luckily, I know where his guard is weak. I've watched him for several bouts now. He's obvious and proud and, worst of all, sloppy.

Callum shifts his weight. He's going to lunge, but I feint forward. Callum shifts his weight backward, a mistake. Not good for backpedaling. He raises his foil to parry my blow, and it's painfully slow. I flick my wrist, driving my foil into a downward crest.

Callum's foil clashes into my guard and is halted, the tip impotently wagging by my ear. My blade pins his shoulder. It's higher than I was aiming, but the buzzer confirms the point is mine.

Callum rubs at where I struck him. He plays it off, but I can tell he's shocked.

"Jeez," he laughs. "It's just a game. Chill out, bro."

That makes me mad.

"Allez!" Rudi calls, starting our second bout.

I don't attempt another lunge, but neither does Callum. We poke and swat at each other, sensing for openings. My pulse is staccato, nettling and sharp. My eyes can't stay on Callum this time, instead shifting to all the minor movements behind him. I find the faces of his friends, smug and so sure of how this will end.

Callum overtakes my vision as he goes for a lunge. He's gotten too close. There's no way I can deflect his blow, so I don't try. All it takes is a burst of power to my left leg and my body shifts to the right. Callum's blade skewers the hollow between my ribs and my raised arm. He's missed me, and his motion carries him forward so that we almost collide. He recovers and hops backward. Right into striking distance.

I slash and lunge, slash and lunge, driving him backward toward the boys he represents. Eagle House backs away from the strip as Callum wheels toward them. I time my final thrust with the moment he hits the edge, and he falls backward.

It's the simplest thing in the world to hop down and poke him, gently, in the heart. The buzzer screams.

"I'm not your bro," I tell him.

Callum looks down at where I've got him, then looks at me. He tosses down his foil, rips off his helmet, and sneers at me.

"You're a little bitch," he says.

"Actually," I say, "I'm a huge bitch."

Bear Hut wins, and when I turn around, I'm facing the strangest thing. Laughing, stomping boys, arms outstretched to pull me into a jumping embrace. As we rise and fall, I think, it could be this simple. But of course there's always a cost when you force yourself to become someone you're not. I can feel my left hand coated in blood beneath my glove. I wasn't careful enough. I'll make sure I take off the glove when no one is looking.

I find Wyatt watching from the edge of our mosh pit, and on his face is an expression of complete disbelief.

Good, I think, and I give him my best, most spidery, wink.

CHAPTER 12

It's remarkable what a little ass-kicking can get you. After I defeat Callum, it's like the boys in my cabin can finally see me. I don't really need to wonder about the *why* of the shift because, as they tell me again and again, they thought I was totally weird when I arrived but, *whoa*, Matthias, what a surprise. And of course they mock Callum within an inch of his life.

They think this is flattering. It's not, but I pretend it is. And back at the cabin I make sure every single one of them sees me apply not one, not two, but three coats of lip gloss before dinner. This earns a few blinks. And the shaky silence that follows me asking *How do I look?* is the sound of a small world that just got a little bigger.

God's work, I tell myself. You're doing God's work, Mars.

Dinner is at the main dining pavilion by Big Lodge. Cabin H's table sits empty, but then I feel that familiar, pressurized ripple skim over the table, and all I have to do is follow the glances to the pavilion's patio. The Honeys sit out there, having their own little gathering, independent from the rest of camp. They don't even come inside for announcements, and by sundown they're gone.

I lie in bed, watching the wooden eyes watch me, and I'm asleep long before they call lights-out.

"Mars."

Caroline's voice. It cuts through whatever I'm dreaming about.

"Mars, wake up."

I don't want to open my eyes. Her voice is thick, each syllable a sucking pop, like something pools at the back of her throat. It must be blood because I can smell it through the cabin's musk. I smell sweet decay, too.

"Mars," she pleads. "Wake up."

I open my eyes.

I can't see her at first. I just see the wide black sky and a scatter of stars. I can hear her breathing, though. Wet. Sticky. Uneven. My vision adjusts. I'm not looking at the sky, but the flat darkness of the cabin's ceiling, and all over it is a mess of glinting glass. Broken crystals. They wink and shimmer. I sit up, trying to see what I don't want to see: the girl-shaped silhouette at the center of the makeshift night sky. The moon won't touch her. Won't show her cut-up face. But I can hear her breathing up above me. Or trying to breathe. Each inhale drowns in a syrupy gurgle. She coughs and it sounds sticky.

I swallow.

"Caroline?"

Her coughing stops.

Something hits my thigh. A piece of crystal. More pieces plink down on my blanket. Then I hear something above me coming unstuck, and I feel a drizzle zip over my shoulder, my cheek. A thread of honey, like spider's silk, wobbling down from the ceiling.

Caroline falls.

My hands fly up, too late, tangling with her arms.

"Shit, chill out, man, it's me. It's Tyler," says Tyler. Not Caroline. I sit up, pushing him back onto the foot of my bed. The cabin is bright with moonlight, and for a moment I see Caroline's ghost hovering in the beams above, but then she's gone. The dream is gone with her. But I can't stop scratching the skin where I felt that droplet of honey.

"Manhunt," Tyler says flatly. "You in?"

I swallow. I let the dream go. I focus on Tyler and what he's saying. Manhunt. Another Aspen tradition. The unofficial sport played by all the campers, usually at dusk when the woods are just dark enough to hide within. But it must be the middle of the night right now.

"What's going on?" I ask. I feel dumb sitting up in bed like this, him kneeling beside me like a parent come to check on their crying kid.

Tyler sighs. "The guys said you wouldn't want to come, but I thought we should ask. So?"

What Tyler says snaps me out of my stupor. I get it. The Huntsmen are sneaking out for a late-night game. What surprises me in this moment is that Tyler was the one to wake me. Maybe my match against Callum won me points with him, too.

"I'll come," I say. "Thanks for waking me. That was nice of you."

"It's whatever. You remember how to play?"

"Kinda."

"Good. You better be fast," Tyler says, and it's the first time I've seen actual humor soften his handsome features. "Wear black," he instructs. "And grab a flashlight but don't turn it on."

I pull on an ensemble of black athleisure. I give in and lace up my goofy white sneakers. Then I join the rest of the boys as we sneak out the back door, beneath the counselor's windows, and into the woods. When we're out of sight of the village, we turn on our flashlights, and deep in the night I see an occasional flash—a trickle of sap on tree bark, or the slimed back of a slug, or a handful of stars spying through the treetops. It all reminds me of the glinting crystal from my dream, but I don't feel fear anymore. I feel . . . solid. Myself. It's something about the forest at night, I think. The woods are different in the dark. Heavy, solid, close. The lush confusion of the day is gone, the whole world gathered into a flat void that presses in all around us. It feels like being held.

Maybe the boys feel it, too. We travel in a quiet pack, not one person's footsteps discernible from another's. The waves of cricket chatter hide our breathing. We stay close, like one large, prowling creature, and just once Tyler's hand brushes mine.

We arrive at the fields sooner than I expect. Eagle House is there, along with a group of Amazons. We're about to start when something draws every-one's attention to the edge of the field, where the moonlight won't reach.

It's more girls. The Honeys, wrapped in oversized sweaters, holding pinkies while they walk. In the night and without their uniforms, there's something undone about their illusory power. Still, we shift nervously as they approach. Like we've been caught. Somehow the game goes from clandestine to official with their arrival.

Ray explains the rules. The game is basically flashlight tag mashed up with hide-and-seek, played with two teams. One team hides, the other hunts, tagging them with flashlights until all but one are found. The last person hiding wins.

There's no discussion about teams. It's boys versus girls. Bria and Ray appear to be the captains, and they use a game of rock-paper-scissors to decide who's hunting and who's hunted. Bria wins twice, and with that the boys, myself among them, are declared the hunted. Bria starts her count immediately, banishing us from the field. I look back as I run, and all I can see is her standing in the light of the flagpole, a coy wave of her hand shooing us into the night.

I put as much distance between myself and the field as possible, letting the dark flood the in-between. The counting ends and, distantly, I can hear the beginnings of the hunt. Flashlights whisk through the trees. Then it gets quiet.

I end up climbing a jumble of boulders in the thin edge of the woods bordering the waterfront. I wait for a while until a commotion deeper in the woods scares me down from my perch, and that's how I end up cir-cling the back of the boathouse.

I hear whispering from the deck. A girl, giggling, and then a guy shush-ing her. I pause in the dark as they stumble away, playfully pulling at each other until he catches her in a kiss. I turn my back to them, embarrassed at what I'm seeing. I dart away from the boathouse, into the tall grasses that fringe the lake's unkempt edge.

Everyone at Aspen knows how to play Manhunt, both how to hunt and be hunted. Manhunt is the unofficial sport of the camp, but it's more than that. It's the black market, the Mafia court—an arena for anything that cannot happen in the brightness of day. Scores are settled; friendships are undone and reforged. That's how it was when we were little.

Now I guess it's also the perfect excuse to pull someone close and suck their face off.

The bullfrogs and crickets are loud at the lake's edge, but I can still make out more laughter from the brush. Another couple, maybe. I start to wonder if anyone is actually playing, or if hunter and hunted have devolved together under the delight of an easy catch, leaving only me to run around in the dark.

I make my way back toward the fields, keeping out of the light, but I feel silly now. Here I am taking everything so seriously, but there's nothing more to this than just a bunch of kids messing around in the woods. And that makes me think again of how Wyatt dismissed my suspicions toward the Honeys. I keep thinking they had something to do with the sheer terror I saw in Caroline's eyes that night, but what if there's nothing more to it than my own paranoia? Wyatt called them bored, pretty girls. I was sure the night would reveal something else.

What scares me is the creeping conclusion that I'm wrong. About all of it. About who Caroline actually was. Maybe this was all she wanted after all. Ice-cream socials and cornhole tournaments and nocturnal games of tag that end in sweaty palms, steaming breaths, and no witnesses except the wink of a crescent moon.

A twig snaps to my left.

I stop walking, listening. I wait for the flashlight to sweep over me and for a girl to call *You're out!*

Instead, footsteps rush toward me, and before I can even see what it is I'm thrown to the ground. I land hard, my shoulder grating against brambles. I stumble up but they come at me again, this time pushing me into a tree. The low branches slash at me as I wrestle free, spinning until I see the vaguest shape of a person standing over me.

"Callum?" I ask.

The next shot is aimed toward my head. My wounded ear. I block it and manage to back up a bit. I can't seem to get my feet under me and I'm back on my ass. I'm sure it's Callum now; a narrow glow from the field cuts through the trees and falls upon his sneering face.

"Got you, *bro*," he says. Then he points his flashlight at my face, but he doesn't turn it on.

"We're on the same team," I say, but I know it's pointless. This isn't about teams.

"I don't think so," Callum says. "Maybe you want to run a bit more and find out."

He's dead serious. If I stand my ground, he hits me again. If I run, he chases me down while enjoying every second of it, but maybe I can make it out into the open.

I try to run, but Callum grabs my neck in one hand and throws me sideways into a wide oak. I crush against my injured hand, bending back barely healed joints. I scream, but it's muffled by a palm over my mouth. I taste grit and blood, some wound on my face bleeding through Callum's filthy grip.

"This is what we do," he says, "to little bitches like you."

In that moment, all I understand is the fact of Callum and the violence he promises. He is what I hear and what I smell and all I feel. He is a heaviness that replaces the night's embrace, crushing me down between the unyielding roots.

And then he's gone.

I hear a crack and Callum yells, "Who's there?"

He's backed away from me. He turns his flashlight on and drags it over the trees around us. He's frantic.

"Who did that?" he asks. His hand is in his hair. He pulls it away and it's black with blood. Callum glares at me, like I somehow hit him. He steps toward me, when there's another crack. This time, he goes down on one knee. Red stripes down his face.

"Who's there?" he growls, but there's fear in his anger now. Maybe it's a trick of his swinging light, but I see new shadows moving in the trees. They pull apart and merge, pulsing as they drift closer. Then they pause, and I make out the vague shape of a girl in the dark. It's the hair, floating up around her head, like she's underwater.

Callum sees them too. He points his flashlight but illuminates only air. I don't know what I'm seeing. The shadows just melt, then re-form in the dark, even closer.

Another crack and Callum's nose is dripping blood. The shadows sweep around us and even though they're nothing more than negative space in the dim light, I get the impression that they're smiling. Callum's flashlight weakens, then blinks out. *Crack. Crack.* Callum cries out one more time, is choked off, and then there's only the wet sound of skin being bludgeoned open.

I scramble backward, finally finding breath enough to scream for help, but then a beam blinds me.

"You okay?"

It's Bria. I can't see her behind the brightness, but I recognize her voice. It's the same professionally concerned voice from when she was in my foyer.

"Yeah," I say. "But Callum . . ."

"He's so annoying."

I jump at the voice behind me. Bria points her light at the ground and there Callum lies in a shivering heap. Standing over him are two more girls. I can't make out their faces for some reason. When I try to look, they blur, like they're vibrating too fast for my eye to keep up with.

"I think he's cute," says one. Her voice is impossible to place; it sounds like words made out of humming. "In like a brooding, broken sort of way. Superb ex-boyfriend material."

Bria clears her throat.

The girls look at us. Their facial features are nothing more than splotchy cavities in the ever-shifting blur of their heads.

"Kill, or just maim?" one girl asks.

"Neither, Mimi, oh my god. You know the rules. Just a purge for now," says the other blur.

Are they Mimi and Sierra? I try to look at them again but a pressure builds in my eyes, like I'm trying to see the wings of a hummingbird as it hovers.

"But he was going to hurt Mars," Maybe-Mimi protests.

All three girls turn to me.

"I'm okay," I say quickly. "But—"

"Purge Mars, too," Bria says.

"But the sun is down—" says one girl.

"We have no choice. We'll just do our best."

Bria lifts her fingers, poised for a snap. Maybe it's the glare of the flashlight, but her features begin to quiver and vibrate, her own face starting to blur. The girls sulkily mirror her, and they snap as one. The sound they create is a singular crack, like too-close lightning, and I can't even hear myself scream as the night tears itself into brightness. In its wake I hear that hum, the one that I heard when I first arrived at Aspen. I'm sure it's that hum, vibrating and hot and saturating the air. But this time it's *loud*. All at once it's inside me, crawling on the inside of my eyes.

I'm looking into a flashlight beam.

"You okay?"

It's Bria. I can't see her behind the brightness, but I recognize her voice. It's the same professionally concerned voice from when she was in my foyer.

I turn in a circle. We're alone in the woods, her flashlight revealing a gnarled mound of roots and a rash of ruby-red mushrooms crushed beneath my muddy shoes.

"We're playing Manhunt. And you're out," Bria says. She switches off her flashlight and runs off, leaving me alone with my wonder. I realize she's right. We *are* playing Manhunt, and I *am* out. I pace the small clearing, something about its emptiness strangely sudden. Wasn't someone chasing me? Didn't I fall? I'm covered in debris and my skin itches with fresh scrapes. There's blood in my hair. When did my ear bandage come undone?

I get no further in my curiosity before shouts from the field pull me from the woods. I make it up the hill just in time to watch as, one by one, the boys are chased away from the trees, out into the open, running their hardest only to be spotlit by the girls, who seem to materialize from the shadows themselves. The boys swear and buckle over, panting from the chase, but the girls don't seem tired at all. They clap together in celebratory hugs, then escort their catches to the flagpole. I see Tyler and Ray and the others. And Callum. He's slumped against the pole, shirt off and bundled into a makeshift bandage. He presses it to his nose. Even from a distance I can see the blood striped down his face and neck.

I walk up, captivated by the sight of Callum and his bright blood. My eyes throb with the memory of a sight I can't seem to see. One of the girls sees me staring and says, "Callum fell."

"He fell?"

I lock eyes with her. I don't know her name, but she's a Cabin H girl. I can tell from the way she looks barely touched by the heat, only a gauzy shine to her skin. I wonder what it must be like to be so beautiful, so easily. What it must be like to walk all the way back to the meadow with these girls, singing and laughing and teasing, and wake up in the morning as part of their cozy sisterhood. I almost reach out and take her hands. I almost beg her to take me when they go.

"He fell," the girl repeats, and in her words I hear a silvery overtone. Like a needle of sound slipped right through my skull.

I shiver. I know she's right. Callum fell.

Right?

Earth to Mars.

I don't know why that phrase comes to me now, in Caroline's voice, but I hear it somewhere far behind me. Not in space, but in time. And I doubt what I've been told. I know Callum fell, but I know there was more to it. A moment when he stood over me in the woods, sneering, then another moment when he cowered beneath a shadowy swarm, and then . . .

I'm still looking at the Honey. The frequency in her voice dissipates from my mind, and I realize she's lying. It's like reaching into a thinning dream and grasping, for just one second, the reality of something only imagined. But I didn't imagine it. It happened. I see it: Callum was bloodied and cowering, and tearing through the darkness were those blurry, bright shadows. I still can't quite make sense of what I saw, but it's left me sure: There was a moment in the woods in which I was watching a boy being killed, and I was sure the Honeys were doing it.

The girl from Cabin H gives me a kind, questioning smile that doesn't touch her eyes.

"Yeah," I say. "Callum fell."

And she walks away to tell someone else.

The game ends. *Olly olly oxen free* is called, the signal for all those hunting or hiding to come out, come out, wherever you are. I walk with the boys back toward our Village. I watch them. I watch Callum. Even bloodied, he's in high spirits. He brags about some moment in the woods with a girl I don't know.

"Earth to Mars," I whisper to myself, like a mantra. A phrase, heavy with memories, rooting me within the suspicion that something here is not right. Something, I'm sure, has been altered.

A mosquito whines in my ear. I wave it away.

Altered, or concealed?

Clever, I think.

Wyatt believes what he said about the Honeys. That they're insubstantial. That they are here to play small, petty games. That there's nothing more to them than the acceptable amount of bored sadism society likes to read into the inscrutable rituals of girly girls. Heaven forbid there's something more beneath the powder, the perfumes, the performance.

But I know better. Maybe it's because I was raised with a sister, or maybe it's because I've spent my life on the outside, peering through a yearning distance at the games girls play, memorizing every turn and trick with the desperate hope that one day I'd be invited to play along, too. So of course I know better. And of course a beast of cunning and misdirection like myself recognizes what's happening here.

Camouflage.

Something hides within the hive, and I, Mars Matthias the Third, will carve it out myself. But if my conviction is a knife, the blade is a mirror I must face myself in as I raise it. Who could I be, if I were one of them? How beautiful? How bad?

And how secure? Maybe I, too, could be safe, veiled within layers of frivolity and boredom and beauty.

Earth, I think, *to Mars*. Wake up. Caroline must have thought the same way, and look what happened. She wasn't safe. I must not be either.

I let the group walk ahead so that I can stand alone in the dark. The night wraps around me. Holds me together. I stay like that until a bead of light separates from the group and bobs toward me, growing into Tyler.

"You okay?"

"I'm good," I say, following after him.

I say that I'm good, but I'm not sure I believe it.

CHAPTER 13

We're slow to rise the next day, the night's racing excitement congealed to a sticky sleepiness in the corners of our eyes. Mornings are usually chaotic at Aspen, but not today. It's quiet, like a great contemplation has been divided up to be worked through by each of us. It makes me think of the aspen trees, individuals all above the earth, but bound together deep beneath. Instead of roots, the secret of last night binds us.

The counselors must notice our stupor but they don't say anything over breakfast. I peer through my own delirium at Brayden and notice him and another counselor exchanging amused looks when one of the boys accidentally overfills his glass of orange juice. So they know.

I barely touch my food. Instead, I pick at the memory of Callum lying on the ground. It seems to be specifically mine, this memory of girlish, blurry phantoms digging into Callum's shaking flesh. I think I know what put those bruises under Callum's skin. Callum, however, remains unaware. He recounts the story of his fall during chores, and nowhere within it do I or the girls show up. I wonder if he's just saving face for his bros, but no. He believes it. I think, just like I suspected last night, that something has been changed.

Just to be sure, I ask Tyler, "Did Callum really fall?"

"Duh. Did you see him? He fell."

He fell. An automatic lie, but Tyler seems to mean it. I find myself thinking, yeah, he did fall, didn't he? But the bright blood never fades from my vision. Bria was there with me when it happened. But *what* happened? Why should I believe my singular memory when everyone else seems to know different?

I tell myself that she has answers, and let myself believe that this, and only this, is why I'll go to her. Today, maybe. If the hazy sun and cricket-song don't lull me back to sleep.

At Eco-Lab, we're assigned a tree identification task. Wyatt notices me yawning and surprises me when he asks, "How was Manhunt?"

"You know about that?"

"Duh. You think we wouldn't notice the entire cabin just sneaking out into the night? Half the Leaders did the same thing in their time. It's a tradition."

I'm about to ask why anyone bothers sneaking, but then I realize why. It's another small ballet, a dance of deniability with us and our elders. They pretend not to see us break the rules so long as we give them the chance to deny it later if we get caught.

"I'm glad you participated," Wyatt says. "Did you have fun?"

"Not really," I admit. "Something weird happened in the woods."

Wyatt's full focus shines on me, like the beam of Bria's flashlight last night, and I cut myself off. What am I thinking, telling Wyatt this? I barely understand the bits of memory rattling around in my skull, so what's Wyatt going to make of it? He'll assume I'm lying. Or, even worse, he'll know I'm not and he'll tell Wendy. I can't have that. I've got my own plan.

"I saw Callum's nose," Wyatt adds. "That wasn't you, was it?"

I shake my head vigorously. "No, nothing like that. He fell."

"That's what I heard."

Wyatt presses his lips together and then seems to reach some sort of conclusion. Carefully, he asks, "Is there anything else you want to add?"

"Nothing," I say. "That was it."

Wyatt sighs, but he lets it go. Whatever curiosity I sparked is nothing against the dampening discretion Wyatt's been raised to respect. I'm extra focused on trees after that, but I see him watching me out of the corner of my eye. I notice him yawning, too, and I wonder: What do the counselors get up to when their campers are out at night?

After lunch, Wyatt heads out onto the lake for sailing and leaves me with instructions to head to the craft hut. I ignore these instructions. Instead I make my way down to the boathouse, where I find Sylv, the Leader in charge of boat checkout. She's dark-eyed and yawning. Further evidence for my theory. I start to make up a story about how Wyatt told me I could join the kayaking elective but she waves me through. I find myself a life jacket and a bright red kayak, then push out into the reeds. Soon I'm careening over the smooth shallows of the lake. Toward the opposite shore, the apiary meadow, and the shaded cottage beyond.

It's farther than I thought. As I paddle, the distance between the shores widens, swallowing me within a black limbo that takes all my strength to cut through. The nose of the kayak bucks and turns. An unseen current flushes over me, but my eyes stay locked on the meadow. It's a bright gold crevice wedged into the rising wall of dark trees. It looks almost molten, as if at any moment the gold will spill forth and bubble over the lake's surface like a pierced yolk.

Grasses and reeds scrape against my kayak as I drift into the shallows. Then come the lily pads, a few at first, and then hundreds of them, interlocking like the waxy scales of some submerged beast. They plaster against my kayak, their flowers cupping into the black water as I fight through them. I end up having to dig my paddle into the muck below to push myself forward.

Every time I look down for too long, I find myself pointing in the wrong direction. I keep my eyes up after that, locked onto the blurry gold of the field. Flashes spike through the glow, shiny things placed in the field. Metal, or mirrors. Whatever they are, they wink like white-hot eyes.

My paddle strikes something heavy in the water, and out of instinct, I jerk away. Whatever it is, it slurps up the paddle and slithers around my arm. I fling the paddle and the thing sucks free. I see, just before it slides beneath the lily pads, that it's a girl's Aspen uniform. Just the shirt, dyed a sickly beige by the rusty lake water. I'm careful as I reach in and take back my paddle, expecting a ghostly hand to grab me.

Finally, I grind against the shore, hidden where the trees bend over the lake. I don't know what I expect as I step into the forest, but it's only quiet that I encounter. That, and the constant thrum of my nerves.

Ahead, the meadow's glow presses through the trees, so hot I can feel it now. Gradually, my vision fills with tall golden grasses splattered with wildflowers, a sea of light and color swirling around a miniature city of wooden towers. They vary in height, each made of stacked boxes, but all of them are topped by shining metal sheets. The sun bounces between them, reflecting into the forest, out onto the lake, and I realize that's the flashing I saw from the water. The effect is a meadow shimmering with light from below, like it's trying to echo the sun.

Everywhere in the air, like swarming starlight, are insects. Bees. The boxes are their hives, the meadow their home. And the hum I have been hearing is—now I can hear it clearly—their song. It's a sound so pervasive, you don't notice it until it's inside your head. And I only recognize it now as I remember the same hum last night, loud and enchanting and everywhere, and before that when I nearly tumbled off a cliff on my first day here.

I'm not scared of bees. Not usually. A bee is a tiny thing, easy to crush. But seeing them this way, as pixels merging into incomprehensible magnitude, my mind can't help but do the math. Crush one, be crushed by millions.

So maybe I am a little scared. Just a smidge.

I keep to the meadow edge, out of the sunlight, walking toward the top of the hill, where I know the house will be. A few times a bee shoots by my ear, and I cover it with a hand, remembering again the faint image of a small golden insect crawling into Caroline's head. My mind fills with the vision of her now, lying inert in her coffin, unrecognizably still. Lying among flowers, lying in this field. So still the grasses curtain over her.

I try to picture her alive and moving, attending to these hives, and I find that I can't.

But that's why I'm here, I remind myself. To know Caroline again. To discover again who she was, and save myself from that final version of her. The false, furious doll that attacked me.

Bria will know, I tell myself.

As I get close to the cabin, the drone of the bees softens to that deep and distant thrum, hard to even pick out among the texture of birds and wind and bugs that thicken with the heat. The cicada song swells, overtaking everything, then hisses away. There's a garden vibrating in the sun, and I see planters overgrown with mint, basil, and rosemary. Other things grow in the earth, their crowns sprouting huge leaves to drink the light. Trellises hold aloft a riot of vines and, passing them, I see green tomatoes nestled in the leaves, as small as eyeballs.

Closer to the cabin, I hear another sound, too. Music. Then the jovial bark of a commercial. A radio left on somewhere, but that's the only sound from within. There's no sign of the girls anywhere. I scan the meadow from above, making sure I'm not missing anything, and then I go to the cabin's porch. Somehow the spark of fear I felt watching the hives has only grown, blossoming into a terror I have to fight off with a stern reminder to myself that, *Mars, listen, these girls invited you here. Here. To Cabin H. So go on. Go in.*

But I can't seem to turn the doorknob, even with my hand shakily grasped around it. Then I sense motion on the other side of the door and get out of the way just before it swings open.

A head pokes out and looks directly at me, where I've hidden behind a wicker love seat.

"This way. Hurry," says Sierra. Not the blurry version of her. Just normal, warm-faced Sierra.

She pulls me into the house, and my questions—all of them—vaporize as I enter a plush and dizzying interior. Low couches of swamp-green velvet, pillows of tufted mushroom-beige, and crocheted blankets cast like pastel nets over chairs and poufs and ottomans. There are trays balancing crystal cups sticky with drained drinks, china plates painted with flowers and dotted with crumbs, and a vast and low coffee table cleared for an abandoned game of Catan. Sierra leads me through the clutter deftly, like she can't even see it, then up a spiral staircase boring through the low ceiling of the cottage. I hear other voices now, and the music is louder, but it's still muffled. People are outside the house, in a backyard I have yet to see. Sierra pulls me down a dim hallway, to a room that is surprisingly similar to the Bear Hut bunks. The same rustic-yet-manufactured bed frames hold up the beds, but these are piled with furry blankets and heart-shaped pillows. Fairy lights crisscross the ceiling.

I don't know what I expected to lurk inside Cabin H. It's all light, all charm. I'm equal parts elated and disappointed.

Sierra closes the door behind her, softly, until the lock clicks into place. I'm about to apologize but she's facing me with a coy smile.

"Just like Caroline," she says.

"What do you mean?"

"She had terrible timing, too."

Sierra shushes me, whispering as she flings open a large, battered wardrobe.

"It's elective hour, right? You didn't take the path. You must have come through the meadow, right? Quick, do a turn for me." I do this without knowing why. "Good, you're good. Just making sure you don't have any hitchhikers. And don't worry, I'm glad you're here. We were serious when we said you should come visit. But we're not used to people just showing up

Bria, specifically, likes to plan. She's a host-type mama bear. You know? It's a good thing you didn't take the path. You would have gotten a big surprise."

Sierra gestures to the window, and I peer out onto the lawn behind the cottage. It's covered in blankets and towels, girls sprawled in lazy arrangements, the whole yard a garden of oiled skin. I look away quickly, but not before I glimpse Bria at the center, wrapped in a white cover-up, reading a book among a sprawling and picked-over picnic that puts the clutter of the living room to shame. I think I saw Mimi with her, fiddling with a portable speaker, but I'm not sure. Sierra was right, though. If I exited the forest into this, I would have either run away with shame, or just died on the spot.

Sierra roots through the back of the wardrobe, gives up on finding whatever she's looking for, and starts her search over with the large upright bureau in the corner.

"Is it okay that I'm here?" I ask.

"Of course! We invited you, didn't we?"

"Yeah, I thought so, too, but Bria ... I don't know ... maybe she forgot?"

Sierra rolls her eyes. "She's just being cool for the girls. Trust me, you're of course welcome at Aspen. And here. Usually. But we're not used to surprises, and if the girls knew you were here it would turn into a whole thing. Next time, we'll come back together, okay? I'll bring you home personally."

Sierra moves to the vanity, which is barely visible among cast-off shirts and shorts, the top covered in wig heads wearing various looks. They shake and topple as Sierra pulls open the drawers. I nearly find the courage to ask her about last night in the woods, but then she snaps upright and faces me with a sudden solemnity.

She's holding Caroline's makeup bag. My questions evaporate.

I know it's Caroline's because I got it for her last year. It's boxy and patterned with small cartoon lemons. They have mean eyes and stick limbs, and they're all fighting. I haven't seen it in forever. I forgot it existed until just now, but my first instinct is to snatch it out of Sierra's hands.

She sits on one of the bunks. I do, too.

"The counselors cleaned out Caroline's bunk, but they missed this. She kept it out so that we could use her moisturizers and serums. She always brought us such nice things."

Sierra hands it to me, and I tremble as I open it. The insides are perfectly organized, each thing locked into its own tiny pocket. It's impossible to look at them, or to look away from them. My breath scrapes out of me, hot and harsh. These were hers. It's more than that, though. These were the things she wore to make herself, herself. The colors of her beauty, all here in one place.

I pull out a few of the small glass bottles, savoring their clinks and clicks. I recognize almost everything by name. Serums and oils and powders. Mascaras. Then at the bottom, stuffed in a corner, I find the one thing I don't expect.

My heart slows. I sit back.

It's her nail polish, the sapphire blue she always wore. The cap is smudged with a blot of polish, and I distinctly see the edge of a fingerprint. Her fingerprint. She touched this. She touched all of this, but the fingerprint is different. It looks like it was just pressed, like if I rubbed it, I could feel her leftover warmth.

"Here, let me," Sierra says. I give her the bottle but then she takes my hand in hers, locking our fingers together so she can paint my nails in quick, practiced strokes. I'm conscious of how large my hand looks, held in hers. It makes me hyperaware of the dark heaviness I bring to this room, this cottage, this otherworldly existence on the other side of the lake. It's as magical as I thought. More magical. And I can't help but feel like I don't belong.

"Nonsense," Sierra says. "It looks great on you."

"What?"

"The blue. Caroline's blue. It looks good on you."

I'm quiet as she starts my other hand.

"We did this all the time. Not just me and Caroline. All of us. We have a rule here. No one paints their own nails. We do it like this. Together." She finishes the first coat on one hand, then takes the other.

"We don't ask each other for help," she goes on. "Because we help each other without asking. Do you get what I mean, Mars? We don't make people ask if we know what they need. We just give it."

We aren't talking about nail polish, I don't think. Or maybe that's all we're talking about. What Sierra says reminds me of all the people who approached me after Caroline died and asked, again and again, *What can I do to help?* As if I could tell them. As if it was my job, my burden, to ask. I wonder about this as she applies a second coat. I notice how simple it is, the interlocking of our fingers. How quickly I yield to help offered without pretense.

"Caroline used to paint my nails like this, too," I say.

"What color?"

"Black. She always wanted me to try blue, but it felt like it was hers."

Sierra sighs. "She wore it so much. I don't think anyone dared to ask her for it. It *was* so much hers."

Sierra suddenly takes in a huge breath, and it comes out shuddering. Her shoulders shake, her eyes glass over with tears. Her emotions surprise me, but then they don't. She knew Caroline for years, here at Aspen. They grew up together, the other side of Caroline's bright orbit away from me. It hurts to watch her cry, and it hurts to feel this ugly jealousy that prowls around the territory of my heart. Sierra shakes off her sniffles and keeps going with the polish, finishing without a single smudge.

"There," she says, capping the polish. Then she takes my hands again, and we sit in silence as my nails dry. I listen to the sounds of the girls out-side. They're laughing, always laughing, and singing along to a new song. Sierra has her eyes closed. The lace curtains rise in slow swells, causing the shadowed pattern to swim over us, and I smell the golden aroma of beeswax candles. They're all over the room, unlit but fragrant anyway.

Suddenly Caroline is so close. Whatever it was—the ritual or the makeup box or just being in a place that was so familiar to her—it's like she's back in this world for just a moment. Just beyond the door, or down-stairs on the low couch napping, or on the lawn waving a lazy hand to the sound of her sisters singing. She's outside. She's happy and unaware. I want to go find her, and I won't say a word just in case it sends her away again. I'll just look, and know that she's finally okay.

The tears come quickly. For once I don't try to hide them. I can't, with my hands locked to Sierra's, and it doesn't matter because she's crying, too. The tremor of emotion passes between our hands, back and forth, back and forth. Shared. Divided. Lessened. The songs outside keep chang-ing, and finally the tears stop.

Finally, my nails are dry. I manage a look at Sierra and she's as much a mess as I am. We both blurt an apology at the same time, the sound crack-ing open our grasp, and we're laughing together. She quiets us as best she can, but it's funny. Just the two of us, crying in the quiet, holding hands like that.

"Here," she says, shoving the makeup box into my hands. "Take this with you. None of us can bear to use any of it, but Caroline would want you to. Promise me you will? Or better yet, I'll come find you one night, and we can use it together, okay? You've got her skin, you know."

"I know."

"Of course you know. All right, then. You ready?"

Sierra leads us back through the house, stopping to make sure no one is in the kitchen as she sneaks me to the back door.

"Mars. Did Caroline. . . . tell you anything about Aspen? About us?"

"You mean you and Bria and Mimi?"

"The Honeys. In general. What did she share?"

"Just that . . . that you were her friends. Her best friends. Like sisters to her."

"There's more," Sierra says. "Too much to say now. Keep going, okay? Whatever happens, keep going. Okay?"

Her stare is imploring. I'm compelled to assure her I will keep going, but I don't know what she's saying. Maybe I do, though, if I came all the way here on my own. Maybe I know exactly what she means.

Sierra boots me from the cottage. I go down through the meadow, through the forest, through the sucking muck until I find my red kayak. I don't look back until I'm beyond the lily pads. Faintly, I make out the flashing hives under the midday sun, and above them the bees, everywhere yet invisible, like glitter imagined into the air.

CHAPTER 14

I get back to the boathouse and it's empty. Even the porch is free of its usual cast of slow-roasted sunbathers. Elective period must have ended. If they thought I'd drowned, they'd be out on the lake right now, but the lake is empty. The only sound seems to be the scrape of my kayak as I drag it up the pebbly shore, back to its taffy-colored family. And of course the ever-present hiss of cicadas. But then I hear the crying.

I find her in the back of the boathouse, between the aisles of canoes. It's the counselor who runs the kayak rentals. Sylv. We scare each other as I nearly stumble upon her.

She turns away. "The boathouse is closed." She pulls the heels of her hands across her face, wiping away smudged mascara.

"I'm sorry, I lost track of time and just wanted to return my kayak. I thought I should let someone know."

"Jesus," she whispers, like she's just realizing I wasn't back. "I didn't—I'm sorry. You should go. Second bugle already sounded."

"I'll go," I promise her. "But are you okay?"

Now that I've asked, there's no need for her to hide that she's crying. She looks at me and says nothing. She doesn't need to. Past her watery gaze is a deeper weariness. A devastation I recognize. She isn't okay. Not at all. But it's not the kind of thing you can talk about with a stranger. You just hope someone else sees it, and knows better than to ask you to dig it up for them.

I know better.

"I'm sorry," I say again. "I'll go."

Her expression softens, something like gratitude or relief taking away the raw edge of hurt. I don't wait for a thank-you. I turn and leave the boathouse, clutching Caroline's makeup case to my chest. But I think about her for a long time. The rest of the afternoon and the next day, I look for her. I look for the Honeys, too, but they don't make an appearance at camp. On Wednesday night there's an improv show in the amphitheater, but most of the older kids skip it to hang around Big Lodge. I drift from room to room, still searching. I end up back before the taxidermied elk. I'm peering into it's mouth when, like a bat, Wyatt swoops down upon me.

"Ready for Outbound?"

"What?"

"The Huntsman Outbound trip. Three-day backpacking trip. Been talking about it all week. You packed yet?"

I remember now. One of the many excursions we'll be taking as a Village this summer. The younger kids typically travel by bus to sites around the Northeast, touring DC or Boston for the day before staying over at a hotel and then coming home in the morning. But the older kids go on hikes. Or canoe trips. Or survival retreats.

By the time we're back, I'll have been here for almost a week, I realize. Part of me hadn't even considered lasting that long.

"Not yet," I tell Wyatt.

"Better get to it. We leave at the ass-crack of dawn. If you see any other Huntsmen, can you remind them?"

I head back to the cabin. Wyatt, or someone, has left Aspen-branded backpacks for each of us at the end of our bunks. There's a list of what to bring. It's not much, and nowhere on it does it say to bring a hive tool, but I slip it into a side pocket anyway.

Ass-crack of dawn, here I come.

Wyatt was wrong. We leave before the sun is even up.

A puttering bus pulls right into Hunter Village and we pile into it, then drive yawning and dozing through the sunrise to our starting point. In an unpaved parking lot at the end of some orphaned road, in the gray-green dawn light, we sit on our backpacks and share a breakfast of pre-packed egg sandwiches. There's equipment to be divided up and carried—they give me the first aid kit—and rules and procedures to review, plus a lecture on sticking together. The counselors are chipper. Too chipper. They clap and chant like strange birds as they pass out Aspen bandannas and Aspen canteens. By the time we're ready to go, we look like a cohort of mascots at boot camp.

"Line up, men!" Brayden bellows as we heave our packs onto our shoulders. The straps cut right through the thin fabric of my uniform. We waddle into a single-file line, then start through a sallow, flooded field that fringes the mountains we'll call home for the next three days.

The hike starts out flat. Easy. The boys bump and jostle one another, seeing if they can tip someone over due to the heavy packs. Outside Aspen, off the campgrounds, the boys are different. I feel it, too, a sudden sense of freedom, a released tension now that we're away from the manicured grounds and out in the woods. The actual woods. It's true that Aspen is in the middle of nowhere, but that nowhere ends in suburbia if you walk long enough. These woods feel totally remote. This nowhere feels endless, and that's both scary and freeing.

After a few hours my shoulders are already knotting up, and the climbing sun has pulled sweat out of every single one of my pores. The hills rise beneath us, slow and smoothed by pine needles, then suddenly steep and rocky. The chatter dies off as we focus on placing our steps. "Root!" someone will shout, and the call gets passed back to make sure no one twists an ankle.

"Rock!"

"Root!"

The rest of the morning is a silent trudge punctuated by these small, breathy alarms. When we stop for lunch I'm panting, and I nearly float into the sky when I let my pack fall to the ground. I've spent the last hour suspended between the conclusion that I can't do this hike—absolutely not for another two days—and my own determination to not show a second of doubt to the others. Thankfully, the boys are in a similar state, which is a relief.

Lunch is dead quiet except for the sounds of tinfoil crinkling, and chewing, and the occasional belch. We get to refill our water, and then it's back to the trail. I keep my eyes down as I walk, willing the incline to level out, and it actually does. When I look up, we're walking through a realm of the forest that feels far more ancient. The trees here are massive and spaced out, the small hills between them neon with undulating ferns. They brush my bare knees and tickle my ankles. The air is dark and sweet.

Absurdly, I'm enjoying this. Enjoying *nature*. It reminds me of something I read when I was researching grief. From a physicist's perspective, a person is never really gone. They've just changed forms. The energy and particles that make them up have disorganized, merged back with the world, united with nature in cycles that are eternal. It's easy to believe that out here—in woods that feel heavy with eternity. But I don't let myself peer through the shadows to gather evidence of my sister. I fear that I'll see her, like I do in my dreams, lying in a crater of shattered ferns. So I keep my eyes down on the single unnatural thing here: the path carving through the forest.

The path widens. The boys walk side by side, louder now. Bolstered, maybe, by the alien terrain, they begin to discuss Aspen with scientific authority. Mostly this means they dissect the girls they think are hot, in fantastical comparisons. Gruesomely, they begin to build new girls from the parts of known ones. Bria's nose. Kyle's legs. Amanda's breasts.

I don't know most of the people they mention. The girl who comes together in my mind is a tortured patchwork, and I tune the boys out.

We reach a summit, we take a break, we take a photo with a big, Aspen-branded banner. We're then informed that the remaining trail is only two miles, and downhill. Even I cheer for this, but my excitement winks out with my first step down the mountainside. My legs tremble, and at any moment I feel like I'll pitch forward and roll into one of the many black-bottomed drops that keep yawning open beside the twisting path. I fall into a strict focus as I walk, ignoring the boys as they continue to rub themselves raw against the kaleidoscoping fantasy of girls made of other girls.

I walk right into Wyatt when we stop suddenly. He catches my arm and keeps me from toppling over.

"We made it," he says, and we have. The boys throw down their packs in a clearing that edges a wide, slow river aflame with late-afternoon light. It's gratifying to see Wyatt slick with sweat, like me. His eyes follow a trickle down my jaw, my neck. His hand on my arm lingers. Unguarded as I am, I feel a flutter in my gut. I try to think of something to say.

"I can't believe Brayden lets the boys talk like that," I say.

"About the girls? That's all boys talk about."

"You don't," I point out.

"Maybe I'm allergic," he says.

Wyatt lets go, and my skin throbs with the sudden loss of touch. I stow away this strange emotion, too tired to analyze it. We join the others, commencing upon the complicated ritual of "making" camp. Which, for me, means gathering kindling from the rotting brush around the clearing. While Eagle House handles cooking, we bathe in the river. The boys swim to the middle, taking turns letting the current carry them through glassy braids of waters sweeping over slick rocks. I sit in a shallow stretch, dragging a sliver of soap over my sunburnt skin, watching the suds twist away. I watch Wyatt, willing him to watch me back. He doesn't, but later around the campfire, he sits next to me. It sends a bolt through my tailbone.

Ah, I think to myself. *Mars has a crush.*

I decide no, I don't, but thank you anyway.

We eat beef-and-barley stew, and sun-dried tomatoes submerged in steaming polenta. There's even basil as a garnish. I taste only the after-taste as I take long pulls from my canteen, and then suddenly I'm exhausted. Wyatt's shoulder is warm against my own as the fire slowly overtakes the meager remnants of sun. Then it's all black-blue above, molten orange below.

I surprise myself when I realize once again that I'm kind of content out here. It makes me distrust the wonders of nature, knowing how easily I've been lulled from my usual, prickly paranoia. Maybe it's the woods, or maybe it's Wyatt's unrelenting cheer for all things green. I shake off my sleepiness and sit up, making sure not a stitch of my clothing is touching Wyatt's. He, of course, doesn't even notice.

Brayden and the counselors surprise us by passing around s'more ingredients and everything unsettles again as the boys wrestle for prime marshmallow-roasting positions. I watch the white blobs of sugar go brown and then black, dripping into the fire, bubbling on the coals.

Of course ghosts come up.

"Do you guys remember Bone White Man?" The Chuckster asks, and the boys around the fire groan in recognition. Even I remember Bone White Man. He's Aspen's bogeyman, a somewhat cruel tradition told to the Bandits to get them to go to bed.

"In the forest there is a cabin . . ." Ray begins.

People jump in to correct him.

"In the woods there is a lake—"

"It's *forest.*"

"It's a cottage."

A debate breaks out about the details, which Wyatt settles by telling the official version.

"In the woods there is a lake, across the lake there is a field, atop the field there is a house, and outside the house, knocking at the windows, is the Bone White Man."

The circle quiets. Wyatt goes on. "The Bone White Man is as old as Aspen. No one knows what he did to deserve his fate. Not even he remembers. But it's fact that a crime was committed, the forest witnessed it, and the forest judged it. One night, under a moon so white and cold it could grow frost on your bones, right beneath your skin, the forest lured the man from his warm cabin."

"How, though?" cuts in Callum.

"Crying," Wyatt says. "A child crying."

"It was singing," Tyler says, and the other boys contribute *chanting, howling wolves, laughing, humming.*

I don't catch who said humming. But that's what I thought, too. I remember being told it was a girl humming. I forgot until just now, but the alignment chills me. A frost forms under my own skin.

"It's crying. In some versions he has a daughter who he abandoned, and it's her crying that pulls him from the warmth of his home," Wyatt says. "Anyway, he goes out into the forest, and he never comes back. He gets so cold that he can't even die. And it's said he's still out there, searching for warmth. If you look at a dark window for too long at night, he'll walk in front of it. Ice white. Hair clumped with frost. Eyeballs frozen solid. That's why we turn our lights out, so that he never finds his way back."

The boys are quiet, and then the commentary resumes.

"Such a dumb story."

"That shit used to scare me."

"It's not a story." This is from Wyatt again. "I heard him once. His frozen fingers tapping against my window. I turned off my light and I saw him, just a few feet away. Then he left. In the morning, my window still had frost on it."

"Oh, shut up, Wyatt. As if you would ever turn on a lamp after lights-out. There's no way you were up."

"You can hear the sound of his teeth chattering, too!" Wyatt sucks in a shivering breath.

"That story gave me so many nightmares," I say. "I still can't look at a window when I turn the lights out, just in case he's standing there."

"It's the opposite for me," Ray says. "I can't look into the cabins from the outside. You guys ever hear the story about the Cabin People?" Ray sits up. "Same start. In the woods there's a house, and all that. But it actually *did* happen at Aspen. And I think it started on an excursion like this one. A bunch of the girls were playing with their flashlights in one of the tents, making shadow puppets. Their counselors kept telling them to go to sleep but the girls wouldn't, so the counselors decided to scare them by casting shadows from the outside.

"The girls talked about it all the way back to their cabin. But once they got back to camp, the shadows kept appearing. It happened anytime there was a light left on. Like in the bathroom at night. Just a detached shadow, like a hand or a head. It got so bad that one night the girls all raced outside, where there was no light. The counselors tried to calm them down by telling them it was a joke, but when they looked back into the cabin, the shadows were still there. Except it wasn't just shadows. They were looking at themselves, people with their faces standing at the windows, waving and smiling."

No one contributes to Ray's story. It receives a silent ovation. Maybe we're each imagining those ghostly hands skipping along the edge between shadow and light.

Finally, Brayden speaks into the silence.

"Do you guys know why it's called Aspen?" The question shifts the tone of the night, like a key change from minor to major.

"Aspen is sacred land," Brayden begins. "Has been for thousands of years, long before the camp was built. A lot of legends exist but the first and most fundamental is that of the aspen trees themselves. Aspen trees grow in groves. It's said they're all connected, just one ancient organism under the earth, and the black whorls in the bark are their eyes. They watch us, making sure we respect this place and one another. It's said that no secret deeds exist among the eyes of the aspen trees."

"Like the Bone White Man?" someone offers.

"Right. Exactly." Brayden nods. "This is why Aspen was built. It's a place where we can be honest with ourselves, and with the forest. It's a place founded upon a tradition of trust."

Brayden looks at each of us, the firelight rimming his eyes in gold. "This Outbound Excursion is all about trust. You trust me and Quinn, your Leaders, to guide you through these woods. We trust you to follow us. We trust one another like brothers because out here in the wild, that's what we are. Brothers. That bond is what will last long after we leave Aspen. The eyes of the forest stay on us."

I feel that Brayden is right, as one by one we break the circle and crawl into our tents. I feel the eyes in the bark, never blinking, never averting. Their unyielding pressure follows me as I brush my teeth at the river's edge, spitting into the moonlit water; it follows me as I step into my muggy tent and pick over restless, anonymous bodies; it follows me as I drift right up to the edge of dreams.

Then it follows me further.

CHAPTER 15

I wake up entombed in soreness, every muscle calcified beneath aching skin. By the sounds of it, I'm the first up. My eyes sting, like I didn't even sleep. I vaguely recall a dream of Caroline, though that's hardly new. This time, though, I couldn't see her. She was in the woods, crying, laughing, crying, and when I stepped out of the firelight to find her, a shadow took my place.

I emerge from the tent, stopping as soon as the clearing comes into focus. All around our tent is a wreath of trash. Brayden and Wyatt pick through it, swearing as they go.

"We would have heard bears," Wyatt is saying. "And raccoons couldn't get into the packs like this."

"Maybe. Who was in charge of securing the garbage bags? I bet it was Ray, he's so fucking lazy," says Brayden. Wyatt shushes him, seeing me. A few other boys have emerged, too, and they blink at the mess.

It's not just garbage strewn all over. Whatever it was, it got into our food and supplies. Flaccid backpacks sit in piles of torn-through packaging, food scraps fuzzy with flies and ants. My pack is one of the few that's fine, and I relax when I find the cold metal of the hive tool deep within it.

"We should be okay," Wyatt is assuring Brayden. "Ravenskill is near where we're making camp tonight. We can take a detour for some help, and—"

"We don't need help," Brayden says, jaw clenched.

That morning, breakfast is cold, gluey oatmeal and a lecture from Brayden on camping etiquette, teamwork, and weakest links. One of us messed up, all of us suffer. It reminds me of my dad. *We before me.* The mood is decidedly grim as we get back on the trail. We hobble on stiff legs, yet Brayden sets a grueling pace. Even Wyatt emanates a tamped fury. It spreads to all of us, rising as the blazing sun burns off the morning mist.

I'm hungry. I'm tired. I push all my energy into staying upright. Eventually I fall into a rhythm, stumbling and uneven, the beat of my swollen feet finding their way across rocks and roots without me even seeing them.

I daydream of the meadows, and the gem-bright colors of everything inside Cabin H. I imagine the girls gathered on the porch, still bundled in blankets against the morning's chill, windows pushed open to let out the smoke of bacon and home fries. Then they'd crowd into the bathrooms to stand at the mirror and pull at their hair, their eyelashes, before shoving socked feet into sneakers the colors of pastel candy. Down into the meadows they'd go, maybe singing, maybe holding pinkies, to open up the hives and wake up the bees inside.

I flirt with the hazy half-memory of Manhunt. Callum crouched in the dark, cupping his hands under a nose dripping with blood, but it feels so strange. Those dark, saturated colors amid the washed brilliance of Cabin H. They don't go together at all. I leave Callum behind in his dark little forest and wonder again about the bees.

I know some things about bees and beekeeping. Not a lot. Just what I looked up as I packed for Aspen. The hives are completely sealed from sunlight, rain, and wind, except for a small porch at the bottom, where the bees enter. Sometimes it gets clogged with corpses; bees are hygienic. They remove their dead in daisy-chain funerals. The inside of the hive is loud. And dark. And cramped. The bees build their honeycombs vertically, the sheets of interlocking hexagons starting at the top of the hives and dripping down. It's different than people. We build up toward the sun.

We seek to scrape the sky itself. Bees, by sourceless unanimity, take all the fruits of a life borne from flight and use them to build down, deeper into the darkness.

I start to understand what Caroline must have seen in them. The bees. They operate within such an urgent, simple logic. Unbothered but also determined. Like her. Their world feels pure, unbound from creativity or pride or rebellion. All those vices live within me, so maybe I couldn't live within a hive after all.

But what about grief? Do bees know loss? Humans have a hundred mythologies to dissect death. When a bee dies, I wonder if it anticipates the moment its curled body will be passed down through the sweetly scented darkness, toward the light that waits below.

I have never prayed until Caroline died, and now that she's gone, I only have one prayer. Just one. *Wherever you are, let it be bright.* I hope it's light that greets us, in the end, after everything. The alternative is unbearable.

I stumble. I recover.

No. There's nothing after, neither bright nor dark. No disorganized energy or dissipated particles. That's what I tell myself. Anything more than nothing leaves too many questions. Conditions and bargains I can't deal with. There must be nothing. I need to know that there is nowhere left to look, otherwise I'll never stop looking.

I stumble again, recover again.

And then I fall.

My hand strikes an upturned rock and the pain snaps me out of my trance. I clutch my hand to my chest, feeling warm blood carve over my knuckles, dripping down my arm. I look up to see if anyone saw.

I'm alone.

I stand and turn. No one is beside me or behind me. I'm not even on the trail.

I'm alone.

"Hello?" I call.

Nothing.

I call again, panic scraping my voice. I turn and turn, trying to figure out the direction I was walking from, but it's too late. I'm lost. I pick a direction at random and just go. Up the hill. At the top I feel a flash of doubt and turn, peering down into the trees. Unlike the aspen trees, these are faceless, like the woods have turned their backs on me.

I see, far off, a thrash in the green.

Bears. Raccoons. Something big cuts toward me. I tighten my pack, ignoring my bloody hands, and get ready to run; then I hear a shout.

It's Wyatt!

I skid down the hill, meeting him at the bottom.

He's breathing hard. "I told you . . . not to . . . go off alone."

I'm torn between crying with relief and snapping to my own defense.

"I just zoned out. I'm sorry."

"You do that a lot," Wyatt says. "Just . . . zone out."

I can't deny that. I'm still reeling from the surprise myself. He looks at me, and his eyebrows furrow. "You're bleeding."

I hold up my hand to show my bloody palm, but he's looking at my head. I touch my bandaged ear and my fingertips come away slick and red.

"I . . . fell. I think. I don't know. I was walking, and then I started thinking about bees and *death*, and . . ."

Now I do cry. I don't get what's happening or why. I don't know how I got here. I try to stop but twin tears push out of my eyes. I wipe them away, mixing my blood with their salt.

"Hey, hey, it's okay. The others are just over that ridge. We stopped for lunch anyhow and that's when I saw you walk away. You just kept going." Wyatt tumbles forward, like his words can put a stopper on my emotions. "We're not far. They're right there. I swear. Look, look at me. We'll walk back together. And we'll find the first aid kit. It's okay. Hey? It's okay, right?"

I'm embarrassed by my emotion. I feel a little empty, a little dizzy. Very silly. I do believe him, though, about being okay.

"I have the first aid kit," I mumble. "It's in my pack."

"Great." Wyatt smiles. "Here, we'll get you patched up."

I shrug off my backpack and he starts digging through it. I remember the hive tool a second too late, right as his hand finds something deep in the backpack that causes him to tense up. He pulls it out slowly, sitting back on his haunches, but it's not the hive tool.

"Mars, you can't have this out here. It's going to attract bears."

In the murky light of the forest, it glows like molten gold. Honey. A tiny, single-serving jar like from the dining hall. How did it get in my backpack?

"I didn't know I had it," I say. I take it from him while he extracts the first aid kit. The jar is heavy in my hand, a crack running through it. The smell is subtle, but there. Floral. Rich.

"I'll dump it out," I say.

"You can't. Leave no trace, remember?"

"Then I'll put it in the bear bags."

"You want another morning like the one we just had?"

I'm tempted to point out that my pack was one of the few left alone, but then I catch a playful warmth in his features. He's joking. I relax a little.

"What do we do with it, then?" I ask.

Wyatt's smile is slow. Easy and practiced. "You could eat it. I won't tell."

"You eat it," I shoot back.

"And when I get dragged out of my tent by a bear in the night, it'll be your fault. You want that?"

While we spar, he blots my hand with iodine.

"A bear would never go for you," I say.

"Why?"

"You stink."

"You're not exactly the freshest daisy either, scout."

I wince as he blots my ear next.

"Question. What's this from?" he asks, offhand, which tells me he knows. Or I'm imagining things.

"Answer. I fell," I say simply.

"Must have been a nasty one."

"The nastiest."

"Nastier than I smell?"

The thing is, Wyatt smells great. Like sunscreen and citronella and, yes, the tang of sweat, but fresh sweat. It's familiar and foreign, and I don't mind it at all.

"You're not so bad," I say.

Wyatt applies a new bandage, then stands back, pretending to observe his work, but he's observing me.

"I owe you an apology," he says. "I've been watching you since you got here. Did you know that?"

"Noooo, really?" I gasp, for the drama. "And here I thought Wendy paired me with her nephew because she wanted to emphasize the Aspen core value of nepotism!"

Wyatt laughs, the quick kind where you exhale out your nose but refuse to break open a smile.

"Seriously," he says. "The directors were worried you wouldn't . . . I don't know, fit in? So they asked me to keep an eye on you. And at first, I thought they were right. But you're tough, Mars. You keep up."

"I thought I zone out."

"And fall. And never take anything seriously. But it's clear people underestimate you."

I have known this literally my whole life. People decide they know everything about me the second they see me, and then reward themselves when I prove them wrong.

"What I mean is, I'm sorry," Wyatt says.

"It's cool," I say. "I'm used to it."

"You shouldn't have to be."

And yet I am. Whose fault is that? I don't say this because I think Wyatt already knows it. My point has been made in the hairpin reversal of his assessment of me.

I decide to change the subject.

"What about the honey?"

Wyatt picks up the jar, carefully unscrewing the lid.

"Bottoms up?" he says.

Then he tips back his head and I watch his throat as a trail of spindly gold tips from the jar, into his mouth. He swallows twice without closing his mouth, eases the flow, and hands me what's left.

"Think you can finish that off, Matthias?"

"You're underestimating me again?" I fire back. I take the jar carefully, tipping it toward my lips. The honey's taste is powerfully rich, not like the honey we get from the store. It's deep, full of light and flowers and heat, like eating summer.

I watch Wyatt watch me. Out here, his mismatched eyes are so much brighter. Past the amusement, past the smugness, there's intrigue. A longing unknown to him, maybe, but clear to me.

I think. I hope.

Now the honey jar is empty except for an amber glaze. Wyatt dribbles some water into it, then dumps it out before bundling the broken jar in some gauze and stashing it back in my pack.

"Our secret," he says.

"A spider's promise," I assure him with a wink.

We walk back toward the group. Wyatt offers to carry my pack and I let him. I notice that the silence between us is clouded with something. A tension. There's something Wyatt wants to say, so I let him work toward it as we pick through twisty mountain laurel.

"Mars, I don't know how to say this, but I'm really sorry about your sister. She was a good person."

For once I don't stop short. Maybe it's the strangeness of the ritual we just performed with the honey, but I feel light. Clear. Talking to Wyatt about this feels okay.

"Did you know her?"

"Yeah. Yes. We were friends, actually. Last year and the year before."

"What was she like? Here, I mean. At Aspen."

"She was . . ." Wyatt swats away a bug. He focuses on the ground as he talks. "She was kind and smart. She paid attention to everyone. She wasn't like . . ."

"Like the Honeys?"

"Yeah. She wasn't just part of one group. She was part of every group, it felt like. We got close because of sailing. She was my sailing partner."

"Don't tell me you had a crush on her," I tease.

Wyatt exhales a laugh. "Nah, it wasn't like that. She was more of a sister—oh. I'm sorry."

I wave his shame away.

"It's okay. I know what you mean."

We hear the boys finally, shouting in the distance. Their laughter filters through the birdsong, and it causes Wyatt to slow.

He says, "Actually, I wanted to tell you something. I lost a sibling, too."

I get quiet. All of me. Even the small hum within me lessens to near nothing. I stop and Wyatt doesn't, stepping out ahead of me before turning around. He looks up into the branches, squinting against the dappled light.

138

"My little brother. He was really sick for a long time. He made it ten years, even though the doctors said he wouldn't. He was a fighter, you know?"

Wyatt's voice is small by the end, cramped and strained. He doesn't go on until the emotions have passed.

"Cancer sucks" is all he adds.

I realize that Aspen, like everyone, thinks Caroline was killed by brain cancer. And for a moment, I do too. I saw the scans. I saw the shadowy blots riddling her body. The constellation of voids, like a prophesy for all the emptiness she'd leave behind.

"I'm sorry to hear about your brother," I say. "That's way too young."

It sounds hollow. So practiced. I mean every word but all I hear are the flat apologies of the people who tried to comfort *me*. I wonder if maybe I heard them wrong.

"Jeremy," Wyatt says. "His name was Jeremy."

I close my eyes.

Jeremy, Caroline. I want to imagine them out there, together in some unknowable brightness. Maybe they're watching, maybe they're not. But I hope they're not alone.

For a moment I think I'm going to cry, but I don't. I can still taste the sweet honey on the back of my teeth, and that roots me in the reality of right now. In the woods there is a valley, in the valley there are two people, within them both a person-shaped emptiness. Wyatt and I understand each other.

"I'm sorry," I tell Wyatt.

"I'm sorry, too," Wyatt tells me.

There's no need to say anything more. We leave it at that, hiking back to the others in shared silence.

CHAPTER 16

That afternoon we make camp near another river. Or the same river. I don't know or care. The mood is decidedly less celebratory than yesterday as the boys slough their packs off and stretch. The hike to get here was downhill and treacherous, sliding us like marbles between blades of rock and jutting trees, and we're hungry from a meager lunch. There's no food for dinner.

Brayden announces a plan. He and Quinn will hitch a ride into town with a few volunteers to pick up supplies. Wyatt of course volunteers. Kenny, the Eagle LIT, offers to stay behind. The micro-expedition sets out, Wyatt leading them with a map and his silly compass watch, which I guess isn't so silly after all.

The boys strike up a game that involves tossing small stones underhand at someone with a large stick, seeing how far they can whack them into the river. I sit in the shade, sipping water. My hand is throbbing under the bandages Wyatt applied. I'm afraid to even look, sure I'll find some sort of bubbling infection. Then the game gets boring and the boys get restless. I don't hear the start of it, but someone kicks off the whining and it spreads like wildfire through the dry kindling of everyone's irritability.

"It was Ray," someone says. "Ray was the one who was supposed to tie up the bear bag."

"Screw you, Nico," Ray fires back. "I did it right. It's not my fault."

"Bears don't just walk into camps like that," someone says.

"Wyatt said it could have been raccoons."

"Or maybe it was the Bone White Man."

This gets some wry laughter. Despite the heat, I find myself glancing at the woods across the river.

"What do you think, Mars?"

This comes from Callum, across the circle. He's swinging around the stick from the game, like a sword. The bruises on his face have deepened, and his eyes are still puffy. It makes it hard to read his expression, but I don't like the way his attention, and the attention of his goons, settles on me. They look hungry.

"I don't know," I say. "Probably just raccoons or something."

"It's weird, though," Callum says slowly. "Most of the food was on the ground. Not even eaten. Mars, you're always following Wyatt to the Eco-Lab. What do you think about that?"

"Maybe they think a camping meal that comes with a basil garnish is for sissies," I say, hoping the joke deflects and defuses, but it doesn't work. Callum takes it personally, standing up and squaring his shoulders.

"Did *you* just call *me* a sissy?"

"Literally, no," I say. "Semantics, Callum."

"So you're calling me dumb?"

Here we go again. The circle goes quiet as Callum levels me with a bitter stare. Revenge sparks in his eyes, echoing those phantom memories from Manhunt. For me it feels like déjà vu, but for Callum the payback I incurred when I beat him at fencing is still owed.

"Maybe it wasn't an animal," Callum offers to the circle. "Maybe it was a person. And come to think of it, wasn't your pack one of the few that wasn't touched?"

I immediately think of the jar of honey smuggled into my belongings. Anyone could have put it there, slightly cracked, to attract all sorts of creatures.

"I didn't touch your stuff," I say.

"Maybe there was something in your bag that brought the bears, then?"

So it was Callum who put the jar there. Time for a bluff.

"Check my bag," I say. "You're not going to find anything."

"I wouldn't dare," Callum says. "Your little boyfriend Wyatt would run to Wendy right away and then they'd get rid of Outbounds probably. Just like you got Battle of the Sexes canceled."

By the way some of the guys in the circle react, I figure about half of them know my backstory, and the other half know enough to understand the accusation Callum is making. I stand up, intending to leave the circle, but Callum's not done.

"You know," Callum says, "*Marshall* here is the reason they had to change Battle of the Sexes to the Village Victory Cup. It's the same thing, but *Marshall* here couldn't handle it because he wanted to play with the *girls*, and when they wouldn't let him, *Marshall* set fire to the scoreboard. Isn't that right?"

I turn around. Blood pumps in my ears. My hand is throbbing.

"What's it going to take to get you to leave me alone, Callum?"

"How about a rematch?" Callum says, so quickly I feel like I've stumbled into his trap. He lobs his stick at me and I fumble the catch. I should leave it at my feet but he's got another stick ready.

I look for Kenny, but he's watching just like the rest of the boys. Even Tyler seems fixed on observing. I know Wyatt would intervene, but would anyone else? Aspen prides itself on letting campers settle their own disputes. From experience, I know how far these disputes can go. Someone is always bound to get hurt.

I pick up the stick, if only to have something to block with when Callum inevitably swings.

"I went easy on you before," Callum gloats. "Just because they told us we had to be nice to the freak with the dead sister."

I swing first. Callum blocks. Then hits back. The sticks are unwieldy.

Not the serpentine grace of a foil. My right hand stings as I fight to hold on with each assault from Callum. He's prepared and I'm not, and in no time he's got me backed up against a tree. He's using two hands against my one. I'm overpowered, just like he wants.

"Not so tough after all," he spits.

"You win," I grunt. "We're even. Just leave me alone."

Callum grinds into me. There's no mercy in his stare.

"Say you're a little bitch. Say it."

I punch Callum with my left hand, my broken fingers against his broken nose. I'm so mad that I only feel the splintering click of bone against bone. Callum wheels backward, dropping his stick so he can cover his face as he howls. Through the cracks in his fingers, I can see one wild eye rolling in pain until it locks onto me, but his friends hold him back.

"Fine. You're a little bitch," I say, tossing my stick at Callum's feet. "Happy?"

Kenny finally steps in to break up the fight. The second it's clear Callum's not going to attack me from behind, I leave the clearing. The boys let me go, stunned or maybe impressed. I don't care. I end up at the riverbank, out of sight, so that I can finally crumple over my throbbing hand. It's like trying to hold a small sun, the heat so ferocious that it purges the tears out of me. I brace myself until it finally eases, and gradually I begin to unwrap the bandages.

There's blood. Enough that I scoot to the water's edge to let the icy river whisk it away in rosy swirls. It helps, and I let the soaked bandages bloat and unravel. Sucking in a deep breath, I peel them back, sticky dark clots coming loose along with shards of my ruined nails.

But . . .

I blink.

Under the shards is a brand-new smoothness. New nails. Completely healed. I'm so alarmed that I flex my fingers without thinking, but the crackling pain is gone. My knuckles are fine, too. Even the cut on my palm is gone, save a pale seam. Like the skin has just closed itself.

I gingerly cup water over my hand, washing away the rest of the blood. Aside from a tingling rawness, my hand is fine. Better than fine. It feels powerful. Solid. Like I could punch one hundred Callums.

"You shouldn't do that."

I jump, hiding my hand as I twist to face Tyler, who followed me.

"Do what?"

"Antagonize him."

"He started it."

"But you swung first."

I did. The element of surprise is one of the few advantages I've got. Tyler looks at my hand trailing soaked pink bandages. "How is it?"

"Fine."

Tyler sucks in a slow breath. "Look," he tries again. "Just some advice. I think you'd have a lot easier of a time if you weren't so . . ."

My back goes pin-straight and my chin rises. "So what, Tyler?"

"Sensitive. Not everything is always about you being gay, I mean," Tyler says. "I don't make a huge deal about it. I don't use it as an excuse, and I get along with the guys just fine."

"I'm not using anything as an excuse. I just . . ." My mind reaches for some way to make sense of the frustration storming in me. "I exist. And they don't like that. And evidently you're not a fan either."

"I'm just trying to help you here, Mars."

"Thanks." I bite the word out. Tyler gets the point and he leaves. I look back at my hand.

My newly healed hand.

How is this possible?

I sniffle, swallowing back my tears. And, like an answer, I taste it again.

The drowsy richness of the honey Wyatt and I shared. I feel its warmth still lining my stomach, spreading out within me in minute golden threads, pulsing in my hand like a glove beneath the skin.

I swallow again, and the taste is gone. The feeling of power remains. I pull my hand into a fist, my tears forgotten.

"Wake up."

I'm shoved. Hard. I lurch from sleep, sitting up into the damp nylon of the tent wall. It's pitch-black, nowhere near morning.

"Shoes on. Let's go," the voice says. I don't recognize it. I fumble as I pull on my shorts. I grab Caroline's hive tool from under my pillow in case it's Callum back for more, but all of us are being pulled out of the tent. Someone asks what's going on and they're shushed.

Outside, we stand shivering. I hear the other boys hustled from their tents. I find my boots and lace them up, slipping the hive tool into my sock.

"Line up. Let's go."

This is Brayden. He stands over the embers of the fire, behind a veil of smoke with Quinn beside him. Wyatt and the other LIT corral us into parallel lines.

"Welcome, Huntsmen, to the Night Hike."

My instincts tell me I can relax. This starts to make sense. Just another Aspen tradition. So long as I stay away from Callum, I'll be fine. And seeing as how he barely even looked at me during dinner and the campfire, I have high hopes he's learned his lesson, Tyler be damned.

Brayden shushes our whispering.

"You've each earned your spot here, but you will have to fight to keep it. To be a Huntsman means facing nature in her fearsome dominion and coming out victorious. There will be many tests, and many chances to give up this summer, but if you endure them each you will have forged an unbreakable bond with one another, and an incontestable authority over nature herself. Can I get a hoo-ra?"

The boys give a half-hearted hoo-ra.

"Louder."

This time the night vibrates with our voices.

The Leaders nod, and Kenny and Wyatt hold up fistfuls of black canvas sacks. They pull them over our heads. When Wyatt gets to me, I expect him to pause, but he doesn't. He hoods me just as brusquely as any of the others. My lungs fill with my own panicked breath as the meager light from the moon is choked off. Then something cold is shoved into my hands. A flashlight.

"Your task is simple," Brayden says. "You will be led into the woods. You will begin a count to one thousand, nine hundred, and twenty-three. The year Aspen was founded. Only then may you remove your hoods and use your flashlights. Find one another, then find camp. From now until sunrise there will be no talking. Are we clear?"

We say nothing.

"Good," Brayden says. "Have no fear, men. You have all that you need. Trust yourselves and your brothers."

I hear them lead the first few boys off. I nearly rip off the hood. Someone clears their throat authoritatively, a warning as my hand rises to my face, and I decide not to try it. I stand still and straight, determined to show no fear. This is just another game, another test. If I remind myself of that, I won't panic.

It's a long time before we hear footsteps, then there's a hand on my neck and I'm pushed step by step through an unfamiliar path. I don't think it's Wyatt guiding me. I can't smell his smell. Whoever it is, he says nothing. Not even when I stumble and he has to heave me forward. If anything, his pace quickens. We go in circles, double back. Then we march along a slope, forever it feels like, until we stop. I still hear the river, so we can't be that far.

"Start counting," my guide tells me, and then I'm shoved to the forest floor. I slide down the slope until my foot braces against something moist and sharp. Roots, upturned. I don't make a sound. I won't give them even a whimper.

I start counting in my head.

At one hundred, I think I hear footsteps up ahead, but they're washed away in the sound of wind and crickets.

At one hundred and fifty-six, something snaps right above my head. I duck, but nothing touches me. I keep feeling the invisible threads of spiders on my neck, my ear.

Between two hundred and three hundred I only hear my own shaking breaths. I lose count, I resume. I don't skip a single number. If this is a test of rigor, I won't cut corners. I'll make sure they see me walk out of this darkness victorious. Without fear. Tyler is wrong about me; I'm not using anything as an excuse.

Somewhere past one thousand, the crying starts. It's so faint, at the very limits of my hearing, but the clipped, choking cry stands out from the soft uniformity of the night. I hold my breath, listening. My hand finds the hive tool in my sock.

A minute later I think I hear it again, but then it's gone. Probably just an animal, or a warped echo.

Then, very close, a girl screams.

I stand and tear off my hood. I aim my flashlight right where I heard the scream and click it.

It doesn't go on.

I click and click and click. It won't work. I unscrew it and there are no batteries.

Another scream, like the night tearing open right before me.

"Who's there?" I call. "Callum? This isn't funny."

This time when the scream comes, it's all around me. Thick and wet

with terror. I fall over myself trying to get away, to do anything to pu
distance between myself and whoever—whatever—it is. Visions of floatin
girls rise over me, and I run. Branches and brambles score my legs an
arms and my shirt tears open, but I don't stop. I don't look where I'm
going. I can't see. I can only hear as the scream multiplies, layers ove
itself, rising to a sobbing, sputtering plea.

MARS

It calls my name. It reaches for me, sliding through the forest as easil
as mist, snipping at my ankles as I tear a path forward. I'm too slow.

There's a break in the trees and a moonlit expanse beyond, and I div
toward it. Anything to be out in the open. My feet splash into water and
wade into a shallow stream. Then I turn, caught between two dark banks
to face whatever follows me.

MARS?

Between my name and that keening cry, I hear scraps of laughter, o
crying, of laughter. I hold up the hive tool like a knife, like it can save me
It burns in my sweating fist.

MARS?

The laughter comes again. Now that I'm standing still, I can finall
focus. The sound is gruesomely mutilated, stretched nearly beyond m
recognition, but as it echoes over the sliding of the water, I become sure o
what I'm hearing.

It's Caroline.

Or it was Caroline. It's her snorting cackle mixed with her bellowing
guffaw, the two pitched inhumanly low and wailing over and over, in a
loop. The hair on my neck rises. The cry comes again, but it's stopped following me.

I adjust my grip on the hive tool and take a step toward the scream
By the time I've negotiated myself back onto the bank I'm nearly calm. O
the illusion of calm. Though my steps are steady and careful, a fur

builds within me. Each time the cry comes, I flinch less. I can hear the skips and breaks in the loop now, seams where the recordings are spliced together.

I find the speaker near the hill I started on, wedged into the hollow of a tree. It's the size of a softball, but loud. Very loud. I reach for it to turn it off when suddenly it shuts up, and an impartial robotic voice says:

Bluetooth disconnected.

A bush nearby tears apart as someone runs deeper into the forest. I sprint after them. They will pay, Callum or whichever one of his boys he got to help him with this. The forest was full of my sister's screams; anyone who heard them and did nothing is complicit. And whoever started this, they will suffer. I will *make* them suffer.

I think I see them for just a moment as they slip through the moonlight, and that's all I need. I draw my arm back and let the hive tool fly. It thunks into something soft, and they fall, but when I reach the spot where it hit them, the tool is all I find. It's sticky with blood, oil-black in the moonlight.

I try to see where the person ran, but the night is quiet again. I'm alone. I crouch, shaking and cold. Soaked. Defeated. A whimper of frustration escapes me, but I snuff it out as I rise.

No.

I start the long hike back to camp, and I remind myself that only one person bled tonight, and it wasn't me.

———————————

All the boys make it back before sunrise.

My eyes roam their bodies for scratches, for anywhere the edge of my tool might fit, but I find nothing. Not even on Callum, who glows with the giddiness of adventure like all the others strolling into camp.

None of them will look at me.

They look at one another. They look so proud. They shine with silvery,

149

invincible smugness at having completed the hike. I split in two, wanting so badly to be strong and impassive before my secret attacker; wanting also to break down and scream—to maybe even beg—for them to tell me who did this.

"You've all passed your first test as Huntsmen," Brayden declares over the fire's coals. The night is breaking beyond him, fading upward toward a gray-blue sunrise. The boys meet the sunrise with straight-backed bravado.

"We return to Aspen, and we never speak of this again. Not even to one another. Your bravery tonight is sacred. Defile the secrecy of it, and the forest will know. *We* will know."

The time to tell the truth is ending. The sun will rise, and, just like Manhunt, the events of the night will cure with their own radiant lore. A glorious, glowing lie will replace the cold, dark truth. It disgusts me.

I realize why: It's a form of indulgent memorialization. It's like my parents and the adults of Aspen telling me what Caroline would have wanted, what she stood for, what her death means. The eulogy replaces the person; the story told takes the place of the life lived. The secret of tonight will replace these silly nocturnal antics with a forbidden luster. The truth will lock up behind the fraternal hush that I'll never be invited into. And I can't do anything about any of it, just like I can't stop the sun from rising.

"Are we clear, Huntsmen?"

Everyone gives a solemn nod. Everyone but me. The warped screams of Caroline still echo in my ears, so clear I can almost imagine her in her final moments again. But I pull myself away from the memory, knowing every second I spend staring back at her half-lidded gaze brings me one step closer to running. From all of this.

I will not run. I have to believe I'm getting closer to understanding something crucial about what happened to her. Manhunt, the jar of honey, this cruel prank; they add up to something. An answer waiting for me to ask the right question.

Brayden lifts a hand, calling out: "Aspen before and ever more!"

The boys echo it back. They yell, again and again, jumping and stamping until they fall out of sync, until the words are lost and it's just chaos, a cry, the braying tantrum of animals marking their territory.

CHAPTER 17

Wendy's office is exactly the same, not a thing so much as moved since I was here last. I know because I spent hours in this sagging wingback chair silently contemplating the shelves of wobbly pottery, the walls fluttering with watercolors and potato-print art. Projects from campers, displayed like trophies.

Wendy is in her chair, hiding behind her computer, her face locked up. Brayden sits at the window. I've told them, second by second, all that happened during the Night Hike. If Wendy is surprised about such a ritual, she doesn't show it. She barely even yields pity when I describe the part where someone used a speaker to bombard me with edited audio of my dead sister's laugh. She just stares at me, unblinking, unrelenting, like if she can push her eyes through me, I'll vanish. Pop like a bubble.

"This is . . . a lot, Mars. You understand that?" Wendy asks.

I didn't expect an outright apology, but she says it like she's giving me notes for the next time I try to tell this story. *Love the enthusiasm, Mars.*

"It was a lot to go through," I say. I'm not looking for an apology, or even revenge. Quite unintentionally, the Night Hike has given me the leverage I need to get something else. "Or do you mean it's a lot of effort to go through to target someone? Because yeah, once again, I agree."

"No one is telling you it wasn't scary," Wendy says, placating and sad. "Anyone would be frightened, out there in those woods."

"No," I say. "No, this isn't about the woods. It's about someone using a speaker with prepared audio."

Wendy's lips twist. "Where would they plug it in? Mars, I'm sorry, sweetie, I'm not following."

I look at Brayden, but he's looking sideways, out the window. He's pissed. I thought about talking to him but remembered his threat on day one. And I decided, no, this jerk can't have a chance to try to cover this up. So I went to Wendy, had him called here, and made him watch as I revealed how poorly he'd managed our Outbound Excursion.

"Bluetooth," I repeat. "It's a Bluetooth speaker. It probably uses batteries. It connects to a phone."

"Where is it now?" Wendy asks.

"I left it in the woods," I say. "I thought I heard whoever planted it and chased after them. I left the speaker behind. It's probably still there."

"You want us to go and look for a . . . what did you call it? A speaker with a blue tooth?"

I set my jaw. "No. I want you to believe me."

Wendy fans her hands at her empty desk, like she's pointing out my lack of evidence.

"Listen." Wendy leans forward. "We all know how much stress you've been under. And given your . . . history with Aspen, I have to ask: Are you being completely honest with us?"

"Yes."

"And?" she probes.

"And what?"

Wendy sighs. "And there's nothing more?"

My jaw aches. She's probing for some lapse on my part, some way to make Aspen pristine. Unfortunately for Wendy, I know better.

"Someone is targeting me," I say.

Wendy leans back. She tilts her head to Brayden but keeps her eyes on me.

"Brayden, do a bunk check. If Mars is telling the truth, someone broke our electronics policy. That's a big no-no."

"Will do," Brayden says without inflection. When he glances at me, I think he hates me.

Well, I hate them both. This isn't about electronics in the woods and they know it. I swallow back harsher words and instead say, "Your response to targeted harassment is to do a bunk check?"

Wendy turns conciliatory. "I'm not sure what you want us to do beyond that, Mars. At Aspen, we can't monitor every child twenty-four seven, especially out in the woods. Our policy is to encourage conflict resolution between campers, and I hate to say it but it sounds like you haven't been all that gentle with some of our more . . . excitable boys."

She's talking about my fight with Callum. I hear Tyler once again telling me that I swung first.

Wendy smiles when she says, "We will of course step in when safety is a factor, but *you* seem fine. How's your hand?"

There isn't so much as a bruise on the hand I punched Callum with. Even my ear feels better. To Wendy and Brayden, I look fine. Callum can't say the same, and it's my fault.

"My hand is okay," I say. "Look, talk to any of the other boys. Callum has been at my throat ever since I got here. If anyone did it, it's him."

Wendy's gentle smile sours. She shakes her head sternly. "Now I know Callum. He's been attending Aspen ever since he was a Bandit. His family has been coming here for generations. I find it hard to believe he'd hurt anyone without, well, some pretty intense provocation. Perhaps this is just a matter of boys being boys?"

This catches me off guard. I physically recoil, and it wins a pinched smile from Wendy.

"Mars, we want you to know we're so glad you're here with us, but if you no longer feel that this is the best place for you, we aren't forcing you to stay."

I stand. Wendy and Brayden lean away, like they can feel the heat radiating from me.

"I'm staying," I say. For a moment I feel tiny, even though I'm the one standing. I feel like a child atop a chair, crying and pouting, like at any moment I'll be scooped up and laid behind the bars of a crib. But I push the feeling away and focus on the sureness I started with when I first arrived here. I put both hands on the edge of Wendy's desk and lean in, lining up the words I've waited years to say.

"You let me get hurt last time. I haven't forgotten that. You, and every adult here, knew what was happening and did nothing. My family could have sued. I wish they had, but they didn't, and I left. But now I'm back. And I'm not going to be chased off again by *boys being boys*. So either you help me, or you watch me get hurt again and deal with the liability of this *and* the last summer I was here. It's that simple, Wendy."

I stand up straight. I drink in Wendy's wide-eyed disgust and Brayden's openmouthed shock.

"That was four years ago," Wendy says.

"And the statute of limitation for reckless endangerment in the first degree is five years. It's a felony, Wendy."

It's Wendy's turn to recoil. "I didn't *endanger you*." The contempt in her eyes is broad and encompassing, taking in all of me.

"You didn't, but the parents of whoever did aren't going to be too keen on undergoing a very public scandal for their boys, all of whom are applying for college this upcoming fall. And I doubt they'll want to pay legal fees plus Aspen tuition."

Wendy recovers some of that patronizing composure I know so well. "You're threatening us, Marshall?"

"No, Wendy." I stand back. "I'm doing mathematics. I checked your Conservancy's filings. This place is barely profitable as it is. By my calculations, you're just six campers away from the red."

I say all this sweetly, like a Honey would. Wendy's frown looks carved. Eternal. Her actual face beneath the pleasant mask she's always wearing. I smile. Before I turn to go, I have one more thing to add.

"Oh, and I've picked a major. I'll be joining Apiculture. Have a *blessed* day."

Before they can say no, I spin and grab the doorknob, swinging it open in a great gust that ruffles the drawings plastering the walls. Wendy's trophies. I almost want to rip one down as a keepsake, but I don't need to. I've already gotten what I wanted.

Both Eagle House and Bear Hut endure a surprise bunk check that Saturday afternoon. No speakers are found, nor phones, but The Chuckster gets busted for pot and Callum is called up to Wendy's office for some unknown offense. They're not back by late afternoon. By the way the boys refuse to look at me all throughout dinner, they must know I've broken the sacred silence we all agreed to after the Night Hike. Then, that evening when I come back from showering, I find Caroline's candle lit. I snuff it out with my fingers, and once the lights are out, I hide it under my bed.

The next morning, Sunday, The Chuckster's parents arrive to take him home. And my candle is gone.

I try not to react. I keep my face a mask of polite interest during chapel, then breakfast, then announcements. Brayden is a superb actor, too. He briefly acknowledges the pain of losing a cherished Huntsman, offers a moment of silence, and then off he bounds, reciting this upcoming week's exciting bevy of Aspen offerings.

"Village Victory Cup!" he intones. This finally raises a reaction from the sullen Huntsmen.

"That's right. This afternoon is the opening ceremony for one of Aspen's most cherished traditions, and every challenge this week is for points that'll go to the victory board. Now I don't know about you, but I've seen our competitors this year, and those girls are looking fierce. I think we can show them a thing or two about superiority, though, don't you? Am I right, boys?"

A warm, derisive jeer. I bite my tongue. They've renamed the tradition, but the bones beneath it are as old as Aspen itself. Which is to say: sexist. A sexist skeleton, beneath it all.

Brayden explains the events, even though it's the same every year. There's capture the flag, tug-of-war, canoe races, archery, but also debate forum, trivia, a mural contest, and a bunch of other tiny, terrible tournaments. I'm stuck envisioning the victory board. It'll be set up near the waterfront, a fifteen-foot-tall monstrosity of pine. Its base will be wreathed in garlands of hemlock and juniper, its blank face painted forest green and buttercup yellow. Aspen colors. A stripe will cut down the middle. We will fill the emptiness with achievements, awards scrawled on construction paper, laminated, and shot into the wood with a staple gun until it looks like a taxidermy Muppet.

I wonder if they'll set it up where they always do. Has the grass grown back in that one spot? Or did the flames dig too far into the dirt?

After chores, I walk to the waterfront to see it. The sky over Aspen is gray and low, blurring the treetops. Steam drifts off the lake, but I see the shadow of it from far off. It's in the same spot. I make myself go all the way up to it. The grass has grown back. The only difference is that now it's made of plywood, and they've removed the traditional garlands of hemlock and juniper. Less to burn in the event a rogue gender-fluid camper decides to go on a flaming crusade against the binary, I guess.

I stand there for a long time, and I don't hear the footsteps until they're right behind me.

"Hey," Wyatt says.

"Hi," I say.

"I heard what happened. I'm sorry."

"I don't know what you heard, but I guarantee it's not the whole story."

I wonder if Wyatt will debate me on this. I imagine the push and pull within him between his loyalty to this place and the obvious toxicity it breeds. I wonder if roots that deep can ever be dug up.

"I figured," he sighs. "What happened?"

I walk, Wyatt follows. We end up on a bench under the pergola, looking at the victory board from behind. I eventually tell Wyatt a quick version of my Night Hike and then my meeting in Wendy's office. When I'm done, he whistles.

"You probably don't know the full story of what happened four years ago either," I begin, but Wyatt clears his throat.

"Actually, I do. Most people do. Your sister made sure of it. For some reason she didn't think you would ever come back to set the record straight."

"She was right. Almost," I say.

Wyatt picks at a scab on his knee.

"It must have been scary," he says.

I won't say it was, but it was. Even seeing the victory board drives a stake of dread into my stomach. It's exactly the same, like I'm back in my own memory. I think that if I traced a finger down the board's edge, I'd find the spot where a taut rope rubbed off the paint. And I'll hear the boys laughing as they pin my arms, knotting me to the board's scaffolding before they threw down one of the spitting tiki torches. It was a dry summer that year, and hemlock burns quickly no matter what, but no one remembered that until the flames were out of control.

That's not true, actually. I knew. And it's why I was able to burn the ropes off before the whole board collapsed where I'd been. The boys were gone by then, but there I stood among the cinders.

"How come you let them blame you?" Wyatt asks.

I guess that was the part of the story Caroline never had right. I took the fall for the inferno. Willingly.

"Because it meant I could leave," I say.

Caroline, righteous as she was, forced the bullies to confess after I was gone. I don't know how. Aspen begged for me to come back when they realized their mistake, but I wouldn't.

"You wanted to go home that badly?"

How do I tell Wyatt that those early summers at Aspen were never the idyllic glory days everyone seems to build their entire lives upon? His whole world sits atop nostalgia for a place that never existed for me. I could peer into that world; it showed in the smiles and joy of the kids around me, but it wasn't mine. It wasn't meant for me. And I knew it for a long time before the incident with the victory board. I knew it, and I fought to stay anyway, because I thought Aspen was going to be like the rest of my life. A battle I just had to keep winning.

And then, for all my grueling, play-along patience, I was punished.

I just say, "Having people try to burn you like a witch kinda ruins the whole summer camp thing, Wyatt."

Wyatt sucks in a sharp breath, but I smile to show him I'm not being as serious as my words. He swallows, takes a new breath, and tries to restart the conversation.

"Want to go pick outfits for the formal tonight?"

"I thought we had to wear our uniforms."

"We do. I'm asking if you want to get away from this thing."

He grins. I find myself smiling, too. We walk back to the Village together, speculating about the conversations currently happening between Wendy and Callum, and likely Callum's parents.

"Even if he admits to sneaking in a speaker, that's common stuff. No one gets in trouble for that," Wyatt says, a rare frankness toward bad conduct that I plan to take full advantage of.

"The real mystery is: How did he get Caroline's voice?" he asks.

"I've been thinking about that since we got back," I say. "It wouldn't be hard. He just needed a phone. Then he could strip the audio from any of her content online. All her socials are still up."

That hurts me to imagine. All those videos and photos and posts. Caroline was never shy. If someone wanted to piece her together from remnants on the internet, they'd have plenty to work with. Definitely laughter, maybe crying, and more than a few moments of her dragging me into the frame of her camera, begging *Mars, Mars, look at this* or *Sing this with me* or just *Smile—no smile bigger*.

"I'll talk to Brayden," Wyatt offers. "But I don't think he'll get sent home. I'm sorry, Mars."

"Don't be," I say. "He can stay. I don't care."

"You're not worried he'll try something else?" Wyatt asks.

A cloud of gnats envelops us. I wave them away as we walk.

"He won't. The fact that I went to Wendy just proves what he needed proved, which is that I'm weaker than him. If he's allowed to stay, he'll leave me alone. In his head he's won, and he can't risk drawing me into another fight. I've already publicly kicked his ass. Twice. He won't risk a third."

"Okay, that's hard-core, but I still figured you'd want to get him sent home."

"I was never after that."

"What were you after, then?"

I wonder if I can trust Wyatt. I like him, and he likes me, I think, but that's different from trust. After a moment's consideration, I decide it doesn't really matter. I already have what I want.

"Leverage," I say. "Brayden and Wendy know I'm right. They can't let anything else happen to me or else they'll be liable. And this time they know I'm not taking the blame."

Wyatt considers this. His eyes—brown and blue-brown—reflect a coy and cunning understanding. "You're a bit of an evil genius, aren't you, Mars?"

I smile. "I believe you were the one who told me that there's nothing evil about doing what you've got to do to survive."

Wyatt lifts an eyebrow. "Should I be worried you're going to try to eat Callum?"

I shake my head sweetly. "I'd never. I simply could not."

"Allergy?" Wyatt offers.

"Standards," I answer.

From the way Wyatt stops talking after that, I can tell that I've maybe spooked him. But as Hunter Village comes into view, he surprises me. "It's so messed up," he says, staring at the handsome buildings behind the rising gloom. "The way you have to think just to survive. It's messed up, Mars."

I shrug because, yeah, it is.

CHAPTER 18

Late Sunday afternoon, it's the Village Victory Cup opening ceremony. The whole camp pours into the amphitheater, boys on one side, girls on another, a cacophonous shouting match boiling the air between them. Even the Honeys are there, bundled among one another, clapping and yelling. A few times Sierra sees me watching them, but her eyes never stay on me for long. I want to run to her and tell her everything that happened, that *is* happening.

Instead, I stay on the boys' side, clapping and chanting with them. It may be my paranoia, but I think they watch to see how I'll react, as if the gendered competition will cause me to go haywire or burst into hives. So I'm extra loud, and I clap with extra gusto. I want Callum, who arrived back from Wendy's office within a cloud of shame, to hear me chant every word.

After the ceremony, we have Sunday cookout in the dining hall, since the grass is too wet for a picnic. Then there's the formal. Campers are allowed back to the cabins to get ready. I change into my sandals and briefly consider Caroline's makeup, but leave it stored away in my drawer. If the boys know I have it, they'll take it. The rest of our war will be small annoyances like this, so I'll have to be careful with anything I show preciousness toward.

Big Lodge has been transformed for the formal, the back porch strewn with yellow and green streamers, and paper lanterns hung throughout the trees. The behemoth building pulses under the muddy sunset, spilling folksy music out in the dusk. As we walk up the stairs, I hear the twinkling sound of laughter from within. All of Aspen is here together before our weeklong competition splits us apart.

Inside, the music is loud. Catering staff in black aprons dot the crowd of white-uniformed kids, holding up trays of bite-sized desserts. A soda bar has been set up on one side of the main room, an ice-cream bar on the other. Younger campers race through the lodge's dark halls, screaming and laughing, but the older kids adopt a more aloof approach to the party. They sit on the stairs, or on the back patio, looking bored and cool, sipping their Sprite like it's fine champagne.

I don't feel like pretending right now, so as soon as my cabin arrives, I hide upstairs on the back porch, alone. It feels nice to be by myself again. I let my raging thoughts cool as I nurse my own soda.

Just as I predicted with the sunrise after the Night Hike, the boys of Bear Hut and Eagle House move with a new, ridiculous swagger. Their moves are greasy with self-satisfaction, made all the slicker by the darkening rumors about what happened, what they faced together in those woods, what got a boy sent home and another in trouble. The irony is that the rumors are so much cooler than the truth—people speculate about a bloody ritual of bonding, a sacrificial killing of some sacred pig—and this locks the boys into secrecy that isn't just fraternal, but also desperate.

It's fucking funny. Clout like that is fragile. Masculinity is, too, I guess.

In a way—actually in a lot of ways—this formal reminds me of my mom's fundraisers. The sticky heat, the muffled music, the sprinkled laughter, and most of all the glances between clusters of people, shot back and forth like blow darts. At parties like these, there's never any dancing. There's hardly even any fun. There's just tension, low and intoxicating and smothering. I guess people prefer potential to action. I don't know. But I wish there was dancing.

A memory bubbles up from this wish. Caroline and me, standing in the garden back at home, out of view of the veranda but close enough that we could hear the music from inside. In the memory we're young, probably too young to be by ourselves, but it was late and the party had reached the point where the remaining adults all sat down and took their shoes off, some even sitting on the floor or the granite counters that we weren't allowed to play on. The laughter accelerated into drunken screaming. Any kid would want to escape that.

In my memory I'm plucking at my little suit, which I hate. Caroline hates her dress. By some unspoken agreement, we trade outfits. Even shoes. Caroline unclips the bow in her hair and puts it in mine. Then we dance. Not real dancing, though. Kid dancing. I just remembering turning and turning, captivated, forfeiting my balance so I could press my small palms against the bell of my dress.

Our uncle found us, I think. Or it was Dad. It was a man, and I only remember the shame I felt when he stepped into the bushes and told me—specifically me—to cut that shit out.

We were still little enough then that switching clothing the first time was seen as adorable antics, but the second time we got caught I got reprimanded. Not Caroline, though. It was like I'd tricked her into going along with my own wicked perversion. We stopped switching clothes after that. Still, we'd often sneak out of those parties to our spot in the garden, bow to each other, and twirl. Even if it was just for a minute.

The ice in my Sprite has melted. The bubbles are gone. My heart burns and I swallow back a whimper as I step away from the railing. I was leaning against it so casually just now, and for a moment there was such a heaviness pressing down on me I thought the railing would snap. I'd land right there on the stone patio, and this time there would be no one to break my fall.

If I didn't back away, I would have looked down. I'm sure I would have had another vision of her down there, sprawled out, invisible to the people stepping over her. A vision—a warning—only for me.

I try to leave the memories in the past—the small, dark garden, the

164

gory crystal of my home's foyer—and rejoin the present as myself. To be *hard-core*, the way Wyatt thinks of me. But I can't. I race into the dark halls of Big Lodge, pinballing away from the sounds of people until I find a bathroom at the end of a long corridor, and slip inside.

I barely register the room. Everything swims as the tears finally overwhelm me. I sink to the floor, tucked into myself, the shaking already starting, when I hear someone say, "Mars?"

I'm so surprised I forget my emotions and jump up, hitting my head on a towel rack. At first I think it must be a ghost, but then a curtain pulls back and sitting in the bathtub is a person with three faces. No, three people. Bria, Sierra, and Mimi, a smoldering joint between Mimi's fingers. She blows her breath toward the narrow window cracked above. I finally smell the stink of weed through the perfume they've sprayed.

"I told you to lock the door, Mimi," Bria says.

"I did."

"You obviously didn't."

"What's wrong?" Sierra asks. She stands and steps out of the tub so she can cup my face in her hands.

"Nothing," I say.

The girls exchange a look, then snuff out the blunt. Bria perches herself on the edge of the bathtub. Mimi sits on the closed toilet. Sierra leans on the sink. The three of them stare at me, but not with pity. With something more like understanding.

"You miss her," Sierra says.

I nod.

"We miss her, too." Sierra rubs my arm. "Do you want to talk about it? We'd love it if you would."

I still fear these girls. The last time I had a conversation with them was my first night here, under the pergola, when Bria acted like she'd forgotten I existed. Sierra and I spent those few minutes painting my nails and crying. Total opposite interactions. This one somehow feels like a third opposite. The girls—their faces, their energy—seem to change from scene to scene, room to room.

"I . . ."

Why not, Mars? Why not? Because of a dreamt moment in the woods during Manhunt? Who has hurt you? Who hasn't? And who else but Caroline's chosen family deserves the truth?

I tell them about the garden and the clothing swap and the dancing. After I'm done, their eyes are glassy. We all sit in the silence, listening to the party outside, and then suddenly the girls are taking off their clothes. Just pulling their shirts over their heads and stepping out of their skirts.

"Try this." Mimi thrusts a skirt at me.

"No, Mimi, you're too petite." Bria shoves in front. "Try this one instead, Mars."

Suddenly my fists are full of clothes still warm from their bodies. I'm backed into a corner, but I don't want to run. The three girls, standing in just their underwear, emanate no threat. They don't even seem self-conscious. I avert my eyes and they don't mock me for my bashfulness. They turn around, facing the tub, so I can change.

I end up in Bria's skirt and Sierra's shirt. They wear parts of my uniform. Sierra delights in the oversized cut by knotting my shirt to show her tanned belly.

"Wait!" Mimi claps gleefully as she pulls out a purse beside the toilet, dumping it into the sink. Out comes a clutter of makeup, hair ties, and tampons. The girls have me crouch down as they lean into my face, plying it with soft powders and shimmering tints. I permit this for a few minutes and then take over when they get to the eyeliner. They coo and clap as I swipe on a wingtip sharp enough to cut someone. For drama, Mimi gives me a small beauty mark on my cheekbone.

I look at myself in the mirror. For the first time in weeks, I'm looking at me. The way I see me and the way I want to be seen.

"Shall we?" Bria asks, swinging open the door, invading the bathroom with the sounds of the party beyond. I nearly say no, but I can't quite form the word. Also, I don't *want* to say no. I feel powerful as myself. Invincible in my newly familiar shape. I want to be seen. I want those boys to know what they're dealing with. And I want these girls to hold on to me like they are right now, pulling me along into their circle. Finally.

We step into the main room and the whispers start right away. They're drowned out by the cries of joy that rise out of the other Honeys, who pull me into their knot of hand-holding and hugging. I pause on the patio when I see Tyler, and his eyes go dull with disappointment. I stumble on something, but they just tug me farther inside their huddle. They smell amazing, like melons and roses and cupcakes. We sit together around the firepit, where the staff are passing out Styrofoam cups of hot cocoa. We huddle over our steaming cups, and even though their conversation is mostly talking through one another in one large, incessant stream of consciousness, I feel included. It's the way they check to make sure I get the reference, or stop to explain the backstory of a joke, or ask me what I think and actually wait for me to respond.

At a certain point the LITs come around with sparklers. When I see Wyatt, I again feel the urge to hide, but he spots me before I can. He looks at me embedded in the circle of girls, taking in my new skirt, my makeup. Then he smiles and hands me a sparkler.

"Love the new look, Mars," he says.

"Really?"

"Yeah." Wyatt doesn't seem to notice that the girls have hushed themselves and are absently paying very close attention to our conversation. His eyes roam up and down my legs, my face.

"You look . . ." He pauses, thinks, nods. "You look happy."

Wyatt leaves and the girls erupt in stifled giggles.

He loves me, they decide. He's obsessed with me. He'll dream about me forever.

I let them believe it. They nearly make me believe it, too. We light our sparklers in the coals of the fire, using them to light one another's, seeing how long we can keep the chain going, cackling as they sputter to life in our hands.

"See, I told you that you were welcome," Sierra whispers to me at one point as we cup our bodies around our sparklers, blocking out the wind.

"I'm glad you're here," she adds. "We all are."

"Me too," I tell her.

The sparklers hiss and crack. Pinprick stings fill my palm as the spark is passed to me and I pass it along to another.

I forget about Caroline and me dancing in the dark garden. I forget my sadness completely. I almost forget my doubts, too, but they lurk just out of sight, like a body in the blur of my periphery, sprawled in the middle of the patio, head turned toward me, chapped lips parting to ask me: Why? Why are they all being so nice?

The phantom of my past, willing me to ask more from myself in the present.

But I'm happy.

So I don't.

———————————

Nothing is different on Monday. Not Callum, not the Huntsmen, not Hunter Lodge, and not the dusty light that drapes over breakfast. But I feel different among all the sameness. I feel collected, like all that had broken off and scattered has been magnetized back together. It's how I used to feel, I realize, before I got here. It's nothing more than the euphoria of feeling like myself.

Brayden is doing announcements. Today begins the first day of challenges in our eternal battle of the sexes, which due to an unnamed queer vigilante of yore must now be called the Village Victory Cup. Then, as Brayden is passing out schedules, he pauses over me.

"Matthias?"

I sit back. My eyes are still muddy with makeup. I serve Brayden a long, cold look as he hands me a piece of paper with my name printed at the top. I don't take it. I make him hold it as I slowly lean forward to read what's been printed on the previously blank line next to "Major."

Apiculture.

The mythic major. The major that never existed.

I take the paper from Brayden with a sly smile. Nothing more needs to be said, and he moves on without a word. I can't stop smiling, though, as I fold the paper and slip it into the pocket of my shorts.

Apiculture.

Again, I feel those lurking doubts. The dark suspicions willing themselves through the ripening skin of my confidence, like bruises, like blight. They implore me to know better, to pause, to ask: Why?

But I don't.

IV

CHAPTER 19

At the far side of the waterfront, just past the boathouse, there's a path through the willows. It's lined with fallen logs and sprays of goldenrod, and sometimes it dissolves into the water's reedy banks. Sometimes it vanishes completely under nets of ivy. And yet it still manages its way all around the southern corner of the lake, to the bottleneck, where it's swallowed by a narrow covered bridge. Thereafter, nestled deep in the woods, Cabin H lies.

I peer at the start of the path.

Mars, what on earth are you doing? Caroline's voice asks me this for the sixth time this morning. As of yet, I have no answer for her.

"Lost already?"

I spin around. Wyatt waves down at me from the boathouse deck. A blink later he's down on the ground, clapping me on the shoulder and guiding me through the willows.

"You're following me?"

Wyatt navigates the path with ease. He seems . . . tired. Irritable?

"*Actually*, I'm going to my new major, thanks to you."

He produces a piece of paper, the same as mine. There it is. Apiculture, in place of Eco-Lab.

"Orders from the mountaintop," Wyatt says. "I guess you scared Wendy bad enough that she decided I should tag along."

"I'll be fine. You don't need to come."

"Ah. So stalwart, young Mars. But I'm not here for your protection. I'm here to *watch* you."

Despite the heat, a chill zips down my spine. We've reached the bridge quicker than I thought. I see it's not really a bridge. It's a covered walkway over a dam, and it's ancient. The lake slides through the sunbaked concrete in ribbons of jet black. The interior of the bridge is black, too, but the other side glows with a sweet warmth, like glimpsing a candlelit room through a keyhole.

Wyatt is silenced by the sight of it, too. I pick up the discarded thread of our conversation.

"I thought the whole private chaperone thing was until I was settled."

"I think you gave the adults the distinct impression that you're unsettled. Wendy wasn't having it when I told her you wouldn't like this."

I sigh. I figured Aspen would make sure I had eyes on me, but I didn't think they'd re-up Wyatt's bodyguard contract. I feel bad for Wyatt, but on a more selfish note I'm a little excited. I didn't realize I missed hanging out with him in the woods until he hailed me from the boathouse deck. And here we are. Hanging out. In the woods.

Wyatt swats at a cloud of gnats.

"It's simpler than you think, actually," he says. "Remember I told you I grew up here? My grandfather showed me how to work with the bees when I was little, and I help out Leena sometimes. Like right now, when suddenly she's got one more wannabe beekeeper to keep track of. That's the reason Wendy gave anyway."

It makes me smile to see Wyatt flustered like this. He's actually a little mad, instead of that usual unrelenting cheer. My laugh must surprise him because he looks confused before, begrudgingly, he cracks a smile, too. I start through the bridge and he trails after.

"I'm sorry that you're now being instructed to escort me places. But really, if you just want to go back to Eco-Lab, I won't tell. Oh, wait, I'm sorry, that would require you to think for yourself. Can't have you using your own brain! That's not very Aspen, now, is it?"

Wyatt slips in front of me, jogging backward on the dusty path. "Mock me all you want, but adaptability is an Aspen value. So I'm *adapting*. And besides, I actually *like* the hives."

"Maybe I do, too? Not that you'd believe me."

"Oh, please," he laughs. "I saw you getting along with the H girls last night. Don't tell me this isn't part of your big, master Mars plan."

I narrow my eyes in playful offense. "They're nicer than you think. Definitely better than the boys."

Wyatt spins back around when we hit the woods so that he can focus on not tripping over any roots.

"I get that things haven't been easy for you," he says. "Before or even now. But are you sure about this? Maybe you got off to a bad start with the boys, but if they got to know you, I think they'd really like you. Instead, you're trying to join up with Bria and her gang."

"Get to know me? What do you want me to do, set up a slide show about myself and present it to Hunter Village for Embers? The more they know, the less they like me, Wyatt."

Wyatt scratches at a bug bite on his neck.

"No, it's like . . ." He reaches up to the trees, as if he can pull down an answer. "I don't know, participate in their stuff. Sports and poker night. Show them you're, like, chill."

"Wyatt, that's not being chill. That's performative heterosexuality."

The forest path cuts away from the lake to become a slanting uppercut through rocks, roots, and a maze of mountain laurel.

"Don't take this the wrong way." Wyatt is breathy as we climb. "But you could learn a thing or two about compromise."

"And I would learn this valuable life lesson by, what, playing Ultimate Frisbee and objectifying women?"

"Would you do that? Play Ultimate Frisbee, I mean."

"If it got you off my back, absolutely."

Wyatt stops, so I have to stop. He thrusts a hand at me. He grins. I take his hand and we shake, our dumb deal made.

"I'm glad you went with Frisbee," Wyatt says. "Because I actually am terrible at poker. I don't have the face for it."

We walk the rest of the way, avoiding the subject of compromise, talking instead about Wyatt's childhood of beekeeping, honey harvests, and woodsy loveliness. It's nearly a mile until we spot Cabin H's clearing. No wonder the girls don't always come into camp. Treacherous during the day, the hike here would be deadly at night.

They're outside when we arrive. The girls, stretching and yawning like they just woke up. They see us and wave lazily, the rings on their hands flashing in the white sun. Already I can see the bees floating over their hives. As we near, I feel that lurking doubt again, the sense of fear that used to reign over my idea of this place. But there's nothing scary here. Just sleepy girls holding up ceramic mugs of coffee and tea as they introduce themselves. I catch a few names—Kyle, Juliette, a pair of twins named PJ and CJ—and I miss the rest. There are many more girls than I thought would fit inside that house, and still more drift down the porch. Bria waves from a hammock.

Leena gathers us and assigns tasks. She's short and compact and so are her instructions. I catch little of it, but Wyatt leads me off toward a hive at the bottom of the hill. Mimi is there and she pulls me into a great hug.

"You *made* it!" she screams into my ear.

She looks at me, looks at Wyatt. Her smile is so big it somehow shows up on my face.

"Where's Sierra?" I ask.

Or I think I ask. Mimi proceeds without responding, instead bubbling on about safety.

"You didn't eat bananas today, did you?" she asks gravely.

We shake our heads.

"Good. They don't like that. Bananas smell like death to bees. Remember that."

I make a note. I make *many* notes as Mimi tours us through the apiary. All around us the girls work diligently while they talk and laugh. Their industriousness doesn't clash with their usual hyper-femininity; it simply combines with it. Reveals that both can exist in the same body. I make gloating eye contact with Wyatt. *Not so bored and useless, are they?*

"Each of these is a separate hive with its own queen," Mimi explains. "The hive bodies are made of individual supers"—she taps one floor of the wooden tower we're next to—"and in each super, we place a bunch of frames, which the bees fill with comb. Some of the cells have brood, some have honey."

"What's brood?"

"Babies, basically. Larvae," Mimi says. From nowhere she produces her own hive tool and starts to pry the top from one of the towers. I spring back as several bees dart out, and she and Wyatt both laugh.

"Don't we need, like, beekeeping suits?" I ask.

Mimi shakes her head. "Do you want a suit? I can grab you one. But you won't need it. The bees are very gentle."

"They don't care if we take their honey?"

"They hardly know," Mimi says. "We only take the excess, and we let them keep just the right amount to maintain the colony's numbers. Too many bees, they outgrow the hive and swarm. Too few, and they can't function."

"Symbiosis," Wyatt adds.

I don't care about any of that. I just need one question answered: "So they *won't* sting us?"

Mimi giggles. "Bees only sting if they find a cause worth dying for. Don't flatter yourself. You'll be fine—just don't move too quickly."

Wyatt nods, assuring me, but I can tell that even he feels beyond his usual spunky confidence. It occurs to me that the last time he managed these hives, he would have been a kid with his grandfather. I don't know how long bees live, but it must not be long. The bees within this box are generations beyond the ones Wyatt knew and trusted. Maybe that's what he's thinking as Mimi proceeds to pry their home apart with efficient zeal.

Mimi lifts the top an inch, peeks inside, then removes it completely.

I'm not prepared for the warmth, nor the sound, nor how they feel like the same thing. Before us is a maze of frames, like Mimi said, but carpeting everything are minute, furry bodies, an innumerable chaos that looks more like one alien entity rather than a thousand individuals. They don't buzz like I thought they would. Instead they hum, low and thick. Calm. There's no anger as Mimi waves good morning at them.

"Mars, you hold this," she says, and she hands me a strange tin can with a smoking spout. Dried leaves smolder inside it. I smell hickory and molten sap.

"Like this," Mimi says, moving me into position so the smoke wafts over the hive. Some of the bees have floated up from their depths, curious or angry, but the smoke calms them. The drone goes lower. I feel it in the bottom of my skull.

"Smoke makes them easier to handle," Wyatt says.

I hold the smoker while Mimi works her tool into the orange wax built up over the frames. She calls it propolis. Then she has us stand back as she works the frame up and out of the hive.

"You can get closer," she urges. I clutch the smoker, my eyes full of tears but wide open with alertness, and follow her painted nail as she points.

"This is brood. See? Do you see how the cells are capped? Don't they look funny? Soft, right? They're not. Larvae grow in there and make their own little cocoons, then bite their way out."

I maybe see what she means. Mostly I'm overwhelmed by the density of the living thing crawling upon the frame, the twitching static of bodies flowing over one another in perplexing, frantic paths. It's disordered and choreographed, and nearly silent. There is always the humming, but I can't figure out where it's coming from. It feels like it's coming from everywhere.

"These frames have honey. See it? Here, let me move them."

Mimi brushes the bees away with her knuckles. They tumble away and disperse, like nothing. "Here, look. Move a bit, it's clearer in the sun."

Mimi shifts and the light slides into a thousand hexagonal wells. It's unnerving, like a wall of eyes opening up, wet and unblinking, but so precise. There's a warp in the pattern, though, a moment where the interlocked cells pinch together, casting a ripple into the mosaic.

I ask what it is. Mimi stares at it for a long time before asking Wyatt to close up the hive. Then she carries the frame away, toward the shed. Wyatt and I wait awhile, watching the bees land on their little porch, their legs packed with orange-yellow pollen. Mimi doesn't come back.

Eventually I decide to go look for her.

"We can't go in the shed," Wyatt calls after me.

"Why not?" I call back, still walking.

"Equipment," he says, which is a lame reason, so I leave him behind.

Up the hill, around the house and pushed back into the forest, the shed is a long, low building. Away from the din of the hives and the house, the air feels clear and light, like I can hear so much more. In the calm I catch the frayed edge of a whisper. Hushed voices slip from a barn door left ajar.

"A disruption," someone says.

"Local, national, or global?"

"It's hard to say. Local, with wide ripples. See?"

This last voice is Mimi. I peer through the gap in the doorway and see her sitting in a pool of lamplight with three other girls, the honeycomb frame on a contraption between them. It's held up like a book on a pulpit, and they look upon it like it's made of letters.

"An interloper," Mimi says definitively.

"So what's the impact?" one girl asks.

Mimi's easy smile is nowhere to be seen as she says, "Disruption. Not political or financial. Here, at Aspen."

"Do we . . . do we need to tell *them*?"

"No." Mimi shakes her head, hair bouncing vigorously. "Per the codes, we have to handle it ourselves, our way."

"What about that?" one girl—Lya, I think—asks, pointing at a section of the comb. "Doesn't that mean death?"

"*Violent* death," another girl clarifies.

Mimi doesn't say yes, but she doesn't say no. The silence the girls share is a consenting one, though, like the truth is so obvious it's not worth stating aloud.

I drift too close to the door, and suddenly my shadow passes over the narrow beam of light. Lya jumps, swinging the door open, but I get around the corner of the shed a split second before. The door closes, fully this time, and locks.

I make a wide circle back to the meadow, through the woods, so that anyone looking out the shed's windows won't see me. At the top of the meadow, I halt. Wyatt sits where I left him, staring off over the lake like he's lost in a reverie, but standing around him are five of the Cabin H girls. Just standing. They quiver in the heat rising off the meadow, their faces blurring for just a moment, and then Wyatt stands, too. They walk over to me, all together.

"Ready?" Wyatt asks.

"Ready for what?"

"Lunch? The bugle sounded. I missed it, too, but the girls just told me it's time to head back."

I glance at the girls. Despite the morning's work, they all appear uniformly cool and unbothered. The sound of the shed opening pulls my eyes that way. Mimi and the others step out, no sign of concern in their faces as they join us. I take that moment to look back at the shed and memorize it. The roof is corrugated metal, the walls cheap plywood painted white. The grass leading to it is worn down, and another path juts from its side, out into the woods in the opposite direction of Aspen, toward the mountains.

We walk back in one loud, laughing parade. The girls commit to a barrage of senseless, flattering questions about my life—*What will you major in? What's your workout routine? What percentile were your math scores? How many other kids do you know who can repair antique calculators?*—and I realize they're acting as one huge wingman in my developing crush on Wyatt. When they finally turn to teasing Wyatt, I think about what I overheard in the shed. It sounded like the girls were inspecting the comb. Deriving some meaning from the warp I pointed out. Death. Violent death. And an interloper.

I look up suddenly when the incessant chatter halts. Wyatt and I are alone beneath a willow tree. And then, sliding through the shade in brisk confrontation, is the boathouse. I jump in surprise. The sudden sight of it, the *discord* of people playing games on the deck and strumming guitars and turning up the radio, is jarring. So at odds with the soft eeriness of the meadow.

"You zone out a lot," Wyatt observes.

I didn't even notice we'd crossed the covered bridge. I look around for the Honeys, but they've flitted away, into Aspen. I blink, wondering where the last half mile of my life went.

"Sorry. I was thinking," I say.

"Thinking? Even *more* thoughts?"

"Yes, one of the major setbacks of having a brain."

"Anyway," Wyatt laughs, steering us toward the dining pavilion, "I was asking you who Sierra is. You mentioned her to Mimi."

"Oh, she's nice. She was one of Caroline's friends."

"From home?"

I tilt my head. "From Aspen. She's in Cabin H."

Wyatt mimics my confusion. "You mean Bria?"

"I mean Sierra."

Wyatt looks off across the lake, not toward the meadow but toward the mountains beyond. He says, "But Mars, there's no Sierra at Summer Academy."

CHAPTER 20

I ask.

I ask again.

It doesn't matter who answers. The answer is always the same.

"Who is Sierra?"

Maybe a head tilt, maybe a squint, but always that distance in the voice, that emptiness behind the eyes. It's so consistent that by the end of the day I nearly believe I did get Sierra's name wrong. Or worse, that I made her up. But that night I'm washing my face and I glimpse the brilliant blue of my nails and I remember the way she held my hands and cried with me, and I know. I know I'm not wrong.

What is it? Another prank? Another demented tradition? Or was it like this when I suddenly left Aspen four years ago? Just the same sinister erasure that Aspen likes to treat all unsightly truths with.

It's when I see the guarded, glazed-over stare of Callum at dinner that I begin to believe something horrible happened to Sierra. When I see him, I still see the whites of his eyes against the blurring black of the woods, blood flowing from his nose. Him, Caroline, Sierra; I can connect them each to the Honeys. But in tandem, my fear of those girls has evolved into wonder. Intrigue.

I stare at Callum until I feel my dread return. Deepen. Solidify.

The next day, things feel too normal once again. I go to breakfast, I walk with Wyatt to the apiary, and Mimi greets us with a big hug. We resume our tour of the hives. Today, the enveloping frequency of the bees feels muted, maybe because the light in the meadow is dampened by an overcast sky. I spend the lesson analyzing Mimi's face—wide cheeks and pointed chin, like a heart—and I find only sweetness. None of the dire tone I heard in the shed, with her sisters wreathed around her and the warped frame. As a test, I ask if I can use the bathroom in the cabin, and she says duh, of course, why would you even ask that?

I enter the cabin and it's quiet, like the first time I was here. At the back windows I can see the shed is wide open as a few girls carry crates into it. Even from here I hear the clink of empty jars.

Leena said they were getting ready to harvest honey. She said Wyatt and I would be asked to help.

I sneak upstairs. I find the room Sierra and I hid in, and the bed we sat on. It's neatly made, the corners tucked. Pictures have been jammed between the slats of the top bunk showing the girls sprawled on towels, or swathed in blankets. I'm not surprised to spot Sierra in a few of them, but I am relieved. I steal one, then slip back outside to finish the morning session without drawing any more attention to myself.

I'm now sure of two things.

First, I cannot trust what I see. In the shining Aspen sun, all colors fade, and all doubt fades, too. But at night the doubts embolden, and without the sun making me squint I feel a clarity I can't always find during the day. It's that clarity that I need to hold on to, above all else. Even now I feel it fading beneath the pressurized brightness of the overcast sky. I want to check Sierra's face in the photo again, but I don't because of thing number two: I must be more subtle. Subtle is hard for me; I've never had the kind of grace or patience it requires. But I'll need grace and patience now, if I want to know more. So, subtlety it is.

At lunch, Wyatt makes a big show about announcing that day's Cabin Challenge. It is, of course, Ultimate Frisbee. He grins at me when he says it. I give a false, dazzling smile. Oh, joy.

"A deal is a deal," he says to me as we head down to the main lawn. "What'd you call this? Perforated heterosexuality?"

"*Performative.*"

"Is everything an act to you?"

"Everything is an act to everybody."

"Well then, can you *act* good at Frisbee?"

I am awful at Frisbee. Comically bad. The plastic disk just shoots away from me at random directions no matter how I aim, and the boys are left swearing and sprinting. I even manage to score a point for the other team.

"You're a terrible actor," Wyatt says, face dripping with sweat as we gather around a water cooler.

"Juilliard trained, thank you," I say. "Can't we do something else as a group? Like tie-dye? It's just these wrists of mine. They're so limp. Perfect for wringing things out."

A few of the boys chuckle. I don't mind. If I can't get them on my side with Frisbee, self-deprecation will have to do.

"Ha-ha, very funny," Wyatt says. "New plan, boys. Ray and Andrea, keep yourselves open and get ready to catch."

"What about me?" I ask.

"Try getting in the other team's way instead."

The play works. It works twice in a row, actually. I even intercept the other team's throw and manage a short toss to Andrea, who scores. Suddenly people are patting me on the back at the water cooler. And I'm sweating. Like, on purpose.

We're about to resume when someone calls my name from the other edge of the field. A Bandit girl I don't know. She jogs up to us and blurts, "Bria wants to talk to you."

She's looking at me. I look at Wyatt.

"Sh-she says it's important," the girl stammers.

I'm torn. I'm just now hitting my stride with the Bear Hut boys, but my instincts tell me to go. Sierra's erasure, Caroline's death, my dreams, the danger that keeps finding me—they connect in a pattern I have yet to

185

understand. So, sorry, boys, and sorry, Frisbee. I give Wyatt an apologetic shrug and follow the girl through a copse of pine trees to a small clearing of dappled light and soft moss. Bria and Mimi and a few other girls sit on a patchwork quilt, a picked-over picnic heaped in the middle of their sprawling bodies. They lift their heads lazily when I arrive, then lie back down, faces angled toward the sun.

"Welcome, Mars. Have a seat. We're just finishing a game," Bria says.

I sit automatically. I have every intention of asking about Sierra, but I remind myself about doubt, and subtlety. I tell myself that's why I don't say a word as I sit, but in the moment, I feel an uncharacteristic shyness, like when I first approached the girls under the pergola. Even though I was invited then, and here, that sense of intrusive monstrosity is back. I feel ugly and alien among their languid sprawl. If I speak, my deep voice will ruin the soft weightlessness of the scene. So I say nothing.

The game they're playing is unlike anything I've ever seen. Between Bria and Mimi is a system of circular coasters and saucers made of thick ceramic and painted in bright, radial designs. Upon each is a cluster of tiles, all different shapes, like piles of candy. There's some system to their placement, I sense, but that's it. The objective of the game is unclear. There doesn't even appear to be a board.

"Resume," Bria says.

A girl off to the side lifts one willowy arm into the air, holding up a faceted crystal cup. She moves it from side to side until it catches the sun just right, projecting a flurry of rainbows onto the blanket. They skim over the saucers and tiles. Slowly, she twists the etched glass, and the rainbows resolve into warping shapes. Ovals and arcs that overlap in abstract patterns.

It's a board for their game, I realize.

Mesmerized, I watch Bria and Mimi whisk their hands across the coasters, plucking up tiles and placing them into saucers with definitive clinks. I can't figure out the goal, or the points, but it's clear that Mimi is winning. Bria's moves take longer and longer to execute. The board of light slides imperceptibly, and I only notice because Bria swears as she loses a coaster to Mimi. At least that's what I think I'm seeing.

At first I think the movement is due to the girl holding the glass, but she hardly even blinks. It's the sun, I realize, moving slowly through the sky. The board slides as a result.

Eventually Mimi and Bria sit back, Bria releasing a heavy sigh.

"No one can beat Mimi," CJ tells me. The glass is lowered, but the brightness of the board remains scored into the backs of my eyes. I blink, and it spins in my memory.

"Want to play?" Bria asks me.

"Oh, Mars, you have to!" Mimi says, pulling me into her spot.

"I don't know how," I say. My voice is so much lower than I expect. I clear my throat, pitch it up, and say, "I'll try if you don't mind explaining the rules."

Look at me. Subtle. Lovely. I'll play dumb until they grow bored of the game, and then I'll ask my questions. I'll ask about Sierra, and Callum, and maybe that will help me figure out what I need to ask about Caroline.

"It's more a game of instinct," Bria says as she resets the arrangement of tiles.

"What's the goal?"

"Depends on who's playing."

"How do you win?"

"That's not really the point," Bria says. "It's more about cooperation."

The girl lifts up the glass and gradually the board comes into focus. Up close it's just fragments of sun bounced into shards, just bevels of light and color. Not really a board at all.

"You can go first," Bria says.

I look at her but she's looking at the game. The light reflects off the tiles, placing bruises of pastel on her throat, her cheeks. The same flecks wink in my eyes as I shift back and forth, wondering what to do.

It's a test. I know that much. They're not seeing what move I make; they're testing to see if I make a move at all.

I reach for a tile of deep sapphire, like my nails, on a coaster close to Bria. I pick it up and wait for her to react. She doesn't. Fine. If I want them to tell me the rules, I'll have to break them, so instead of placing the tile on my saucer I drop it into a teacup off to the side, beyond the glowing board's edge.

Bria smiles faintly, striking three tiles from three coasters and placing them, with gravitas, on my saucer. Then she waits.

I glance around. All the girls have sat up on their elbows, watching. I look back to the board. I pick up a flat black tile and place it in the middle, right on the blanket, as another experiment. Again Bria smiles. The girls—all of them—inhale quickly.

Bria shushes them.

"Why that move, Mars?"

I stare at the black tile. I feel like it's staring back. Among all the color and light, it's the only thing that doesn't shine. That's why I picked it. For its ugly, for its alien, and for its singular nature. That's why it gets to go in the center.

"Dunno," I say.

We play quicker after that. However senseless my moves are, Bria responds with clear intention. It's maddening. I count the tiles, add up each of the colors, and do whatever I can to parse the connections, but I can't crack the code. Eventually I just start creating designs. I make a triangle, then a star. The gilded borders of light rotate gradually, too slow to see until we've morphed into a new shape. I notice Bria only touches tiles along an iridescent hoop two moves in a row, and from that I guess her next move. When I make it for her, I win another faint smile.

We fall into a rhythm. I focus less on figuring out the game, and more on the inching light, the sharp clicks, the graceful swoop of Bria's hands. Did Caroline play this? Was she good at it? When we sat in the parlor and had coffee with Mom's donors, did Caroline think of this game every time a teacup was set on its saucer? She must have. She loves games.

Loved games.

I picture her again, in that eternal dusk. The end I hope is bright.

"Not yet," Bria says.

I have the sapphire tile pinched in between my fingers, but I lower it back into the teacup. My hand drifts elsewhere, making another move. I hardly look at what I'm doing now. My mind feels miles above Aspen, deep within the cloudless sky.

"Mars, you want to ask me something, don't you?" Bria says. Her voice doesn't bring me back down to earth. It joins me, up wherever I am.

"Yes."

"So ask."

There's Caroline in the dusk. There's a new void next to her, in the shape of a different, missing girl.

I ask: "What happened to Sierra?"

Bria scoops up a quartet of tiles and then snaps them down, pinning the points of an irregular diamond that's appeared in the refracted light. I stare at it. The black tile—my tile—is trapped within it.

"I was hoping you could tell me," Bria sighs. "What do *you* think happened to Sierra?"

"I don't know," I say. "I thought maybe I made her up."

"You didn't. So *think*," Bria urges.

I remove a point on the diamond, but when I put the tile elsewhere, the line of light stretches to join it. I move it again and the same thing happens.

"I saw her," I say. My own voice sounds far away, far below wherever my mind is now. "She was at the formal. We lit sparklers together."

"And then?"

"And then I went to bed."

"No. Again."

"And then I went to . . . I walked back to my cabin. And went to bed."

"No. Again."

I want to look at Bria, and can't. The whole time our hands float over one another, snapping the tiles into new shapes. Patterns I can barely perceive. Not diamonds and squares, but interlocking flowers of light that rise up from the blanket. They rotate as the sun rotates, and I feel as though I move with them. Physically, mentally, I'm shifting apart. Petal by petal, I'm opening up to Bria.

"I walked back to the cabin. I brushed my teeth. I removed my makeup. I went to bed."

"What did your dreams show you that night?"

I'm there, watching myself sleep. I'm hovering over myself. I'm drifting down. I'm sinking into my own scalp. I'm tossed by a frothing interference—the anxious rumination of my brain falling asleep as Bria and I enter my mind—and then I'm in the dark beyond, the dark within, watching. Dreaming, maybe. When Bria speaks, it's like she's right next to me in that dark.

"The lace favors you, Mars. It shows you things. Show me what it showed you."

I don't want to. I know what she'll see. The aspen trees and their eyes. Caroline, falling toward me, through me, her body crushed beneath mine. I am a heavy, crushing, deadly burden. Again and again, we collide with the tile floor.

The tile floor.

The tiles remind me of the game. We are in my mind, but we are also in the woods, in a clearing, upon a blanket, playing a game.

I say no to Bria, but not out loud. Not with words. My hand reaches into the pulsing glow of the game and, finding a tile that hums and skips on its coaster, I pull it out. It burns, the magnified light sizzling on my knuckle, but I'm quick. The pattern tumbles into a new shape, and Bria's voice falters.

"Show us. Please."

She's frustrated. I can feel it. It's not just *frustrated*, though. That's just a word, a finite arrangement of shapes with limited meaning. Words are senseless containers for things like the emotion Bria is feeling. What Bria feels is indescribable. Vast. Illegible in all languages except intuition. Like this game. I place a tile, change the pattern, and Bria's mind opens to me. I know all that lies beneath *frustrated*. I see into it, into a new darkness. Into the darkness within Bria this time.

"You can't find her," I intuit, but that's not quite right. I sense further through the feeling. "You're missing Sierra. Like, you're *without* her."

"No further," Bria says. Or she says nothing. Her hands have lost their weightlessness and now shake as she rearranges a coaster. A pointless move. The game remains in my control.

"She's . . . lost? She's . . ." I stumble on. I dig through Bria, past her, toward a vast brightness she guards. *The lace.* It weaves into visions. I see a winking moon glimpsed through serrated trees. I run in a body that is not mine. I fall, go limp. I'm rolled onto my back so that I'm staring up into a starry night, and the hulking shadow that caught me. I taste metal. My own death. My fluttering eyes close.

No further, Mars.

Now we watch through the trees. Sierra—the body I was just within— lies on moonlit rock beneath us. She wears my Aspen uniform shirt, knotted at her belly. Her eyes are still wet but no longer moving. Though it's nothing but a dripping blackness in the starlight, it's clear what cradles her is a splash of blood, thickest at her head.

We scream.

We say, over and over, *No.*

No no no.

Get out.

Get out!

"GET OUT!"

A cold pain shoots into my ear. I twist away from it and the world flinches beneath me. I hold on to the picnic blanket with white fists. The game—the coasters and tiles and saucers—are in disarray beneath me. They are dull in my shadow, nothing but cheap glass and ceramic. It's over. I don't know what it was, but it's over.

For another few seconds, Bria and I are in sync as we breathe in, breathe out. Then we unlace, and I finally feel like I'm my own again. I look at her just before she slides a hand across her cheek, swiping away a teardrop. Her hand comes away sticky, threaded in gold. The same gold that flows in her eyes.

The gold of honey.

"Sierra is in the woods north of Hunter Lodge," she blurts. "He found her. She's dead. The lace showed us."

The girls are racing over me, bombarding Bria with questions.

"What do we do?"

"Who did it?"

"Should we tell—"

"We tell no one," Bria says, swiping away tear after sticky tear. "Our codes are clear. We handle this ourselves, our way. Tell the others to stay out of the woods at night. Something hunts us."

"What about Mars?"

Bria's eyes lock to mine. The blanket spins beneath us, like the light spun around our game. Or only I spin. Bria appears immovable now, though her face begins to blur.

"Purge it," she commands. "Purge it all, this time."

I turn to run. I feel like a tiny thing in a huge machine, my body heavy. Clumsy. I look up at the girl who was holding up the crystal cup, the one that formed the board. The crystal sparkles through her tan knuckles as she pulls it back, then swings it forward.

It's lovely, I think, as it connects with my temple.

It's lovely.

It's

―――――――――

"Up you go."

"Do you have him?"

"Get his arm."

"*Their* arm."

"Whatever. *Its* arm."

"Dude, not cool."

That was Wyatt. The other voice is Ray. Maybe Brayden. I feel their fingers digging into my armpits. I'm dragged upright, we hobble a short distance, then I'm allowed to lie down again, this time in a patch of shade.

"Should we call the infirmary?"

"No, look. He's fine. Mars, you there? Wake up, buddy."

Wake up?

It's like a mundane prophecy. I hear it, I do it. I open my eyes, just to see if I can, and look into the shaded faces leaning over me.

"How's your head?" Wyatt asks.

My hand rises to my temple, where a bright throb pulses.

"Ninetieth percentile."

Wyatt blushes, the other guys laugh. Making the joke makes me think I'm okay. I search backward through the wobbly memories, wondering how I got here. I remember playing Frisbee, I remember huddling up at the water cooler. Then, in too-bright Technicolor, I see the dark disk whip down from the sky and connect, solidly, with my temple.

Later I'll wonder why this memory is in third-person, like I'm someone else watching it happen, but right now it doesn't feel important.

I push myself up, the wooziness fading now that I'm out of the sun's unbearable brightness.

"I'm fine," I say.

Wyatt calls off whoever was running to the infirmary. I'm handed a paper cup and it's full of too-cold water.

"Take it easy," the boys tell me. "Just hang out."

They resume their game. I watch them throw the disk back and forth, back and forth, the metronome centering my tilting mind. Sometimes the Frisbee passes in front of the sun and my mind fills with a frantic whir, like all my neurons are lighting up at once. But I just close my eyes and pull back into the shade, and it fades.

"Don't go to sleep," Wyatt says, nudging me. I guess he's beside me. I forgot.

"I'm not."

"Do you think you have a concussion?"

I laugh and it hurts a little bit. "From a Frisbee? No, I don't think so."

"Good," Wyatt says. "That would have made me a pretty shitty LIT. I hope you had fun, though."

I think I had fun. I remember having fun. I also remember something else, a terror as fleeting as the sparkles reflecting off the lake. There and then gone, replaced by the vision of the Frisbee smacking into my head. *Thwack!*

I'm fine by the time we head back to the cabin. No dizziness, hardly any pain. There's just one moment, though, when we pass by a sunlit clearing in the pines around the athletic field, where vertigo sweeps through me and I'm sure it's all wrong—all of it—but it passes, and I'm fine again, and we head home.

CHAPTER 21

When we show up for Apiculture the next day, Mimi surprises us with beekeeping suits, presenting them to Wyatt and me like couture gowns.

"I wasn't sure what sizes," she says as she lovingly unfolds them. "I washed a few, just in case."

The suit is made of thick white cotton, the fit so baggy it slides right over my uniform. It's heavy. I like its heaviness. Last night and today I've felt haunted by this strange sensation, like I'm drifting out of myself. The suit's weight feels secure. I feel better within it, despite the heat.

Dressed, Wyatt and I look like two deflated astronauts. Mimi has us try on our hats next. They're wide brimmed, with a dense mesh veil.

"You're probably thinking, hmmm, why are we wearing these when Mimi said we didn't need them? Did she lie? And the answer . . ." Mimi pauses for effect as she leads us down into the meadow. ". . . is that I have uttered no such lies! You don't need them if you're just watching, but today the two of you are gonna lead. You ready?"

A thrill rises through me. I didn't think I'd get to do this so soon! Am I ready? How could I be? I hardly know anything about working with the bees. I don't even know what Mimi is going to have us do.

"We're on swarm watch," Mimi says simply.

I gesture at the air congested with bees. "Isn't this a swarm?"

"No. Well, kind of. Actually, no. Look, here's the deal. When a hive gets too big, it'll swarm. That means the queen will leave the hive and take, like, half the colony to a new location to start a new hive. That's called swarming. It's how the hive reproduces itself and it's super cool, but to most people it just looks like a threat."

Wyatt chimes in. "You can find videos of it online. Thousands of bees will just create a cluster on, say, a stoplight."

"Or under a porch," Mimi adds. "Wherever the queen goes."

I'm already confused, and I'm already stressed.

"So we're going to stop a swarm of bees?" I ask.

"No. I mean, kind of? Depends what we find. Here," Mimi says as she hands me a hive tool, but I've got my own. I show Mimi and her eyes linger on it, like she recognizes it. Then she goes chipper again.

"Good. Let's open up the hive, then."

I use the tool to pry open the top of the hive, and again I'm overcome by the humming warmth that exhales out. It smells sweet and close, like a deep breath within a tight hug. Mimi stands back as she instructs. We pull out the frames for inspection, and I'm amazed at how heavy they are, how the bees themselves drip from them like liquid. My veil is dotted with them in seconds. Their sound rises from a hum to something angrier.

"Wyatt. Smoke," Mimi calls. Wyatt moves the smoker over the frame I'm holding.

"Good. Mars, what do you see?"

There's too much to see. I have no idea what to look for. I say, "Bees?"

"Okay, true, but, like, *anything* else? Describe it."

"I see . . ." I maneuver the frame toward the sun. The comb is perfectly aligned, no warps like last time. On the other side, though, I find a corner where the cells bulge out, like fingers pushing through the comb. I tell Mimi and she claps gleefully.

"Queen cells!" she says. "They look like teacups, don't they?"

They don't. Like at all.

"The hive is feeding some of the babies with royal jelly, turning them into queens," Mimi recites. "Do you know why?"

Wyatt raises his hand, all eager, but Mimi focuses on me. I shrug, my shoulders burning with the weight of the heavy frame.

"It's a common misconception that the queen bee rules the hive," Mimi says. "Her power is in name only. In reality, if she's not doing her job, the workers will kill her and simply create another. Sick, right?"

Mimi's eyes glint with comedic malevolence as she takes in my equally exaggerated gasp.

"Hives aren't monarchies," she says, taking the heavy frame from me. "The queen isn't an authority. She's just a priority. Like an organizing principle. The real authority is in the colony itself."

Wyatt can no longer hold back. He blurts, "Superorganism! A bee colony is a superorganism."

"I was going to say *democracy*, but sure," Mimi says, throwing a wink at me. She raises the frame. "So. *This* hive is trying to raise some new queens. It's because their numbers are too high. We have several options. We can eliminate the queens and give the hive more frames to fill with comb, diverting their expansion efforts and preventing a swarm. We can split the hive, taking the queen cells and relocating them to a new hive. Or we allow a queen to hatch, and she'll fly away and take a swarm with her, making a new hive somewhere else. Maybe in our apiary, but maybe not. So! What should we do?"

I understand about half the words Mimi says, and even less of their meaning. The insects on my hood are multiplying, the spellbound calm from the smoke breaking.

"Swarm naturally?" I guess, because it seems like the least likely option.

"Ugh, that's what Bria says," Mimi pouts. "I think it's wasteful, letting them leave. Less honey for us, you know? But Bria says sometimes letting nature take its course is the best thing we can do."

We reinsert the frames. I have chosen for us to do nothing more, evidently, so Mimi talks through hypotheticals for the remaining time while we ask questions. I learn that if I had chosen differently, we may have spent this time breaking the teacup cells off the comb and discarding them, dooming the larval queens inside.

On our walk back, Wyatt and I excitedly discuss what we saw. The way it felt. The sounds it made. We make it to the covered bridge in record time, and before we reach the boathouse Wyatt slows, like he's reluctant.

"What?" I say.

"Nothing," he says back. "Just, you seem really into it. I'm sorry for doubting your intentions."

I feel that floating sensation again, and I pull myself back down to earth. It's a lightness I haven't felt in . . . a long time, it feels like.

"It's interesting," I say.

"It is," Wyatt says, but I feel like he's talking about me, not the bees.

The Village Victory Cup turns out to be not so much a battle as it is a strange carnival of sideshow competitions. One afternoon it's a show-down to see who can pick up more ice cubes with chopsticks, the next it's who can burn through a taut rope with just a magnifying glass. There's a whipped-cream-pie-eating contest—which an Amazon cabin dominates—and a debate bout—which Bria wins, no surprise there. There are more strenuous tasks, too, like capture the flag, relay races, and something called the Aspen Trifecta, which is a mix of swimming, archery, and rock climbing. Somehow, I get stuck doing this one.

They start us on the float, out in the lake. A Leader sits in a kayak, telling us to ready, set, go! I throw myself into the water, barely registering the chill as I thrash to shore. I'm fast but not first. I make up for it at the makeshift archery range they've propped up on the fields, when my third arrow hits a lucky bull's-eye. I fall behind again at the rock-climbing tower, but the girl ahead of me keeps giving up halfway and plunging back down. For once I don't think about how I must look as I heave myself up one hold at a time. Shining, sweating, muscles full of blood. I feel good. I feel powerful.

At the top I twist to take in all of Aspen, spread below me in a panorama of neon greens and baked butterscotch and those pristine white uniforms dotting the distance. The rush of it all dazzles me, makes me grin. I can see all the way into the meadow on the other side of the lake, and across the open athletic fields to the woods. I can see smoke from the kitchens and, closer, a rash of glitter cast across a tennis court where a lone girl has fallen, so still I almost stop to wonder why. Then my hands slip from the holds and I fall, the jerk of the rope snapping me up before I'm lowered into a mosh of cheering Bear Hut boys. They chant my name. *Mars, Mars, Mars!*

I'm not sure what's changed between me and the boys, just that the change started with Frisbee. I guess Wyatt was right. They seem less bitter toward me the more I participate in these little games. It helps that I win them, I realize. Maybe that's all that mattered all along. Not that they knew who I was, but that I didn't get in the way of who they wanted to be. Which is Bear Hut, Bear Hut, big bad Bear Hut!

We stamp and cheer this every evening at dinner when the day's points are tallied, the awards for the challenges handed out. I notice Wyatt watching me more and more the louder I yell, the harder I stomp. Sometimes he watches me even when I'm quiet, like when we're helping Mimi put new frames into the hives, or listening to Leena talk about wildflower varieties native to the meadows. He watches me, and I watch the Honeys as they drift in and out of main camp. They participate in the games, but sparingly, like the antics amuse them only in short bursts. Then they vanish.

When I see them, I feel shame. I don't know why. But they're nice to me. They say hi, they know my name. At one point they're short a person during a match of volleyball, and they ask me to join their side. The girls' side. I suck at serving, but my height helps nonetheless, and we beat the boys. It's my favorite moment of the week, until Friday.

Friday afternoon, our task is to cross a pit of lava using a hanging vine. Not real lava; it's a mire of mud created with a hose, since it hasn't rained in days. Not a real vine; it's a rope, knotted to an A-frame of fallen logs. We go one after the other, launching over the lava, but Andrea misses his landing and we lose him to the lava. The rope settles in the middle, stumping us. Finally, I think to remove our shoes and string them together to grapple the rope over, and it works. I'm the best at it, so I end up crossing last. When I do, it's Wyatt who catches me on the other side, and though my feet land safely on the ground, his arm stays around my waist, like he's not sure I'll stay put without him.

When I shower, my hand travels to where he touched, and though the water is cold my skin stays warm.

Saturday comes and the battle ends, not with cannon fire and war cries but with a tie-breaking challenge involving using a straw to pick up marshmallows and drop them in a bucket. A ferocious Bandit named Bonnie wins it for all the girls, and the screaming is earsplitting. The Bears glower and cuss about it, but I think it's nice. I want to cheer with the girls, but I don't.

That night is the New Moon Party, when the sky goes dark so the stars can shine their brightest. All of Apsen, now united, meets for a full-camp sleepover on the lawn. Towels and blankets are spread out over the field, and telescopes are brought out so we can look at the winking constellations. The little kids get to go first, peering through the lenses at my namesake, at Venus, at the waning sliver of the moon, and then they're ushered into waiting tents. The older campers remain, watching the sky for something in the heavens to shoot sideways.

It's an Aspen tradition, I'm told, for the older kids to watch until sunrise. Some of us attempt this, but most nod off. Brayden and the other Leaders hang around a firepit, ignoring us, and eventually they fall asleep, too. I don't, though. I find a way to sit near Wyatt as he names the constellations, though I spend less time looking at the stars than I do staring at his profile drawn in starlight.

At some point, someone brings up the heat wave that's been broiling the camp. In the night it's not so obvious, but in the day the plants look dull and wilted. Someone else brings up swimming. The contagion is immediate. Suddenly, silently, a group of us are stumbling out of our clothes and racing down to the waterfront. Even Wyatt, though I'm sure Brayden is depending on him to stop us. He doesn't, though. He jumps in first, shattering the moonlight collected on the lake's placid face. We tumble in after.

"This is, like, when we all die, isn't it?" Mimi keeps saying. "Like in the movies, this is where we die, right?"

"Shut up," Bria jokes. "You have to be hot to die first."

"Or have sex," Mimi counters.

"Well, you haven't done that either, girl."

We churn the silver water, reveling in the strangeness of the dark shore, testing how far we can swim from it before Wyatt calls us back. I swim a little farther, hoping he'll call me by name. Inch by inch, I lead a small cluster toward the raft, then past it. Finally, I hear him yell, and faintly I see him waving from the boathouse deck. In the still night, his voice is crystal clear as it sweeps across the water.

"Mars. We're heading back."

"Swim with us," Bria says somewhere in the darkness beyond me.

"I can't," I say.

"Oh, come on, just come home with us, Mars," Mimi begs.

I look at them—just featureless faces drifting through the night's watery reflection—then I look back to Wyatt.

"I'll be back later," I call to him. It's dark, but I think I see his head shake. I imagine I can hear his disappointed sigh.

"Oooh, rebel," Bria croons. The girls laugh and splash.

"Come with us," I call to shore. I want to see if Wyatt follows. I keep looking back as we reach the lake's middle but Wyatt isn't there. Maybe he's watching from the Hunter Village hill, seeing if we make it.

We reach the lily pads, the lake floor rising to fill our toes with muck as we push through the tough, slimy cords. The girls splash one another, laugh and scream, but we all get quiet as we reach the meadow's edge.

"Don't wake the bees," Mimi jokes. I giggle like I get it, but the whole walk up the hill I wonder if the insects sleep. And if they do, would they dream? Their hum is quiet, but when I put my ear to the cool wood of one hive, there's a faint vibration within.

Once we reach the cabin, it's back to chaos. The girls rip off their soaked underwear, pushing their damp bodies into big sweaters and fresh leggings. Clothes are thrown at my feet and I end up in a lavender camisole and, ironically, boy shorts. Dry and changed, the girls find a sudden energy, and I watch transfixed as they start one hundred separate tasks. Some of them start to heat up cider on the stove. A few resume a game of Catan on the coffee table, and a few others involve themselves in another game involving coasters and tiles.

"Don't bother," someone says when I ask about it. "Mimi wins every time."

I hear popcorn popping. I smell honeyed wax burning. Someone turns on a record player and someone else keeps bumping it, so it skips and jumps through Vivaldi's "Summer." I know it because Caroline has the same record. She must have heard it here.

Remembering her amid the chaos is a sudden, frigid slap. It nearly knocks me backward. I grip the arms of the chair I've embedded myself in to keep from running right out the door and back into the lake. She sat here, maybe in this chair, maybe with her legs pulled under her just like me. She stood at that stove, or touched that record. If I doused the lamps and observed the cottage in black light, it would glow with her fingerprints.

My breaths quicken. I need to get out of here. I make it onto the porch, then down the stairs, but stop. I don't have shoes. My toes curl and flex as I will myself forward, but no amount of willpower is going to make up for the mistake I made in coming here. I can't swim alone. I can't hike through the woods in the dark, barefoot. All I can do is stand at the edge of the porch's light, the hundred ghosts of Caroline blazing at my back.

The music inside halts. A literal record scratch. The murmuring rises in frantic questions and then the door opens. Bria joins me on the bottom step.

"Come inside," she urges.

"I can't be in there," I say. It's all I can manage, and it comes out cramped and sullen.

"It must be hard," Bria says after a few seconds. "Being here. Being with us."

I nod. It wasn't, until it suddenly was. And now it's impossible. I feel the culmination of every mistake that brought me to this doorstep. Staying home would have been harder than following Caroline all the way out here, but if it could have saved me from this, it would have been the right choice. I was a fool to think I could find her here. What I've found instead is just another girl-shaped void with the silhouette of my sister.

"We can stay out here, then," Bria says. She sits down, and I follow. Someone comes out with a quilt and wraps it over Bria and me. Someone else hands me a heavy mug full of spiced cider—small, perfect stars bobbing in the steam.

"We use cardamon, cloves, and the stars are star anise, obviously," Bria informs me. "Try it. It's good."

It *is* good. Dark, spiced, fragrant. It's a new taste for me, something that belongs entirely to right now.

A few other girls come out onto the porch, then a few more, until the din of the house quiets to just the girls overseeing the popcorn popping. From the sounds, I can practically see the big steel saucepan they're using, the ricochet fire of the kernels muffling each time they clamp down the heavy lid.

"Do you want to talk about her?" Bria asks me.

"No, it's okay," I start to say. But the truth is, I do. I want to talk about Caroline.

Ever since she died, people have tried to comfort me with prayers of healing, of calm, of perfect and everlasting peace. All of it has added to the terror of her loss, like first her body was cremated, and now her memory must be incinerated, too. Death, twice, first the body and then the heart. But I'm not ready to move forward. And it's not that I can't admit that she's gone. It's that if I move on, I leave her behind.

I don't want to move on just yet. I just want to sit here a little while longer beside her ghost, and try to hold her hand.

"It's like . . ." I say, swallowing. "It's like she's everywhere, and nowhere."

Bria rubs my shoulder. I don't have the words for how I feel, probably because this is the first time I've been asked. But I'm not self-conscious as I stumble on.

"And everyone acts like it's easier if we just don't talk about her, like they're doing me a favor. But it feels like she's dying all over again. People tell me that it's going to be okay," I whisper. "But right now, it's awful. It's so awful."

I shake and I shake, and Bria rubs my shoulder. We look up at the stars together.

"Love has a weight," Bria whispers. "And so does loss. Sometimes it can all be so heavy. But look at you, Mars. You're holding it all up."

I am. Sometimes I stumble, but every time I get back up, I'm lifting everything that's holding me down. Bria is right. It's heavy, but I'm strong. I don't know how I never noticed.

When the worst of my sobs subside, I find the energy to sip my cider, thankful for its warmth in my fingers.

Bria says, "We talk about Caroline all the time."

"You do?"

"All the time."

The girls on the porch murmur in agreement.

"Can you tell me about her?" I ask, and I don't care that I sound so pathetic. Like I'm asking about a stranger, or a long-lost grandmother, and not my own twin.

They don't act like I'm pathetic. Instead, miraculously, they oblige.

"She was funny," Mimi says. "She wouldn't stop until she got you to laugh. Sometimes when I was sad, she would just give me that look, and I'd smile before she even made a joke. I just knew she was going to be funny, and that was enough."

"She gave good hugs," Bria says. "Really good hugs. I remember one time she hugged me so hard that my back cracked."

"She always ate the butts of the breads," Kyle says. "We pretended it was a huge favor, but I think she secretly liked them."

"She liked them. I know she did. When we made pizza last year she asked for my crusts."

"She pretended she could talk to birds and that's how she gave Leena feedback when Leena needed to be told her natural deodorant wasn't cutting it. A message from the birds. She even wrote it on paper and signed it 'The Birds.'"

"She hated moths. She said she could hear them flapping around her at night."

"She was kind to me. My first year at Aspen, she was the first person I met on my first day, and at the end of the session, she was the last person I said goodbye to."

"She did a really good frog impression."

"But she couldn't sing."

"Oh my god," I laugh. "She *so* couldn't sing. Did she ever tell you that she got kicked out of choir in seventh grade? Not even the show choir. Just . . . regular choir."

The girls are appalled. They laugh as I tell them about Caroline's horror at finding she'd been rescheduled to stage crew, and how for every single shower for the next month I heard her belting out "Edelweiss" like her life depended on it.

"Will you tell us more about her?" Mimi asks me.

I pause for just a second—it feels like the memories of her that are only mine are all I have left—but then I turn and look at all the girls on the porch with me. They sniff as they smile, also crying. This sadness is unlike what I started with. It feels spread thin, a bit in each of us. Shared. Not so heavy anymore.

So maybe it will feel good to share even more.

"Okay," I say. "What do you want to know?"

"All of it," Bria says.

So I start as far back as I can, and I tell the story about us changing clothes in the garden, and the parties we ditched in high school, and the time I made her cry at Niagara Falls because I said she should go over the edge in a barrel, and bit by bit I retrace her life. Our life. Our together.

And the Honeys listen.

CHAPTER 22

The sun.

Oh, fuck the sun.

It's suddenly everywhere, under my eyelids, soaking through the crochet blanket bundled around my face. Now that I'm awake, I feel the stiffness of my joints, all knotted on the low, sunken couch in the Cabin H common room. I bolt upright, sending a swarm of floating fibers through the bright morning air.

Late morning, I guess, because the world outside is lit to full radiance.

I remember falling asleep just before sunrise, and being so tired that I didn't care if I got in trouble for not making the trek back to Hunter Village. How could I, without shoes or even clothes? The Honeys decided I would stay anyway, heaping so many blankets and pillows onto me that it was impossible to leave.

"Oh good, you're up."

The voice startles me. I twist to look behind the couch and into the kitchen, and I'm surprised to see not one but many people standing there. Not just standing, moving. Cooking. Now that I see them, I can hear them, too: the scrape of a whisk in a bowl of batter, the thud of a wooden spoon knocking around a French press before the top sinks on with a sucking hiss, the ancient toaster throwing forth toast.

"We didn't want to wake you," Mimi says. "OJ, coffee, or tea?"

"Coffee," I mumble. "What time is it?"

"It's late. Leena let us sleep in."

"I should go," I say, but all at once the girls are full of protest.

Not without breakfast! Coffee first! No one walks out on brunch, dummy!

Bria cuts through the chatter. "Leena radioed to your cabin; they know you're safe. I bet they're sleeping, too. No reason to rush back."

One girl hands me a mug painted with butterflies and beetles, another fills it with fragrant coffee. A third places a claw-footed bowl of sugar on the side table, then a jar of cream that's sweating in the heat. Yet another hands me a wooden-handled teaspoon. All of this in a few sleepy blinks.

At the same time, several others pull the blankets off the floor and tidy the living room. Girls slide into the cleared couches and chairs, and suddenly plates are being passed around. Forks and rumpled cloth napkins follow. Then, the food. It daisy-chains from the kitchen, simply appearing from the dense clamor of girls at work. They sit in shifts, eating and laughing and teasing one another. More food manifests—scones, and a bowl of blueberries, a questionably gray smoothie, chia seeds in a little clay bowl.

The cabin is small and lively but the girls move among one another in a way that feels cohesive. I realize it reminds me of the bees among their comb. Or maybe I only think this because the spoon I'm using to stir sugar into my coffee pricks my thumb, and I find upon its handle a small metal bee. The napkins are embroidered with small blue-gray bees, too. The knobs on the cabinets are painted ceramic bees, fat and cheerful. Everywhere else, too: the coat hooks, the cross-stitched pillows, even the inlaid design of the hexagonal bathroom tiles. The motif is all I see as I maneuver through the cottage. I find it cute, if not a little cloying. It's no worse than the profound dankness of Hunter Lodge's taxidermy animals, or Bear Hut's carved mascot, Bernard. My mom has a donor whose whole house is full of Santa Claus figurines.

I prefer the bees.

A scream cuts the din, not in terror but in playful warning. Girls rush over me, bounding across sofas to get out to the porch, then rush back in. They're dragging someone with them. Wyatt, wide eyed, hair mussed, carrying a garbage bag full of clothes.

"Oh, *thank you*," the girls say, pulling their discarded uniforms out of the bag and tossing them into the corners. They sit Wyatt down and put a plate on his lap. He looks completely shell-shocked by the business of it all, and it's a minute before his eyes even settle on me from where I'm watching. When he sees me, he reaches into his bag and pulls out my uniform. He even has my shoes, the socks tucked into them, and wags them at me like a scold.

We head out shortly after, the girls making us promise we'll come back, as if we're not scheduled to show up on Monday.

While Wyatt and I walk through the woods, the buzzy glow of Cabin H fades and I start to feel sheepish.

"Am I in trouble?" I ask.

Wyatt shrugs. "You shouldn't have swum across the lake. It's not safe."

"Everyone was swimming."

"And everyone returned to the correct shore. Except you."

"I don't subscribe to binaries like shores."

Wyatt does that quick-exhale laugh. "So what? You'll just float forever in the middle?"

"Yes. In my little nonbinary canoe," I say.

Wyatt tilts back his head and ponders this. Then he asks, "Question, Mars. What's that like, floating in the middle?"

I wait for him to laugh, or to indicate somehow that he's not really asking, just continuing our banter. But he wrestles the mischief from his face and replaces it with an almost-academic curiosity.

"Okay. Answer. It's like . . ." I pause. My mind is still spinning with the business of Cabin H. My usual explanations slip away. "It's more like I

drift back and forth. Sometimes I'll get out, stay a while on one shore, bu
a part of me is always waiting to get back to drifting."

"You don't get tired?"

"I don't," I say. "Or I guess I do. But it's not drifting around in the
middle that makes me tired. It's staying too long on either shore. People
have these specific ideas of what a boy is, or a girl is, and it's so exhaust
ing to play along. People make themselves so unhappy trying to get it
right. But it's not even real. So I reject all of it. I'd rather be happy and
adrift."

"What's do you mean, it's not even real?"

"Hate to be the one to break this to you, nature boy, but hardly any
thing is real," I laugh. "Gender, the idea that there are two shores directly
across from each other. The lake has a ton of hidden shores, but you don't
know that if you're stuck standing on the land."

"You lost me," Wyatt laughs. "Back on the subject of actual, non
metaphorical shores, it's my job to make sure you don't do that again. You
could have drowned."

I put on a posh voice. "Better to drown as myself than to breathe the air
of someone else's life and drown all the same."

Wyatt shakes his head; his curls bounce. Exhaustion has deepened his
eye sockets. He smiles, though, when he says, "Brayden didn't even realize
you were gone until Leena radioed. Not a good look. I doubt he'll tell
Wendy."

I relax. Just a little, though.

"You should have come with us," I tell Wyatt as we walk through the
quiet camp.

"Did you have fun?"

"Kinda," I say, and that's the truth. I had a great time, but not a fun
one. Fun wasn't the point. "We mostly just talked."

"About girl stuff?"

"About Caroline, actually. And it was really nice."

Wyatt gives a thoughtful nod.

"Then I'm glad you broke this one rule. Just don't do it again, okay?"

I smirk at him. The shadows in his eyes are for sure from staying up all night. I wonder if he slept at all, or if the sunrise found him waiting on the boathouse deck, watching for the moment I stepped out from the covered bridge.

We don't talk about the night swim. It passes behind the opaque veil of discretion that seems to swallow so many things at Aspen. But at the same time, there's a twinkling in Wendy's eyes as she watches us yawn at dinner, a *knowing*.

I don't like that. And it's not that I'm against lying. Trickery is the first defense of people like me, who need to outmaneuver the dangers of telling the whole truth. But when everyone is complicit in a lie, aware of it yet pretending otherwise? I'm suddenly uncomfortable with deceit. Lying should be personal, I think. It shouldn't be so easy to deceive, at such a large scale. Yet Aspen does it all the time.

I try to think of other examples, but I can't. That feels off. I know there were other things in my catalog of conspiracies—from both my first stint at camp, and during this redo—but the sunny days have sapped the color from my convictions. I'm left with the impression of suspicion, but no real evidence. For hours at a time, I forget why I'm here. What I'm looking for. And when I remember—usually because something reminds me of Caroline and the low-grade agony turns suddenly stinging—I'm disgusted with myself.

Something happened here, I remind myself, marveling at how I could have forgotten. But then I ask what happened, and I don't know.

Then I find the photo.

It's returned to me, actually, on Monday, in a stiff white envelope that's been pinned to a bag of freshly laundered uniforms. A note says it was found in my pocket. There's a little smiley face accompanying the anonymous handwriting.

By now I've spent so much time with the girls in the cottage that I recognize them in the photo, but there's one I don't know. She's in the middle, giving the camera a peace sign. She looks familiar, but it might just be the Aspen uniform. Maybe the photo was taken last year. That doesn't explain why I have it, though. Vaguely, I can imagine myself in the Honeys' cottage, in a hallway upstairs, opening a door into the back bedroom, but I open the door to a bright nothing. The memory, if it's a memory, goes no further.

No further.

Yet another loose end strung off into the distance. But this thread feels taut, like if I tugged it, something would tug back.

So I don't tug.

On Tuesday, as Wyatt and I are getting ready to leave the apiary, the Honeys ask us to stay for lunch.

"Oh, sure," Leena says when Wyatt asks if that's allowed. "The dining hall doesn't need more mouths to feed. Besides, it's about to rain."

She's right. Thunder has been grumbling in the distance all morning, small spats of rain peppering the lake. We had to be careful inspecting the hives because the wind dug right into the mounds of bees, carrying a handful away each time. Mimi said they would find their way back, though.

Wyatt and I stay, sitting on the porch as the clouds finally break and rain flushes down the meadow. The other side of the lake vanishes in grayness. Wyatt feels nervous next to me, tapping his foot, eyes boring into the fog, like he mustn't lose sight of Aspen.

"Leena said it was fine," I say.

"It's not that."

"What, then?"

"I don't know. I've just . . . never been allowed in Cabin H so much."

"What, really? Not even during the off-season?"

"Nope."

I can't help it. I grin. "Wyatt, are you scared of girls?"

This gets him to relax, even if the sudden nonchalance is an act. "What? No. Why? What does that even mean? Scared of girls."

But Wyatt proves me right when Bria dashes up the stairs and he stands up, like a soldier at attention. She's carrying a large basket of red peppers, their waxy skin jeweled by raindrops.

"A job for you both," she says, handing Wyatt the basket. "Chop these."

I open the door wide for Wyatt. "After you."

For some reason I never quite realized that part of living all the way out in Cabin H meant the girls prepared their own meals. There's no dining pavilion, no staff. Not even Leena makes an appearance in the kitchen. And thank goodness, because it's a small room. Every inch of the counter is crowded with ingredients, but I'm amazed at how once again the girls fit against one another without jostling or competition. There's hardly any seams between them.

Wyatt and I are stationed at the kitchen table, wooden cutting boards before us. We chop the peppers in half, extracting the seeds and stems. The peppers are snatched up and thrown on a griddle somewhere, and we're told to chop red cabbage next. Then green onions, then carrots. The vegetables are misshapen, and I realize they're not from a store. They must grow all their food here.

"God no," one of the girls tells me. "Some grows here, but not all. We pick recipes at the beginning of the week and Leena grabs supplies from camp. Whatever Aspen doesn't have, Leena gets in town."

213

I can't imagine carrying groceries through the hike between Aspen and the meadow.

"Me neither," says Mimi. "There's a service road back behind the shed."

Lunch is ready just as the sun comes out. The peppers we cut have been charred and brushed with spiced oil. There's a slaw of purple cabbage, ginger, green onions, and carrots, served alongside black-charred barbecued duck. And finally, each of us is given a single fried zucchini blossom drizzled in honey.

We eat on the porch, watching the mist rise off the dripping garden. It's the best food I've had since brunch a few days ago. Wyatt hardly reacts to the feast, but he finishes everything he's given. Even the blossom.

After, we stay to help clean up. The second I say I don't mind doing dishes, I'm parked before the deep porcelain sink, up to my elbows in lukewarm suds. Wyatt dries. Mimi and several others put the dishes away. We hardly talk as we work through the mountain of plates. I hum to myself. A notice a few other girls hum, too, just loud enough to notice as they bring more and more for me to scrub. It's meditative, the way we work together. It's like falling into a groove made perfectly for your shape. Within that groove I feel safe. Content.

I meditate on this. Contentedness is a party I leave early every time. It's not often that I feel invited to begin with, and even rarer that I feel welcomed enough to stay. I've learned to never test any group's hospitality. Patience like that is finite for someone like me, and it's dangerous to indulge in it.

But I don't feel that here, in the daisy-chain apparatus of Cabin H. The groove I fit within is perfectly my shape, no wishful warps imposed upon me. I feel more than just welcomed. I feel essential. Needed. And instead of running from it, I want to see how long it will last. Maybe it could last forever, so long as I keep doing my job.

The dishes are suddenly done. It feels like a kick to the stomach, to have nothing else to do. The familiar threat of being dismissed is heavy in my empty hands, and like clockwork I hear myself say to Wyatt, "We should go."

"Yeah," he says, "the rain stopped, too."

I don't know if it's just an echo of my meditation, or if what I hear in Wyatt's voice is actually there, but I sense disappointment in him. The same simple pleasure I felt, fading fast.

CHAPTER 23

Now when I dream, it's about Cabin H.

Nothing important ever happens in the dreams. We do chores, or we bake bread, or we watch the bees. Curiously, no one speaks. In the dreams there's hardly any sound at all. Just a submerged muffle, a whispering like wind in trees. I always know the dreams are about to end when the sound speeds up, rising until it verges upon a familiar hum.

This week Aspen is getting ready for the July Jubilee. When I was little, the July Jubilee just meant a chance to see our parents halfway through the summer. It's really more of an open house, though. Prospective families will come to tour Aspen, while current families get a weekend to see what their kids have been up to. The theater kids put on staged productions, the culinary majors make meals, the ecology kids lead educational hikes, and the craft kids show off their pottery and paintings. The sports kids will, I assume, play their little games for an audience, finally.

A new feature is a farmer's market set up on the lawn of Big Lodge, or perhaps it was always there but I never noticed it. During Apiculture, we're told that we'll be selling honey at a little stand. Wyatt and I still aren't allowed in the production shed, so we spend an entire morning using twine to tie parchment labels onto jars. The labels say BOTTLED BY THE BEES OF THE ASPEN GROVE in elegant scrawl.

Our Cabin Challenge that day, and every day, turns out to be various chores to get Aspen ready for the weekend. Gone are the hours of fun, games, and budding camaraderie. Here are the hours of scrubbing moss from the shady side of the log cabins. And sweeping decks, which feels pointless. And prying mushrooms out of the stone walls, which feels evil.

The girls are given chores, too, but it's things like making garlands and painting banners. I watch them enviously until, as though hearing my SOS, Bria saunters over to us.

"Brayden, can we borrow Mars?"

Brayden is much older than Bria, but she talks to him like an equal. And he looks at her like he thinks he has a chance.

"For what?"

"Apiculture prep. We're making signs for the farmer's market. It'll just be for the day. Please?"

Brayden relents, and Bria grabs my hands and pulls me away.

The girls make working fun. They're quick at it, too, and we finish early enough to win a few hours to ourselves. We lie in the sun among the freshly painted signs, talking and making small bracelets of grass, and I feel that limitless contentedness return. The girls are interesting. Sensitive, and smart, and funny. I want them to like me. I want them to never know I thought they were vapid, even if it was just a momentary doubt. I feel a terror that they'll find out anyway, and I feel a strange guilt strung through it all.

It's hard to place what exactly makes them so alluring. They are all so different that there's no consistent trait unifying them. Yet it's their togetherness that emanates a strange pressure. As I spend more time with them, I begin to believe that it's nothing more than their matching sense of self-possession.

"Bitchiness," Bria sighs. "That's the word you're looking for."

We're on the back deck of Big Lodge, the signs handed over to the craft hut for mounting. The girls have vases with long, slender necks, and they're arranging flowers in them. I don't know where they're getting the flowers. Every time I look away and then look back, a new blossom bobs in the breeze.

"I don't think you're bitches," I say.

"You probably did, though, right? Before you talked to us?"

I don't have to say yes. Bria already knows, I guess. But she's not mad.

"It's okay, everyone does. Just comes with knowing who you are and what you're worth. It's easy for people to perceive a threat, but that's usually their own insecurity talking."

"I understand that," I say. "Sometimes I think the way people react to me has nothing to do with me, and everything to do with them."

Bria slots a flower into a vase, twisting it around the neck so that it faces the sun. "People tell on themselves all the time," she whispers. "They tell you the truth about themselves, one way or another."

After the impromptu flower arrangements, the girls go to the dining pavilion and knock on the back door until a cook opens it. She's not surprised to see us and lets us into a low-ceilinged kitchen humid with the steam of an industrial dishwasher. The girls find the freezer and pull out Popsicles, then out to the boathouse we go.

We do the same thing the next day, Brayden not even protesting Bria's requests for my "help." Being with them is like traveling in a pack of ghosts. The walls of Aspen are immaterial to them; we float through restrictions I once found so claustrophobic. We are invisible to the eyes of authority, becoming an ethereal, roaming pressure just at the edge of the camp's periphery. People seem to know we're there and to be interested in what we do, but indirectly.

I love it. It's thrilling. The next day when they invite me to join their crafting, I don't even bother telling Brayden. I just go, and we spend the afternoon painting terra-cotta plant pots.

The girls are fascinated with themselves, too. Almost as fascinated as I am. The way they talk about themselves—with such frankness—it feels like all people are wet clay, all the shapes that define us self-imposed. I realize this fits into the way I've always seen myself, which is: art, attempted, though often spoiled by the demands of another's taste. It makes me wonder what shape I'd be if I'd never met another human being.

"I think I will be famous," one of the girls might say, or, "I want to be an internet poet," or, "Maybe I'll revolutionize ballet." They say it with such easy authority that it feels practically real, like the hardest part is believing and, once that's over, the actual task of acting it out is just mundane paperwork. Inconsequential to the dream itself.

It's thrilling, and it's powerful. I see why Caroline loved them, but what I can't see is what replaced that love with fear. What could have been so dreadful that she wouldn't have wanted to come back to Aspen at all? The past is the strangest thing to imagine, as I sit here among them, watching them boss about the dolls of the future.

"What about you, Mars?" Mimi asks me on a golden afternoon as we sip honey-sweetened lemonade at the edge of the athletic field. All of us are crowded onto a few blankets, legs kicked out into the grass. "What's in your future?"

I nearly give some dreamy projection, but I sense the Honeys would clock the insincerity. From experience, they have a taste for truth, even if it's a little bitter.

"I don't know. I don't think any of us know. I think it's pointless to try."

"It's not pointless. It's manifestation," Mimi says studiously. "You put that energy out into the universe, and the universe hears you. There are studies on, like, positive thinking and subconscious action."

Bria scoffs. "So what, people who get into totally random car accidents just weren't giving the right vibes? That's a hideous way to blame people for things they can't control."

The conversation devolves into a philosophical debate about energy. Our higher selves dancing in higher dimensions of pure light and love. God. Gods. Unfathomable forces that drive us, divinely of course, toward our destiny or our doom. Magical thinking, Bria calls it, before sliding a cool hand over my wrist to get my attention. She says: "Mars, help me. You're into science and stuff. Tell them it's all bullshit."

I stare skyward. A fleet of butterflies floats over us. "Actually, there *are* higher dimensions. We use them all the time in math and physics to make sense of complex problems."

"Like astral projecting," Mimi adds, vindicated.

"No," I laugh. "Space-time. Einstein stuff. String theory requires at least ten dimensions to work out. Theoretically, I mean."

"Ten dimensions? And not one of them astral? Mimi, I'm so sorry, you must be crushed."

"Shut up, Bria," Mimi says sweetly. "Call it math or call it magic, but it's the same. There are higher dimensions, and if we influence them, we can manifest our own reality. It's possible, right, Mars? *Theoretically?*"

Bria and Mimi turn toward me in unison, like it's up to me to settle this debate.

"Maybe," I say. "But we wouldn't know. We experience reality as a three-dimensional projection in our brains. Our geometric instincts are 3D. So things in higher dimensions are kinda impossible for us to even visualize. That doesn't mean other dimensions aren't real, though. It just means we aren't able to comprehend them."

I fully expect silence, or to be outright declared a nerd and booted from the blanket. But instead, the Honeys have sat up around me. Their interest makes me desperate to keep going, but I'm not sure what else to say. Then a butterfly flits down onto the blanket to probe a fallen droplet of honey. It gives me an idea.

"Here, it's like that game you play. With the tiles. Hand me that glass."

I'm passed one of the curved glass cups we smuggled from the dishwashers. I raise it so that the sunlight passes through the water in its belly, projecting a glowing shadow onto the butterfly.

"Imagine that butterfly can only see in two dimensions. Its world is flat. If we asked it to describe the glass, it could only see that 2D shadow and tell us 2D things about it. But we humans, one dimension up, understand the glass's shape and depth. Our world is 3D. But what if we're like the butterfly, and we're trapped in what we can perceive? What if our world is just the light and shadow of some higher dimension's design? And if only we could comprehend it, we could change it? Well, physics tells us that just might be true. But we can't grasp it, so we can't change it, so we're just a butterfly. Trapped, but unaware. *Theoretically*."

I look around, like a magician at a children's birthday party. *Ta-da!* And my confetti falls to no applause.

"Now *that's* ridiculous," Mimi scoffs.

"It's theoretical physics!" I insist.

Mimi shakes her head. "I don't like the idea that we're trapped in a design. I have free will, don't I? I make choices."

"She does," Kyle says grimly. "Those bangs from last year prove it."

The girls dissolve into laughter and Mimi lunges for Kyle, but it's playful. Fun. The philosophy of manifestation is abandoned. But I remain within the riddle of perspective and illusion.

I stare at the pastel shadows curving over the butterfly, transfixed at the way I can pinch them together by adjusting the glass in my hand. Does the butterfly know the rainbow is just the shadow of something greater? Would we? What beauty in our reality is simply an unfathomable refraction across space, light, and time?

Maybe ghosts, I think, as I watch the rainbows pull together upon the butterfly's wings. Maybe magic.

And then the butterfly erupts into light.

"Mars!"

I snap from my trance as the girls rush to put out the tiny, smoldering fire that's appeared on the blanket. Right where the butterfly was.

Oh no.

The glass of water in my hand and the sunlight magnified through it. It must have formed a beam, and . . .

The smoke curls away from a pile of blackened, ruined wings. I'm shocked at what I've done. I drop the glass, and beads of water crawl down my thighs. I—

"Mars."

Bria, her voice cool and calm. I look up. The amusement in her lips douses my panic. It's just me and her for a second as she raises a hand and there, on her knuckle, quivers the butterfly. When I look at the blanket, the crumpled body is gone. It's just a hole eaten away by the light. Just a void in the curious shape of wings.

"Close call," Bria says. She's scolding me, but there's a playfulness behind the warning. Like we share a secret.

The butterfly flits away, and it seems like the most marvelous thing in the world as I try to remember what just happened.

"Oh, Mars, here," Kyle says, pulling us back to the others. She's brought me a bundle of clothes, which she's been promising to do. I forget the butterfly and, right in front of them, exchange my wet uniform for a cute little crop top.

"I wish I had arms like that," Kyle sighs, flexing.

"Your arms are great, Kyle. Shut up," Bria says. "But she's right, Mars. You should go sleeveless all the time. I bet Wyatt would finally make a move if you did."

Again I catch that sly amusement just under Bria's words. Are we friends with inside jokes now? I swat her knee, playfully. She swats back, and my heart sings.

"You should try to talk with him more," Bria urges. "Maybe we've been too selfish, hoarding you to ourselves. I think we frighten him away."

"I don't know," I say. "It comes and it goes with Wyatt. Sometimes I think he's into me, sometimes I think he's just curious."

"Could be the same thing," Mimi says.

"Could be," I say.

The Honeys involve themselves in a complicated scheme to lock Wyatt and me in a cedar closet together, or somewhere in the dark behind the theater's curtain, or the damp tile maze of the pool locker rooms.

"Would you?" Mimi asks. She deepens her voice when she does, filling it with the scarlet of scandal.

"He's older," I say.

"By a year."

"By nine months, actually." I'm blushing.

"See?" Mimi claps. "It's love. You're in love."

"Answer the question, though," Bria says, much cooler. "Would you?"

I never answer, because Wyatt himself appears at the edge of our dreaming little bubble. I half expect him to knock, as if the partition between us and the rest of the lawn is physical.

"We're heading back to Hunter Village," he says, jerking his thumb. He's clipped and mechanical, like he gets around the girls. For a second, I don't move—I pretend that it's me that makes his nonchalance fumble, stretched atop the blanket in a crop top. Comfortable. Myself.

He walks off, blushing.

"You say you can't manifest the future," Mimi murmurs. "But that crop top implies otherwise."

We stifle our laughter so that Wyatt doesn't hear. Then I gather my things and saunter after.

The next day, the girls don't come into camp after lunch, so I hang with the boys during Cabin Challenge. Our assignment is to drag kayaks out of the boathouse and into the nearby woods so they can make room for some sort of presentation. We turn it into a race, and Andrea and I dominate the others. Eventually the boys get into one of the kayaks and slide it down the grassy hill. We take turns until Wyatt gets us to stop, but when he's gone, we just do it again.

It's strange, playing with them. Fun. Nice. It makes me wonder: Why oh why, Mars, didn't you become friends with them sooner?

Tyler is the only one who hangs back now. When I crawl from the toppled kayak, breathless with laughter, the sight of him glaring at me from the shade snatches the air from my lungs.

The Honeys asked me why he and I hate each other. I said we don't. We just survive in different ways. Tyler assimilates, and since I can't do that, I resort to exceptionalism. We both cost the other their advantage if we circle too close.

When we break in a circle below the willow tree, the boys resume their pastime of discussing, in grotesque detail, the girls of Aspen. This time is different, though, because they ask me to join.

"Mars, be honest. Who's actually the hottest?"

The boys stare at me with a remote hunger that I know isn't for me, but for what they assume I've seen. Still, it's me they're staring at. I'm not being ignored or dismissed. Inside myself I register the faintest, darkest glee in response to their invitation. I shiver. Who am I becoming?

"Ew, fuck off," I laugh, hoping they listen.

"Oh, come on," Ray says. "We won't tell. We Bear Swear it, right, guys?"

They shout *Bear Swear!* and shower me in macho begging. I wave it away and they switch to badgering questions.

"You're close with Mimi, right?" Mitch asks. "You think she'd be into this?" And he rubs his palm down his stomach. Then lower.

"Nah, man," another boy answers for me. "Mimi's a prude. You gotta target the sluts."

"Stop," I say. I think I say. They roll on until Wyatt cuts in and tells them, *Guys, cut that shit out.* I'm glaring at Brayden, who's lying against the

224

willow trunk grinning as this happens. Finally, I catch his eye and he just looks away. But he's still grinning.

"They're all sluts, I bet," says Mitch.

"Not Mimi; not when it comes to you," Ray claps back.

"Stop," I say, louder this time. "They're my friends."

"Yeah, but you're not one of them. You're one of *us*. So come on, man." Mitch puts his hands on his hip. The power pose. "Play matchmaker. What are they into?"

I stare at Mitch. He just keeps that smug smile on his lips, testing me. My jaw hurts from clenching so hard. I'm furious with myself. I don't want to be in with the boys if this is what it costs.

I take in a long, slow breath.

"What are they *into*? Not a seventeen-year-old with weapons-grade halitosis."

Mitch's smug face ices over and the boys erupt in laughter. It makes me even madder. I point at the next one.

"And not those marshmallow-puffed gums. Try flossing."

And the next one.

"Not that inbred-looking Hapsburg jaw. You look like a deep-sea fish."

And the next. *Chinless lawn gnome with haunted Victorian doll hands.*

And the next. *Anthropomorphic stubbed toe.*

Until I've snipped off a portion of each of their bodies.

"Not any of you," I say. "None of you have any idea how disgusting you are."

The laughter peters out long before I get through them all. I'm ready for them to strike back, but they don't. I dare them to with my glare, then look to Brayden.

"Not cool, man," he says, shaking his head with well-practiced disappointment.

Man.

"Are you kidding me? What about calling a group of girls sluts?"

Brayden keeps shaking his head. I don't see who, but one of the boys murmurs, "Well, they *are*," and this gets a dark chuckle out of the down-turned faces.

I sweep aside a curtain of willow branches and leave the circle. Wyatt chases me down.

"You can't just run to them," he says.

We're at the maw of the covered bridge. I'm breathing hard, and angry tears push through my lashes. Confused tears. I don't know what I'm becoming, here at Aspen. I barely look at Wyatt until he grasps my shoulders and turns me toward him.

"Don't listen to those guys," Wyatt says. "It's nothing. They're just being boys."

"What about Brayden?" I say. But I want to say, *What about me?*

I ask Wyatt: "What's a man got to do with the bad behavior of boys?"

Wyatt's jaw flexes like maybe he's thought about this, too. He doesn't ask me to get back to work, but I do, dragging out one kayak after another with no help as the boys murmur behind my back. I'm soaked with sweat by the time I'm done, and sore, and I take too long in the showers. The boys are quiet when I exit the bathroom, and even quieter when I get to my bunk. On my sheets is Caroline's candle. I'd almost forgotten that it went missing.

Taken, I remind myself. After I reported Callum.

When I pick the candle up, it slides apart, shattered like a bone still connected by the sinew of the wick. I have to cradle it. It can't be fixed. It's no longer a candle. It's a message, received.

CHAPTER 24

The first wave of parents arrives on Friday, just before dinner. Mine are not among them. Thank god. Part of me thinks that if they see I'm out here having fun in the woods, they'll stage an intervention and drag me back home.

Dinner will be in the dining pavilion. With the parents attending, there's an added air of performance to the routine, something dire about it that makes the Leaders nervous as we get changed. Our clothes are examined by Brayden and Wyatt for rogue grass stains, our hair is combed and gelled, and a few of the boys even shave. When Wyatt passes me during inspection, he only taps his nose. I make sure my septum ring is hidden. No one can see, but I also wear a crop top beneath my collared shirt. Just because.

At the dining pavilion, the banquet tables are clothed; the plastic plates and cups are swapped for ceramic and glass. Rather than the mad scramble to fetch platters from the kitchen, the staff has multiplied into a uniformed army that sweeps through the aisles, placing the platters before us. The food is performing, too. Summer salads bejeweled with cranberries and mandarin orange, cannelloni bean tartine, fillets of rosy salmon, and there's the whispering scent of forthcoming apple pie in the air.

"Culinary majors did a great job, didn't they?" Wyatt has turned into a one-man show for the few parents seated with Bear Hut. "I smelled them baking this bread this morning. It's amazing, right?"

The parents look so odd at the table. Like huge children, grinning at nothing and everything. Wyatt and Brayden ply the conversation with prompts, and the Bear Hut boys thaw into a performance of brags, playful jabs, and good-spirited teasing. It's not their usual electric cruelty. All the points are rounded off so that nothing pierces, only bruises. It's like the conversations I'm used to at my parents' house. Everything awful in the subtext, the surface kept clean and classy.

I'm silent. I haven't said much to these guys since the other day when I said way too much. They haven't spoken to me since. The candle was enough for now.

Wendy and the other directors take the parents for a sunset walk after dinner, which will end in the amphitheater. The night activity is yet another performance. A talent show, with the campers singing, dancing, reciting poems, and doing improv. Most of the parents are here for this.

Our cabin is in charge of setting up the amphitheater. With the adults gone, the boys revert to their usual coarseness. In fact, they seem intent on making up for their polite behavior. They start talking about which girls look like their moms, which moms they'd fuck. Wyatt makes a half-hearted effort to stop them, but Brayden just laughs, and it bolsters the boys.

"Hey, what about you, Mars?" Ray smirks at me.

They go quiet, the swell of crickets filling in. It's a hungry silence. I glance at Wyatt and his eyes are wide with fear, but I'm not losing my cool this time.

"Any daddies you got your eye on?" Ray presses.

"Yeah, yours," I say.

"My dad is dead," Ray says flatly, barely keeping a straight face as the boys erupt in snickering. His dad is fine. His dad was in the *Time* 100 last year. He mentions it all the time.

I shrug, and let the boys roll on with their porno hypotheticals. Soon the rest of the camp is filing into the amphitheater. The parents and little ones are given the front rows, and we're pushed to the very back.

It's like there's nothing onstage for my eyes to see. I sit off to the side, my anger stoking itself as I watch, clap, and watch. It's not the bright fury that made me snap under the willow tree. It's a low blue flame licking out from beneath the boulder of self-control I've dragged back into place. I should have never let it slip.

A screech returns me to the amphitheater. Feedback from a mic as the next act is introduced. I sit up when I see Bria waltz onstage holding, absurdly, a cello. I recognize two other girls from Cabin H, both with violins. Then there's a boy with what I think is a viola.

They begin a piece so quiet that the audience hushes. Even the crickets pause their incessant singing to listen. I forget my anger; I'm riveted now, too. I didn't know Bria played the cello. She never practiced in front of me, but she's incredible. Her cello emits a robust, hypnotizing hum. Together, the quartet layers over it, weaving together a sonic net that bundles my mind and lifts me up and up, out of my swaying body. Everyone else sways, too. Even the boys.

There's a small commotion at the edge of the stage, and from the wings bursts a figure swathed in lilac organza. A dancer. Then several dancers. They wear veils of sheer, frosty blue, their faces gasping and ghoulish as they lock hands, twist, and writhe. The music is classical, the dance is contemporary.

Then the music changes, skipping into something diabolically fast. The dancers back into a circle, each of them taking a solo in the middle. The girls are all different, some with balletic grace, some with jazzy gusto. I watch one girl who refrains, like she's nervous, until the swaying mass spits her forward. She glances back at them, betrayed.

She does dance, though. The music breaks through her nerves, and like a raindrop on a window she tumbles through her movements. Shy at first, fluid the next, then suddenly captivating. Wild is what she becomes, spinning so fast her veil rips away in the rising winds.

It's the girl from the boathouse. Her name is Sylvia, but she goes by Sylv. As I watch her dance, I feel dizzy and elated. I feel anchored, so deep within the earth I can sense its pulse in the roots of the aspen trees. But I'm in the sky, too. My perspective stretches across time and space, catching on the memory of Sylv crying in the boathouse. Then she's walking backward, rewinding through her own life. Sinking into her bed, rising in the night before. Manhunt Night, but Sylv is in a different, darker part of the woods with the other Leaders. I smell the stink of beer, and I feel the rough pads of greedy fingers digging downward. I'm watching it all happen to her, and I sense the Honeys watching with me. They want to know what makes Sylv cry; that's why they've made her dance.

I try to twist away from the memory that I know isn't mine; I ask to be shown something else. Anything, please. Where I land is a moonlit stretch of rock. I have no feet. I have no body. I'm only here as a watchful consciousness, as eyes that can't even close. There is something to witness—just for me, I feel—but I don't know what. Maybe the serrated edge of the trees closing over the sky? Maybe something below? Maybe the sticky splash of black driving down the rock, into the soil.

Maybe the girl, laid out on her back in the center of the bloody mess, watching me as she dies.

I don't know her name, but I know her face from a photo I once found. And I've seen this scene before. When? I sink backward, upward, outward. Now I'm watching myself in a sunlit clearing, playing a game of tiles with Bria. I see myself gathered in the mesmerizing lace of light as our hands form designs, see Bria dig through my thoughts, see myself retaliate and dig through hers. Then I see her push me from it all, slapping me back to earth, and the girls swarm over me.

They did something to me, took something from me. Carved the doubt from my insides. But from the outside their motions are barely even visible. Just microscopic twitches in their fingers as they pet the blood off my scalp, and I just lie there letting them.

My doubts. My dread. Destroyed. Incinerated, like the butterfly on the blanket.

I think again of the girl on the rock, and now I know her name.

"Sierra," I whisper out loud as applause overtakes the amphitheater, the dance finished.

Sierra. Her name is Sierra. Of course I know Sierra. The memory of her breaches my mind with violent recognition. I know she was here this summer, and that she painted my nails, and that she dabbed blush onto my cheeks at the formal. What about after that? Where did she go? To that rock, to her doom. But how?

I stand with everyone else to clap as the cast bows. The vision of Sierra on the bloody rock passes over the memory of Caroline in the foyer. The two fallen girls eclipse each other, aligning with an evil, breathtaking symmetry. They speak in one, imploring command.

"Earth to Mars," I remind myself.

Wake up.

Come back down.

Help us.

I know I'm clapping but I can't feel a thing. It's like my first night at Aspen, during the evening Embers, when I searched the crowd and found Bria already watching me, a smile on her lips. A smile that knew about things I couldn't even begin to guess.

One of the Honeys is helping Sylv stand from where she's collapsed, panting at the stage's edge. No one seems to notice, or to care, that she is crying. Through the forest of clapping hands, through the bowing dancers, I lock eyes with Bria on the stage. She's watching me once again.

This time, she isn't smiling.

CHAPTER 25

I don't dream, because I don't sleep. I lie in bed and stare into the unblinking eyes in the wood, slowly suturing together the fragments of my memory. The more I focus on the vision of bloody Sierra on the rock, the greater the stain around her grows, dripping through my memories from the last week until they're soaked through. Then comes the fear.

I knew it, and they made me forget. And the moment in the woods with Callum, too. It rings with the same threatening frequency. A warp in the comb of my memories.

I don't know what time it is when I decide to get up. I barely even decide. I just sit up and dress in the dark, then descend the creaking staircase as quietly as I can. Brayden and Wyatt's door is ajar, like always. I push it open, but I don't wake them. Reason finally reaches me.

I can't trust these two either. I can't trust anyone but myself.

I arrived at Aspen knowing this, and then I forgot. But now I'm back to being me, free from that smothering lace that swaddled my mind. And as myself, I know what I've always known: I can only depend on what I can provide for myself. Nothing more, nothing further.

I grab Wyatt's keys from a hook on the wall, a new plan forming in my mind as I slip from Bear Hut. By now my feet know the path through the forest. I jump along the bars of moonlight falling through the trees. I push myself to think, despite the dread. I have to, if I'm going to figure out what's happening here.

I need to be rational, but in the darkness it's easy to conclude that whatever spell I've surfaced from is supernatural. Out in the woods, with nothing but the steam of my own breath and the mournful plea of the loons off the lake, phantoms feel material.

This doesn't scare me. I don't fear the dark. I know the dark, and it knows me. Within it, I'm safe from the sun's lovely illusions. I know what I've always known: The monsters worth fearing are the ones that are dangerous enough to hide in daylight.

Camp is trapped in snapshot stillness when I arrive. The banners for the July Jubilee hang lifeless in the humidity. I jog to the Eco-Lab and use Wyatt's fob to unlock the doors. I lower the shades and find the light switch, flicking it on for long enough to see what I need—the surge protector for the computers, a chair, some paper, a pen—and then back into the dark I go. Soon I'm sitting in an icy glow from the monitors, an empty search bar blinking before me.

I type: *aspen conservancy deaths*

I wince. The first results are, of course, news coverage of Caroline's death. Lots of articles about my mom. I scroll past them, but only hit more memorials. Obituaries, mostly of rich people, attributing their best memories and friends to Aspen. Yuck.

One obituary stands out. It's of a young girl who couldn't have been more than a year older than me and Caroline. And she died last year. I squint at her photo—she has big cheeks. Freckles. She looks so familiar, I find myself placing her in the photo I found with Sierra. Was she here at Aspen as recently as last year?

According to her obituary she died at home, in August. The same August Caroline came home scared. The cause of death isn't noted, but after some searching, I find an online fundraiser in her honor. The cause: a fund to research cancers of the brain.

A chill rolls through me. I push myself to keep going.

Next, I look for accidents or scandals around Aspen. There's an article about a car crash that claimed the lives of six campers, but it's a different camp. Several other stories like it—a bus crash, a drowning, a few freak accidents—pop up, and they all have one thing in common: None of the stories I find have anything to do with Aspen.

Aspen, a camp that's been operating for over a century, exists beyond blemish. That's strange to me.

I broaden my search: *catskills missing persons*

There are many results. I open a spreadsheet and start typing. An hour later my spreadsheet is full of dates, names, and personal details. I add whatever I can find, including area of residence. I pull up a map of the Catskills, list out the towns near Aspen, and cross-reference that against my list. I make a few pivot tables, too, but I'm not sure what I'm looking for. Anything, I guess.

My cursor hovers in the empty search bar, my previous searches glaring back at me.

aspen conservancy deaths
aspen conservancy scandals
catskills missing persons

Sierra once told me: *There's more. Keep going.* What did she want me to find?

I skim my list of other people vanished by the Catskills. I remember the stories the boys like to tell, about hunters who just walked into the woods and never came out. And I think of Brayden's insistence that the aspen trees, ever watching, claim only those who would do the forest harm. What could these people have done?

I begin to look deeper, past the tributes and articles covering ongoing cases, into the lives of each person prior. I'm not sure what I'm looking for until I find it for each person, but I know it when I see it.

One man killed a family in a drunk-driving accident. He went missing the next summer.

There's a SUNY student who was implicated in the death of another student, through hazing. She went missing in the summer, too.

All over, I find guilty people vanishing into summer's maw. Soon I have a new list with only a few names on it. Each person on my list went missing in this area, one per year, right around now. Just like Sierra.

I sit back and look at the list, my eyes throbbing from staring into the glowing screen for so long. It's hard to know what I've found or if I've found anything at all. A few hours of research in the dead of night is, I realize, not the airtight case I was hoping for. But it's not nothing either.

I find some paper and a pen. I scribble the names, dates, and details into a hand-drawn grid. Then I delete my spreadsheet and close out all my windows. All but one. Yet another write-up about Caroline's death, but from a local paper. It's not the article that stops me, though. It's a related piece at the bottom. Another click and I'm looking at what caught my eye: a photo of my mom at some long-past fundraising event. And there, smiling behind her, is Wendy.

At first I don't understand. Then I do. Wyatt's family manages the Conservancy, but the state owns and protects the land. Mom's a senator; she does all sorts of press events for the New York State Department of Environmental Conservation. Ironically, most of it is against her will. "I don't trust them. They care more about trees than people," she used to say all the time.

I suspect there's more truth to that than she could have known. I close the window and clear the browser history before shutting down the computer. As I lean back in the chair, I stare at my reflection in the blackened screen and finally see the person sitting behind me in the lab.

I run for the door, my chair crashing behind me. I hit a table, swear, try to keep going. The person slams me into the painting of the cage of the back wall. *How big is your wingspan?* I think absurdly as we wrestle. Then I hear their voice.

"Mars. Mars, it's me. *Stop.*"

I stop struggling. Wyatt lets me go.

"Quiet," he says.

"*You* be quiet."

"I was. For, like, ten minutes while I watched you. What the hell are you doing here?"

I can barely see Wyatt in the dark of the lab. The urge to throw open the shades itches in my hands. I need to see his face. I need to see what he knows about this.

"Something is wrong," I say. "Something is wrong with this place."

"With Aspen? What are you talking about?"

"I'll prove it," I assure him, spreading my crumpled list onto a table. I urge Wyatt closer. He doesn't move. From his backlit shape alone, I can tell he thinks I've truly lost it. It makes me realize how frantic I must look.

"I'm not crazy," I say.

Wyatt tilts his head. "I watched you break and enter so that you could make an Excel spreadsheet in the dead of night, Mars."

Okay, point. I start to feel very, very silly.

"How did you know I was here?" I ask.

"Followed you. Where are my keys?"

"Sorry," I say, tossing them back.

"Why, Mars? What's going on?"

When I don't answer, Wyatt strides to the door. He flicks on the light and then snatches up the telephone from its mount on the wall.

"This goes to the offices, and the office line forwards to Wendy's cell. Tell me what's going on or I'm getting her on the phone."

"No!" I rush to the phone and hold it down. Wyatt peers at me down the line of his nose. He's in just a white shirt, his hair pressed sideways from his pillow. He looks tired, and mad, and betrayed. But he doesn't look sinister.

"I'll tell you," I say, my hand still on his, both our hands on the phone. "Just turn off the light."

In the doused chill of the Eco-Lab, Wyatt and I sit on a table across from each other, bell jars of insects floating around us like silvery bubbles. I start with the strange vision I had at the recital, and how it reminded me of Sierra. I have to tell Wyatt who Sierra is because he still can't remember her. Then I show him the list of people who have vanished, and finally I tell him my theory.

"People go missing near Aspen this time every year, and I think the girls in Cabin H have something to do with it. I think Sierra tried to warn me when she told me there was more to the Honeys, and they made her disappear. Maybe Caroline did the same thing."

Wyatt holds the list up to the moonlight, squinting at the names.

"If she was actually a camper, Aspen would have reported Sierra missing the second she didn't show up for something."

"Not if it's Aspen that's covering it up," I press.

"Aspen isn't covering anything up," Wyatt snaps. He turns away from me. I can see by the rigidity in his shoulders that I've lost him. Maybe I can pull him back.

"What about the missing people?" I ask.

"The woods are dangerous, Mars."

"But what about the dates?"

"You're really shocked people are in the woods during the *summer*?"

He's past listening. Wyatt grabs up my list and heads for the door. I run after him. Our debate resumes in the heat of the night as Wyatt walks us back toward Hunter Village. I almost have to jog to keep up with him.

"Just think about it, Wyatt." I'm begging now, and I don't care. "How does an entire camp just forget about a girl? A *popular* girl? She was here and then she was gone, and no one even cares."

"Did you look her up?"

I stumble over a rock, barely catching myself. Wyatt doesn't slow down. "I don't know her last name."

"So you broke into the Eco-Lab and instead of looking up the person you're seeking, you just created a list of a dozen *other* missing people? Did Aspen forget about them, too?"

"No, that's not what I mean. Or—I don't know. Maybe. Look, I'm sorry for stealing your keys—"

"And breaking, and entering, and—"

"But, Wyatt, listen to me, *please*."

We both halt, because I've grabbed Wyatt's wrist. He looks at where I hold him, disgusted. He looks like one of the boys. Anonymous among the Aspen Elites. I was an idiot, telling him all this. This is his home. I let him go.

"Sometimes people die, Mars," Wyatt says in a low growl. "When Jeremy died, I was desperate for explanations, too. But you know what? Sometimes people just die, and there's no mystery to it, or conspiracy, or cover-up. There's no reason at all. Trust me, I of all people know how hard that is to hear, but you're not doing your sister's memory any favors with this."

It's my turn to pull away.

"This isn't about my sister," I say.

"That's right. It's about you."

Wyatt bears down on me. His finger rises to jab at my face.

"If this was about your sister, you'd respect her memory and let her go, but this is about *you*, Mars. You can't accept that she might have actually loved this place, so now you're rationalizing it, and it's driving you crazy. You've made enemies with your cabin, with Brayden, with Wendy, and now with me. And none of it satisfied you, did it? So now you're making enemies out of those girls. Next, it's Aspen. And then what? Are you going to really blame the fucking Catskill mountain range?"

Wyatt blows out a breath, steam billowing in the silence that gathers between us. I can't even blink.

"I know that grief can make you feel crazy," he says. "But you can't let it get away with it. You've got to let it go before it takes you down with it."

"This isn't about grief," I say. I choke on the lie. It is—all of it is—about grief for me. But there's more, just like Sierra said. And I'm so, *so* close. I know it.

Wyatt goes to hug me and I push him away.

"Fine," I say. "Let's just talk about it tomorrow."

"Okay."

"Are you going to tell Wendy?"

Wyatt takes a while to respond.

"I woke Brayden up before I left. I'm sorry, Mars. I had to. I think this has gotten to a point where safety is a concern. Maybe Wendy was right. Maybe this isn't the best place for you right now."

"They'll make me leave," I whisper.

"I know," Wyatt says. "I'm sorry."

Wyatt's words have the impact of cannon fire. My anger, thick as it is, cracks apart. It's over. I'm done. I'm going home, and all of Aspen's mysteries will remain, blazing bright and unknowable. I wasn't careful enough. I wasn't smart enough. I wasn't focused enough. I'm losing Caroline again, no closer to understanding her suffering now than I was the moment I saw those bees crawl out of her head.

The remaining hike back to Hunter Village is painfully short. The cabin looms dark and dead, no lights on, like a sealed verdict. Wyatt wordlessly escorts me up to my bunk, then makes sure I get under the covers before going downstairs. He takes my list with him.

I find Caroline's hive tool in my cubby and hold it against my chest until it's as warm as my skin. Then I imagine it's actually the metal that's warm, and I'm the lifeless weapon.

I'm not tired in the morning. I'm not anything. The emptiness pervades all of me, like my skin is a thin balloon that's slowly collapsing. Wyatt won't look at me during chapel. I wait to see Brayden appear in the Hunter Lodge doorway during breakfast, to tell me to pack it up. But he's not in the Village. Probably he's with Wendy, at the Welcome Center, waiting for my parents to answer their phones.

I perform my chores. I hook my hive tool to my belt, pretending at normal. We head into camp and find a mob of parents on the main lawn, polo shirt dads and tennis skirt moms towing after their excited kids. Aspen has put out a table with copper cisterns of coffee, water for tea, and mountains of jewel-bright fruit. Wendy shows up on the porch of Big Lodge to welcome everyone, but she's there and then gone, leaving her staff to organize the day's activities without her. I almost follow her, wanting to get my own execution over with. I only stay put because a lifetime of training tells me exactly what to do, which is to pretend that nothing is the matter at all.

The day's activities are announced. There will be tutorials in the morning, athletics in the afternoon, and tonight a production of Shakespeare. Instructors for the majors are called out, each raising their hands in a big wave so parents know who to follow. Leena isn't among them. In fact, I don't see any of the Cabin H girls here.

By force, I make myself think of anything other than those girls. I have to pry them out of my mind. The ragged devastation they leave behind is sticky with gore. But if Wyatt's right—if this is a delusion inspired by my grief—all I can do is purge the infestation and hope that the scars heal quickly.

I tell myself all of this, but I still spend the morning at the boathouse, my eyes ticking from the colorful sails slicing over the black lake, to the meadow, to the covered bridge. No one crosses it. None of the parents venture out to Cabin H, and the girls don't come in.

Somehow, I'm still here at lunch when Wyatt pulls me out onto the dining pavilion porch.

"We need to talk," he whispers so the milling parents don't hear us.

"Is it time?"

I have to lean in to hear his next words.

"When we got back last night, Brayden wasn't in the cabin. I assumed he went to meet with Wendy, but Wendy just asked me where he is."

Wyatt's jumpiness sneaks under my own skin. I don't know what he's saying, but I start to shiver despite the heat.

"Wendy doesn't know about last night," Wyatt whispers. "Like, at all. Because Brayden never made it to her. He's missing, Mars."

CHAPTER 26

Brayden is missing.

I blink, and I think my eyes widen, but I manage to keep my face absent of my spiking anxiety. And glee. Wendy doesn't know, so I have more time. But . . .

Brayden . . . is missing?

I've seen Wyatt both angry and kind. Playful and pensive. But never scared. This is new.

"Say more," I urge.

"I told Wendy no one's seen Brayden since last night, and she just brushed it off. She says he probably just has the weekend off."

"Could he, though?"

Wyatt shakes his head. His curls vibrate with his worry. "No one gets Jubilee Weekend off. It's a big rule, and Brayden has jobs to do that I've been covering all day. Plus, why would he just leave in the middle of the night? It makes no sense."

I don't really think Brayden took the weekend off. I just want Wyatt to hear himself admit he knows Wendy is lying to him.

"So what do we do?" I ask.

Wyatt stands up straighter, gives me a stern look. "Nothing, Mars. This has nothing to do with us. Or your list of names. It's probably just a coincidence."

I have a choice here. I can remain a drifting deflation in Mars-shaped skin. Or I can pull myself together. I choose myself, together, and it keeps my voice low and sure.

"If this has nothing to do with last night, you would have gone to

Wendy and told her about me sneaking out yourself. But you didn't. Because you think there's a connection between Brayden and the people who go missing near Aspen. You think I'm right."

Wyatt shakes his head. "No. I don't."

"Then why are you coming to me with this when you *should* be getting me kicked out?"

Effortlessly, Wyatt's face clicks into a dazzling smile for a pair of parents who float too close to us. We are both flickering between selves—our conditioned performance and our hidden reality. I want to take his hand and ground him here. We're discovering something real.

"I promise you there's an explanation," he whispers, false smile still on his lips. "Brayden has gotten in trouble before for sneaking out. Other shit, too, I think. I'm telling you this so you don't go looking for him in the middle of the night. It's dangerous, Mars, and my job is to keep you safe. I can't do that if you keep going rogue. You do what you did last night again and I *am* telling Wendy myself. Please don't hate me."

I roll my eyes. I'm not nervous anymore. Wyatt is shitty at bluffing. He won't rat me out, because now he's seen enough with his own eyes, and the right conclusions are unavoidable. Doubt is the gift I've given him, but Wendy is the one who unwrapped it. She's lying, and now Wyatt knows it.

There is something very, very wrong happening at Aspen.

I sit through lunch, looking for any clues among the counselors at the banquet tables. If they know what's happening, they don't show it. The only hint I see is when Donovan, Aspen's co-director, decides to accompany our cabin over to the athletic complex. I bet he'll stick around for the rest of the day to cover for Brayden's absence.

All afternoon I wander between activities, but I never see the Cabin H girls, or even Leena. I only see Wendy once, chatting with parents on the porch of Big Lodge, and her act is perfectly jovial. Donovan sits with us at dinner again. He's loud and quick-witted, and he fills the conversation with a jack-hammer laugh, but by now the other Hunters are whispering. Brayden's absence has been noted, but not explained. When I ask Donovan on the way to the theater, he shrugs it off.

"Dunno," he says. "I'm sure he's around. Don't worry about it."

It.

Not *him*.

While we file into the theater building, I think about the moment last night when Bria locked eyes with me over the applauding crowd. The memory adds to the strange surreality of Brayden's erasure. And the moments before—when I watched Sylv dance, and my mind floated elsewhere, saw things I can't explain but know are true—what was that? It felt . . . familiar. Like the stolen memory of playing tiles with Bria. It felt like washing dishes in Cabin H. I felt *joined* to some vast and tangled knowledge, and now, a day later, I catch myself missing it. Just a little. But enough to make me doubt my own intentions as I scheme.

The play begins. We sit in polite attentiveness as students waltz across the set with great import, spewing absolute nonsense with breathless conviction.

What am I not seeing?

I explore all that I can recall of Cabin H's insides for anything I missed. A trapdoor leading into a secret cellar, or maybe a spot of blood on the lace. But when I think of the cabin, I feel the same intoxicating longing, so I veer from it. Pan out. I view the meadow and its hives, bank around the cabin and finally come to . . .

The shed.

At intermission I tell Donovan I need to use the bathroom, and Wyatt jumps up, offering to go with me.

Donovan gives us a double thumbs-up. "Buddy system. I like it."

"You don't have to use the bathroom, do you?" Wyatt says as soon as we're outside the theater.

"Nope."

"Mars. Come on. Don't do this again."

"Go back if you want," I tell him as I march toward the boathouse. Wyatt must know what I'm thinking because he runs in front of me to block my path.

"Stop. I'm going to go get Wendy right now if you don't turn around."

I sidestep Wyatt. "Get her. I want her useless ass to see something."

"See *what*, Mars?"

"The shed."

Surprise flashes across Wyatt's face, like he's just now remembering the lone shed back up against the trees of the Cabin H property. It's the opening I need.

"It's the one place we aren't allowed to go. Isn't that weird? The girls even let us into their cabin, but not the shed. Why not? Did you ever use it when you helped your grandfather?"

"It's new," Wyatt says, and now he sounds unsure. "Leena built it a few years ago."

I march on. Wyatt pads after me. We pass through the covered bridge and this seems to bolster his protests.

"What do you think you'll find? Evil beekeeping suits?"

"I heard the girls in there once, talking about some sort of violence. Maybe they were planning something? I don't know. That's why we're going."

"*You're* going. I'm stopping you."

"You're doing a very bad job."

Wyatt scoffs, but he's still with me. We're in the forest now, dusk turning everything into a net of dark greens and blues that crisscrosses the burning orange sky. He has a tiny flashlight on his key chain and he plays with it, but leaves it off.

"The way I see it," I say through heavy breaths as we climb uphill, "you know something is up with Aspen, but you're too conditioned to actually break a rule. So you're using me to break all the rules for you. You want to know just as bad as I do."

"That's absurd."

"Then go." I stop, teetering on the slope. I sweep my arms out at the forest, back toward the way we came.

Wyatt huffs. "I'm not letting you go alone."

I can't help but grin as we pick up our pace. We end up reaching the clearing just as the sun drops behind the horizon, darkening the field before us. Dots of neon zip over the high grass. Fireflies. The cottage's lights are all on, and shapes move behind the thin curtains.

I pull Wyatt into the brush, but it's him who leads our slow progress toward the shed. Approached from behind, it's bigger than I thought, with plywood rooms barnacled to its back. I'm barely breathing as we reach the dirty windows and look inside.

"I don't see anything," Wyatt says. "Happy?"

"Never."

"You should work on that."

"You should accept people as they are."

Wyatt ducks down and drags me with him, holding me still. He points, and through the gloom I see someone running in the woods. As she gets closer, I realize she's on the path I spotted forever ago that bypasses the shed and leads off into the woods, away from Aspen. The shed blocks it.

The girl bounds up the steps of Cabin H and darts inside. A second later the night is full of squeals and screams. The commotion boils out of the cabin in the form of many girls, all in fresh white Aspen uniforms. Their laughter fills the dusk as they wind into the woods, linked by their pinkies, back the way the girl came from.

"What's that way?" I ask Wyatt.

"Nothing. Wetlands. Then the mountains."

The girls have vanished, but we can still hear their laughter. We follow after on the narrow path. It pulls us away from the lake, down a gentle slope, to a swamp. The sky opens up as the forest dissolves into sopping puddles and grassy islands. The pine trees retreat, and soon everywhere I look I see the spindly gray-silver aspen trees, black sockets winking in the moonlight. They are utterly still, until a faint breeze breathes a tremble into their branches.

Wyatt reaches for his keys and clicks on his tiny flashlight, but I jump to cover it.

"They'll see," I whisper.

Wyatt nods and we continue in the draining light of the blue-plum sky. We follow a path that converts to an ancient wooden boardwalk cutting through the tall swamp grasses. Out here, the fireflies are everywhere. I'm afraid the girls will spot us, but we can't even see them anymore. Or hear them. Instead, the air is thick with croaks and chirps, and the needling whine of mosquitoes that feast on our bare arms and necks. Soon it's too dark to continue. We're about to have to feel our way forward, when finally the clouds unveil the moon, and out of the darkness rises the inorganic structure of a building. We've reached the swamp's opposite border.

It sits at the far edge of an overgrown lawn, beyond a boulevard of noble conifers. Even in the darkness I know it's abandoned. Entire sections of its outer walls have rotted away, and the moonlight fills breaches like cavities rotting a tooth. It's utterly quiet now, no laughter to follow. We approach the building, spellbound and reverent, like we may wake it up.

"What is this place?" I ask Wyatt.

"A hotel, I think. There's a few of them in the Catskills, left behind like this. But I didn't know there was one on the property."

We pass through a graveyard of wicker chairs and a tennis court cracked open by saplings. I feel that if we screamed, the silence of this place would swallow it up. I don't want to go inside, but I need to know more. Everything.

An outdoor pool wraps around the building's back, furry with moss, a playful breeze rippling across a low tide of ferns. We keep out of the moonlight as we ascend a crumbling staircase to a wide doorframe absent of doors. Pitch black waits beyond and, with a nod, we venture into it. We stay close as we shuffle over carpets squishy with mold, to a lobby completely exposed to the sky. Moonlight pours in, bathing entire trees that have grown from the floor. We find a staircase and climb, the whole time listening for any indication of life within. I only hear drips that echo in the dank air, and a sweet breeze gasping over the walls of ivy. Beneath it all is the muffled thrum of my own heartbeat.

"Mars," Wyatt whispers, and I realize I've ventured off. He's in a vast dining room near what I think is a fireplace, except . . . different. *Wrong* is the word that pops into my head as he clicks his meager flashlight onto something I can't make sense of. The mantel bulges from the wall in papery mounds, like a monstrous fungus has been poured down the chimney.

"Listen," Wyatt says.

What I hear is a new thrum. Not my heartbeat, but something beyond me. A sonic richness so low I can feel it more than hear it, and it's coming from the wall.

"Bees," Wyatt says. "It's a beehive."

We step away automatically. The hive flows up into the fireplace. Bees build downward, I remember, so likely they started at the top of the chimney and descended. I wonder how far it goes down into the building's rotting body.

"The basement," I say.

From the lobby comes the echo of laughter. Wyatt turns off his light.

We creep to the lobby, keeping hidden as the halls fill with chatter and footsteps. The girls appear a second later from a side passage, chained together by their pinkies. They make no effort to be quiet, and as soon as they're gone the silence sucks back into the space. It's like they were never there at all.

I still feel the tingle of the hive we just witnessed. I still feel the need to go deeper.

"This way," I whisper.

I lead us down the way the girls came. Immediately I sense the temperature rise. It ticks upward as we enter a kitchen, Wyatt's flashlight blinking on to reveal grimy tile floors and butcher-block counters fuzzed in fungus. I feel for the heat's source and find a stairwell. Warmth rises up like a hot breath, carrying the smell of beeswax.

We descend. Wyatt goes first with his light. Small bodies dart around us, invisible outside the illuminated cone. I feel the tickle of one land on my outstretched hand. A honeybee. We can hear their drone distinctly now, and the ceiling actually drips with honeycomb in places. When I nearly stumble and fall into one of the structures, Wyatt grabs me and holds on, driving the light directly into the dark before us. We progress like that, with only a few feet of visibility, the walls twisting and enfolding, until the passage opens into a room so big that the flashlight's weak beam can't find its ceiling. Instead, great curtains of honeycomb hang down, growing thicker toward the room's back, folding over one another to form a lacy stalactite.

Wyatt aims the light back down, just in time to stop us from walking into a sudden drop. It's the edge of the basin over which the hive hangs. I shiver, peering into it, because I know what it will contain.

Honey. Dark, glassy honey.

Wyatt's arm remains around me as he raises the flashlight back up to inspect the monstrous hive.

"Where are the bees?" he asks.

The air hums with their drone, but he's right. The bizarre structure is oddly desolate of any visible swarms. A hive this big would have millions of them, but only a few lone honeybees halo our heads.

"I can hear them," Wyatt whispers. "It's like they're everywhere . . ."

As though he can surprise them, Wyatt flicks the flashlight into the corners, back and forth, until it snags on something moving along the honeycomb near us. A fluid twist, like many small bodies crawling over one another. But under the glare it's just honeycomb.

Until it opens its eyes.

"Help me," it says. "Please help me."

It twists again, something huge beneath the comb. Encased in it. A mouth, a nose, a strangely bent arm, a crumpled hand.

A person.

"Brayden," Wyatt whispers.

"Please. I feel—" Brayden shudders, and the honeycomb creaks. "Please," he begs.

I hack at the comb with my hive tool and Wyatt just uses his hands. The light whips around us as we pull down the delicate, sticky structure, digging until we find the naked body below. Brayden whimpers. He's badly hurt, though I can't see where. But I can smell the hurt. Blood and a darker odor. Sweet and rotten and thickening as we pry him out.

The bees, invisible as they are, let us know they're angry. Their drone rises into an undulating siren, then a crackling threat. I drive my hands into the sticky shards, desperate now. Honey fills my nail beds, webs between my fingers, drips to my elbows. But Brayden is nearly free. Just another chunk and . . .

Brayden's weight does the rest. He slides from the comb, falling into Wyatt and blotting out the flashlight.

I go to help but then freeze.

The flashlight has become a harsh glare caught between them. For a moment it appears to pass right through Brayden, taking on the golden-scarlet hue of his flesh, embryonic and quivering as he clings to Wyatt. Within him I see a squiggly network of veins twisting together into a mass that, quite clearly, pulses.

His heart.

"Wyatt," I say.

"Help me with him," Wyatt snaps, and I rush forward. I grab Brayden's arm, and when I pull, his flesh slides right off the bone.

I scream until I get the flopping sleeve unstuck from my hands. Brayden has crumpled between us, golden threads strung between him and Wyatt. Wyatt fumbles until he recovers the flashlight, aiming it at Brayden.

Holes. Everywhere, Brayden's flesh is pocked in holes, clean and precise and *weeping* with honey. He cradles the bones of his hand with his remaining arm. His bones are soft, too, like warm rubber. He looks at us and his eyes are scoops of yellow jelly in his skull.

"I don't feel—"

He jolts and gags. A tooth drips from his lips and lands without a sound in the honey pooling around him.

"I don't feel so good. I don't—"

"We're gonna get you to a doctor!" Wyatt yells. He has to yell. The drone from the hives is loud now. Furious. I feel a prick, then a needling pain in my neck. I've been stung. Another one gets my knee. I pull at Wyatt's back.

"Wyatt, we need to—"

"DON'T LEAVE ME!" Brayden leaps at us but his legs buckle beneath him and he falls. His skeletal hand drags over Wyatt's chest, catching on the keys, tearing them off. The flashlight thuds into the honey, aimed upward into Brayden. The light passes through him. Like a jack-o'-lantern, he glows an eerie gold, his bones black and twisting below his viscous, dotted flesh.

Brayden screams again, his lower jaw yawning wide until it falls to the floor. Brayden implodes with it, smothering the flashlight. The light flickers beneath the quivering mass, flickers again, then goes out.

CHAPTER 27

A new light rises, one from within the honeycomb. It's not the harsh white of the lost flashlight but something more organic—a pulsing, waxy buttercup that gushes over us as we run. The walls themselves throb with it, the entire cavern vibrating as we stumble through the folding hallways.

When Wyatt falls, I'm down with him in a flash, heaving him up. But his foot is caught. The ghastly light shows us what's got him; a leg twisted into the comb, the shin drilled open with tiny holes. Within each I see a small white bead. Larvae.

I grab Wyatt's ankle and pull hard, cracking open the comb. The buttercup light flickers like a jostled light bulb.

"Run!" Wyatt screams.

Now I see them all around us. Phantom figures melted into the walls, the floor, the ceiling. The yellow light breaks around the shadows of shoulders, hips, skulls, and hands. Blurry bodies in the comb. I don't think about it as we run. The stings are incessant now. Clots of bees cling to my flesh like they're trying to burrow beneath it.

We hit the stairs, bounding up them two at a time. The kitchen feels icy compared with the damp heat of the basement, and this alone seems to repel the bees. But we don't stop. We run through the moonlit lobby, through the hallways of molded carpets, out to the waving ferns and the rotting wicker furniture. We run until we're flying over the narrow planks of the aspen swamp, fireflies streaking past us. We run until we reach the forest and realize in unison that what lies ahead is as bad as what lies behind. Cabin H, glowing between the trees, dark figures visible through the sheer curtains. Like those bodies swimming in the comb.

"This way," Wyatt whispers, driving us off the trail and into the woods. We walk until we can't see the cabin. When we find a stream, we stop to wash the honey from our hands. I scrub all the way up to my shoulders. Then I splash my face, the bracing cold a gift against the encroaching white dots that throb in my vision. We sit. We don't speak for minutes, until Wyatt asks, "Are you okay?"

"I got stung" is all I can say. The understatement is so vast that I almost laugh, but I don't. My skin feels so tight, like if I move it'll split over my cramping muscles.

"Are you okay?" I ask.

Wyatt doesn't say anything at all. His hands shake in his lap.

I reach for them because, suddenly, I need to know that his flesh is solid. And it is. I press my thumb into his palms until he blinks, focusing on me. His grip tightens. We stay like that until our fingers are stiff and our palms sweaty. Then, like my hands weren't enough, Wyatt hugs me.

He pulls away, the last of his tremors fading. I turn his wrist over so that I can check his watch. I press buttons until it lights up.

"Show me north," I say.

This tiny task shakes Wyatt out of his shock, but barely. He stares at the watch, turning it in a small circle, then points into the woods. "North."

He turns a quarter to the left.

"That way to the lake."

But we don't start walking. Both of us stand there, staring out into the vast night, the invisible borders of Aspen far beyond. It's like we can feel Aspen's bucolic dreaminess, and beneath it that candied, buzzing core.

Wyatt's hands are shaking again. He lets me take one, and that's how we finally move forward.

Walking up to Bear Hut is a strange parallel to the night before, except this time the porch light is on.

"What do we say?"

It's the most Wyatt's spoken since he found north in the woods.

"Do you have a radio? Can we get in touch with Wendy?"

"But the Jubilee," Wyatt mumbles. He sounds hollow. I can tell he's just barely standing at this point. I am, too, but I guess I'll have to be the strong one for now.

"Fuck the Jubilee," I groan. "We just watched Brayden *dissolve into honey*. We need to . . ."

I don't know what we need to do.

"I'm—" Wyatt slumps against me. I push him up and shake him until he opens his eyes, their usual mix of colors dull. Fading. In the porch light I can see that his face is covered in angry welts, each with a pinprick black stinger at the center.

"I'm tired," he grumbles.

Now that the pain has lessened, I can feel each throbbing welt on my own body. Still, I help Wyatt climb the stairs. I expect Donovan to be waiting for us in the common room, but it's blessedly empty. The clock on the kitchen oven reads 2:48 a.m. The numbers contract as another wave of exhaustion rolls over me. Carefully I guide Wyatt to his room and slough him off into his bed. I don't know if I should remove the stingers—I remember some note from Mimi that doing so injects even more venom into the body or something. I don't even know if the venom is deadly. For all I know, we'll both fall into comas in a few minutes.

Well, if I'm going to be in a coma I want to at least be in my bed. I trudge upstairs, to the dark dormitory, and halfway across the room the lights snap on.

Applause. The boys sit up in their bunks, clapping. I think, oh, I'm already in a coma and this is a dream.

Then Ray says, "So, you guys finally did it?"

I blink at him.

"They totally did," Charlie says. He sounds disbelieving, and repulsed.

"What?" I say.

"We covered for you," Mitch says. "Well, for Wyatt. He's our man."

The boys snicker. I sense subtext but don't understand it.

"We . . ." I don't know what I'm even about to deny. They think we had sex? They think we snuck away from *The Tempest* to . . . hook up?

"You owe us," Ray says. "Just remember that. You owe us, asshole." He snaps off the lights. The boys don't settle down, though. They carry on, riffing on hypotheticals of Wyatt and me in the woods. They whisper, but I can hear every word. Then just some words, my bed suddenly beneath me. Then nothing.

I awaken upright, hours later, as I'm standing in the shower numbly scratching at the welts on my skin. The stingers fall out one by one. Each barb I remove inches me closer to the surface beneath which I'm submerged until, gasping, I'm myself. I can think again.

I dash from the shower, pull on a uniform, and go to Wyatt's room. Donovan is kicked back on Brayden's bed.

"Goooood morning, Hunter!" he bellows. "Feeling better? The boys said you were *mighty* tired. Can't say I blame ya. That play, man."

"I'm okay, thank you," I manage. I'm about to rush to Hunter Lodge when I knock into a person right behind me in the hall.

"Mars. I'm here."

Wyatt pulls me into the kitchen. He looks fine. Totally fine. Or—no, not quite. Beneath his skin there's a feverish heat, and small rosy circles

259

show where the bees got him. He looks like I do; swollen and confused, like a newborn.

"Act cool," he whispers.

"Wyatt—"

"It was real," Wyatt says, but it's an open question.

"It was real," I confirm. "I mean, I think. I—"

Wyatt hushes me.

"Meet me after breakfast."

Wyatt leaves. I stand in the kitchen, gripping the counter's edge. The sink drips, drips, drips. And there's the mug I used my first morning here. I used it in a dream, I thought, but it's been here the whole time. It's a mocking reminder of a time I truly knew nothing about the beast I was begging to notice me.

That wasn't a dream. None of it was. I can't see how I ever got so confused, or how I ever thought the most sinister thing about Aspen was the sweet taste of its water.

I wash the stupid mug and place it, with shaking hands, in the hutch.

"What did you do, Caroline?" I ask the empty sink, as though the black of the drain will gargle forth a response. "What did you become?"

Breakfast is served in Hunter Lodge this time. A special treat for the families sticking around for the final day of Jubilee. Just families of the Hunters, though. It's indicated that the Amazons are having their own special breakfast, except Donovan calls it a "brunch" and chuckles at the idea of it. How cute.

Everyone is full of chuckles this morning, actually. The boys, Tyler back among them, elbow one another and glance between me and Wyatt with panting expectation. Wyatt does an okay job of acting normal, but he freezes when Wendy appears behind him, her hands falling onto his shoulders.

"I'll need to borrow some muscle for the morning," she says to Donovan. "Think you can spare a few?"

Donovan salutes her. Wendy picks Tyler, Mitch, and Ray. And of course Wyatt. I lift my hand to volunteer but catch an invisible shake of Wyatt's curls, and a look in his eyes urging me to stay put. My hand stays in my lap and I watch him go, hunched in apprehension.

He's right. No more focus on us, for now. Not as all of Aspen watches. All we can do is play along with the mass denial and wait for our chance to run. I keep my hive tool on my belt, brushing my knuckles over it every few seconds as we walk into camp. I wonder: *Was this a gift, too, Caroline? Did you know I would come here despite your warnings, and did you know I'd need it to pry myself back out?*

I don't remember the Jubilee farmer's market until I'm standing right below the banner. ASPEN FARMER'S MARKET it reads in big bubble letters. Then beneath that: FRESH VEGETABLES, ARTISAN CRAFTS, RAW HONEY. Small bees are painted looping around the letters. I painted those. I helped make this sign, just days ago with the Cabin H girls.

All around me, people are milling through farm stands boasting pastoral bounty. Farms from all over have traveled here, setting out overflowing displays of their harvests. Artisans, too. There are booths draped in quilts, and shelves overgrown with chunky ceramics, and of course a whole section of items produced by the craft hut kids. I step into the shade of one stand, overwhelmed by the scent of earth, of green. There are twisting carrots nicked in dirt; onions from amethyst purple to bone white; voluminous, corrugated kale bouquets.

I turn, trying to find Big Lodge in the background, but the market goes on in every direction. For a moment I'm completely lost. Then I smell it. The warm perfume of beeswax. I go still, and the crowd parts around me, revealing a stand at the market's middle.

It's under a high white tent, and the stand itself is a hexagon of rough wooden crates. Laid out are candles, ointments, soaps, lip balms, creams—all of it a creamy yellow that absorbs the day's brilliance, mutes it, wraps in the cloying scent of golden honey. There are, of course, jars of the stuff everywhere. They form molten pyramids, taking in the light and gilding everything around them. The girls working the stand hover in the golden light, appear to drift just outside accessible reality, like mirages. Like angels.

I tell myself to run. But I can't. I'm watching as the girls hand an older couple a jar of honey. The light catches it and I see that it's not a clear citrine, nor a lustrous gold, but a darker, deeper, red. Like mahogany wood stain. Like liquid garnet.

Like Brayden's melting body.

Like blood.

I back away and, in unison, the girls at the stand look at me. All of them but one. Bria, her back to me. But she must know I'm there, because after she finishes exchanging a pair of candles for some cash, she turns. We lock eyes. The pressure sets in right away, strands of the whispering lace reconnecting me to Bria's will, wrapping around my wrists, my neck, pulling me toward her.

But I step away. Bria's eyebrows knit in a kind of pity. She holds something up for me to see.

EARTH

Dangling between her elegant fingers is Wyatt's abandoned flashlight, clinking on its snapped key ring. I can hear it, because Bria can hear it, because something connects us now.

EARTH TO

A network spreads out from her, like she's the spider and I'm the fly straining against her web.

EARTH TO MARS

Something crosses in front of the sun, and the pressure in my mind

262

lessens. I can look away from Bria. It's Aspen's flag, snapping in a sudden gust of wind that quickly ripples through the market. The tents billow and lift, forcing people to cling to the posts to keep them from flying off. The girls scream, holding down their hair, but Bria's eyes are glued to me. In the time I've looked away, she's somehow crossed through the display, so that only a few steps separate us.

Her face twitches and blurs.

I run. I feel her eyes buzzing at the back of my skull. I don't look back. I dodge past the parents laughing at the windy pandemonium. I slip between the stands, and finally make it to the market's outer edge. Big Lodge is off to my right, but on the porch I see those ghostly white uniforms. A trio of girls, watching me. They wave when I see them. I run the other way, past the dining pavilion, past the boathouse, past the athletics complex, and into the woods. The rise of the valley slows me. My throat burns as I suck in shallow breaths, fighting a tightness in my chest.

I keep running until my legs are trembling so bad I have to stop. My sides ache with cramps. I pull myself a few more steps upward, then collapse in the crook of a tree jutting from the hill.

"Mars."

From above, hands drop onto my face. One hooks around my chin, another around my neck. They pull me up with so much force my teeth crack shut. My feet kick the air, my toes jam into a branch. The pain is nothing compared with the tightness of my skin ripping beneath their grip, like small nettles glove their palms. More hands clap over my mouth, my eyes. The nettles dig deeper, burrowing into my eyelids. Everywhere my skin erupts in aching fire. It's not the needling sting of the bees this time, but a thickly spread agony. Dull. Huge. Enveloping me as my senses shut down.

Then I can't feel anything at all.

CHAPTER 28

"Wake him."

The light comes for me all at once, dissolving the numb dark and resolving into a pastel rainbow just beyond my eyelids. The sense of being dragged skyward dissipates, like the sensation of falling in a dream. I jerk awake in a sea of plush velvet pillows. The sun winks at me through a sheer fabric canopy. Aspen trees, frail and trembling, reach up all around me. I shield my face, feeling for those burning hands, but my skin is cool. Free of fire.

I fight the dreamy vertigo and try to sit up. The hands find me again and I flinch, but they're cool this time. Gently, they pull me forward and place pillows behind my head. My eyes roll across the scene before me.

I sit at the head of a long table. It's actually a fallen tree split in half, its warps leveled and buffed to a glassy sheen. Streaks of moss swirl down the middle, like a table runner, and from the moss bursts colorful blooms in conspicuous arrangements. I get lost in the details until the small shifts in my periphery alert me to a major detail I've missed: Seated all around the table are people, so still I at first think they're statues. But now I see they're watching me. Waiting.

Their faces are blurry behind dark veils hanging from wide-brimmed wicker hats. The wicker weaves down over their shoulders like armor, forming breastplates and corsets with elaborate interlocking designs. Under the wicker, some wear dresses, some jumpsuits, but all of it is an incandescent white where the sunlight touches.

"Veils off."

In unison they pull off their hats, placing them on cushions at their sides.

"Welcome, Mars."

This time I see who's speaking. Bria sits across from me at the far end of the table. Her features swim in the super-heated air of the clearing.

"We're sorry to bring you here like this. Please understand we have as little choice in this as you do. The hive is higher."

Here. The aspen trees are spindly and spaced apart. Hints of sulfur and rot intermingle with the aroma of pollen, grass, and wildflowers. The sky is huge here. I'm in the swamp, out in the wetlands beyond Cabin H.

I try to speak but my mouth already feels full. I can't move my tongue.

"Remove it," Bria says.

Two girls sitting to my right and left lean over me. One opens my mouth, the other reaches in. I feel nothing as she gives a tug and out comes a small wooden star. Anise, like the fragrant stars that floated in the warm cider they gave me. With it out, I can feel my tongue again. I can taste the fading licorice on the back of my teeth as I chew away the numbness.

I try to talk. "What . . . ?"

The girls watch me. Faces still, their eyes shine with barely concealed hunger.

"What are . . . you?"

The girls turn to Bria. Bria is clearly in charge here.

"A sisterhood," she says. "Nothing more."

"Where . . ." I swallow. ". . . is Wyatt?"

"Safe. At Aspen. We won't harm him."

I feel more myself with every second. The clumsiness melts from my fingers. I can wiggle my toes. I'm sore, but I can move. I think about running and the second the thought forms, one of the girls beside me whispers, "Don't run."

265

"Please. Don't," Bria says. It's not a command, but an honest request. Still, authority underpins her every word and motion. She lifts her eyes to the trees around us, then raises a twinkling glass bell. Things move among the trees. People. People I know. Boys, from Eagle House and Bear Hut. They drift through the trees with half-lidded stares, carrying platters in their arms. They lean over the seated girls to place the platters on the table.

They bring cutting boards of shining meats rolled into roses, baskets of bread dotted with baked seeds, and plates of sweating cheese drizzled in oil. There are peaches, split open and cored, their middles wet with sugar, served with bowls of whipped cream, yogurt, and crushed almonds. Several of the boys carry crystal pitchers of water that they decant into translucent goblets. As one leans over me to fill my cup, I whisper, "Help me."

It's like I've said nothing at all. I glimpse into his ear. I see the wriggling backside of a bee. Another nestles into his cartilage. Several more cluster in the hollow of his jaw.

"Drones, under our control," Bria says simply as yet more platters are set down. The girls pick at it, filling their plates, but no one takes a bite.

"You have questions," Bria says. "We can try to answer them."

"Try?" I sit up. The anger in my voice surprises me. I make myself go still. Focus. All around me I sense that stalking menace, the aura of predators. I cannot lose control now if I want to survive. My whole life has trained me for a moment like this, maybe, where the lurking threats of my mind have become inexplicably material.

I know what survivors of all kinds know. When there's a real threat, you cannot waste time denying it if you intend to live through it.

"Brayden is dead, isn't he?"

She doesn't answer.

"You killed him," I say. The girls glance across the lavish table at one another, like they're afraid to get between Bria and me.

"We had to. Something stalks our hive. We've lost too much this season already—first Caroline, then Sierra. We needed to fortify ourselves. I don't deny what you witnessed was shocking. You saw a portion of one of our most holy rituals. Nothing I say to you will make any of this make sense until you see for yourself. Really see, I mean. With the eyes of all. To be shown is an honor. Our greatest honor . . ."

Bria hesitates. Then, with a new resolve, she raises another bell—this one gold—and the drones return. They work in pairs now, setting down platters covered in glass domes. The glass is ornately etched, though a familiar crimson slides through the facets as the domes are positioned in front of the girls. On cue the boys remove the covers, and the faces of all the girls fill with a faint red light.

Honeycomb sculptures, like those we glimpsed in that subterranean hive. In the light they're hardly as sinister. It's just their color—that deep crimson in each tiny well, like a lattice of gold beaded with blood. But the shapes, too, feel wrong. They aren't the strict planes of the apiary hives, and they're not the folding curtains of a natural hive. They're something in between, and familiar, and *wrong*.

The girls look upon the comb with dreamy hunger. The two closest to me drink the air in deep inhales. I hold my breath until I have to breathe through my mouth, but the sweetness finds a way in anyway, coating the back of my throat.

"We're not used to interruption," Bria says. "We do our work away from the world on purpose."

"Your . . . work?"

She means the comb. She must. The energy from the girls isn't just basic hunger. It's intelligent desire. The look of artists gazing upon their work with pride.

"Ask," Bria says.

But my eyes are stuck on the edge of the closest platter, where within the comb I can see the clear impression of a nose. I follow the slope up to a brow bone. The socket is empty, the eye melted away.

Bria sighs. I'm staring at the face in the comb so I don't see what she does next, but suddenly the pent-up hunger of the table breaks into frenzy. The air is a flurry of reaching hands. The face is pried off the platter, gilded strands flailing behind it, and crammed into a moaning mouth. Hands dig into the other comb, taking fists of the glazed gore, catching the viscous goop and lifting it high over parted, panting lips.

Run, Mars, I tell myself. *Go. Now.*

But I can't move. Or I don't. Because I'm not numb anymore; my hands are clenching and unclenching. I can feel my insides quivering with each breath. Nothing supernatural holds me down. What has me pinned, like a butterfly in a bell jar, is simple terror. Like prey, I am immobilized by the inevitability of my own extermination.

The girls chew and chew; they feed one another small morsels from their plates. They laugh, and they laugh, and they *laugh*. Their laughter is like a bell that rings another bell—a bell in each of them, a bell in me. The more I watch them and the more I hear them, the brighter the vibration is within my own chest. I can feel it right between my lungs. A bell, bright and happy, begging to ring with them.

For a moment I forget my doubts. I let it ring, and the girls all around me seem to hear it. They smile at me—beautiful smiles, smiles so radiant that my cheeks hurt trying to reflect them—and they take my hands in their sticky grips, and they pull me forward. It's like we're all reaching together, our arms woven into a single appendage that stretches into my future without hesitation, with only hunger. Our grip opens, and together we scoop up a crescent of the dark honeycomb. It's heavy—no, dense. Like it has its own gravity, but we work together to lift it up, so high the sun pours into it and splashes a red shadow over my face, over my closing eyes, over my parting lips, my reaching tongue, my stretched jaw.

"It's easier to just show you," Bria says.

The honey hits my tongue, plunges through me, fills me to the brim with its dark gravity.

CHAPTER 29

She is running through the woods.

Actually, she's being chased.

Not all can see the difference right away.

You can, if you know what to look for. It's the way she gathers her skirts with indelicate desperation, like she would rather the bramble shred them than slow her down. It's the smell of her fear, hissing between clenched teeth when she reaches the swamp's edge. And it's the decision to push forward anyway, for surely anything is better than going back. That's the difference between running, and running away.

We know what she wants before she wants it, and we're ready to give it before she asks. We don't usually make them ask.

She arrives before us as many do. Fallen, purging frustration and anger through her tears, spitting rapid bargains meant for invisible ears. Prayers, we think they're called. She doesn't see us yet. Her attention is on the narrow path behind her, and the shadow lumbering after, ripping through the wildflowers with predacious intent. Her panic rises as she drags herself just a few feet onward, on hand and knee. She is trapped. She is thinking, *Do not let me die here.*

We let her see us. Whatever she sees, it's lovely. Or lovely enough to cool the molten terror of her heart into a cold steel. She may know who we are, after all. She may have come here on purpose. Her eyes, a brown one and a blue-brown one, shine with long-held resolve. Maybe this was her plan all along, to bring this man to our domain. To feed us.

Her assailant arrives in our clearing. He smells different. A noxious odor of entitlement. Anger, too. A violent lust. We're in the clearing with hem now, among the swaying aspen trees, but he sees only her. And she is staring, embittered and imploring, up into the quivering bows of the aspen trees. At us.

We won't make her ask, but we will wait for the precise moment she understands what she is asking for. For her, the revelation arrives in the plinking snap of seams being ripped open, amid the sobs of *No, no, please don't*. It's a revelation as sharp and thin as the knife upon which she balances now. The kind of revelation that, if not grasped, falls into you, down and down and down, cutting forever.

We won't make her ask. Too few know they can ask. Our answer is our action, and we hope they forgive us when it's done.

They always do.

She sits beside the hotel's pool, refracted light catching on the pout of her lips. Like her lips, all of her is poised to allure. It's the sort of coy game she's learned to play her whole life, without ever once knowing what it'll win her. It's what girls are expected to do, she knows.

We know, too. We play the game. It's less a game and more the choreography of survival. It just feels like a game in all its mysterious rules and mundane choreography. You sit, your legs together. You laugh, but not too loud. You speak, but only in answers. You reveal all things through subtext. You're the closed flower, the lidded jar, the blanketed birdcage. Someday, usually as it's happening, you realize that all along the thing you've been flirting with is your own destruction.

The girl beside the pool skims her toes across the water, eyes dreamy with the bouncing light. It's an act—her whimsical stare at the turquoise water, her bored aloofness when the boys name her after her body parts, the polite detachment at dinner. An act. She is nowhere but right here, listening closely for the sound of laughter.

Our laughter.

We call to her with it. Really to anyone who will listen. We feel her stare and we know the violent longing that enriches her daydreams, because it once enriched ours, too. Longing that insulated our isolation, made it bearable, until we heard that laughter. The laughter hummed in our heads until we found our way back to it.

She spoke to one of us, once. She said, You girls go to the camp by the lake, yes? We said yes, but we like to sneak into the hotel for the pool, and the buffet, and because the kitchen staff let us use the basement for parties. It's so easy, we say, to get here through the boardwalk path in the swamp. (We do that sometimes. Add, somewhere in our polite conversation, how to find us.) She said, I wish I had eyes like you. One brown, one with a dash of blue. And we said, Oh, how sweet, it runs in the family.

And then we asked her how long she was staying, and if she wanted to join us for a party. She waited too long to say yes and ended up insisting no, no, she'd better not. And then she took up her post at the pool's edge, mourning her decision, hoping for another invitation.

The girl at the pool is called over to her father's table to say hello to his friends. It's their last day at the resort. She will be back next year and, depending on where she is along the continuum of her own destruction, maybe she will finally say yes.

She gasps, falling from the lace in a violent, enveloping numbness. It's always like that when she exits the lace; a sudden, heartbreaking loss of sensitivity, like every bright nerve in her body has died. She breathes, wipes at the sticky tears on her cheeks, and reminds herself that this living deadness is what it's like for most humans, all the time.

Pity. She always feels pity for anyone who isn't one of her sisters. They have no idea how much more there is to feel, to see, to *know*. They cannot even perceive the lace, never mind ask it questions.

She dips a cloth napkin in water and drags it over the sticky honeycomb residue on her fingers, her lips. Her sisters do the same as they roll back into their individual bodies, sitting up off the pillow-strewn cottage floor. None are keen to speak, to break the unification and set themselves apart again. Alone again. They clean up in comfy silence until the sun has set and it's time to report what they've synthesized.

She, the Leader, dictates while another writes. There's not much to say. They've asked the lace for many things this summer—locations of missing people, the identity of killers, facts lost to time and many other hidden histories—but they have only just learned that the memory of all the world goes backward *and* forward.

So they asked for the future. To their delight, the lace answered.

She recites the six numbers for the hungry ears of her sisters. Six numbers worth millions. Worth everything, to girls like this.

They'll need an adult to enter the lottery for them, but that's easy. By now the sisterhood goes back generations. Sharing will mean less to go around for each of them, but that's okay. There are many, many lotteries to win, and there is plenty of the dark honey left to win them with.

And if they run out of honey?

They won't.

The world will never run out of predators worth turning to prey.

She cannot unsee the version of herself in that photo. It's the awful way the flash makes her look like a smear against the forest's dark, like a wraith. She begins to unsee her actual self, her reflection replaced gradually by that naked, glowing wraith in the woods.

He was supposed to delete the photo. He said he would if she went all the way with him. She did her part; he ignored his. She should have watched him delete it. Made him do it. But, of course, she didn't. She blames herself for that, and eventually for everything else, too.

Even after camp ends for the summer, sometimes he texts the photo to her. Usually in the middle of the night in his time zone. For her, in California, she's often sitting with her parents watching TV. She keeps her phone flipped over in her lap between responses.

Her: Haha, very funny. delete that

Him: I tried, it just keeps coming back.

Him: what's up

Her: with my family

Him: take a new pic.

Her: I'm busy

Him: it'll take 2 seconds...

Him: hello?

Him: ????

Eventually, she plays along, because she knows there's a limit to how long she's allowed to resist. She's afraid of what happens if she trips over that limit without knowing it. The person who enforces it does not have reasonable limits of their own, not when it comes to retaliation. She didn't believe the stories about him, and now she's become a story she's sure no one *else* will believe. So she rises from the couch and goes to the downstairs bathroom.

Considering the mirror, she sees instead the photo he holds over her. They weren't even supposed to have their phones in the woods. Camp policy. But he always had it somewhere in all those pockets. Months pass and she resents anyone in cargo shorts; the sound of keys on a carabiner clip makes her nervous. When it's time to reapply for her old job at Aspen, she feigns disinterest and gets a job at a sandwich shop near her college. But somehow he finds out, and he's mad, and he sends her pictures to her new coworkers.

So she goes back to camp. To end it. She writes it all out on the plane ride. She rehearses it silently at night, and during the empty hour of her shift manning checkouts at the boathouse, and in all the spare moments she's not attending to her Bandit girls.

But when she tries to talk to him, she only gets in a sentence before he calls her crazy. Still, the next night at the bonfire, he's there. Watching her with that same leering lust. And when she risks a glance back, he's got his phone out, a pale glare lighting the grins of the boys grouped around him.

The next day, a camper catches her crying, and she's terrified they'll tell someone. She shuts off her emotions just in case. She resolves to be strong for her own girls, but anytime she looks at them she feels shame. It makes her cry harder. She hides more. The next people to find her are a pair of girls. They ask, How come you're not instructing dance this year? And she says she doesn't do that anymore. And they beg her, Please, please, join us. It would be their honor. Call it a favor. Just, please, dance with us.

She *does* decide to dance with us. She's unsure about it right until the moment we push her to the front of the stage for her solo, warming her back with encouragements. We believe in you, Sylv. We *believe* you, Sylv.

They want the old you, she tells herself. Not what's left. But then she sees the flash from a phone's camera, from many cameras as the parents watch, and she sees her cabin of Bandit girls in the front, and she understands that this, painful and familiar, is the chance she needs to reforge herself.

So she dances like she used to, like she's wanted to for a while now.

The lines of her body tell us all we need to know. When you're us, you learn to read many things, most of all the messages that are hard to say in the clumsy language of words. You watch the body instead.

Dancing is one of the many ways we enter the lace.

After, we act quickly. The boy with the photo makes it easy, walking right through the woods in the middle of the night. When he wakes up already encased in the comb, he spits at our feet and asks us first, how dare we, and second: Do you know who I am?

Why yes, we say. You were Brayden.

———————

Is it justice?

We don't complicate it with ego. What creature congratulates itself for eating? That's a human habit, and one you'll learn to leave behind. What matters in nature is hunger and the instincts that satisfy it.

But he deserved it, didn't he?

They all do.

But what exactly do you do to them?

We purify their flesh. The umbral honey flows from corruption, from the sacrifice of darkness to the light. That's what makes it so potent. That's why it takes just a drop to join us, here, within the mind that connects all things. We call it the lace. You've been here before. We can access it in many ways, but umbral honey is the purest. It unveils within us our most connected self.

Connected to what?

One another, Mars. We seek nothing greater than the connections to one another. Alone we are outnumbered and temporary, but together we are infinite. Each of us has access to all of us. And what a blessing this is. Don't you see? Our means to survive has always hinged upon our ability to outsmart predators who seek to isolate us, consume us, annihilate us. Our service to nature is as a net, swollen with the weight of the world, rocking above the maw of a void that will never stop hungering for our sweetness.

———————

She knows exactly where to look for the booth at the farmer's market. Even from inside the car, she can smell it. And the silvery strands of

276

tension are thicker up here in the mountains, crisscrossed at the horizon, woven forward toward their nexus. It's a lovely weave to be within, she thinks as she scoots her walker, inch by inch, toward the booth. Her granddaughter skips ahead, fascinated by the soaps and lip glosses being sold by the older girls, who are pretty and kind and so, *so* cool.

She, the older woman and not the little girl, waits to be noticed by the girls behind the counter. Of course we've already noticed her, though. We've felt her impending arrival for hours now, and we clasp her hands with muted adoration. She gives us a few dollars and we give her a jar of honey. Not the golden variety. Her jar is from the crate at our feet. It hums with a heaviness of the mind. It is warm, and it is red, and it is very, very fresh.

She accepts the jar and thanks us. She introduces her granddaughter. They have the same eyes. One brown, one bluish brown. Just like her grandmother before her.

It's nice to meet you, we tell our elder.

He sits at a vanity, dabbing starlight onto his cheekbones. He likes it when the afternoon light catches on the skull beneath the flesh, because it makes him feel solid. Material. Not the abstraction people seem to fear.

If he sits just right, he can see his sister in his reflection. It takes just a turn, just a tilt, and there she is. Caroline, blinking back.

We would like him to turn away.

He turns away. A minute later he is applying lipstick when, oh, there it is again! A flashing resemblance beneath his skin. Now he can't unsee it, lips half-bloodied by the lipstick, a halo of Christmas lights twinkling behind him like stars. Her lipstick. Her stars. He reaches out and the tube clinks on the mirror as he tries to draw her into being.

We would like him to turn away now.

earth to mars.

That's what he writes.

He reads the words and wonders about the girl who used to summon him with them. It used to annoy him when she asked, over and over, if he'd join her on one of her silly adventures. But with her gone, he thinks that maybe he should have spent more time with her, and less time making her ask.

We would like him to turn—

She was a good person. She was a good person. Whatever she did, she did not deserve whatever was done to her. She did not deserve to die.

Caroline did not deserve to die.

I know that Caroline did not deserve to die.

I put the lipstick down. I push away from the vanity, but I stare at myself until I'm sure it's me. Just me behind those eyes. I stand up. I walk downstairs. The Honeys are waiting. They stare at me, dumbfounded, like they're seeing a real-life ghost float through their living room.

HowHowHowHowHow? their thoughts echo in my head. They are frantic. They are searching for me, not my body but my mind, pulling at the radiant tethers that had me bound.

But I'm myself again. My focus is faultless, without a single crack for them to hold on to. For this handful of seconds, at least.

"Mars, we—" Bria starts.

I slam the back door and make myself walk calmly down the stairs and through the apiary. It's a hot afternoon, the cloudy sky a singular, unrelenting brightness.

When I hit the forest's edge, I run.

CHAPTER 30

I run so I don't have to think. I run so hard that my throat fills with fire and my muscles turn to ice. I am aching, shivering, swearing as I reach the covered bridge. The damp cool within slows me down and I linger, reluctant to reenter Aspen but knowing fully I cannot go backward. Trapped, I pace the creaking bridge, a marble sliding between two gravities.

Think, Mars.

How much time has gone by since I awoke in the swamp? If it's still daytime, not much. Or it's tomorrow. Or who knows.

I try to walk backward through my memory. Back up the path, through the apiary, into the cabin, up the stairs, to the vanity, but after that my memory becomes a rope unraveling. The timeline frays into dozens of strands, then hundreds. Hundreds of other lives, simultaneously playing in the eye of my memory, impossible to parse coherently.

But it wasn't like watching another person. It was me, in those lives. I was soothing a child. I was sitting by the pool. I was popping a zit. I was singing along to the dealership jingle on the radio. I won the lottery. I took a cake order. I stopped short, thinking, *Hmmm, did I lock the door?*

The memories are a swarm that I cannot comprehend. Not anymore, now that the intoxicating sensitivity of the umbral honey is fading. But I remember the feeling of being spread through that brilliant network. The lace. It was like there was nothing to me at all, no body, no weight. I danced with the fluidity of thought, arcing like light between the small windows of other worlds. I felt all of them with the rich, casual certainty that they were mine.

And there was no *Mars*. No *I*. Just a thunderous *us*. A voice made out of all the voices, speaking in words made of pressure. A willpower that called itself *we*.

I can still feel it now, hissing in the gaps of my brain. Its words were edged in static. I can't understand them, not even the memory of them. It's like falling out of an embrace, trying to trace the shape of another via the emptiness you now hold. My connection, if that's what it was, has been cut.

I spit, trying to get the taste of honey out from between my teeth. I think of the comb on the platters—faceted, red, wrong shaped—and I want to feel revulsion, but my mouth waters. I spit again.

Think, Mars.

I run out of the covered bridge, to the path fringing the lake, toward the boathouse. I can't stay here. They'll come for me. If I'm not here, they'll come for Wyatt. He was one of the few boys not catering that demented little swamp banquet.

Think, Mars.

Aspen roars with sourceless insect chatter, dead-still beneath the racket. It's the limbo of afternoon, so the cabins must be off doing their individual activities. I hear commotion at the athletics complex and closer, music. The only life I find is a group of staff unfolding blankets on the lawn. Sunday cookout. Of course.

I nearly run to the adults. Then, thinking better of it, I recede back into the woods. I need to focus on finding Wyatt and getting out of here.

I find Hunter Village empty, too. The door to Bear Hut is wide open. Mayflies drift inside, wondering what all the fuss is about.

Invite the outside in, I think as I pass Bernard the Bear.

I pause in the doorway, listening. The cabin feels so still, so strangely evacuated. I'm tiptoeing as I check Wyatt's room—empty—and as I sneak upstairs to the dorms—empty—and as I go to leave. Then, descending the stairs, I crash into a person racing out of the kitchen. Ray. Normal Ray, not the droopy-eyed puppet from the swamp.

"Mars, man, where ya been?" he asks.

"Craft hut." An automatic lie. "Is Wyatt with you?"

"Yeah, we're up in the lodge. He's kicking our asses at poker."

Ray turns to the door and I focus on his ear. No bees that I can see. I edge around him, scanning for their furry little bodies.

"You want in?" Ray asks, a little nervous now.

"Fine, yeah." I smile. We head up toward the lodge.

"Actually."

I stop. Wyatt could never kick anyone's ass at poker. He told me so himself. He doesn't have the face for it.

"I'll be right there," I say. "I forgot something."

I jog down the hill, and after a few steps, Ray calls out, *"OLLY OLLY OXEN FREE!"*

Boys in white uniforms materialize at the tree line. Andrea, Mitch, Charlie, Tyler. Even *Tyler*. A shot of betrayal super-heats my blood, seeing him stride toward me with the rest of them, trapped in unnatural synchronicity as they break into a charge.

No more thinking.

Run, Mars.

The boys dart after. I'm quicker than them. I have to be. But there's too many, and they steer me away from the trail back into camp. I'm forced uphill, past Hunter Lodge and into the trails above. I can hear them crashing at my heels, shouting in strange, stretched voices, and then one tackles me from behind. We skid down the hill and his hand claps over my mouth. I choke on dirt and my own screams. He's heavy, too heavy.

I'm caught.

"Mars. It's me. It's Wyatt."

Wyatt!

Wyatt folds into me, pinning us down as the other boys race past. We lie still until their shouts are only echoes bouncing among the trees. He relaxes, sliding his hand from my mouth, and that's when I roll us over so I'm the one pinning him down. A rock the size of my skull rises in my hands, pulled from the brush.

Wyatt's eyes go wide. Those eyes. One brown and one bluish-brown. I stared into generations of those eyes, in the lace. Wyatt isn't a Honey, my instincts say. Not yet at least. But I need to be sure of at least this.

"Turn your head," I tell Wyatt.

He turns. I stare into his ear, make him show me the other one. No bees, but then again, I didn't see any in Ray either.

Think, Mars.

"Question," I say. "If a spider could wink—"

"Answer," Wyatt snaps back. "Spiders don't have eyelids."

I drop the rock and spit out the dirt he packed into my gums. We pull each other up and I hug him. Hard. Wyatt whispers, "I came back for you."

"I came back for *you*."

"So competitive." I can hear the grin in his voice. He sounds tired, but just that scrap of humor puts a beat back into my heart.

"What happened?" I ask.

"Quiet," he warns me. "I'll tell you later. For now, do you trust me?"

Those eyes. Familiar *and* new, like all of Aspen's deceits. But behind them is the boy I've known all along.

"Yes," I say.

———

Wyatt knows the woods better than anyone. He guides us into invisible grooves that cut across the dense miles of forest until we're finally released into a wide, overgrown field. At the far edge is a barn, and we keep to the field's perimeter as we head toward it.

"They won't know about this place," Wyatt whispers. "It's just outside Aspen's property. But I used to camp around here. I stowed some stuff away before heading back for you."

The barn is huge up close, and falling apart. The roof has caved in and the outer walls look about to as well. We slip inside through a gaping hole where doors once hung.

"Careful," Wyatt murmurs. He takes my hand and leads me around a mess of scorched wood and rust-eaten machinery, to a ladder. It's rotting, like everything else, but it holds as Wyatt helps me up. We crawl onto a loft that's been swept clean of debris, a sleeping bag laid out alongside a backpack and some supplies. There's a door, just right in the middle of the wall, and through it I can see across the shifting ocean of treetops to the lake. Aspen's lake, flashing *mayday, mayday* as it burns beneath the setting sun.

"Here, sit. You're shaking," Wyatt says as he coaxes me to the floor. He rummages through his pack until he finds two granola bars. He makes me eat one, then drink from his water bottle.

"Better?" he asks.

My mouth still tastes like dirt, but it's a welcome bitterness replacing the sweetness from before.

"Better," I tell him. "Tell me what happened to you."

Wyatt must decide I'm not going to pass out or float away because he finally flops down next to me and starts talking, chewing at his own granola bar.

"I'm not sure I even know, to be honest," he says. "Wendy knew something was up right away when she pulled me out of breakfast. She told me to meet her at the Welcome Center, but she never showed."

She separated us, I think. Wendy didn't want her precious kin involved.

"Finally, I went back to Hunter Village and it was just Donovan there. Acting normal. Or normal for Donovan." Wyatt pitches his voice down.

Puffs out his chest and squares his shoulders. *"Heyyyy hey, mister man, how's it hanging?"*

I laugh. He has clearly been practicing his Donovan imitation for years.

"Anyway, I asked where you were," Wyatt says, a little bashful. "Donovan said you were off with the boys on a hike. *Willingly*. And that's when I knew something was *definitely* wrong."

I punch Wyatt's arm.

"Good to see you've still got your charm," he laughs, rubbing where I hit.

"They came back without you." Wyatt goes serious again. "And when I asked where you were, they acted like you weren't real. Like . . . that girl you knew."

"Sierra."

"Yeah. Sierra." Wyatt lets out a long exhale. Shame tilts his head down and away from me. "And I almost believed them. I tried to tell them what we saw, about Brayden, but they just kept laughing at me and saying I made it all up. And you know what the worst part was? I wanted to agree. It was like the more I tried to explain it, the less it made sense. Until it felt like this mess I'd made up to scare myself. A ghost story. I know how that sounds, but—"

"I get it," I say. It's the same—the way the Honeys buff away doubt and dissent, and Aspen binds its children in agreeable untruths. It's pressure and persuasion, and if the Honeys wield it as some supernatural power, it's only because they've concentrated the perfume Aspen has doused us with all along.

"I asked myself what you would do," Wyatt says. "I decided to think for myself, and run. I packed a bag and grabbed as much of your stuff as I could, to prove to the police that you were real. I didn't know what else to do. But then I got here, and I was going through the stuff, and . . ."

I nearly laugh at what Wyatt pulls out of his bag. There's Caroline's hive tool, and her candle, but also something I had totally forgotten. The 1973 Mayfair calculator. It is potentially the most absurd object to have while sitting in an abandoned hayloft while running for your life.

"I decided to go back. Then I heard them call *olly olly oxen free*, and, well . . . I'm just glad I went back."

"I'm glad you went back, too."

"But I shouldn't have left."

I tip Wyatt's chin up so that he looks at me. "You came back, and we made it out. That's what matters."

"Where were you?"

I tell Wyatt about waking up in the aspen wetlands, and about the feast, but my words fall apart in my mouth as I try to describe whatever transpired between the feast and the moment I surfaced in the mirror.

"I don't know," I finally say. "I don't know what to say. It was like being connected to everything, and it was like I was everyone, at once. Yet I was still Mars, because I was talking to myself. And we were . . ."

We were together.

Again I feel a longing for that incandescent harmony, if only for the glimpse of Caroline I met within it. I wish I'd stayed longer, seen more. Could the lace show me what happened to her? What drove her away from Cabin H? Did she try to invite me in, like Sierra, and was she punished? Did she want me there all along?

I stop there and Wyatt doesn't make me go on.

We make a plan. Town is only a few miles away, but we'll travel just before sunrise. We'll call my family, not Wyatt's. He'll stay with me. We will never, ever come back here.

We unzip the sleeping bag and spread it open to sit on. We eat granola bars and watch the sunset burn through the cracks in the walls, laying ruddy bars of light into the dusty air. Birds dip in from the sky, startle at us, and cry out to warn the others.

"No offense," Wyatt says after a while. "But your sister's friends seem a little homicidal."

I snort. "No offense, but your beloved summer camp seems a little culty."

Wyatt gives me a pained grin. "I hate that you were right."

"I hate that I was right, too."

Wyatt chucks an acorn into the rising dark of the barn. We lean back on our elbows and watch the crisp periwinkle sky ripen to red.

"I bet you wish you never came back."

"Actually, I'm glad."

Wyatt glances at me. "Why?"

"I needed to . . . to know all of this. To know what she went through. And there were moments when it felt like she was there. Like, *right there*, next to me. Helping me find my way back out."

The blue of my nails is chipped, but it still shines. It reminds me of the game with Bria in the pine grove, where I reached into a board of bent light and picked up a perfect azure tile. Now I know why I reached for it first.

"I just wish I could have been there for her," I say on a shaky breath. "Whatever she went through, I should have been there."

"You couldn't have known," Wyatt says.

"I could have," I say. "I *should* have. We . . . used to tell each other everything. But these last few years, we hardly talked about anything real. She was so busy and she was always so stressed out, and I guess I was, too. We fell out of sync and there was never a good time to fall back into it."

I can taste the falseness in what I'm saying. I ball my fists. How come even after she's gone, I can't bring myself to tell Caroline the truth? Will I be like this forever, smothering my sister's memory in self-serving fantasy? First I lie about her death, and now the lie has reached backward to taint her life?

"Actually," I start. "It was worse for her. I knew it was worse. My mom and dad had all these dreams for her that I never had to deal with because I'm, well . . ." I gesture at my body, kick out a foot and point the toe, and Wyatt snorts. "So she had to do it all. Student council. Tennis. Pre-law, then law-law, and so on. She was chosen for everything. And even though I knew *she* didn't make the choice, I still found a way to resent her for . . ." I swallow. "For not choosing me. That's how it felt. And it seems so ridiculous now."

And here it is, the gruesome thing I never wanted to admit but have known all along.

"I knew she was struggling and that she needed help, but I was too proud to offer it. I wanted her to ask. I wanted to feel needed again."

Wyatt puts a hand on my back, because I'm shaking. There are no tears, though. It's like I'm empty of emotions and this—this ugliness I can barely even stand to articulate—is all I've got.

"And now she's dead," I whisper.

I picture her face. I try to picture her smile, but it's hard. Her smiles became so rare toward the end, and I stopped fighting for them. That's the true horror, I think; that I gave up. That I let her go onward, into unimaginable horror, alone. But I didn't know any better. I swear, I didn't.

"You couldn't have helped her, Mars," Wyatt says. "She didn't even know she had cancer. You couldn't have done anything to stop it."

Here is another shroud we'll pull over my sister: the lovely lie that what crushed her into an early grave was her own rebelling, monstrous body, and not her twin's. But I crushed her. Or she caught me.

I still don't know.

I've danced through that night's violence ninety-nine times trying to find meaning in it. I dance through it a hundredth time right now, expecting nothing, but I surprise myself as a new pattern emerges. My hand, my ear, the hive tool, the candle—the ways Caroline hurt me add together with sudden importance. Combined, they are the variables that woke me up over and over when the summer's spell pulled me under. Dulled me. Blissed apart my doubts. Earth to Mars in a handful of cuts and collectibles.

Oh, but I don't have a meaning for the calculator.

Unused, it sits half out of the bag. An ironic upset to the desperate calculus of my grief.

I realize I'm no better than anyone else who chose to romanticize Caroline's tragedy. I'm worse. I'm making her save me once again, because I can't for the life of me accept the obviousness of oblivion. Sometimes people just die, and it will never, ever make sense.

I put it down, all of it. The heavy mystery I will never understand. Just like Wyatt said, I have to let it go or it will take me with it.

"I know I couldn't have saved her life," I say finally. With finality. "But still. When she died it was like saying goodbye to a stranger. I realized I barely knew her, in the end."

"Is that why you came back here?"

"Yeah, to look for her."

"What did you find?"

I found Sierra's hands in mine as we inhaled the chemical aroma of nail polish and listened to the girls sing along to the radio. I found Bria crying with me on a stoop while we watched the fireflies over the meadow. I found Mimi holding up a hand to block the sun from my eyes. Overtures of Caroline echoed in each of them. Her soul scattered among her sisters, like puzzle pieces for me to fit together.

The Honeys will scare me forever. But I owe them at least this. They were there when I was not; they never asked to be asked. I'm honest when

I finally say, "I found enough to know that Caroline wasn't alone in the end, after all."

I squeeze my eyes shut, and the tears finally fall.

———

I feel lighter after.

Wyatt thought of everything, including toilet paper, and I unspool reams of it to dry my eyes and blow my nose. Then, in an adorable display of environmental stewardship, Wyatt makes me put all the used paper in a bag he brought for garbage. Leave no trace, he tells me, winking.

We lie on the sleeping bag. At the far edge of the sunset, stars are appearing. We watch them. They watch us back. Wyatt goes through the constellations for me again. I make up new ones like Orion's Jock Strap and Wyatt goes along with it, but all he can contribute is: Orion's Other Belt.

He has to clap a hand over my mouth to stifle my teasing, but he retracts it just as quick, going very still. Like I've stung him. A few minutes later, he takes a steadying breath.

"Before we head back out there, I wanted to share something with you, too."

I sit up.

"You were right. About me and rules."

"What do you mean?"

"When you—" Wyatt sits with his legs crossed, hands limp on his ankles. "When we were on our way to Apiculture that first day, and you said I would rather let someone else think for me than use my own brain and break a rule? I thought that was the craziest thing ever, but then I started thinking about it and, yeah, you were right. I didn't want to see what was going on here. Aspen isn't what I thought it was. *I'm* not who I thought I was."

I can feel it, the nervous energy shivering over Wyatt's skin. His jaw is clenched, all of him tense. I nearly take his hands.

"You know what I think about all the time?" he says.

"What?"

"When we stood in the woods and ate that honey together. I haven't stopped thinking about it, to be honest. And after we saw what happened to . . . what happened in that building, I thought, *Oh, what I was feeling wasn't real*. It was, like, drugs or something. Magic."

Wyatt finally looks at me. Looks me right in the eye, with such surety that I won't even let myself blink.

"It wasn't, though, was it?" he whispers. "It was a real feeling."

"I don't know. I don't know what you felt."

"I felt . . ." He clears his throat. "I *feel* . . ."

Wyatt's still looking at me when he turns his hands over, facing his palms up to the night like an offering. A question. My hands move to answer. They hover, trapping an excited heat between our skin. He's the one to close the gap. His hands are rough, his grip unsure, until I squeeze back. Then the grip is absolute.

"What do you feel?" I ask again.

Wyatt's answer is a deep breath, a lean, an unsure, upward tilt of the chin.

A question.

An answer.

I kiss him.

Wyatt pulls away. He's staring at me like I've stung him again, but then his fingers rise to my lips and tentatively trace their shape. He studies me. It's the same wondrous concentration I've seen him apply to the mysteries of the natural world, except now I'm the mystery. *We* are the mystery. His fingers graze down my jaw, to the back of my neck. He pulls me in, and then he's the one kissing me.

I let him. I want him to. I return his yearning with the full force of my own. Restraint dissolves in the wet heat of our shared breaths, evaporates in the crush of our bodies pulling together. Restraint has done its job; in the slow language of patience, we learned about each other from afar, and grew toward this moment with slow, organic chance. When we crash together now, there's no awkwardness of discomfort. Just an instantaneous intimacy, too perfect to be crafted. Perfect enough that it could only have evolved.

Wyatt gets my shirt off before I even get his pants undone. He tugs at the crop top but I yank at his shirt's hem, and he lets me drag it up and over his raised arms. My hands explore the mystery of his skin, feeling the prickle of hair on his chest, the curve of his stomach, the needful arch of his spine, the flex of his shoulders as he pulls me into him. He holds me with such force that for a moment I feel that wheeling levitation from before, like the world has dropped away and we're falling upward, into the net of stars.

Wyatt's hand dips between my hips. I place a hand on his chest, slowing him down, but barely. My nails drag down the back of his scalp, to his neck, to his back, pricking across a scar.

He shudders.

"Oh, sorry," I whisper.

"It's nothing," he urges me.

But my fingers trace it again. A straight line bitten out of his shoulder. Not an old scar, but a wound that's barely scabbed.

"It's nothing," he whispers, his hand cupping over me and squeezing gently. I gasp. I fall into him, forgetting the cut, but a low buzz cuts through the steam in my head. A question.

If I took the hive tool, if I placed its dull blade against Wyatt's scar, would it fit like a key to a keyhole?

I think it would.

I detach from Wyatt. His eyes flutter open and, seeing the question on my face, his eyes give me the answer I need.

First, guilt.

Then: malevolence.

"It was you," I say. "You set up that speaker up in the woods. You lit the candle. You—"

We're so entwined, it only takes the smallest shift and Wyatt has me pinned to the gritty floorboards.

"You should have left when you had the chance," he says. It's not his voice, not his face. Veins bulge in his forehead as he fights to keep me pinned. The boy I kissed has flickered away, and now something else has me trapped. Something wearing his skin this whole time.

It's stronger, but I'm smarter.

Think, Mars.

I headbutt Wyatt. Hard. I feel his nose crunch against my skull. He howls, falling backward. I snatch up the flashlight and pin him in the spotlight.

"You were never going to make it here," he says. Blood drips over his lips, onto his uniform. Then, quite clearly, a bloody glob inches its way back up into Wyatt's nose. Another craws over his cheek.

Bees.

"You're a drone," I whisper.

We dive toward the hive tool at the same time.

VI

CHAPTER 31

Wyatt is too fast. Too strong. He slaps a hand over the hive tool.

But I grab the calculator.

I smash his hand and the tool skids across the floor, down into the shadows of the barn. This choice—a choice Caroline made for me, maybe—gives me the seconds I need to get out of his reach. He curls against the ladder, holding his broken hand, so I go for the strange door in the wall. An ancient rope dangles down into the dark waves of wild grass.

"Mars?" Wyatt pleads. "What's happening?"

I'm stunned to hear his voice. *Wyatt's* voice. But then he flickers away, replaced once again by that furious imposter.

"Your sister was weak, too," Wyatt says. But it's not Wyatt. This thing isn't like the boys who chased me or served the Honeys in eerie unison; Wyatt isn't just brainwashed. He's fully possessed by someone or something. It wears him, extending throughout his body with alien awkwardness. He shivers and jerks. More bees escape the carnage of his nose.

My heel inches over the drop. Will the rope hold me? I have to stall him.

"Who are you? Tell me!" I demand.

"It doesn't matter."

Wyatt lurches at me.

I know what happens before it happens. I see it all over again. Caroline smashed against our hallway mirror, stumbling toward me, her feet twisting in the carpet as she dives at me and the banister. Wyatt's boots catch in the sleeping bag as he leaps. Caroline's arms wrap around me. Wyatt's arms engulf me. The moon swings above us, the starlight like falling glass and crystal as we drop through my memories, the three of us falling as one.

I have spent every second since the accident trying to purge this very sensation from my body, but it's never come unstuck. And now, as we plunge, my body remembers in vivid detail how to twist just right. How to maneuver the sickening flip of gravity so that when the ground finds us . . .

We slam into the earth, Wyatt first. I remember this, too. The muffled snap, the meaty thud, and then: that steely embrace going rubbery. I drag myself off Wyatt—*Not-Wyatt*, I think—but pain somewhere in my leg dwarfs everything, so sharp I fall sideways. I know better than to look at Not-Wyatt, or my ruined leg. I focus forward, dragging myself through the grass, willing my adrenaline to numb me for a few seconds longer, a few feet more. There's a moment where I hear Not-Wyatt stir, a wet, choking cough, and the crush of grass as he drags after me. I swallow back a scream of frustration, moving as fast as I can, until his sounds are buried beneath the seething night.

At the forest I pull myself up with the low bows of a tree and limp onward, crying so hard I can barely see. Somehow I reach the edge of a pond full of moonlight. And aspen trees. I choke on fresh despair. Wyatt, or Not-Wyatt, or whoever—they led me right back into the wetlands.

"*MARS.*"

He tackles me from behind and we crash into the shallows. The aspen trees fill my view as I look up at him, so that he becomes a silhouette printed into the wall of unblinking, white eyes. I try to find Wyatt within it—I find his pupils, the only color left—and I'm close enough to see the fragile skin of his eyelid quiver as a bee squirms out like a living tear.

"*You are too weak for us,*" Not-Wyatt hisses. "*Caroline was too weak for us.*"

He straddles me, like he straddled me only a few minutes ago. His hands lock around my throat and slowly, slowly, he pushes me below the water. The night muffles, the trees ripple and merge. I thrash. I punch and scratch but he doesn't even flinch. I dig my own hands around his throat, but it doesn't matter. There is no regard left in him for his own life. The bees will make Wyatt kill me, and they won't care if he dies, too.

He pushes me deeper and my vision pulses like it's trying to escape my skull. Upturned muck blots out the moon. Bright dots swarm the edges of my eyes. I hear my throat gurgle and creak.

I hear myself begin to die.

A hand, soft like starlight, slips through the water and cups my cheek. I open my eyes and see a strange new thing through the cloudy water: a brightness growing behind Wyatt's head. Even down here I can feel its warmth, can hear its hum, rising and rising until Wyatt is suddenly pulled away. And I'm wrenched upward, choking and gasping and kicking, onto the reedy bank.

I take my first real breath in minutes. The dots clear. Not all of them, though. A handful of bees swarm in the moonlight over the pond. And girls in white uniforms hum beneath them.

The Honeys.

Mimi is the one who pulled me up. Her soaked body hugs mine protectively as she cries, "What happened? We've been looking all over. What happened?" And then, "Oh, Mars, your *leg*."

"Back up," Bria says, appearing over Mimi. Her voice is strained. Her eyes glow that gilded brown. She grips the air with a flexed hand and the bees draw into a slithering lasso. They lash at Wyatt, forcing him into the pond. More girls join Bria, and it's like all the particles of the forest dance to their command. Soon Wyatt is dragged into the pond's middle. Something holds him in place despite his thrashing. A pressure that vibrates the water into a simmer.

Prolonged thunder crackles over our heads. The hum of the Honeys, turned all the way up.

"What do we do?" Mimi cries.

"Mars first, then the boy," Bria says. She places a hand somewhere below my knee, plucking at a chord of white-hot pain. My scream cuts through the hum.

"Mimi, hurry!" Bria commands.

"But the sun isn't up—"

"Now!"

Mimi appears above me. She holds a small jar with a cute little bow. Honey. She's going to force me to eat it.

"No!" I scream.

Mimi unscrews the lid and dips her finger in. Two girls pry open my mouth and she swipes it over my gums. Instantly, the skyward gravity of the honey wrenches me out of my body, my pain, and I'm left watching myself from above. From within.

The rest of the girls dip their fingers in the jar, dragging the dark syrup over their lips. Then they connect their pinkies, and the hum changes. Focuses. It points itself at me. *Into* me.

"Let us help you," Bria urges. "Trust us, Mars."

I try to block them out but the hum is under my skin now, crawling through my nerves. It's in my bones, in the gaps of my joints. I stiffen as it pulses against my leg, the vibrations turning dissonant as they wash over the broken bone in my shin. But then, slowly, the dissonance pulls itself back in tune. I let it. I want it. The pain eases. I can feel the bone twitching within my muscle until, with a hiss, it pops back together.

The hum pulses through me, snagging on other breaks in my skin. I sink into my skin and sit up in a body that feels brand new. Even the dirt beneath my nails has been dissolved.

Around me the girls have quietly fallen to their knees. Only Bria remains standing, but barely.

"Up. Get up. We're not done yet, girls," she says through gritted teeth.

They help one another up, swaying to the water's edge. Wyatt cowers among the lily pads. Maybe it's the honey in my blood, but Wyatt appears to me now as a mass of legible energy. I can feel the terror jumping in his heart, and the confused whir of his thoughts. I can even feel the prickling insects hiding deep beneath his skin.

"I knew it. *He* killed Sierra," Mimi says.

Wyatt, or Not-Wyatt, stiffens. A confirmation. The epiphany circulates through the other girls, and then through me. I remember seeing him the morning after Sierra died, right as I was walking to the apiary to discover she had vanished. Wyatt was tired. This was why.

"It doesn't matter that he's Wendy's kin," Mimi says. "The hive is higher."

The girls nod. They glare at the boy in the pond, but he stares toward the sky, silvery light pouring into the dark sockets of his face.

"Help me," he whispers.

"Help you? We're going to *kill* you, asshole!" Mimi shouts. "Girls, get ready—"

"He's a drone," I shout.

Stillness takes the clearing. Even the thunder falters.

"Impossible," Bria says.

"He is. I saw them. They're in his head."

"We would sense our own drone," Kyle says. She joins Mimi to resume the hum.

"No," Bria commands. "We'll test him. Mars, can you stand? We need your help."

I test my leg. Other than a faint itch deep within the bone, it's fine. Two girls, CJ and PJ, help me up. When it's clear I'm okay, they join my pinkies to theirs. Wyatt stiffens, then jerks as the hum intensifies again.

I find myself humming, too. It's not a sound from my throat. It's a vibration that emanates from the microscopic layers between my skin and the skin of the girls beside me. A repelling pressure between two magnets.

The pond begins to glow. It's a jade luminance rising from the bottom, and soon the forest is awash in its trembling light. The lily pads skip and slide, their blooms sighing open. Wyatt tenses in some unseen embrace, resisting as it drags him down, inch by inch, until he's up to his shoulders. In the cold light I can see tiny bumps darting under the skin of his throat, trying to escape the waterline as he sinks. The Honeys hum louder, push him down farther, and soon only his face breaches the vibrating surface. Then, right before he's fully submerged, his mouth splits open and out twists a writhing, buzzing fog.

Bria quickly snags an unseen cord in the air and the swarm drifts toward her, like a kite. It hovers over her palm.

The girls whisper. *A splinter swarm? Someone splintered?*

"Who?" Bria asks, never taking her eyes off the bees. Even I can tell these are unlike the bees of the apiary. Whatever escaped from Wyatt is much angrier, much more sinister.

The girls are silent.

"Who did this?" Bria asks again.

When no one responds, Bria purses her lips and produces a susurrous whistle, like wind through grass. The raging swarm calms into a drifting eddy. She steps back and releases her hand. We all watch as the bees dip and swerve, their bodies ruby red with blood. Then, like a snaking necklace, they squiggle through the air and loop around one girl's hair.

The rest of the girls gasp.

Bria makes a strangled cry.

"Mimi?" she whispers.

Mimi cowers in the small swarm, looking with wide eyes at her sisters.

"I had to," she whispers. "For the hive. I had to. They were *weak*. They needed to be purged so the rest of us could thrive, but I couldn't do it myself, could I?"

"Oh, Mimi, what the hell?" Bria pushes her hands against her temples.

"I had to!" Mimi stands up straighter. Her lip quivers as she puts on an air of defiance.

"Caroline was *weak*. She never should have been queened. We all knew it. Even *she* knew it! It's no wonder the throne rotted her from the inside out. And then Sierra invites *this* into the brood?" She shoves an accusing finger at me. "A queen must be a *queen*. If she is anything less, the hive exterminates her!"

"Have you lost your mind?" Bria shouts back. "We don't hurt innocent people, Mimi. It's our *one* rule!"

"I'm not hurting people," Mimi pouts. "I'm hurting *boys*."

Bria, to her credit, throws me a sideways glance and asks, "What are your pronouns again?"

"Uh . . ." My throat still feels raw from being choked within an inch of my life. "I'm cool with really anything. I'm fluid."

"See?" Bria throws her hands up in the air. "And what about Sierra? You knew she was going to recruit Mars? So you took her out with a drone?"

Mimi doesn't deny it. She thrusts out her chin proudly.

"Sierra created a liability and I moved to solve it. It was her mistake for getting in *my* way. I did what none of you could, and I did it in a way that gives you all plausible deniability. In other words, *you're welcome*."

"This is not how we decide things," Bria says. "This is not who we are."

"That's right," Mimi snaps. "I am what none of you are. *Strong*. We can't afford another failed queen. The sisterhood requires honey, and we're barely producing enough for just *ourselves*. If we pick wrong again, the hive will collapse. Bria, why can't it be you? Haven't you served the longest?"

"The throne is not a privilege," Bria says. "It's a burden."

"Then *I'll* be the one to bear it. You know I'm strong. None of you can beat me at tiles. None of you even sensed what I was doing through the lace. That should prove I have what it takes to lead us."

I think Bria almost gives in. I can see Mimi's logic working into her, but then she shakes her head.

"No." Bria claps her hands twice, officially. "Mimi, you have murdered your sister and forged a splinter swarm, and thus you have imperiled the hive's unity *twice*—"

"Wait," Kyle cuts in. "She tried to kill Mars, too."

"Twice and *a half*," Bria corrects. "You know what the penalty is."

"Stop!" Mimi cries. "You can't! You think you're so high and mighty, but you don't give the verdicts, Bria. The hive is higher."

Bria shrugs. She lifts up her fingers, ready for a snap.

"The hive *is* higher, Mimi. So why don't you shut the fuck up and let it speak?"

"You wouldn't," Mimi whispers.

Bria snaps. All the girls do, at the exact same time. Mimi blinks, all her childish affectations falling away as she glares at her accusers. Then she turns to run, but halts. From the distance comes a dissonant hiss. I feel them before I see them; millions and millions of wings churning the air. They seethe from the woods, from the direction of the wetlands. It's the same enveloping drone that overtook us in the caverns beneath the hotel. The bees, all of them, have been summoned here, but I don't know for what.

"I'm not snapping!" Mimi shrieks. "It's not unanimous!"

"You don't get a snap," Bria says. She sounds sad. I can sense that her thoughts are on Sierra now, and that her sadness overlays a much deeper, much more powerful fury.

The first bee swats against Mimi's cheek. She crushes it. I barely see her next move. She blurs with that uncanny speed and I register a sudden flash of moonlight. Her hive tool. It whistles at me, halting just before my neck, because Kyle's caught it. Mimi shrieks again, crushing several more bees into her scalp.

Then she's gone. In an instant, the girl is just a fuzzy figure as bees coat her limbs. Her screams are wild and furious. She tries to scrub them off, but it's pointless. More fill in the gaps, rounding her out until there's no more Mimi. Just a cocoon of tiny, simmering bodies.

The cocoon rises into the air.

"Mars." Bria never takes her eye off the cocoon. "Don't look."

The drone of the bees rises a key, then another. I sense their billion wings beating faster and faster. The moonlit clearing shimmers with sudden heat. Something in the cocoon begins to glow molten orange.

Mimi screams. Out punches a hand. It's coiled in steam, the flesh pink and peeling. It tears open the cocoon to reveal a burning core, and briefly the pond is bathed in boiled red. The heat is so intense I feel my tears evaporate, but then the breach is sealed, the peeling hand gone, the screaming cut off. The glow seems to intensify and darken at once, like the sun setting behind a raging storm.

Finally the drone quiets. The light fades. But heat still clings to the air, as does a new scent of charred flesh.

"Mars, listen to me."

Bria fills my vision.

"Run," she commands.

"But Wyatt. He's—"

"No one will hurt him."

"But—"

"No, listen to me. You run and don't come back. Every hive needs a queen, and Caroline was that queen. But now she's gone and the hive . . .

it wants . . ." Bria shakes my shoulders. "It wants you, Mars. It has been asking for *you*. You need to run. I can't hold them all off."

Me.

Me, the queen.

Bria stands me up. The swarm boils apart in the air behind her. The girls watch it with rapturous admiration. Within it I see shapes. Patterns. The same seductive patterns I saw when the umbral honey sank into my throat and filled me with its astounding gravity. I feel it locking onto me, pulling me closer.

Bria shakes me.

"You don't want this," she growls. "Caroline thought she did, but she was wrong and it tore her apart. You know far less than she did. The same will happen to you."

I'm not so sure. The song of the hive is singing for me. It searches through my mind and, finding the knot of my pain, it picks at it. Unravels it. Begs it open so that it can fit itself inside.

Bria slaps me so hard I'm thrown to the ground. It's enough to clear my head. When I look up, there's two of her. No, there's Bria and then a double swimming beside her. For a second, I recognize Caroline in the dual glare.

"Run," they say in unison.

For once, I listen.

CHAPTER 32

On new legs, I fly.

The forest rips beneath me.

I have no one now. Everyone—everything—is behind me. All of it trapped in the chill of the pond. All of them, chained together by their littlest fingers, humming and crying and laughing and burning.

They burned Mimi.

When the cocoon burst apart, nothing dropped out. Not even a blackened skeleton. Whatever she had become was smaller than ash.

Run, Bria had said. Like if I didn't, I'd be bundled up within the fist of the swarm, crushed or incinerated or—

Embraced.

Every hive needs a queen, Bria had said, *and Caroline was that queen.*

And it killed her.

I cry out as I run, but I don't stop. My scream and my legs are the same, just the outward expression of something breaking within me. I came here with a question. I promised I wouldn't run this time. But here I am, sprinting, because I was never strong enough for this answer.

The forest thins and I hurtle over a low rock wall. The trees on the other side snap into a grid. I'm in an orchard. A farm comes into view and I slow. I can make out the blinking lights on a grain silo and, below that, the tidy lines of a house. I swallow down my panic, force calm into my limbs, and jog toward it. I briefly consider asking for help but then I spot an ATV in the yard. Even better. I've only driven one once, but I remember marveling that it was legal to move that fast while that unprotected.

I hop on and press buttons until a headlight pops on. I keep pressing things until the beast rumbles to life. With a twist of the handle the ATV gives a bratty jerk, nearly tossing me. After another few tries, I manage a lopsided circle. I even figure out the brakes.

A screen door slaps open and a man yells, "Hey!"

"I'm sorry!" I yell back.

I swerve onto a gravel driveway, nearly behead a rickety mailbox, and swing onto a paved road. As soon as I've got a straight shot, I open the throttle, and *whoosh!* Wind fills my ears. So does the mechanical roar of the engine, and the uncanny silence of the road's black ribbon. And for *once* I can't hear the incessant chirping of bugs. It sounds like freedom. Finally.

I remember the ride into Aspen, all those drops and hairpin turns. I take them slowly so I don't catapult myself into the ravines hiding behind the guardrails. Eventually I exit the deep forest and glide past sloping, manicured fields. Houses rush up against the road. Ahead I see—oh my fucking god, thank you, gay Jesus—a traffic light.

I pull the ATV over in a yard cluttered with lawn ornaments and continue on foot. Whoever I stole this from probably called the police, and they'll be looking for a rogue ATV. Actually, I wouldn't be surprised if they were also skeptical of the bloody, gender-fluid teen in a crop top, short shorts, and hiking boots.

I flip my septum ring down, just to complete the look.

The town is bigger than I thought. I can hear the highway through the thinning trees, and the glow of neon signs up ahead blots out the moon. The stars are still visible, but now they're just scratches on the flat black night. Not the majestic geometry that hangs above Aspen. And thank god. I'm done with the majesty of the wilderness for a long time.

I walk, ducking into the trees when cars pass and wondering what I should do. The police are out of the question for a few reasons: First, there's my fetus-old ATV larceny from Old MacDonald. Second, I'm a

Matthias, not that I can even prove it. I don't have a phone. And with my haircut, I don't even look like my own ID. So, I guess that's three.

I'm still strategizing when I look up and, in the most ironic tragedy of my entire messed-up life, I am standing before Applebee's. In fact, I think it's the exact same Applebee's we stopped in on our way up.

Kismet, karma, or justice, I'm no longer ignoring coincidences, especially of this caliber.

Very funny, Caroline, I think as I walk inside.

"Oh, sorry, but we're closed—"

The hostess sees me and stops short. I'm sticky with sweat and probably filthy. I don't know what she sees but I probably only have a second before she takes out an Applebee's-themed rifle and shoots me.

"Help," I say. "I need help. I need to use your phone, and then I'll go. I promise."

She just responds with a smug "I *knew* it!"

I have time to wonder if I've made a terrible mistake, but then another waitress rushes in from the dining room waving a rag.

"Wait!" she says. "You're Heather Matthias's son, aren't you? Oh, we *knew* it was her a few weeks ago. I swear, we were just talking about how we should have gotten a picture and put it up on our celebrity board."

She points at a section of the wall where two photos hang. I spy Guy Fieri and then in the second photo, also Guy Fieri.

I relax. This I can handle. "Can I use your phone? I need to call my mom, actually."

The waitresses wave me over to a phone inside the host's booth. Before I pick it up, I give them a serious look. They both have their phones out.

"No photos," I say. "You can't tell anyone I'm here. It's . . . top secret."

They give a conspiratorial nod and put their phones away. I dial home.

When I hang up, the waitresses have set a booth in the back for me. They sit me in it, accepting no protest as they set down, grandly, a basket of mozzarella sticks. And boneless wings. There are chips and quesadillas, too.

"We didn't know what you'd like, so we went with a Classic Combo," says one, fidgeting with her pad.

"Love a Classic Combo," I say. "Thank you so much."

This settles them. They eye the empty seat across from me, waiting for my invitation.

"Actually, can I use your bathroom?" I ask.

The waitresses would be honored. They introduce themselves as Greta and Susan as they—both of them—walk me to the bathroom.

"Take all the time you need," they say. "We'll be here if you need us." They give each other big winks and pull away, giggling.

The bathroom is the same as when I was last here, bleeding into the sink. As I wash my face, I try to ready myself for what's to come. Dad was *so* shocked to hear from me. He knew something was wrong immediately. He didn't even ask if I was okay. Just: "Where are you?"

I told him and, after a humiliating pause, he asked, "The *same* Applebee's?"

"I love the Irresist-A-Bowls. They're irresistible."

"Do not move," he commanded. "Do not talk to anyone. We'll call you from the car."

Susan and Greta promise to let me know if the phone rings, but it doesn't. After I've washed myself as best I can, I pat myself dry with paper towels. Then I return to the phone and try Dad's cell. Nothing. I try Mom's and she picks up.

"Mars, sweetie, are you okay? What's going on?"

"Heather, don't." That's Dad. I can hear that I'm speakerphone. They're already in the car.

"I'm fine," I say.

"Good. Stay put. We'll be there in a few hours. Don't call again," Dad says.

"Martin, Christ, you sound like your father," Mom whispers. "Mars, sweetie, are you safe?"

I glance at Greta and Susan, who have started picking at the Classic Combo platter.

"Yeah, I'm safe. Just hurry, okay?"

"You know the drill?" Dad says.

"Yes, sir."

"Good. Don't make any more of a scene."

"Yes, sir."

The line dies.

A few hours later, Greta, Susan, and I are best friends. I learn all about Greta's pet praying mantis named Minerva, her book club, the things that trigger her eczema, and her interest in dogs even though she's allergic and also they scare her. Also, they trigger her eczema. Susan tells me about her nephew, who is trans, but she is so worried about offending me that I never quite manage to parse much more.

We all notice when a car pulls into the empty plaza, pauses, and then circles around to the back. The phone rings, just once, like a doorbell.

"I'll get it," I say, scooting from the booth. Greta and Susan grip each other as if to reassure themselves that *it's happening!* Then they look at the mess of the table. It's covered in greasy baskets and smears of dipping sauces and—yes, fine—an Irresist-A-Bowl.

I walk through the bright kitchen, spooking myself when the decaying decor of the kitchen from the wetlands hotel flickers over my vision. I push on, to the back door, and wave to the dark car behind the dumpsters. After a moment the lights flash, and out rush my parents. My mom reaches me first, crushing me in a hug. Dad waits until she's checked every available patch of skin for a scratch, and then he hugs me, too.

Inside, Greta and Susan stand at attention beside our now-spotless table. Dad hands me a duffel bag and orders me to get changed. Back in the bathroom, I find everything I need for a fresh start. Wet wipes, deodorant, fresh clothes. They even packed my makeup, and a little biohazard bag. For evidence.

Leave no trace.

I have to force myself not to think of Wyatt as I use the supplies to rebuild myself. By the time I'm done, we could walk into church and no one would have any clue what I'd been through.

I find Greta and Susan flailing about my parents in the kitchen, asking again and again if they can get us anything. Mom politely declines. Then the two women spend a tearful few minutes telling Mom how much they admire her, what a role model she is. Dad's patience is faultless for this sort of thing, but when the waitresses start fawning over *me*, he gets restless. Greta is telling us how she didn't know what "a gender fluid" or "a nonbinary" was until tonight, when Dad finally cuts in.

"Heather, we should go. Ladies, we're so sorry to inconvenience you like this. Thank you for feeding our son. Will this cover it?"

He hands them a thick envelope of bills, way more than the price of a hundred Irresist-A-Bowls.

"We won't be needing change, but we would appreciate your discretion in the matter of keeping this between the people in this room. Are we clear?"

The ladies say yes, sir, of course, sir. Then they hug me goodbye and make me promise to come visit.

We leave through the back door.

"We'll talk more once we get to the highway," Dad says.

Mom rubs my back. She kisses the side of my head before slipping into the driver's side. I pop open the trunk to toss in the duffel, but of course the trunk is full of Mom's garment bags. I try to shove the duffel in but I encounter something firm. Rubbery, almost.

A familiar buzzing picks up in my ear.

Out here the night smells like wet asphalt and exhaust as the car starts, but from the trunk drifts an organic odor. Something sticky, putrid, and sweet. As slowly as I dare, I drag the zipper down the curves of whatever hides inside. Out pours that stink, so thick my eyes sting.

I peel open the bag.

I think I scream. I think I leave my body. Hands—my father's—clap over my mouth and I suck in a new smell. Sharp, chemical. The colors wink out of my vision and I go limp. The last thing I see is my mother rushing to close the bag up, the zipper catching once, twice, on Caroline's nose. Then I'm locked inside myself, the vision of her mummified corpse my only companion.

CHAPTER 33

I awaken in pieces.

In blinking circuits.

Each new sensation lights up nerves still drowsy with drugs, connecting me back together. First I'm just my ears: I hear the rolling static of cicadas, scored by the crickets' chorus, and the murmur of a crowd. And the ever-present, far-off undulation of the hive. Then I'm a nose: I smell damp notes of moss, and concrete crumbling to dust, and a mellow, fungal thickness dotted with the spice of hickory.

My brain jams these pieces together until I realize: I'm back at the hotel.

I can't move. I can't even twitch my fingers, but I'm not numb. Not at all. I can feel that I'm upright, encased in something warm and sticky. Honeycomb, folded around me like a cocoon. Just like how we found Brayden.

"Wake him."

It's my mother's voice. My eyes fly open but I see nothing. Just the after-image of Mom struggling to zip up the garment bag and hide the pale thing within. Caroline's body, wrapped in opaque plastic, laid to rest in the back of our Buick. Then Dad shoving a chloroform rag into my mouth. Then the ceiling of the back seat before Mom reaches back to place, with maternal tenderness, an eyeless mask over my face.

Maybe it's the drugs, but I barely grasp the horror of it. Instead, I think: *I can't wait to tell Caroline I was abducted behind an Applebee's, how embarrassing, oh my god.*

The mask scratches as it's lifted away and I can finally see. For the first time in my life, I wish with complete conviction to be back at Applebee's.

I look down into a long, dark room painted in torchlight. Yellowed columns rise to form arches that never meet in the middle, like snapped wishbones. The ground has eaten through the foundation and the sky has eaten through the roof. What seems to hold the entire place together is a web of ivy, but despite the ruin of it all, there's a reverence to it. I'm in a church. All around me are saplings strung with paper lanterns. I'm hanging right above the altar, where the stained-glass window would shine down on . . .

People. People in white jumpsuits stand in a tightly packed, hushed congregation, staring up at me from below. They wear those impenetrable veils, but I know they're looking at me because I'm rocking slightly in whatever holds me, and the congregation rocks with me. I try my hardest to move and all I get is the creak of the honeycomb, and a tickling drop down my eyebrow. Even my thoughts feel seized.

"He's awake," says a person below me. They hold a long, hooked pole, my wicker mask at the end of it.

"Then we await the sun. You may remove your veils."

The people pull off their veils. I stare into a crowd of adults. Parents, I realize, from Jubilee Weekend, wearing the same dopey, excited grins from when they toured our cabins and sat with us at meals, absorbed in the idyllic fabrications of Aspen. I even spy a few of Aspen's senior staff. There's Wendy, close by, and she's holding the arm of a little old lady—the one from the farmer's market, the one called *elder*. Side by side, I see their resemblance, though all the faces blend with united rapture.

That's how I find Mom and Dad. They stand at the very back, and they're the only people not smiling.

What . . . ?

I try to speak. My tongue squirms beneath a weight I'm only just registering. Something prickly in my mouth bleeds the taste of black licorice.

Another star anise. Even though I know what it is—it's no heavier than a coin on my tongue—I can't spit it out.

"The hive is higher!" Mom calls out. The congregation repeats this back to her in one voice. *THE HIVE IS HIGHER!*

"The sun rises," she calls out. "And with it, an end to the old. And with it, the birth of eternity. And with it, us."

AND WITH IT, US!

The reverence breaks, and the adults set to a flurry of tasks. Rather, the men do. They serve the women crystal goblets off ringed disks of wood. Hors d'oeuvres appear and I smell the minted meat of keftedes from my mom's own kitchen, hear the snap-crunch of phyllo dough pastries. It's a cocktail party atmosphere. I'm struck by the familiarity of watching it from afar, like Caroline and I always did, from the banister in our house. I wonder: Was it these same people, but I never noticed?

Wendy raises her glass for a speech.

"Before we begin, allow me a few words," she says, quieting the party. "On behalf of the Aspen Chapter, thank you all for joining us. None of us expected to be back here so soon after last year's queening, but . . ."

Wendy gives a sigh. She's looking at Mom not with compassion, but with well-practiced condescension. A few people snicker.

"It has been a hard, hard year," Wendy continues. "Our umbral yields have been at their lowest in a century. Our prognostications have continued their imprecise trends, all but immobilizing the Conservancy's market operations. And of course the hive has suffered . . . disruptions. A failed queen, and from the Matthias bloodline. Such a shame!"

"Yes," Mom croaks. "It was quite the surprise."

"Oh, I don't know about that," Wendy says easily. "If I recall, almost one year ago at the last queening, some of us tried to raise doubts about Ms. Matthias's suitability? So sad they had to come to fruition. Heather, Martin, we are so sorry for your loss."

"A failed queen is a loss to all of us," Mom says, bitter and barbed.

"Yes, well." Wendy shrugs. "Here's to hoping we chose better this time, then. The hive is higher!"

THE HIVE IS HIGHER!

It's fencing. Feints and lunges. Mom gives a pinched smile, raising her own glass like I might raise my sword. "A shame indeed," she says. "A hard year for *all* our girls. It's unfathomable that so much could go so wrong right here, beneath the *careful* management of the Aspen Chapter. A splinter swarm, right beneath our noses? My, Wendy, if I didn't know you so well, I would say poor Mimi had some help in her little rebellion."

A pause. Everyone has heard the accusations in my mother's words.

"But you'd never allow that, would you?" adds my mother.

"A dim queen leaves ample shadows for dissent," Wendy chirps. It's the effort in her easiness that betrays her now. "And girls will be girls, I suppose. They had to go so *long* without a proper Leader. Rebellion couldn't be helped, but they handled it just fine. We can agree on that, can't we?"

"Can we? I for one would like to hear from the girls myself. Ladies?"

The crowd ripples with intrigue as the Honeys enter. They stay in a clump, staring at everything but me before finally fixating on a dark corner I cannot see.

Help me, I think at them. *Please.*

They're exhausted, and scared, and it makes them look unlike themselves. Absurdly regular.

"Who wants to explain what happened this evening?"

The girls lock together in silent protest. I realize there's no Bria. Did they execute her, too, for saving me?

"Fine," says my mother. "Let's hear from Ms. Lewis, then. Let her speak."

This is directed toward the corner the Honeys have been watching, which suddenly erupts in a commotion as someone gasps to life.

"Brianna Lewis," says my mother in a shade of disappointment. "I've just learned that when you had the chance to secure our next host, you not only held back, but prevented your sisters and our drones from giving chase. What do you have to say for yourself?"

"This will fail!" Bria spits out the words, like she's trying to rid herself of the numbing anise. "What's higher? The hive, or the bureaucracy of the Conservancy? How many times are you going to force an unwilling queen so that you can stay rich with our predictions?"

Several adults rush to quiet Bria but my mother raises her hand, halting them. I see her slip into the charitable pensiveness she adopts when answering dumb voter questions.

"Bria, we force nothing. You know that deep down, don't you? With guidance from the lace, the Conservancy simply creates the *safe* and *necessary* conditions for a powerful hive."

Contempt colors Bria's voice. "Powerful, or productive?"

"Powerful, productive, *rich*. There's no difference, sweetie," Mom says. "It's the way of nature that great power comes with vast appetites. Our power has always been our connections—to one another, to nature, to the lace. The umbral honey fortifies those connections. Without it the network frays, we grow weak, and our apex falters. But starting today, we begin to rise again. Like the sun—"

"Oh, shut *up* about the stupid sun!" Bria shouts. "You forced Caroline to be queen and it was a mistake, and now you're making the same mistake again. Your greed will collapse us all."

The word *collapse* causes whispers to spread. Mom calls out, "That's enough."

After a struggle, Bria's muffled protests vanish. I watch Bria through the Honeys, who adopt expressions I recognize from Caroline's repertoire: intelligent rage tucked behind blank, tired stares. Whatever this party is—the Conservancy or the Aspen Chapter or whatever—the Honeys despise it. They fear it, too. I realize I was wrong, thinking all this time that these girls were beekeepers. The adults are the true keepers, the girls the kept force.

Mom calls for the uncertain crowd's attention once again.

"I know what you're thinking," she says. It's a gentler tone. From experience, I know she is beginning an appeal. "Caroline had her doubts. But I assure you, Mars does not. He returned to Aspen of his own volition, just as custom states a new queen must. We made sure of it."

This, I realize, is true. I fought so hard to do exactly what they wanted.

"Caroline failed," my mother states. "Mars will not. If anything, her failure proves that *she* was the foretold spare, not him. We must trust the lace, complete the ascension, or else we'll endure another season like the last. Ask yourselves, can your industries suffer more losses? Can you afford to operate your empires without the guidance of the lace?"

The whispering lessens.

"And then ask yourself one more thing..." Mom articulates every word with hushed urgency. "Should you have to? I say: You do not. Weakness is a choice. We must choose unanimous strength. That has been our sisterhood's way for centuries."

The whispering has ceased.

"The doubt, if you feel any at all, is the insidious symptom of our fraying network. Nothing more. The throne has merged successfully with the Matthias DNA once. It will do so again. Today. But if Ms. Lewis is correct about one thing, it's that if we cannot move forward together as one, we will fail at once. I lay this choice in the hands of our unanimity."

Mom raises up a hand, a snap poised at her fingertips. The hands of the other Conservancy members go up automatically, along with most of the crowd. Wendy pauses for a fraction of a second, along with several others near her, but they all gradually lift their hands. None are willing to be the one withholding unanimity.

Everyone snaps, the hot summer air bubbling with their consent.

THE HIVE IS HIGHER, the crowd intones, but it's not the righteous shout of before. The unison has come undone at the edges.

"Good." Mom steps back. "Let's hurry. Morning approaches."

The crowd separates, and from the back of the church a group of men roll a large slab forward, its load veiled in lace.

My heart begins to pound.

I know what lies beneath the lace. I know that shape.

The crowd maneuvers the Honeys so that they stand between me and the slab. The girls hesitate and I try to reach out to them again. *Don't! Please!*

But they can't hear me. They form their daisy chain and their telltale hum starts low. The adults produce small jars, twisting off the lids and dipping their pinkies into jewel-red honey, sucking at the substance with indulgent moans. Then the congregation merges their voices to the rising hum, thickening the air with harmony.

The thing on the slab stirs.

I pull away, all my muscles straining to produce barely even a twitch.

People gather at the slab's edges and begin to lift. It rises like it weighs nothing. They angle it toward me.

"We begin with the sun," Wendy calls.

The lace falls away, exposing everything below in the blue-gray of the breaking dawn. It's not my sister. Not anymore. It's curled at the slab's center, nude, the limbs strangely sickled. But her face is the same. Same nose, same lips. Even the eyes remain perfectly preserved.

I pull against my constraints, desperate to put any distance between me and that strange body, but instead I feel myself inch closer. A magnetism begins to collapse the space between us.

Not us. Me, and that *thing*.

"The sun rises!" Wendy cries out. "And with it, us!"

AND WITH IT, US!

The sun arrives as a sideways radiance, punching buttery bars of light through the church's empty windows. The slab lights up, the thing upon it erupting with amber radiance. Everything—the ivy, the columns, every single upturned face—submerges in an undulating, fiery brilliance. My eyes burn but do not blink. My sister's features melt away, leaving behind a neon silhouette of molten glass.

"Higher!" Wendy calls.

The adults crawl over one another as they try to lift the slab up, and up, and up. They crush one another, stand atop shoulders, flow into a writhing mound that hoists their sun toward me.

"Royalty," Wendy yells in a voice that's nearly singing. "Abandon one to fortify another!"

A droplet stings my cheek, followed by a drizzle across my mouth. I try to close my eyes but the golden figure burns even brighter in the dark of my mind. Its incandescence liquefies, stringing toward me. I feel the *pat, pat, pat* of each individual drop until they merge into a silent, sticky pressure. It flows over me. Through me. My eyes stay closed, my mouth does, too, but all across my body I feel tiny pricks of agony, like my pores are being pried open.

I become one wound.

A void, being filled to the brim with light.

CHAPTER 34

In the woods, there is a lake.

Across the lake, there is a meadow.

Atop the meadow, there is a house.

Through the house, there is a hive.

And within the hive, there are bees.

Bees that forge a single teaspoon of honey in a floating dance across one hundred thousand flowers; flowers that push with haughty defiance through the frosted earth to open; the earth, a living mosaic grown from every dead thing buried below; the dead things shedding the particles of their lives; particles that remember sunlight, starlight, moonlight; or sadness, laughter, love. Memories. Particles. The dead, the earth, the frost, the flowers. And honey. The threads between all things pull together in a single drop of honey.

In the woods there is a lake.

Across the lake there is a meadow.

Atop the meadow there is a house.

Through the house there is a hive.

And within the hive lives a bridled vastness. A consciousness old enough to remember the patterns of all things, bright enough to illuminate them, and bold enough to influence them. Hungry, too, for everything must eat to grow.

In the woods a lake.

Across the lake a meadow.

Atop the meadow a house.

Through the house a hive.

Within the hive, everything.

Everything.

In the infinite eyes of everything, the present is nothing more than an intersection made out of space and time and—most important of all—intention. The present is a seam that doesn't exist between what was and what will be. The then, the now, the later? They are colorful shadows cast from a single light, split through the prism of experience. Just reflections and rainbows. Just math, to the eyes of the infinite.

The woods a lake.

The lake a meadow.

The meadow a house.

The house a hive.

The hive, everything.

The true form of reality is not a loop and not a continuum; not a volley between the cause and effect of now and then; not the pleasant idiocy of a path between two predetermined points. It's a lace, intricate and infinite, woven through all things.

In.

Across.

Atop.

Through.

Within.

The weave of the lace complicates inward, layering into a design so dense it becomes invisible. Unknowable. You must be small as a bee to trace it, yet as vast as the hive to comprehend it.

In, across, atop, through, within . . . and beyond.

That is where I am now. Beyond. Watching the churning design of the world from across a cold distance, like the stars watch us. Caroline used to tell me *Earth to Mars*. Well, the earth has finally come to me, and now I am vast enough to return its embrace.

I know who I am, but not what. A collective, a summation, or maybe a hive mind? I don't feel frayed and pulled to pieces like I thought I would. I'm not annihilated. I remember my body, my life, my memories. I remember being alone. That's the one thing that hasn't changed. Even here, within the nexus of all of nature, I'm still alone.

"Oh, *please*, Mars."

Oh?

I heard her. I swear, just now, it was her. I trace the echo, pulling myself down into the scalding lattice of space, time, and everything. I let my memory guide me, and what I arrive within is a dark garden.

It's the garden back home. The windows of the house have been flung open to let out the heat of the party and invite in the cool of the night. We are having our own party in the shadow of another, with secondhand light and scavenged music and a stolen bottle of prosecco. That it's embarrassing and cheap doesn't matter, because we . . .

We.

"There you are!" she says. "Finally!"

She's here.

My sister. She's *here*. Right before me.

I hug Caroline. She's real. She hugs me back and I'm a body again. Not a floating mind, not a sprawling lace, but a body that feels her solid warmth, that smells her shampooed hair, that can hold her one more time.

"I looked for you," I whisper into her hair. "I looked everywhere for you."

"I know," Caroline says. "I was everywhere. But I'm here now."

It's a minute before we break apart, or it's a lot longer. The time here feels unsure of it itself.

"Where is here?" I ask.

Caroline plucks at the bushes, absently picking out dead leaves as we walk together.

"It's a net; it's a map; it's the lace. We don't really know. It's the dimension of consciousness between all things, which the honey allows us to comprehend. Think of it like all the world's memory, but going backward *and* forward."

"Is this a memory?"

"This is." She gestures at the garden. "We're not."

"Are you . . . real?"

"I'm . . . something. I'm trapped, I think. And so are you. Oh, Mars, I'm so sorry you got bound to the hive. I never wanted this for you."

We reach the far edge of the garden, the music fading behind us. The same music fades in from ahead, and we reenter the garden.

"Want to dance?" Caroline says.

"Sure."

"Wait. But first, want to switch?"

I'm in my usual suit, she in her summery dress. The second I consider switching, we've switched.

Caroline smiles. "Gimme a twirl!"

I give her a twirl. I throw a hand out for her and she catches it, and I spin her around. Her tie slaps my wrist. We dissolve into our dramatic routine, finishing the dance in her usual bow, my usual curtsy. What's strange is that no adults come to disrupt us, though I hear them talking louder.

"Look, Mars, I don't know how long we have," Caroline says. We stand still now, just out of the light's reach, holding hands.

"Real or not, I need to apologize to you. The night that I attacked you, I thought I was doing the right thing. I wasn't myself. By then I was . . . I don't know. Confused and scared."

I can see it as she saw it. Caroline in the shed behind Cabin H, sitting in a circle with Bria, Sierra, and Mimi, the melted nub of a candle between them. As they hum, the wick flares to life, and gradually the candle un-melts, pulling wax from the perfumed air. When the candle is formed, Caroline picks it up. Stamped in the cooling wax is my name. MARS.

"The lace tells us so much. Who to target; who to help. The candles tell us who to recruit. When your candle came up, I knew it meant I would fail as queen."

Caroline sits in a row of the Aspen chapel, watching some girls onstage rehearse. Sierra sits with her, talking animatedly while Caroline looks across the empty lake. I know this look. She's deciding on a plan.

"I had been failing for some time. The Conservancy was demanding so much from us. I wanted to meet their demands, but I could feel the hive's power corrupting in my body. I didn't want it, and it didn't want me."

Caroline lies bundled in her bed in Cabin H as Mimi pets her shoulder. Caroline's eyes focus on the far distance, but I'm watching Mimi. I think I see the moment her sympathy runs out. I see, in the lamplight, the first sparks of resentment toward my sister.

"I knew right away that I would fail, too. I never wanted to be queen. I never had the choice. But you know our parents. Not a huge fan of options."

Deeper in the past, Caroline is slumped at our kitchen island, eyes red and nose raw. Mom and Dad stand across from her in a unified front of disappointment. They are telling her that if the hive cannot produce more honey, it will all collapse, all of it. Aspen, the Conservancy's network of wealth and power. The secret sisterhood that runs the world. And it will be because of her. They are suggesting, once again, that Caroline force the Honeys to harvest without those dated, righteous rules.

Caroline is telling them that's not how it works, that the hive has not just an appetite, but *taste*, but she only gets so far in this explanation before they tell her she isn't trying; she's letting fear drive her. They're reminding her for the hundredth time that they raised her for this one reason. And they again mention that no one is irreplaceable to the hive.

Least of all the queen. Certainly not Caroline. Not when her understudy lives in the house with her.

Then they're suddenly laughing to burn away the somber atmosphere, an act to cover up the fight as I walk in from the back door. I don't linger. I shrug off my winter coat, throw it onto a chair beside Caroline, and charge up to my room.

"I told our parents I would attend to the hive even in the winter, but I had one condition: that they leave you alone completely. After what happened to you at Aspen, I never wanted you to come back. But I missed you, Mars. There were a million moments I wanted you there. I'm sorry if my protection looked like exclusion. It was. And it was almost worth it."

I see myself as Caroline saw me. Distant, cold, but ultimately comfortable. Bitter in my solitude but safe because of it.

"When your candle came up this summer, after a year of trying to get ahold of my rule, after a year of failing to produce enough, after all the promises Mom and Dad made to manipulate the Conservancy into ascending me . . . I knew it was over. I knew I was done. If I didn't leave, the girls would have had to kill me themselves. That's the way of bees. So I left."

Now I'm watching Caroline running from Aspen, just like I did. I see her sitting outside in the chilly brightness of a gas station, and our parents' car pulling up. They don't offer her fresh clothes like they did me. They don't speak to her. They drive through the night, all the way home. Inside our house they descend to our basement, to the wine cellar, and then to a room I have never seen. It's lined in aspen bark—the floor, the walls, the ceiling all swirled with eyes. They sit her at a table. It's the only thing in the room, though the empty shelves make it clear this place once held some sort of abundance.

"Umbral honey. The room was supposed to be for our personal hoard. The sole reason we were raised, Mars."

Our parents stand over Caroline's shoulders. They tell her that she can end it, but please, dear, don't ruin your body. It'll be a vessel until Mars is ready. They leave her with a noose. And her hive tool, of course. After they've locked her inside, she cries. She waits for them to regret it, but they don't. Her mind darkens with futility, but one thing halts her from giving in: knowing that once she's gone it will be her sibling's turn.

Think, Caroline, she tells herself. And with her last trace connection to the lace, she asks what she should do.

"There was no escape for me. For either of us. I only saw one option."

Caroline crushes the light bulb and the room blackens. High on one wall the panels are scored with light from behind. Caroline hacks into the soft wood with her hive tool, filling her hands with splinters, prying away the panels to reveal a squat window. Breaking it is easy, but digging her way out takes until nightfall. But she does it. Cut up and crying, she escapes, and she nearly lets herself run, but those final visions from the lace turn her back toward the house. She looks up at the balcony. Our balcony.

"I'm sorry, Mars."

Caroline stands over my bed. Her thoughts scrape through the fried architecture of her mind. All she thinks about is her failure, and what it will mean for her sibling. All she's known is the pain of a legacy she never asked for, and the humiliation of never being enough to fulfill it. It's heavy. It's crushing. It's nothing she would ever wish upon anyone.

Especially someone she loved.

"I love you, Mars," she says, raising the sundial high.

In the dark garden, Caroline lets go of my hands. Tears stain her cheeks. They glow a faint gold in the light from the party.

"I'm sorry. I'm so sorry," she whispers.

I hug her and whisper back, "I'm sorry, too."

"For what? I hurt *you.*"

"But someone hurt you first. And . . ." I think about sitting with Wyatt in the hayloft, before he turned on me. I think about all the heaviness I gave up when I finally told the stars the truth. I reach for it now.

"I was jealous. I thought you were so ungrateful because you had the life I wanted, and you didn't even want it back. And I resented you for it. But I didn't know. I didn't know anything at all. I thought we would have our whole lives to make up. I said goodbye to you so much earlier than I had to."

Caroline squeezes my hand.

"Death isn't the end," she says. "It's just when we become everything else."

"But I don't want everything else, Caroline. I can't apologize to everything else, or hug everything else. Or watch a movie. Or talk. Or see you. I don't know who I am if I'm not your twin."

Caroline laughs.

"So dramatic, Mars. You've never needed anyone to tell you who you are. It's what I admire about you most. No force on this planet can compare to that will of yours." She taps my head.

"Perks of being the evil twin, I guess," I mumble.

The familiar hum seeps out of the distance. The light from the window grows brighter, the adults louder. For a breath I hear the fevered mosh of all those bodies crawling atop one another, lifting the radiant corpse toward the sun.

"It's ending," Caroline says. "Listen, Mars. You're strong. You are the strongest person I know. There's nothing we can change about the past, but you can make your own future. The hive needs you. Not Dad and Mom and all those adults, but the hive. The girls. *We* are the ones connected to the bees. All those other people are the parasites that have built up a fortress around us. They think they're in charge, but the whole system collapses without us. And you're our queen now. The hive chose *you* for what must come next. Do you understand?"

"I think so."

"Know so," she commands.

The window is blinding now, the party a roar at my back. Caroline and I automatically raise our hands against the light, casting shadows across each other's eyes. Together we dissolve in the rising radiance, but together we stay for just one more second.

Before she fades, I think: *I love you. I love you. I love you, Caroline.*

Then I can see only her eyes, and my reflection in them, and I'm falling backward, backward, back through the stars, through the earth, through the watching woods. Over a lake. Across a meadow. Into a house. Into a home.

Into a hive, where a young queen has just awoken.

CHAPTER 35

I fall to earth.

I land in the arms of the Honeys, who have reached up to claim me from the sky. They wrap over me in intricate knots of affection, gratitude, and relief. I look up past their crying faces toward the broken height of the church to see if any traces of that shining golden body remain, but all that's left are motes of glittery pollen and a cloud of bees weaving between them.

I have changed. Something lives within me now. It watches the world through my eyes. When I see the bees, I see the shimmering tracks in the air upon which they flow. Like ghostly threads of starlight.

The girls help me stand. For the first time since awakening in the church, I can move on my own. I discover that I'm dressed in a heavy gown of translucent white fabric. It flows from me in all directions, grand and cumbersome. In the fresh morning light, it sparkles with golden embroidery. I turn and it sweeps the mossed altar where I landed. It's majestic, an outfit perfect for a queen's coronation.

"Help her," Kyle whispers, squeezing my arm.

The girls back away from me and I face the crowd, which is still untangling from its mosh. As I stand, the congregation falls over themselves to reapply their veils and then kneel. The light here is still sideways, the sun still only just risen. So it was only a minute ago that I was dragged into the molten light. That means the time I spent with Caroline in that world, wherever it was, whatever it was, lasted only seconds.

It wasn't enough. I want to sink back into the sky and return to her, but the connection is almost gone. Just a glimmering thread stretching out into the bright abyss that buzzes in my head. I can feel her, though. She's not gone. Just everywhere.

"The hive is higher," says a voice.

THE HIVE IS HIGHER

Everyone rises. They don't remove their veils. But it's like I can see through the netting, through the thin skin of their faces and their brittle skulls, into each of their minds. It's similar to the sensation of consuming the umbral honey, where I felt as though I was simultaneously viewing the world through too many eyes, too many lives. The difference is that before, I felt as though everyone was within me. Now I feel as though I'm within everyone else. When I stare into the minds of the congregation poised in stolid reverence, it's myself I see reflecting back at me.

The hive is higher. And now I am the hive.

I turn to the girls around me. They stare at me with muted urgency. There is something they want me to know. I search their minds for any indication of what it is. Together, we are all thinking *help her,* but I've missed something crucial and they need me to see it.

"Welcome, Marshall Matthias the Third."

My mother's voice rouses the congregation from their stupor. They clap for me. She steps forward, still veiled, but I know it's her. Of all the minds I can peer into, the top members of the Conservancy remain beyond my reach. They appear to me as gray blots among the swirling network. Guarded. Out of my control.

My mother hands me a flat length of metal. A hive tool, much longer than normal and sharpened into a deadly saber. She backs away, as does the congregation. They line the edges of the space, forming a new perimeter around me. And now I see her, a girl slouched on the ground.

Help her.

It's Bria.

"As queen, your first duty is to secure your rule from all forms of subversion," my mother says. "The hive's synchronicity depends upon it. Do this, and your ascension is complete."

She means I have to kill Bria.

Bria knows this. She won't look at me. She doesn't have to, because I can feel the sour fear coursing through her. Death surrounds us, as certain as the sunrise. Bria feels it in the future. So do I. We both know what must be done.

I raise the hive tool until it's level with Bria's throat. She doesn't even flinch. She's scared, but she's too prideful to show anything other than strength. I can feel the iron authority of her mind as it applies its genius to the monumental task of holding herself steady. Authority like that cannot be tolerated in a hive. There is one will, and that will now works through me. Anything more than one and my mother is right. Synchronicity is forfeit; my rule may be ruined.

"Do it," my mother calls from the crowd. "Become queen."

I draw back the blade. It slides through the air with sinister ease, so sharp I know just a single flick could sever Bria's throat. I focus on her neck, watch her breathe. Deep breaths, each of them, like she's not sure which will be her last.

Help her. The girls thrum with a silent protest meant just for me. But it doesn't matter. I have gone this long without the affirmation of others. What was it Wyatt told me in the woods? *All anything in nature wants is to survive. Nothing evil about that.* He said that. I didn't believe him then but I believe him now. I am not the evil twin. I'm not evil at all. I'm only doing what I must, or what I want, if there's even a difference for a queen.

Fast as the wind, I swing the blade. A spray of red arcs up, sparkles in the morning light, then rains onto the mossy ground.

Next come the screams.

The girls behind me screaming with joy, and the congregation before me screaming in shock as one of the veiled figures drops. Their veil topples off when they hit the ground. It's Wendy. The hive tool juts from her shoulder.

Darn, I think. All the mysterious calculations of nature at my disposal, and my aim still sucks.

As the adults rush to Wendy, I stand Bria up. The Honeys help me undo her bindings. They pull her behind me. We stand in a compact formation atop the altar, facing down the furious congregation.

"How dare you!" someone screams. The elderly woman with different-colored eyes. My parents push to the front of the fray. They tear off their veils. "Marshall Matthias the Third, what do you think you are *doing*?"

"Leave," I say.

My father walks right up the altar. The Honeys back away but I can't, not in this dress. He stands over me like he's done so many times before, so that I can see the whites of his bulging, indignant eyes. There's a hatred in there that has always been kept especially for me, and now he doesn't bother hiding it.

"I don't know what you think you're doing," he says. "But this is bigger than one of your little protests. It's time to grow up. You are a part of this family, and it's time you acted like it. Your sister would want you to accept your role with grace and dignity."

"My sister," I say, "wanted to live."

"Oh, sweetie, of course," Mom says. "We all wanted that. But sometimes life has different plans for us. Everything happens for a reason. You can see that now, can't you?"

What I can see is the diabolical design that killed Caroline. A culture of toxic silence. An organization exploiting the lives of young girls. Parents who manipulate their children like disposable chess pieces. And me. A sibling who knew that she needed help yet didn't give it, who she *still* tried to save in the murky dusk of her final moments. Who she fought to hold, and who crushed her in return.

"The reason everything happens is because of *us*," I seethe. "We all failed Caroline, but *you* killed her. And now you talk about her like she wanted it, or any of this. But she didn't! She crushed herself trying to please you and it wasn't enough, and now she's gone and you *still* can't stop using her."

"Mars, your sister was very troubled," Dad says. "I don't know what you think you know, but she only ever wanted what was best for the hive. She would have wanted us to—"

"Stop it!" I shout. "Leave. Her. *ALONE*."

A wash of heat pours into the broken church, the sunlight fading as millions of tiny specks writhe down from the sky. They orbit the church like a living cosmos.

"Leave," I say again.

My father turns to my mother. They survey the sky as though pondering the likelihood of a sun shower. Whatever threat I think I've presented, they don't perceive it. Other members of the congregation slip away, dragging Wendy with them. I let them go.

"No further," my father commands.

I lower the swarm. Tighten the whirlwind.

My father grabs the front of my dress, violently shaking me.

"No further, Mars," he hisses. One of his hand wraps around my throat. Lightly. A promise. It reminds me of the murky nothingness I nearly succumbed to when Wyatt thrust me under the pond water. Like everything else, I can trace the threads—Wyatt's puppeteered violence, to Mimi's embittered betrayal, to Wendy's disdain for my family, to the power struggles of the Conservancy, to my forced ascension, to the grip around my throat.

All I have suffered flows backward from this moment, from this thing that wears my father's skin. Greed. The ravenous hunger that sees all things as consumable. People, lives, love. All of it just honey, all of it for the taking.

This is not survival. No other animal on Earth partakes in such brutal excess. This is a human vice. And now, with my own humanity compromised, I can't stand it.

A bee lands on my father's thumb, another on his wrist. He releases me, waving them away as he steps off my altar. More bees float downward, dizzily encircling my parents.

No, Caroline's killers.

"Girls," my mother cries out. "Control your queen."

The Honeys and I answer as one.

WE ARE NOT YOUR GIRLS

I gather my dress in shaking fists and together we march from the altar, the swarm parting like curtains to let us out into the aspen forest. Maybe it's the morning mist, or the net of tremulous dew cast over everything, but the eyes of the aspen trees shine with a fierce understanding. Then the silvery trees quake with the might of a storm imploding, all the heat of summer sucked past us in one great breath, drawn down into the church's burning belly.

If there are screams, they're buried beneath the drone of a new swarm taking flight, and a new colony rising.

CHAPTER 36

In the woods there is a lake. Across that lake there is a meadow. Atop the meadow there is a cottage, and within the cottage there is a blessed peace. It's the kind of relieved emptiness that falls over a space that has been suddenly deserted. There are signs of people all over—water drips into the sink, the door hangs open, a summer breeze ventures inside to play with the scattered joy of an abandoned board game—but there are no people.

Down in the meadow, there is laughter. The girls race over flashing puddles left behind by the recent storm, pile into a rickety canoe that balances just barely atop the mosaic of lily pads. They shove off—they're still laughing—and paddle their way to the middle of the lake, where we've positioned the floating dock.

"Thank god," Kyle says from the dock, reaching into the canoe to take the cloth-lined baskets from our outstretched hands. Bria and I are very careful as we unload all the things the girls asked for. We're the only pair capable of not instantly capsizing the canoe, so we get stuck doing deliveries, but it's best this way. Bria hates our afternoon ritual of just lying around.

"Like idiots," she adds.

"*Bored* idiots," I tack on.

We secure the canoe and scramble onto the dock. The other girls move to make room in their loose knot as we distribute the goods. We've brought watermelon and strawberries, but also crackers and a stiff block of sharp-smelling cheese. We couldn't find the plastic cups, if those ever even existed in Cabin H, so I grabbed a set of crystal tumblers from the hutch. Bria fills them with lavender lemonade from my frosty glass decanter.

"Fucking divine," CJ says after a sip. PJ grabs her tumbler to try it, but thinks it's too sour, which I anticipated. I unveil the small jar of honey I hid at the bottom of the basket.

"Oh, perfect," PJ says, snatching it up.

I lie back, a tumbler balanced on my chest. Condensation beads on it and soaks into my cropped shirt. I whirl the droplets with a nail painted a fresh, miraculous blue.

"They're here," Bria says a short while later.

"I know," I say. Because I felt them arrive at the Welcome Center. Donovan was there to greet them. He's taken over for Wendy ever since she had that fall—into a pitchfork, can you believe it?—and every day at lunch he gives Aspen an update on her recovery. The last several updates have all been: She's on the mend, and she can't *wait* to come home!

I suspect Wendy can very much wait to return to Aspen. In fact, I wouldn't be surprised if she never comes back at all, knowing we lie here waiting.

"She'll be back," Kyle says, answering my thoughts.

Kyle is right. I'm just being dramatic.

"Incoming," Marisol whispers.

We keep perfectly still, perfectly aloof, until the quiet over the lake is interrupted by Donovan calling my name. He's waving from the waterfront, a pair of unfamiliar adults behind him. They appear unsure and out of place in their dark suits.

"Want to take the canoe?" Bria asks.

"Nah," I say. I hand off my tumbler and dive in. The water is warmer than it used to be. Just like the sun is brighter, the sky bluer, and the trees greener. I haven't gotten used to the hypersensitivity yet, nor the way my thoughts ripple into nature and echo back. I kind of hope I never do, because it makes all things, even the slow paddle toward shore, feel important.

I reach the docks and pull myself up and out. I wave at Sylv as she helps a pair of Bandits pull a double kayak from the shed. A few of the Bear Hut boys are playing volleyball on the beach and they hail a hello, which I return with a sturdy salute. I pick over the grass, climbing up the hill, toward the pergola where Donovan waits.

He gives me a plaintive nod and steps aside, revealing our guests. A man and a woman. I don't know their faces. They wear stiff suits despite the heat and sport official-looking badges. We were making guesses last night about when they'd show up, and who they'd be. I guessed correctly that it'd be today, and they'd be detectives.

I sit down at the picnic table with them.

"Marshall." She says that name like an apology.

"Mars."

"Mars," she corrects. "We have some news that will be difficult for you to hear. Do you want to dry off and get changed?"

"No, I'm fine, thank you. What's wrong?"

The detectives exchange glances. I take a deep breath. It is time to perform.

"Mars, there's been a fire," she says.

They get most of the details right. They haven't quite figured out where the fire started yet (faulty wiring in a hidden room in the basement, the whole thing was lined in wood, it went up like a tinder box!), but I can live with the poetic injustice of this. The rest—the things that matter—are all confirmed. A fire during a storm, a downed tree across the access road, a fire truck that couldn't get there in time, and nothing but ashes left of the couple who had been inside. Not even bones.

When they're done, and when I've regained my own composure, the woman leans forward and takes my hand. She's stoic, but I can see the sympathy at the edges of her professional mask. I feel bad for deceiving them, but proud that my performance landed so well.

"Is there any family you can stay with?" she asks.

I think of my aunts, who I last saw in the kitchen during Caroline's Celebration of Life. I have a living grandmother, too. They were also children of Aspen, per the secret records Wendy kept. I have questions for them. Many, many questions. But I've had enough answers for now. I'm okay asking for nothing else for the rest of the summer.

But summer isn't forever. It will end, and the Conservancy will grow a new head, and if the honey doesn't flow, the blood will.

The girls and I will be ready for that fight. We alone are the hive, and we are done being kept.

I reach into the minds of the detectives, blurring their doubts so that when I raise my chin and tell them, "I'll stay here," they simply say yes, you will.

───────────

I trot back down to the lake, but before I dive in, I feel a familiar presence watching over me. I turn to the boathouse and there he is, in the shade of the deck. Wyatt.

I wave.

He doesn't wave back.

And I don't blame him. Wyatt remembers everything.

"How are you?" I ask. I've been asking. He hasn't answered me yet. But all the other times, he's run away. This time he stands his ground and finally has something to say.

"I tried to fix it."

I don't recognize what he holds up. It's an inorganic, blocky thing, with tape wrapped around it. It looks heavy, even in Wyatt's big hands.

"Your calculator," he says sadly.

"Oh," I say.

What a strange, dumb object. There was a time I saw myself in that calculator, but why? What could a simple machine know? It's nothing compared to the incalculable comprehension humming in my head. The comparison feels offensive now.

But Caroline picked it up. She chose it from all the other things in my room, and I still don't understand why. Of all the mysteries I can unravel, this one stays intact. It could be meaningless. But nothing feels meaningless anymore. Perceived all at once, Caroline's actions seem to add together to form not a path toward Aspen, but a trail through it. To here. To this glorious present.

Still, the calculator befuddles me. I don't like looking at it.

"Keep it," I tell Wyatt. "I don't need it anymore."

Wyatt's frown deepens. The girls are calling me from the floating dock. I wave at them, but don't dive in yet. I linger, watching Wyatt back, waiting for the moment he'll run away.

He surprises me when he blurts out, "Are you going to erase it all? You can, can't you, now that you're one of them?"

The Honeys can do incredible things. Uncanny, beautiful manipulations of nature and all its children. But there are some things too deeply rooted for even their scalpels to tease apart without fundamentally changing a person. Like my memories of Caroline. Like the dark bruise of Sierra. Traumas that become part of us, warping the deliberate pattern of our comb. We typically leave those alone, as a courtesy.

"Do you want me to?" I offer.

Wyatt does back away then, like I've bared my teeth at him.

Instinct tells me to do it right then and there, but shame holds me back. I *could* incinerate this horrible summer from Wyatt's mind. I *could* become something beautiful to him again. Every violation is available to me, and the hive thrums with a pleasant pressure at the chance to eliminate this loose end.

But then I think of the calculator, banged up and inelegant, cradled in Wyatt's hands, and I stop. I ignore the hive's instinct. It's easy to defy, just a small sting in my mind, though I wonder if this is how the ending began for Caroline, too.

"I won't," I tell Wyatt. "I promise."

Once upon a time, in a broken barn beneath the stars, Wyatt looked at me like he saw me. Not the abstraction, not the performance, but me, Mars. The person. When he looks at me now, it's like he's not sure what he's seeing.

I know that look well. It's the way the world has watched me my entire life, and it's nothing I cannot endure. I just wish I didn't have to endure it from him.

I turn from Wyatt and dive into the water, as deep as I can go, to where the murk blots out the light and I can float in the chilled weight-lessness of the dark. To where the constant hum in my head slows to sluggish thunder, and I can be alone with thoughts I know are my own.

I let myself wonder what Wyatt sees. I know he doesn't see me. I know because when I catch myself in the vanity mirror, or see my face stretched in the curved faucet of the sink as I do dishes, I don't see me either. Whoever I'm looking at, they seem happy. At home, even. But they aren't me.

Where does the hive end? And where do I begin?

What have I given away to become what I am?

It doesn't matter, I tell myself, because I'm happy now.

My lungs ache for air.

I let myself float up, up, up toward the light.

ACKNOWLEDGMENTS

This will end on a happy note, I swear, but before I get to all the lovely thank-yous, I need to say something.

I never wanted to write this book. I had to. I had to find a way to pin my own nightmares down and study them after I lost my sister, Julia, very suddenly in 2018. And while my sister's death was certainly foundational to much of this book, it wouldn't be right to simply "acknowledge" her here. For that, of all things. Her death was not a contribution. She did not choose it, want it, or deserve it. She was so much more, and I refuse to acknowledge her through the lens of tragedy. Instead, I'll say this:

In the aftermath of my sister's death, so much love was revealed to me in my own life. Kindness, and sympathy, and space when I needed it. I didn't have the capacity to properly thank people for even a fraction of it, but I've lived in gratitude since and done my best to write with that in mind. I realize now—just now writing these acknowledgments—that I wrote this book not as a response to death, but as a tribute to the love that helped me through the wilds of grief.

And you know what? My sister is part of that love. If there is a tribute to her here, it's for the version of her that will always and forever feel like pure love to me. The version I glimpse in every breathtaking view atop every mountain I climb in remembrance. That new sense of life is what, and who, I thank.

All right. Okay. Thank you for letting me say that. Now let's lighten the mood a little, okay? So! THANK YOU:

To my parents, for cultivating a childhood love not just for big adventures across big mountains, but also for the quiet study of plants and flowers and the small things that squirmed under the bricks in the backyard. I promise I only write about wicked parents because you raised me with love enough to prove queer kids can have so much better.

To Blase and David, and Shoko. And to little Phoebe, too young to read this book but just young enough to not protest the inevitable bee costume I'll make. And to Colin, a part of the family forever.

To my agent, Veronica Park, who I think emailed editors before I even finished telling her about this idea, and to Gordon for coaching me through a book deal while I had a literal blade to my throat (I was shaving).

To my editor, Zachary Clark. Zack, oh my god. Thank you. For championing this book, refining it with me, and putting up with my many rants about bees, dahlias, and pseudoscientific, hypothetical dimensional physics. And to David Levithan! It's a joy to be able to thank you on the page after all your inspiration, mentorship, and friendship.

To my amazing hive at Scholastic! To those responsible for the gorgeous, warped beauty of the book's design: designer Maeve Norton, artist Shane Rebenschied, and art director Elizabeth Parisi; to my publicity and marketing team, who have no clue what they're getting themselves into yet but are getting into it nonetheless: publicist Alex Kelleher-Nagorski, marketeers Rachel Feld and Shannon Pender; to my awesome production editor Janell Harris; to those early readers who gave invaluable feedback and enthusiasm to Mars's story: Melanie Wann, Carlee Maurier, Caroline Noll, Savannah D'Amico, Elizabeth Whiting, Roz Hilden, Jody Stigliano, and Nikki Mutch; and to ALL the rest of the bees buzzing in Scholastic, applying your individual genius to bringing books to humans, THANK YOU! Also, for the record, I know you're not actually bees. At least not all of you. At least not *yet*.

To my friends. All of you! And specifically: The Frals. Before this, I would have said you could never know what your friendships mean to me. But you can know, because you can read about Mars and the Honeys, and their cottage of elaborate meals and games, and recognize what your love has done for me. Thank you, for all of it. Also, I still have no idea how to play Azul. Also, Leah *did* fall.

And to my friends (the writer ones this time), starting with, of course, the WAPera. Claribel, seeing you mid-pandemic to sob and dance was literally life-giving. Phil, I can't wait to send you this book so you can pretend to throw it out. Thank you both for being so freaking hot.

To Zoraida and Victoria, my own personal Honeys. Our Catskill Cabin Retreat clarified and inspired, and I'm sorry for putting baby doll heads on your pillows, but honestly, it was funny. Victoria, you also gave me invaluable feedback on Mars and the Honeys right in time at, ironically, a We Work! Love that.

To my gay group chat, which until recently sported a photo of sexy Quasimodo as the icon. I miss it! Can we put it back? And to John Fram, who I brought with me on a research trip under the guise of "assistant," which, if you know John, is hilarious. To the many, many writers who have cheered me on, asked about this book, and raised an eyebrow at my response.

This'll be weird but: to my summer camps? Yes. I won't name names, but I really did absolutely adore my time at most of you. Actually, I will name Camp Jewell. I adored my time at Camp Jewell—it is *such* the opposite of Aspen; they share a rough layout and that's about it—and it helped me find immense confidence in my identity. Dustin, thank you for helping out on operations details. You're the best!

To Brian Moon at Moon's Gold Apiary in the Catskills, who let me suit up and say hi to his astounding bees. The candles I bought burned beautifully beside me as I wrote this book.

To David T. Peck, PhD and director of research at Betterbee, for an absolutely fascinating conversation about bees, beekeeping, and the sublime intelligence of superorganisms. I promised I wouldn't mention you in the event that this book is as scientifically inaccurate as *Bee Movie*. But you were so helpful, and I . . . hope this book isn't the next *Bee Movie*, so please allow the presumption of my gratitude.

To Andrew Coté, author of *Honey and Venom*, and urban beekeeper mastermind. It was great meeting you at the market, but honestly I'm here to thank you for some delicious honey. Does it come in umbral?

And to you. To my readers. I know I have not made it easy for you, dragging you from dreams and drag queens, to cons and costumes to . . . bees? *Bees?* And yet here you are! I love you all. Every day I look forward to your jokes and heartfelt messages. Most of all, I look forward to what you make with whatever inspiration I can provide.

Finally—lastly—I would like to thank bees. Every single bee. Personally. But there are so many of you! And—oh no!—I've run out of time! So please, if you see me in the wild, show yourselves to me and I will give you thanks without being asked.

—Ryan
Oct. 6, 2021

A sneak peek at BEHOLDER
by Ryan La Sala

The Sunday night of the party, a few hours before everyone dies, a girl with bleached bangs is telling you all about her future.

She is, of course, very wrong about what comes next. Her hand spiders up your leg (she thinks you're older than you are; everyone does). You are uncomfortable (with her, but also in general; the outfit you shoplifted for tonight is way too tight, and you're sitting on the arm of a sofa that's probably worth a year of your rent).

You aren't sure why you're still here, in this exquisite penthouse apartment. Uhler brought you but, old as he is, he probably left hours ago. And your yiayia, even older, is probably still awake at home, praying over her mirror, begging God to deliver you back to her safely.

You, you, *you*.

You are Athanasios Bakirtzis. Reckless, charming, self-destructive Athanasios. Athan to your friends, if you kept any, but that last part—the self-destructive part—usually scares them off. Which you like. It means the next time you burn your life to the ground, no one else gets caught in the blaze.

The girl with bleached bangs squeezes your thigh, and you turn back to her. For a moment, you were just staring off at the wall. Specifically at the wall*paper*. It's a sickly yellow color, infested with a sprawling, golden design that seems to shift every time you blink. It looks like neurons—rotting neurons that flicker with poisonous thoughts. And just for a moment, while your eyes sought some logical escape from the pattern—a break or seam or anything that would disrupt that unending, wretched design—it felt like *your* brain was slowly filling with poison, too.

What's in your future? the girl asks, her hand squeezing again. *What's fate got in store for you?*

Your fate, your future. Two things you refuse to think about, thanks to years of your grandmother's superstitions. You glance at the wallpaper again, and it's like being wrapped in your yiayia's claustrophobic beliefs. Is tonight the night you finally cut your way free?

My future . . . you say, trying out the words.

The girl squeezes, and her eyes focus on you for what feels like the first time in almost an hour of one-sided conversation. She really wants to know.

You make an excuse to go to the bathroom. Alone.

This is the excuse that saves your life.

CHAPTER ONE

I close the bathroom door, shutting out the party.

The room smells like the perfume of the trio of girls who were just in here. It's a tiny, beautiful space. The dark green wallpaper rustles with monstera leaves, and a golden faucet gleams in the candlelight.

It's serene. Safe.

I wish I could match it. I often feel this harsh contrast between me and the artful rooms I pass through, working for a designer like Uhler. Someone arranged this space with love and intention. I wish someone would peer into the chaos of my interior and pull me into peaceful composition. It's no wonder the rich enjoy life; they get to live it in such beautiful spaces. Like this penthouse. It's softly lit and artfully decorated and way, way too big for the bachelor that Uhler introduced as the host when we arrived. It's hard to believe anyone lives in so much gorgeous emptiness.

I'm not threatened by the casual grandeur, though. I've faked my way through dozens of these parties before. It's easy. The guests are always the same: brand-new New Yorkers trying out being fascinating, looking for someone to listen to them prove it. As Uhler's personal party date, that person is usually me.

I'm a good listener, they always tell me, which is true. But the actual truth is that I know if I ask people about themselves, they're less likely to ask about me. By the night's end, I know everything about them.

For instance, Zoey Marie Kaplan, the girl with bleached bangs, thinks she's an empath because she can read "vibes," and for the record mine are immaculate, and she doesn't believe in New Year's resolutions because they're for weak people who don't believe in spontaneous evolution, whatever that is, and she's upset with her boyfriend because he doesn't flush the toilet all the time, which I agreed sounded like weaponized helplessness of the first degree. All this I learned just by letting her talk, and I don't think she even knows my name.

Athan.

I'm still not ready to head back out there. I flush the toilet with gusto and take my time washing my hands.

Athanasios.

My name means "immortal" in Greek, but it might as well mean "survivor's guilt." In my head, I hear the whole thing spoken in Yiayia's pleading voice. *Athanaaaasios.* I should go home—this is far too long to be away from an old woman who depends on me—but lately I can't be around her for more than a few minutes a day. Her rituals, her superstitions, her wards against some all-seeing evil eye that's searching, searching, *searching* for what's left of our family. She's gotten so much worse in the past few months.

Look, just look, my mind whispers as I wash my hands, but I keep my eyes off the mirror. Not yet.

How long can I hide in here? I don't want to go back out to the party until that girl has found another person to talk at. There was a cute boy watching me over by the window, but his eyes were shooting daggers. Probably someone I ghosted. Oh well. I *should* look for Uhler, but he never stays at these things long. And besides, I can't keep running to him every time I start to feel lost. His charity won't last forever. I'm not even sure it *is* charity. All these party invitations, all the checks slipped to me so that Yiayia and I can keep up with our monthly rent—it's got to add up to something, right? I'm not eager to find out what.

Look. Just a peek, I urge myself.

It's embarrassing, but I'm building up the courage to look at myself in the mirror. Most people look at themselves without a second thought, but not me. Of all Yiayia's superstitions, avoiding mirrors is the most important.

Yiayia doesn't want me to end up like her, I think.

Morning to evening, my grandmother clutches a scratched-up hand mirror and prays. Sometimes it's a frantic song, and sometimes it's a quiet mumble I hear through the thin walls of our apartment. For a while we could still go on walks, me leading her with one hand while she used the other to hold the mirror up so she never had to look away. Not anymore. Now she won't leave our apartment. The praying has gone from a few minutes each hour to a constant babble. She even falls asleep with the mirror buried on her chest, clutching it with hands that have gone clammy and stiff since they used to tuck me in. The few times I've tried to slip it away, her grip seizes like a nightmare is blowing through her dreams.

That mirror has her trapped, and I don't need to wonder why. She tells me, in her rare moments of lucidity. *Athanasios!* she'll cry out suddenly, her voice rising like a siren wailing over the din of the city. *Our eyes cast curses!* On and on, her warnings reel with the momentum of a far-off catastrophe rushing toward us. *What we can see, can see us!*

Ever since the fire that took our home and family, she's filled my head with cautions against the evil eye and all the doom its focus brings. *Never let it find you, Athanasios. Promise me you will never look for it.* Greek superstitions, as ancient as the Acropolis. Myths that have turned into a madness I'm afraid I'll inherit.

Dr. Wei says the resentment I sometimes feel toward Yiayia is okay. That it doesn't mean I don't love her, or miss her, or want the old her back. Dr. Wei says that sometimes we self-mythologize to make ourselves big in our own minds, and Yiayia believes her praying is an act of heroic sacrifice. It's called a compulsion. He says that I probably have a predisposition, but I still have the chance to prove to myself that mirrors can't trap or hurt me. Gently, Dr. Wei has asked if I really believe in evil eyes. In mirrors and their magic.

I said I don't believe in any of it.

But I'm lying.

Because it's not all myths. I've known that since the first time I broke Yiayia's rule, found a mirror at the very back of our family's frame shop and saw what our eyes could truly do. I'm not sure if the Sight is a superpower. It feels more like a curse I can't control. It happens automatically in any mirror—in anything reflective—when my reflection's gaze meets my own. It makes living in a place like New York City, an entire world gilded in reflective glass and chrome, a hazard. But I've gotten good at dodging myself.

I've experimented here and there when I'm feeling brave, mostly just to prove to myself that I'm not suffering from some contagious delusion. I'm not. The power, or blessing, or curse, is real. But that's all the more reason to fear it. Dr. Wei says my fear enables the mythology, but Dr. Wei can't see what we can see.

I dry my hands on expensive towels, the kind with tassels. I'm done. Nothing else to do now but face my fears.

Look. Just for a moment. Just for a blink.

I look at myself in the bathroom mirror.

For the briefest moment before it happens, I'm able to see my reflection. It's like looking at a stranger. Someone else's eyebrows in an unsure furrow, someone else's chestnut curls, someone else's fear clenched in an unfamiliar jaw. Then I look into my own eyes, and the Sight activates.

Time reverses in the mirror, showing me everything it has seen this night. I watch my reflection look away, then reach for the towels. I watch me un-dry my hands, then un-wash them; watch the water flow up into the faucet; watch myself back out of the bathroom and the girls from before cram inside; watch a cloud of perfume hang in the air over them before sucking back into their little spritzing bottles.

Now that I've finally looked, I'm captivated. The girls gaze at one another in the mirror as they touch up their makeup, but it feels like they're gazing at me. They smile and laugh. They look so close. I put a hand on the glass and tap, like they're in an aquarium.

Something slams into the bathroom door and I jump. The reflection in the mirror lurches with my shock, jumping into the previous day, showing a man on the toilet, scrolling on his phone. I cover my eyes, blushing.

The slam turns into knocking. "Just a minute!" I shout.

I rush to reset the mirror. My mind scrambles, and so do the images in the glass. The edges glow white-hot.

"Stop," I beg the mirror. "Stop. *Please.*"

I shouldn't have looked for so long. I tap my fingertips over my eyebrows, like Yiayia used to do when I was a little kid and had even less control over our family power. If she'd only let me practice, if she'd just told me how . . .

The slam comes again.

Tap tap tap. Stop stop stop.

A scream squeezes through the gap as the door is pushed open. I only just catch it with my foot. The lock must be broken. I peek, and the mirror is back to normal. This time, I avoid my reflection as I swipe my phone from the counter, put on a smile, and swing the door all the way open.

"Sorry—" I start, but no one is there.

The hallway is empty. The party has gone silent. I turn toward the living room, expecting to find it suddenly vacated, but everyone is still there. Just standing still, like statues. Is it a game? Or a prank? A surprise, maybe? But they aren't huddled in gleeful anticipation, waiting for a person to walk through so they can *explode* with *Surprise! Happy*

Birthday! They look scared. Everyone is facing the walls. Zoey Marie Kaplan, the girl who said she was an empath, notices me standing in the doorway. Tears are gushing from her unblinking eyes, dragging dark stripes of mascara to her chin.

"Help me," she whispers. Her eyes rise to the wall behind me.

I turn, but before I can see what she's looking at, a shadow cuts through the crowd and rams into me, knocking my phone from my hand. It's a person. They grab me around the waist, driving me backward until I stumble back into the bathroom.

I land on my ass, swearing.

"Hey, what the f—"

The person—the boy I saw earlier, the one watching me from the window—cuts me off. "Don't open this door. If you don't open it, they won't see it. I'll come back for you when it's safe."

He slams the door in my face, and I'm left with just the flash of an impression. I recognize him now as one of Uhler's many interns. I remember him because he always wears that bandanna knotted around his neck. Orange, black, and white, like a monarch butterfly's wings. I caught those colors now. I'm sure it was the same guy.

But . . . what the fuck?

I race to open the door, but hesitate. What did he mean? *I'll come back for you when it's safe.*

It's the tiniest pause, but in that time something *unleashes* beyond the bathroom door. It shakes on its hinges as screams flood the penthouse. High, keening cries. Voices pushed to their limits, cracking, breaking, wrenching out of bodies thrown into violent motion.

It's the other party guests, but how could people sound like that? It sounds evil. Rotten. I back away from the door, expecting something foul to gush from under it.

The screams go on.

And on.

And on.

For minutes.

For an hour.

I press to the back wall and stare at the door, imagining myself opening it and running, imagining my phone somewhere on the floor where I dropped it. Could I grab it? Dial 911? Call Uhler, or even Yiayia? Pointless visions. I'm too much of a coward to go for it. Whatever evil Yiayia warned me against, it's found me. I looked into the mirror for too long, and it looked back. I don't know what's happening, only that I deserve it. I ball myself up next to the toilet and stifle my sobs, afraid they'll hear me.

The screaming finally resolves into words. Pleading words. The people scream *Can anyone hear us?* They start to bicker, and it turns into an argument. But at least they sound human now. I nearly work up the courage to swing open the door and try to help, but that's when the fighting breaks out.

Crashing. Breaking. Agonizing moans. I don't know how long this goes on for. An hour? Hours? Time frays and unravels as the sounds of violence shred through the thin walls hiding me.

Then someone knocks.

A very polite knock.

So polite, I nearly shout "Occupied!" Like I would in the single-person bathroom of a crowded restaurant. But the memory of the boy with the butterfly bandanna stops me.

He said they couldn't see the door.

I stay quiet. The knocking moves around, like someone is trying to find the hollow space behind a wall. I creep to the door and just barely make out whispering. It's Zoey! The empath. Was the boy right? Can she not see the bathroom's entrance?

She knocks and knocks, whispering, *"Please God please God please God don't let me die in here."*

She's not looking for a way into the bathroom. She's looking for a way *out* of wherever she is.

I'm scared. I'm tired. But hearing her plead like that . . . it awakens something in me. I turn off the lights so I can see her walking through the glowing band at the door's bottom edge. The next time her knocking takes her toward me, I give a gentle knock back, just for her to hear.

She goes quiet. I can see her shuffling back and forth.

I knock again. If I can draw her close, I can open the door just enough to squeeze her in, then shut it again. Then she'll be safe, too. She'll have a phone. We can call for help.

Her knocks are soft. Questioning. She's close now. I can hear her breathing.

I knock back one more time.

She shouts, right behind the door. "HERE! HE'S IN HERE!"

All at once the bathroom vibrates as an entire crowd stampedes down the hall, ramming against the walls with terrifying speed. People crawl over one another to get at the door. I fling myself against it, holding it shut, but they don't even turn the knob. They just pound their fists, desperate and furious. Their cries layer into a messy chant.

Come out, come out, little Athanasios!

The lights flicker. The mirror flickers, too, like it's responding to the thing in the hall. Not the people, but the *thing* that's taken hold of them. The thing that is searching for me.

Then it all goes wrong for Zoey Marie Kaplan. Within the chaos, I hear her screaming, *Back off! Hey! Stop! You're hurting me!* Her voice slides down to the bottom of the door as the crowd begins to crush her. Her cries turn strangled and then I hear a crack. Then another. Meaty snaps of bones. Bloody, bent fingers thrust beneath the door—the only visual evidence I get. They twitch as the chaos outside pulverizes her.

Then it all goes still.

It's still for minutes. Maybe an hour. I can't look away from the fingers, and the blood drying on shattered nails. Then, with a *schwoop*, the hand pulls away. Gone. I blink, realizing that the light from the hall has turned from gold to white.

It's morning.

I get up slowly.

I crawl to the door, bending as close to the bloody gap at the bottom as I dare. I listen. I can hear the far-off sound of a siren. Traffic. New York, reappearing on the other side of whatever hell the penthouse vanished into for the past five hours.

It's quiet. It's so quiet now. Is it finally over? Has the eye finally turned elsewhere?

I keep my eyes closed as I stand, afraid to even glance in the mirror. My hand finds the doorknob, shaking as it twists.

I open the door and my eyes at the same time.

You should know better, Athanasios. We cannot run from what reflects us. The farther you run from a mirror, the deeper your reflection vanishes into it.

CHAPTER TWO

I step into a burning brightness. Morning pours into the hallway.

The hall is empty except for a dark smear of red where something was dragged off into the living room. I forget my rule of not looking and follow the smear, but clap my hands back over my eyes immediately. I saw my phone, but I also saw something else. On the floor, peeking around the doorframe, I saw one of them. A person. Just the top of their head was visible, but their eyes were wide open. Dull, dead, and staring back at me.

"Fuck," I say, too loud. I lower my voice to a whisper and repeat: "Fuck, fuck, like seriously: Fuck." I chant this as I tiptoe around the smear, hovering a hand out to snatch up my phone, afraid the person will spring to life and grab me. They don't. My phone is sticky and, when I flip it in my hand, badly cracked. I shove it into my pocket and rush backward, down the hall and to the front door. Home.

Oddly, the rest of the penthouse is totally untouched by the violence. The kitchen is a mess of poured-out wine bottles, the trash can overflowing with killed cans of seltzer. The picked-over remnants of cheese, olives, and crackers look like a still-life painting atop a wooden cutting board.

Whatever happened in the living room, it never made it past the hallway. But there aren't any doors. Nothing that could have stopped those people from escaping. So why didn't they run? What held them in that room against their will? A person? One another? I hold my breath as I creep to the exit, afraid that at any moment one of them will lunge from the penthouse's tasteful decor and drag me along the bloody smear back into that room.

But a sound from the outside hallway stops me right before I open the front door. Chattering walkie-talkies. People talking. Careful not to touch it, I look through the peephole.

There are men outside. They exchange hushed orders. One pushes to the front and gives the doorbell a jab. I recoil at the loud buzz and my hip catches the narrow console table, toppling a thin-necked vase of tulips. I lunge for it.

I miss.

The silence shatters.

"Open up!" a voice booms through the door. "Police!" They knock three times, each a demand.

I'm frozen in place.

OPEN UP. POLICE.

I'm a good person, a good boy. I reach for the latch but stop. I'm once again facing down a door that both traps me and saves me. What did the boy with the butterfly bandanna say?

I'll come back for you when it's safe.

He never came back. Maybe, I realize, because it's not safe.

The knocking turns brutal, shaking the photographs hung in the entryway. I step away from the door. They're going to think I did this. *Did* I do this? My power, the mirrors, the evil eye—ancient superstitions whisper inside my head. Did I cause all this? I don't even know what *this* is, but it doesn't matter. I'll be blamed, and they'll take me away, and Yiayia will be alone, and—

Yiayia. I need to get home to Yiayia.

"We're coming in. Step away from the door. Do not attempt to run," the police instruct. Something scrapes against the lock. A key. Of course they have a key.

I need to open the door. I need to hide. I need to run. I need to confess. I can still make this choice. My future is still in my hands. But if I don't act now, that lock will tumble apart and fate will decide it for me.

Fate versus me.

I decide.

I watch the doorknob turn.

I decide.

I twist the dead bolt and slap on the door chain, then run backward into the apartment. I pass the kitchen. My tiny bathroom. I tear down the hallway, careful of the blood, and plunge into the sun-drenched living room. I'm running to the windows—the fire escape—but then the banging stops. Or my hearing fails as my eyes fill with the sight before me.

This is nothing like the room I sat in just hours ago. That room was laid out in a low, lounge style, with a wide couch covered in fuzzy pillows of velvet and bouclé. I remember the carpets, thin and tufted, layered over one another like overlapping lily pads so that the floor shifted beneath you as you stepped around low tables of perfectly clear, tempered glass. There were abstract lamps on heavy marble bases, and bookshelves with no books, and chairs of polished chrome, and little framed mirrors speckling the walls, like unblinking eyes peering out from the wallpaper.

It's all in ruins now. All the furniture has been overturned and smashed and bent into a mountain at the room's center. It reaches upward, toward the only overhead lighting: a chandelier with all the bulbs smashed out. It's like whoever built it was desperate to turn off the lights but couldn't find the switch.

Second, I notice the walls. They've been stripped of their wallpaper, about as high as a person could reach. Small smears of blood edge the barren patches, like someone's nails split while doing it.

And finally, I see the people.

Bare backs, spines flexed under flesh. Legs and arms and faces frozen in shock.

The people are in piles. I only see them now as I circle the mountain of furniture. They're crammed into the back corner of the room, in the mountain's shadow, as though hiding from . . .

The sunlight. It hardens everything into cruel, inescapable details. Makes the dead flesh look like stiff rubber. The sight burns away my ability to think, and a single word blinks in the emptiness of my shock. *Sculpture*. The way the bodies have tangled over themselves . . . it doesn't look like the chaos I overheard. No, there is something verging on artful about the arrangement. Someone did this. A person knotted these limbs together before the stiffness of death set in. My mind is on the verge of making sense of the shape—the limbs all aimed outward, a knot of necks and heads in the middle, but then my footsteps crunch on something.

Broken glass. I look down into a shattered mirror, my lifetime of avoidance saving me from making eye contact with myself. Instead, I gaze past my reflection at the ceiling and see something there. All above me, hovering in the sun-soaked air, are glimmering threads.

I reach up to pluck at one, but jerk away when I hear the front door bang open and the hall fill with footsteps. The police have made it inside. I give the horrific sculpture one more glance before running out of the room, into the master suite. The inside is untouched, jackets tossed onto the bed. I lock the door and rush to the far side of the room—a wall entirely made of windows that overlook the city. If my memory is right, there's a door here and—yes!—a balcony. I rush outside.

New York is a welcome assault on my senses. It's cold and windy and *loud*. Buildings rise all around me. The city shifts below, cars sluggishly braiding around a hundred faceless pedestrians. The air is frigid. Clear. It's another overcast November day, like any other.

I accidentally catch my reflection in the window of an office building across from me—I look terrified, wild, guilty—but a second later the reflection wobbles backward through time, the pane darkening to a square of night. It answers the question hovering at the periphery of my thoughts: What happened?

The reflection rewinds through an outside view of the penthouse, hours before. Bodies fly at one another in time-lapsed violence. A fight, too fast to make sense of.

Stop, I urge them. Urge myself. I have to go. *Now*. I tear my eyes away and look down the seven-story drop. Several cruisers wait below. I whip back and climb upward instead, to the roof. It's easy with the steep metal stairs of the fire escape. The roof of the building is a dead garden. I bound past raised beds of withered plants and grimy patio furniture, onto the next roof. I scramble over the buildings, turning the block's corner, then find another fire escape hidden from the police. I race down it, reaching the emergency ladder suspended above the sidewalk. I drop the last ten feet and roll to a stop, right in the path of a baby stroller.

"Oh," says the lady pushing it.

My charm kicks in. I stand and pretend to dust myself off as I step aside with overacted chivalry. Friendly, a little embarrassed, like *Yikes, you wouldn't believe the night I just had*. Her face eases into a knowing smile, like *Yeah, I've been there, too*, and she passes by.

I force myself to walk now, but quickly, like I've got somewhere to go. Sirens are getting closer. By now the police have probably called in the crime scene. Did they see me as I escaped, or did I really get away? My adrenaline mixes with a sudden wave of sickness, like I'm being flung high in the air on a roller coaster. I hug the buildings, just in case I let loose the mouthful of acid I keep swallowing back.

Those people. Arranged like that. What the fuck?

An ambulance lurches to a halt right in front of me and paramedics spill out. I'm wide open in what's about to be a hive of police. I pull off the sidewalk and into a storefront at the building's base. It just happens to be a coffee shop. I park myself at the counter, my back to the street, and sink my head into my hands.

"Can I help you?"

The barista eyes me with undecided suspicion. I throw on a smile, and the barista's face softens. My smile is useful like that. It's the dimples.

"Depends," I say. "Your espresso machine working?"

"You bet she is," the barista says, slapping a hand on a big chrome piece of equipment right in front of me. In the reflection, I can see out the café window behind me. It's perfect for keeping a lookout.

"Long night?" the barista prompts.

"The longest."

I get a cappuccino and pay with cash, even though the price is painful. The barista gives the espresso machine another pat when he hands me the drink, saying, "Let me know how I did." He winks.

I grin, forcing myself to hold eye contact as I take a sip. I'm surprised how easily charm comes to my defense, but I shouldn't be. I've hidden behind charisma for years.

"Good," I say, licking foam from my lips.

"Darn. Usually I do great," he pouts. There's a double meaning there.

"I'll look forward to great next time, then." I smile. He heads off to help the next customer.

I drop the act right away, my face back in my hands. But then I make myself sit up. *Don't look suspicious, Athan. Look at your phone, even though it's dead.* I hold it up, but look past it, at the reflection swimming in the chrome body of the espresso machine. By accident I look into my own eyes, and my reflection instantly retreats. Backward, out of the coffee shop, into a busy street that quickly empties as the sun un-rises.

Stop it, I demand. *Not now. Not here.*

I'm about to close my eyes so I can tap on my temples again, but then I see something in the reverse world of the reflection. I see *him*.

The boy with the butterfly bandanna.